BALLAD OF BROKEN BANNERS

BOOK ONE OF THE ANOINTED DUET

K. GODIN

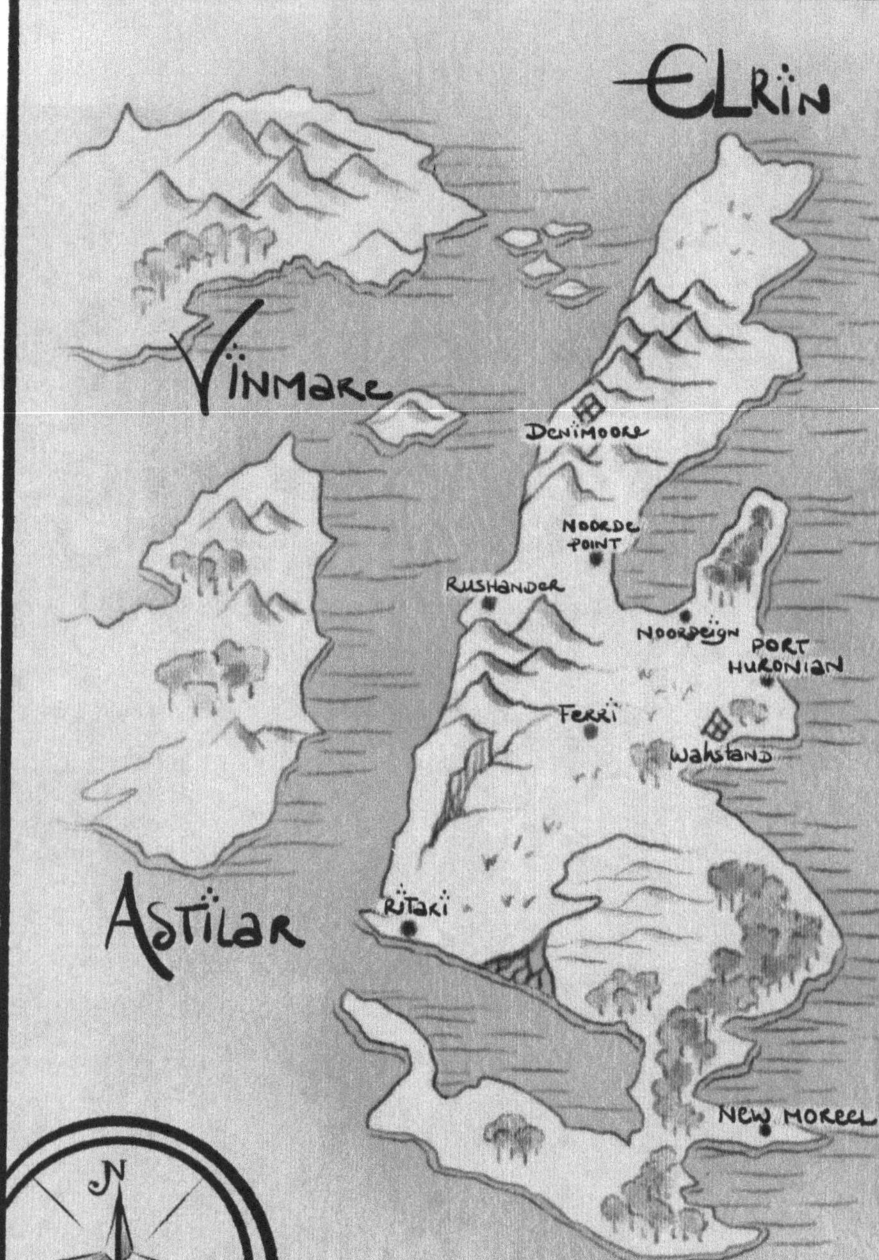

ELRiN
Vinmare
Denimoore
Noorde Point
Rushander
Noordeign
Port Huronian
Ferri
Wahstand
Astilar
Ritaki
New Moreel
N

Lythnals
The Barren Sea
Osallow

BALLAD OF BROKEN BANNERS

K. GODIN

Print edition ISBN: 9781068800702
E-Book edition ISBN: 9781068800726
Hardback edition ISBN: 9781068800719

First edition: March 2025
10 9 8 7 6 5 4 3 2 1

WWW.AUTHORKGODIN.COM

Cover Design by Jaqueline & Jones Florencio
Map by C.J. Merwild
Editor Beth Attwood

To those who remain soft despite the harshness of the world,
Please never change.

On either side the river lie
Long fields of barley and of rye,
That clothe the wold and meet the sky;
And thro' the field the road runs by
To many-tower'd Camelot;
The yellow-leaved waterlily
The green-sheathed daffodilly
Tremble in the water chilly
Round about Shalott.

Willows whiten, aspens shiver.
The sunbeam showers break and quiver
In the stream that runneth ever
By the island in the river
Flowing down to Camelot.
Four gray walls, and four gray towers
Overlook a space of flowers,
And the silent isle imbowers
The Lady of Shalott.

Underneath the bearded barley,
The reaper, reaping late and early,
Hears her ever chanting cheerly,
Like an angel, singing clearly,
O'er the stream of Camelot.
Piling the sheaves in furrows airy,
Beneath the moon, the reaper weary
Listening whispers, 'Tis the fairy,
Lady of Shalott.'

The little isle is all inrail'd
With a rose-fence, and overtrail'd
With roses: by the marge unhail'd
The shallop flitteth silken sail'd,
Skimming down to Camelot.
A pearl garland winds her head:
She leaneth on a velvet bed,
Full royally apparelled,
The Lady of Shalott.

"The Lady of Shallot" Part I
By Lord Alfred Tennyson (1832)

PART ONE

CHAPTER

ONE

THE SCREAMS OF THE DYING MEN STILL ECHOED IN MY EARS AS I pushed my way through the tent's opening, and I blinked at the sudden darkness before lifting my hands to remove the helm from my head.

"Ah, sister, how did our enemy fare on the battlefield? Although I'm not sure you could call that pathetically small farmer's field as much." My brother's head lolled as he glanced at me from the chair he was sprawled across, and I scoffed under my breath before wiping the mud and blood from my face. He was drunk, as usual, and by the look of his tousled hair and unlaced tunic, he had somehow succeeded in finding company to keep him busy while I was gone.

"We managed to take two alive for questioning, but the others were not so lucky," I murmured quietly while I tried to keep my temper at bay.

"My, how exhilarating, a sweet victory indeed. Who would have thought a group of boys and lowly commonfolk would be able to put up such a glorious fight?" He raised his silver cup towards the ceiling of the tent in celebration, not caring that the deep maroon liquid sloshed over the sides, and I inhaled sharply.

"There is nothing sweet about the death of young men who have been led astray by those who prey on their naivety," I growled. "And there certainly is no pleasure in killing those who do not fully grasp the consequences of their decisions. You would know that had you ever been brave enough to leave the comforts of your tent." His brown eyes narrowed at me, and I shifted under his gaze.

Though enraged, my brother was still handsome. The features my father had gifted him made that difficult to deny. However, the cool look of disdain he now sent in my direction was identical to the one his mother wore anytime I was within eyesight. In fact, when he stared at me in such a way, it was hard to see any similarities between us other than the dark colour of his hair, and I was sure he was thankful for that.

After all, producing a bastard within a highborn household was not unheard of, though it brought whispers. But *housing* a bastard who was older than the true heir and allowing them to have any semblance of importance, well, that was another thing altogether.

"I bet the other Anointed and the noble families will think our victory sweet, and our father will be proud. Especially considering we stopped the rebels from ransacking another titled house." Standing from his chair, Skileer ran a hand down his embroidered tunic and then reached for the extra set of armour that sat on the floor, the metal unmarked and pristine as always.

"He won't be proud of your choice to busy yourself with some poor woman while you were meant to remain unseen," I reminded him. "Father will cut out her tongue, or worse, if he finds out."

"That would be a shame," he agreed with a shrug. "But then again, her tongue was not the most interesting part of her."

When I clenched my jaw rather than responding, he smirked. "Besides, she is nothing but a bored farmer's wife looking for some enjoyment. Or rather she *was*. Her husband was probably one of the men you slaughtered today." My stomach churned at his indifference, and I glowered at him.

"You are repulsive," I snarled.

"It's truly a shame you believe so," he sighed. "I must think it's difficult to have such a horrid opinion of the person who will someday be responsible for your fate."

I knew he enjoyed holding that fact over my head, and I scowled as I watched him slip the silver armour on. He didn't bother with the chainmail or gambeson and clumsily fastened the buckles before lifting his cup to finish the wine in one swallow. Now empty, my brother saw no use in the dish and tossed it to the ground before pushing past me as he made a hasty exit from the tent.

With him gone, it felt as if the air around me had finally settled, and I exhaled roughly while turning to the mirror. The glass had been propped against the side of the tent, and I took a moment to study my reflection. My long hair had been carefully braided to keep the strands tucked beneath my helm. Although now, the intricate twists just looked like a matted mess against the sides of my head, and the dark brown colour was caked with sweat and dirt. The skin of my face was also soiled, though the drying splatters of blood and muck only made my sharp features more prominent and highlighted the hooded grey eyes that were staring back at me.

Unable to look at the carnage any longer, I slid my fingers across the filthy metal until they found the leather fastenings and undid them quickly. Piece by piece, I removed the steel and let it fall to the ground with a hard thud before doing the same with the chainmail. My body ached, the muscles tired from wielding my heavy longsword and from being trapped beneath the armour that struggled to fit around my shoulders snugly without crushing my breasts. Our master armourer was talented, the best in all of Elrin, but the suit had been made for my brother, and though we were the same height, he did not have the curves of a woman.

Now that I was released from my metal cage, I sighed in relief and rolled my shoulders before stripping off my sweat-soaked tunic and wrap that secured my breasts. Not caring about the cool autumn air, I strode over to the washbasin, grabbed the cloth, and scrubbed at the skin of my naked torso until all evidence of the battle was washed away. I longed for a true bath, but we would not be home for another fortnight, and I wasn't foolish enough to leave camp in search of the springs that were tucked away in the forest nearby. Especially not when I really considered what other threats could be out there, lurking amongst the shadows that surrounded us.

That would be another surprise we did not need. Not after my misguided assumption that this fight would be against nothing more than a few outlaws who were unhappy with the fate the Gods had given them. Instead, it had been a bloody and brutal battle, and those men were not only beyond displeased, but they had also fought with the courage and skill of a true army.

It would appear that the one they called High Commander had not just taken the fear and suffering of these men and twisted them into radical ideas that threatened the peace the Anointed families had kept for centuries. But he had also educated them on warfare and made certain that they would be a formidable adversary.

A sudden onslaught of gruesome memories from the battle flashed through my mind, and I took a shuddering breath before pulling my breeches down my legs. Once free from the fabric, I ran the cold cloth over my thighs, letting the water race across my skin that prickled in the chilly air. Satisfied that I was somewhat clean, I pulled on a simple frock and turned to the entrance of the tent.

However, before I could duck through the canvas, a head full of greying curls appeared, and I swallowed roughly as I looked at my father. To others, his face may have appeared to be unreadable, but I could see the fury behind the well-practiced mask. After all, it was the same guise I had nearly mastered myself.

"I told you no prisoners, Rígan." The words were quiet, but no less intimidating, and I struggled not to show any uneasiness. My father was one of the only people who could intimidate me in such a way, and my fingers curled into tight fists as I readied myself for a fight.

"They surrendered to us," I explained. "I thought perhaps they may finally tell us who the High Comman—"

"What are the words of our family?" he interrupted me. "What are the words of House Baxteel?"

"Honour, family, duty," I muttered.

"And is duty and family not of the utmost importance to you?" He knew it was; he knew it was the only thing I cared about. It was the only thing I truly clung to after all these years.

But instead of answering, I simply nodded.

"So tell me why you struggle to follow orders, Rígan," he snapped. "Your brother seems to have no problem doing so."

Venomous words burned the tip of my tongue. Nasty, horrid things that I had longed to say for the last twenty-six years but had swallowed down because I knew that they would not help me where my father was concerned. Nothing I said would. My status would forever be Edmyn Baxteel's bastard daughter and my father would not change that. And because of his inaction, no one else would see any worth in me.

No one would sing the songs of my victories, no Grand Elder would write my name rather than my brother's in the pages of Elrin's history. And once death took me, I would be truly forgotten. I would be nothing more than dust at the end of it all. That was my future, and while I knew there was nothing to be done, I still somehow struggled to accept it.

"Did you hear me?" my father barked, drawing my attention back to his stern expression.

"Yes," I whispered in defeat, already knowing what was expected of me once I left the sanctuary of my tent.

"Good. Now fix your face, our men do not need to see that forlorn expression." Smoothing a hand across my mouth, my fingers lingered on the scar that ran across the right side of my lips, and my father grunted in approval.

"Tomorrow, we head for Ferri." Frowning, I looked at him questioningly. Ferri was a small village south of the land we currently camped on, and it was in the exact opposite direction of home.

Realizing I was about to interject, my father lifted a hand, a clear signal that I shouldn't bother. "We were invited to participate in the tourney, and given the victory today, attending will only continue to improve the status of our house amongst the others."

"But," I tried again, "we told our men we would be returning home as soon as this mess here was dealt with. They will be longing to be reunited with their loved ones before winter comes. Would now truly be the best time to attend such an event?"

"Now is the perfect time for a tournament. It would show these rebels that the Anointed and other noble families are united in our effort to keep them from corrupting what we have spent centuries building," my father explained. "The responsibility of maintaining the peace of this world was given to the sacred four houses by the Divine Triad themselves, and despite his best efforts, this so-called High Commander will never be victorious in his attempts to overthrow the Gods' favourites."

My father's eyes narrowed as he searched my face. "And *our men* will be longing to return north, or you are?"

Raising my chin, I forced my face into a more believable

expression of indifference. "I'm not sure I know what you mean."

Scoffing, he glared at me. "Your little trysts back home with the oldest Dansby boy have not gone unnoticed over the last couple years, Rígan."

My cheeks flamed under his scrutiny, and my father shook his head in disbelief. "Fret not, the boy will be in Ferri, and perhaps now is the time we put those whispers to rest. After all, we do not need his father worrying that you will ruin whatever match they plan to make for him."

Finally releasing me from his stare, he focused on the filthy armour I had hurriedly discarded. "We will be entering the tournament. It will prove that this day was nothing more than another minor incident and the other nobles will see that Skileer has only continued to prosper and strengthen our position. That is what we need to focus on now, especially for your brother and the future of this house."

I struggled to resist the urge to roll my eyes. My father and I both knew allowing *Skileer* to participate in the tournament was not a wise choice, and my brother was not at all likely to display any sort of strength. However, judging by the expectant look my father was now giving me, it was clear that wasn't a real concern.

"I will be sure to clean my armour," I murmured.

"It would be best for all of us if you cut your hair as well," he added, ignoring my sullen mood. "It's grown too long to easily conceal."

Taking the strands in one hand, I twisted them together until they were falling down my back and out of my father's sight. He scowled but said nothing else, and then he was exiting my tent and stepping out into the drizzling autumn rain.

THE SPIRITS of the men had lifted as the night wore on, and I strode across the mud while the echoes of drunken singing faded with the distance. Finding the metal cage that sat at the edge of camp, I curled my fingers around the cold bars and peered in at our two captives. They were no older than twenty, more boys than men. However, despite their youth, they were now facing the consequences for playing a game of life and death, and I wondered who had allowed them to march with the rebels in the first place.

"We know you're there. Are you finally here to finish us?" the larger of the two sneered, and I took a deep breath before rounding the corner of the cage until I moved into their line of vision.

"Do you know who I am?" I asked while I glared down at them.

"The bastard born of House Baxteel," the boy muttered while his eyes raked over me from head to toe in a pitiful attempt at a leer. "Though you certainly don't look poorly bred."

Moving my gaze to his, I held his stare, watching as his expression wavered until it crumpled altogether, and then his attention fell to ground nervously. This was a reaction I was used to; most strangers found the sharp lines of my cheekbones and cold steel of my gaze far too unnerving to look at for long, and this boy was no different. Turning my sights on the smaller of the pair, I smirked when I noticed the way he trembled. This would be easy.

"You know my house, so you must know why my father's men tracked you and your group here." The larger boy's lip curled in disgust, but he did not deny it. "Tell me what I ask, and you will be shown mercy."

"Your kind knows nothing of mercy!" he snarled before huddling closer to his friend, who sniffed noisily. "We are aware of what your brother and his men do to captives, and we are certain you are all as cruel as the Goddess you serve."

"We do nothing more than what we have to in order to protect the innocents of Elrin," I argued. "And our hostages are only poorly treated when they refuse to cooperate."

The boy scoffed but said nothing more on the matter. "Besides, the Huntress is not known for viciousness, why would you say otherwise?"

"Perhaps it's because we aren't blind to it!" he spat. "Perhaps we can see things for what they are, and we do not let her gifts of power, privilege, or bloodlines sway us the way you Anointed do."

My jaw tightened as I stared down at the pair. I wanted to argue, I wanted to say they were wrong, and that I too did not let those things hold any power over me. But that would be a lie, and one I seemed unable to tell.

"Nothing to say?" the boy asked while narrowing his eyes in defiance.

"I am sorry that you feel our Goddess has failed you," I mocked.

"Not just your Goddess," the smaller boy finally spoke in a hushed voice. "We have been failed by all of the Divine Triad."

I lifted a brow as I moved my attention to his face. "How so?"

"You truly don't see it?" he asked. "The people of Elrin are suffering and have been for some time. Our crops have not flourished in years and fevers have devastated the larger villages and cities."

"And because of this, you think our Gods have abandoned Elrin? That they have turned their backs on us and that is why we have endured such misfortune?" I presumed with a sigh.

"How could we not? Your Goddess, the Protector, and the

Healer all remain silent while our prayers go unanswered," the larger one growled, obviously enraged by my indifference. "You Anointed say our Gods watch over us, you say they have the power to bless us, to heal us. If that's true, then they are cruel for watching our suffering. And if they do not hold such abilities, then they are not what you all claim them to be. So, which is it?"

I had no answer for him, no sharp retort, and I had been too thrown off by his statement to notice my brother's figure as he crept through the shadows. In fact, I hadn't detected his presence until I heard the arrow hit its mark and I watched as the larger boy grasped at the torn flesh of his throat, his fingers curling around the feathers that stuck out from just beneath his left ear. His friend had been just as shocked by the sudden attack, which left him completely unprepared for his own demise, and I hadn't even managed to take a step forward before he was slumped to the side as his life left him.

Grasping at the cold bars of the cell, I blinked down at the bodies, and then Skileer spoke from behind me. "Father told you no prisoners, Rígan. Perhaps next time you will listen."

His voice was heavy with disappointment. But when I turned to face him, I noticed that the corners of his mouth were curled upwards.

CHAPTER

TWO

MOVING THROUGH CAMP, I WATCHED OUR MEN PREPARE FOR the journey south while the long skirts of my gown blew against my legs, and I looked down at the fabric with a frown. The hem was just long enough to touch the ground, but given the rain and number of bodies who trudged back and forth across the damp earth, at least six inches of the material was now soaked with mud.

"Do you need something, my lady?" one of the squires asked nervously from where he stood outside the makeshift paddock we had constructed prior to the battle, and I glanced up from the dirty hem.

He was not one I recognized, and my lips curled when I noticed his lingering stare. It was not something that would be permitted in normal circumstances, but given my status, even the lowly stable help thought they were warranted in their gawking.

"Go fetch the lady her horse, Samsin." The order came from over my shoulder, and I glanced back at Donigan as he strode through the muck with more grace than I would have thought possible. Startled by the knight, the squire hurriedly nodded his head and then scrambled away, and I smirked as

13

he slid across the wet earth before he clumsily found his footing.

"I thought you knew better than to harass the poor, unsuspecting servants," Donigan chastised me as he closed the distance between us, and I narrowed my gaze at him.

Donigan Taith had too just been a lowly squire when he had come to my father one morning at the young age of ten. He had no family and had been passed from house to house until he finally ended up in our great hall, where he begged for a place to stay. The knight who he had been sworn to had lost his life in a drunken brawl in our village the night before, and thus, he was desperate for someone to take him under their wing.

My father had not been keen on the idea at first. He hadn't been in need of another servant boy, and Donigan was a rather small thing, so pale and thin with his deep brown eyes and raven-coloured hair. He was nothing like the strong and handsome man who stood before me now. However, despite his beginnings, Donigan had proved his worth over time and now was an invaluable asset to our army.

He also had a way about him that was unlike any other man I knew. His smile was known to make ladies swoon, which was typical of a young knight, but there was also something just so pure about him, a true goodness that radiated from his very soul.

Of course my father saw no use in a quality like that, but he had been pleased by the speed at which Donigan had moved up in ranks over the last twelve years. Now being a general, he had a title and money and was what songs were written about. Or would have been if it were not for the fact that he had come to status because of his skills on the battlefield rather than the blood that ran through his veins. My father had grown to be impressed by him, and even rewarded him handsomely. But he could not change tradition.

Just as with bastards, ballads were not written about the lowborn.

"I was not harassing anyone," I muttered before glancing in the direction the boy had fled. "If anything, it was me who was being looked at like a piece of meat."

"Can you blame him?" Donigan laughed softly, and my attention snapped back to him.

"Is that what they teach you when you squire for knights? To ogle at ladies while they are minding their own business?" I growled. "What about honour and chivalry?"

"Those things are all well and good in theory, but a boy of his age forgets himself when standing in front of a woman such as you."

Rolling my eyes, I shoved at his shoulder, and he grinned playfully before turning to the squire who was now approaching with my horse. Taking the reins from him, he shooed the lad away with a flick of his fingers and then came to the left side of my mount and fell to a bent knee.

"My lady," he proclaimed sarcastically, and had no one been watching, I would have kicked him.

Instead, I rested my right foot on his strong thigh while my other slipped into the stirrup. Hoisting myself up, I did my best to gather my skirts as I perched in the saddle uncomfortably.

"I think you're out of practice," Donigan whispered as he watched me struggle to find my seat while sitting sideways on my steed, and I glared down at him as I tried to adjust subtly.

"I'd like to see you try and do it in a gown," I snapped, and he snorted before patting my gelding on the neck and then turned to mount his own horse. Of course, he had a far easier time, and I watched longingly as he swung his leg over his mare before sinking into the saddle.

"Are we ready?" my father called as he approached with my brother in tow, and I lifted a nervous hand to my hair as a strong gust of wind blew against me.

I had not listened to his advice the night before, and was now worried what he would do if he saw the long dark strands billowing in the breeze this morning. However, knowing I could not fight with the wind for our entire journey, I waited until he and my brother passed before moving in to blend in amongst our men.

"What has you so nervous?" Donigan asked as he pressed his horse next to my own.

"I'm not nervous," I retorted, but he paid my poor behaviour no mind and just rolled his eyes.

"That's why you suddenly look like a little spooked filly," he continued, and I glared at him. "What did your father do this time?" His narrowed gaze moved to focus ahead, and I scoffed under my breath.

"He reminded me of my duty at the tournament." I noticed Donigan's jaw clench in anger while his attention shifted away from my father and drifted to my brother's back.

"He's asking you to do *that* again?"

"He can't risk his true heir, and he won't let our house appear weak in the eyes of the rest of the court. Participating in a tournament is a great honour, even more so if we do well," I reminded him.

Finally, he moved his focus back to me. "Fine, then why not have one of us do it? Many houses allow their men to compete in their name at a tourney."

"Houses who do not have proper heirs, or perhaps less noble families. Certainly not one of the Anointed," I pointed out. "Besides, if he allowed one of you to take Skileer's place instead, there is the chance of you boasting about it after you've fallen into your cups."

I shook my head. "It would be an embarrassment if anyone found out the truth."

"Your men are more loyal than that," Donigan disagreed.

"They are not *my* men, and you overestimate your fellow knights," I muttered. "Most are here because of the money and protection my father's name offers. But as this rebellion continues, I worry their devotion to us will waver."

"I wouldn't waver," Donigan assured me.

"I know that," I sighed. "But be that as it may, I still shouldn't have told you anything about this."

"You know I would never repeat it to anyone," Donigan swore.

"It would be your head under the sword if you did," I reminded him.

"True," he agreed. "But you wouldn't let that happen." His grin grew into that same smile that made all the maidens flush and giggle, and I rolled my eyes at the expression.

"And why is that?" I asked.

"Because you like my pretty face right where it is," he replied as his expression turned smug, and it was no wonder how he had the power to send unsuspecting barmaids and ladies spinning.

Leaning over, I shoved him roughly, watching with amusement as he struggled not to fall off his horse.

"Need I remind you of that last time you tried to woo me with that pretty face of yours?" Though it had been a couple years ago, I never truly allowed him to forget it, and I watched as the fair skin of his cheeks reddened.

"You promised you wouldn't speak of it again!" Donigan barked, and I laughed quietly.

"No, I promised I would never tell another soul," I said softly with a grin. "And I haven't—yet. However, sometimes I worry your obsession with yourself makes you a tad forgetful, and it is my duty to bring you back to your senses."

The nasty look he gave me would have been intimidating if it weren't for the blush that still lingered on his cheeks, and I ignored his sour mood as I clapped him on the shoulder gently.

"Don't worry, Donigan." My smile grew. "There will be many ladies who would happily listen to your drunken sonnets about their eyes. Remind me again how you rhymed *grey* and my *lay-day*?"

Shrugging out from under my hand, he pressed his heels into his mount's belly, and I snickered as I watched him canter off for a moment before I shortened my reins and chased after him.

GRABBING AT MY SKIRTS, I gingerly sank into the rickety chair that was placed across the table from my father, and I looked at the dinner that had been laid out for us. It was amazing the luxuries my father gave priority to when we were meant to be keeping a rebellion at bay.

"Eat," he ordered me with a pointed glare, and I instead opted for the goblet of wine. Sipping at the crimson liquid, I glanced at my brother from the corner of my eye as he entered the tent. Swallowing down the large mouthful, I took another and prepared for this meal and the conversation that would no doubt come along with it.

"Where have you been?" my father growled at Skileer as he fell into the seat next to me. The smell wafting off of him and the sheen of sweat that covered his face was enough of an answer, and my father straightened in his chair while those dark eyes narrowed. "Fucking another woman? Who was it this time, a blacksmith's wife or another rebel?"

"I don't know what you're talking about," Skileer whispered sheepishly, but his lie was too blatant to ignore.

"When will you learn?" my father questioned. "When will you become something other than a useless idiot who only thinks with his cock?"

Snorting into my glass, I slammed a palm onto my chest

while the wine burned the back of my throat and my brother turned to me.

"Easy, sister," he hissed. "I would hate to have to tell Gwain that his whore choked to death before we made it to the tourney."

My body stiffened and I carefully placed my cup back on the wooden surface of the table while the silence filled the tent. He was taunting me in order to take my father's attention off of himself, and I hated that it was working. Clenching my jaw, I inhaled through my nose and then glanced at my father.

As predicted, his stare was fixed on my face, and I felt my heart race.

"It wouldn't be much of a waste, would it, Father?" Skileer continued, obviously thrilled that his scheme had worked.

Unable to help myself, I dug my fingernails into the arms of my chair and then lifted my chin. "But what would you do without me? We both know you're too cowardly to face our enemies yourself. If not for me, you would be the laughing-stock of court."

Skileer's jaw went slack, and my lips curled as I took in the bewildered look on his face.

"Finally, you look as foolish as you are."

"You ungrateful bitc—" Skileer began as he made to lunge for me, but the pounding on the table was enough to bring him to a halt, and we both turned to face our father once more.

"Enough!" he roared while rising from his seat, and I winced as the chair fell backwards and crashed to the ground. "I will not have you squabbling like two common fools!"

"Only one of us has common blood in our veins," Skileer murmured, and my father pointed one long finger at him.

"You will keep your fucking mouth shut and your cock in your breeches from here on out. Should I learn of any more incidents, I will be sure to teach you a lesson you won't soon forget."

Though I tried, I was unable to keep my smugness from showing on my face, and Skileer snarled at me.

"And you." My spine stiffened as his attention moved to me. "You will learn your place, girl. I will not have my bastard make a mockery of my family or our name any longer. The Dansby boy is not yours; you are not worthy of him. You will accept it, or I will make certain you no longer hold any appeal for him."

The scar that ruined the right side of my lips tingled at the threat, and I lowered my eyes to my lap.

"Now get out of my sight!" he snapped, and I hastily stood from my chair, offered him a shaky curtsey, and then fled while my brother snickered.

Tearing at the laces of my gown, I growled as my fingers struggled to loosen my binds, and I turned my back to the mirror. Watching my hands, I finally managed to pull the ribbon free, and I shrugged out from under the fabric before falling onto my bedroll.

Pulling back the furs, I crawled beneath their heavy weight and let my body relax. It would only be a few more days until we finally reached Ferri. And though my stomach still churned at the thought of my father's threat, my heart pounded within my chest when I remembered that Gwain would be there.

The thought of being reunited with him after having been separated for so many weeks made my body ache with longing, and I told myself that I would make certain we would be able to sneak away for some time together, despite my father's warnings and wrath. Grabbing at my shift, I clutched the material that covered the thudding in my chest and leaned over to reach for one of the saddle bags. Unclasping the buckle, I searched blindly until my fingers stroked across the folded piece of worn parchment and pulled it from its hiding spot before lifting it to my face.

The ink was faded, and the creases were deep, but the words were just as beautiful as they had been the first time I had read them. In fact, I didn't even need to look at the parchment to know what they said, the declaration of his love was imprinted in my mind now.

>*My darling,*
>
>*I miss your warmth, your touch, and the sound of the beating in your chest that is the only match for my own. Food has no taste; the world seems duller without your secret smiles, and I feel as if I will cease to exist without you near.*
>
>*I pray each night that the Gods will bring you to me in my dreams.*
>
>*Do you ask for the same?*
>
>*I am desperate and desolate without you.*
>
>*Sincerely,*
>
>*Lord Gwain Dansby*

He loved me and nothing my father said or did would change that. I was sure of it.

It did not matter that others whispered behind our backs. It did not matter that no one approved, and I was sure whatever match his father chose for him would mean nothing in the end. He did not care that I was illegitimate, he wanted me as I was. I would be *his* choice.

"Are you looking at that letter again?" Jumping at Donigan's hushed voice, I tossed the parchment aside to press a hand against my belly while I gasped for air. Realizing he had startled me, he offered me a sheepish smile before ducking into my tent.

"Are you mad? What are you doing?" I whispered while narrowing my eyes at him. "If my father catches you in here, he will kill you, and I won't be able to stop him from doing so."

"I think you are confused about your father's priorities. He may kill me if I disclose your secret, Rí, but I am not a simple foot soldier. I think sneaking into your tent may be lower on his list of concerns," Donigan drawled. "It's not as if he worries for your virtue any longer."

My cheeks heated at his pointed stare. "I don't know what you're talking about."

"I hope you lie to your father better than that." He grinned again before reaching for Gwain's note. Lunging forward, I tried to snatch it from his fingers, but I was not quick enough, and he avoided my flailing arms as he held it close to his face.

"My, what pretty words," he murmured with a roll of his eyes. "Who knew Dansby was such a poet?"

"Don't be jealous," I murmured, but Donigan paid me no mind as he folded the parchment up and shoved it back into the saddlebag.

"Trust me, I've long since let go of any of those particular feelings." The words were quiet, but I felt the weight of them on my shoulders.

Growing uncomfortable in the silence that now fell over us, I turned to him. "Gwain may not be a bard, but at least there is no mention of the colour grey."

My teasing did not have the effect I was hoping for, and I watched as his brows furrowed before he tossed the leather bag aside.

"I just want you to be careful," he sighed as he turned to look at me. "Gwain Dansby is charming, I suppose, and I am sure he has some qualities you somehow found endearing. But I'm not certain that he is everything you have imagined him to be."

Annoyed, I glowered at his warning. "Donigan, I can

promise you, I am nothing but careful. I would not care for him if he hadn't earned it."

"And how did he do such a thing?" my knight asked. "Tell me what it was that won you over."

I didn't know if I could explain it, and I was fairly sure Donigan would not understand even if I tried.

He and I may have had things in common, and even shared a similar fate, but it had never hardened him, not in the way it had me. Thus, I was not certain if he could truly grasp what exactly I was on the inside. Where I was cold and sharp, Donigan was soft and gentle. And while we were alike in so many other ways, we were counterparts in that aspect, and he somehow could not see or fathom the biggest difference between us.

If he had, I was sure he would flee from the frigid jagged edges that made up my very core.

"He does not care about my status." It was a pitiful explanation, but it was the best I could come up with for now.

"Yes, I am sure you being a bastard matters very little when you already warm his bed," he said softly. "Besides, why should he care? It's not as if he would ever marry you."

There was a sharp intake of breath and then that cold, familiar mask fell over my face, covering any reaction his words may have roused, and I looked at him with a single lifted brow. I could handle the judgement from my father, or from any other person for that matter, but for it to come from Donigan, well, that cut me deeply.

"If you are done with your warning and insults, you can find your way out." Donigan shivered at my tone and kept his eyes downcast.

"I shouldn't have said that, forgive me," he whispered while he shifted under my glare.

"Don't have regrets now," I scoffed while that frigid sensation curled in my chest. "You said exactly what you meant, have the courage to stand by it."

Donigan began to shake his head, his palms raised like he was trying to placate a wild animal. But it was too late. His words may have wounded me, but I was no frightened creature. I was the predator, and I saw my mark and lunged for the kill.

"Though I am surprised a lowly orphan from the streets would have the courage to speak to noble blood in such a way," I snarled, not caring for the way he was now searching my face desperately. "I suppose your rapid and rather surprising rise in ranks made you forget yourself and what it is you *are*."

There it was, his jugular bared for my teeth to sink into, and though a small part of me screamed out to stop, I couldn't help myself. I would come out the victor of this match and I could no longer be concerned about what he may see when I did so.

He had hurt me and now I would make him bleed for it.

Turning my eyes forward, I stared at the canvas of my tent and then I uttered the final blow. "Even after all this time, you have never truly learned your place, though I suppose I am partly to blame for that. I let you believe we are equals when that could not be further from the truth," I growled. "I may be a bastard, but you, *you* are nothing."

A soft breeze blew against my hair as he scampered from his spot with more speed than a man of his size should possess, and I heard the soft rustle of his exit as I kept my gaze locked on the fabric, though I felt something crack inside me.

As I suspected, Donigan fled when he saw what was beneath my surface, and I was left alone to dwell in the massacre I had left in my wake. And while his departure was unsurprising, it still made my bones ache in the bitter cold that filled me once more.

It was a pity; I had somehow hoped he could withstand it.

CHAPTER
THREE

The journey across Elrin would have been a dull and exhausting affair as it was, but since my spat with Donigan nearly a fortnight ago, it felt unbearable now that he no longer sought me out for conversation. After all, there was not much to look at besides the long expanse of barren fields and cloudless sky. And though we neared the end of our travels, I was certain our destination would not offer much of a view either.

Ferri was a small village, one often overlooked as it was not a major trading post or port. There had, of course, been a rather grand castle that once stood proudly on the outskirts, but it had sadly been burned to the ground, and now there was nothing notable about the town at all. Well, besides the whispers.

The blaze was said to have been a horrible tragedy, that some servant had been careless with a lantern or maybe a maid had mishandled a candle. But I knew the noble houses had their doubts. There had been far too many rumours of rebels entering the village for it to have been a coincidence, and Lord Fareham had just been given his title and lands only a month prior to the fire. It had been a gift from the Anointed families in hopes of starting a strong alliance.

It was a wise choice. Aerdian Fareham was a charismatic man, though I truly thought the only reason people looked to him as a leader was because of their fear. He was tall and strong, and I had once seen him kill a man with one well-aimed strike of his fist during a tournament just two years prior to his coming of status. And while he was not the wisest lord, he was ambitious, and thus an easy choice when it came time to appoint the next powerful house. However, it would seem that even he could not keep the enemies at bay.

Sighing, I focused back on the road ahead and shifted in the saddle before glancing at the men. Donigan may not have sought me out, but he had been visible amongst the group during our journey. However, now I could not seem to spot him. Searching the party for his form, I steered my horse to the closest bannerman who trailed along behind me in hopes of answers.

"You," I barked, and he jumped at the sound of my voice before halting and then bowed at the waist.

"M'lady?" he questioned nervously and his eyes darted around as if he was making sure we were not within earshot of anyone else.

"Have you seen Donigan?" I asked while I scanned our army once more.

"Donigan?" One of his dark brows lifted, and I realized my mistake in addressing my friend with such familiarity.

"Sir Taith," I corrected. "Where is he?" The man's own gaze moved across the fields that surrounded us and then he pointed east.

"He rode with the scouts earlier this morning." My rough sigh was more obvious than I had meant for it to be, and the man took it as a sign to step closer before resting a hand on my horse's shoulder. The placement was dangerously near to where my leg rested, and I glared down at him.

"Is there something I can do for you, m'lady?" The

unspoken offer in his words was obvious and my scowl deepened.

"And what exactly is it you're suggesting, sir?" My tone was cold, and yet he still didn't have the decency to back away.

"I saw him come out of your tent in a huff after the night after the battle," he explained while his palm slowly stroked across my horse's neck. "And you need not worry, I won't say a word. But, if it's company you are looking for——"

His words stopped abruptly with a sharp gasp as I dismounted, and I watched his face slacken the moment he felt the tip of metal nudge against the tiny gap in his armour just beneath the arm that was raised. Waiting until his brown eyes met my own, I pressed the dagger against him with more force.

"You overstep, sir," I seethed, noticing the colour leave his face, and then it was me who crowded him. "I am going to assume you misspoke, and that is the only reason why this dagger is not lodged into your flesh. However, make that mistake again, and I will cut out your tongue and then I will let my father do with you as he will."

His throat bobbed roughly, and his lips parted as he searched for a response but decided to nod shakily instead. Angling the blade, I aimed the tip upwards and watched as the steel wedged itself into the middle of one of the small silver rings of his chainmail before a tiny spot of red bloomed across the light fabric of his gambeson.

It was not proper for a lady to be armed or to toss around threats so flippantly. But I would rather be punished for my behaviour than allow one of these lowly men to see me as weak.

"Be sure to quietly pass on the warning to any of the others who think such an offer is warranted." Removing my weapon, I spun on my heel and led my horse in the direction where I noticed a few men making their way back to us. Donigan was ahead of the group, and I could see the moment he spotted me. Frowning, I watched as he urged his horse to canter around the back of the group rather than taking what was obviously his original path.

I knew our argument had not been one for the faint of heart, but we had both drawn blood. I had hoped now that we had space away from each other and a chance to lick our wounds, we would be able to move past the heated words and the hurt they had left behind.

Donigan apparently had other ideas.

I shouldn't have been surprised really, he was known to avoid those he was cross with. And though we had never had a spat quite like the one in my tent, I figured a direct approach would be the best way to sort out this mess we had created.

Keeping track of his horse, I halted my steed and hoisted myself back into the saddle before making my way towards him. Donigan looked exhausted as he rubbed his forehead with the back of his hand, and I observed him for another heartbeat before I urged my horse to close the distance between us.

"Anything suspicious?" His spine straightened, but he did not meet my eyes.

"No." His tone was clipped, and I frowned before I tried once more.

"I suppose we will make it there by nightfall then, if there are no problems on the road."

"Yes." Growing irritated at his dismissal, I leaned over to grab at his arm and tugged on the limb until he met my gaze.

"Really? Is this how you plan on speaking to me for the rest of our journey?" I asked, noticing his brown eyes were guarded as they looked past my shoulder, and then he roughly pulled from my grasp.

"Well then, it is a good thing we have only a few hours' worth of travelling left," I continued, sitting back in my saddle with a frown, and Donigan narrowed his gaze before shaking his head.

"What?" I demanded, no longer willing to play this game with him.

"Nothing," he answered, but my irritation grew.

"Now you have nothing to say?" I sneered. "You certainly didn't have this issue last time we spoke."

"If I remember correctly, neither did you," he pointed out before he began to move his horse around my own.

"And yet I'm here trying to move past it," I argued as I followed.

"Is that what this is?" he asked with a dry laugh, and I felt my chest tighten at the unfamiliar cold sound. "Tell me, why must we all move past things on your terms? What if I want to be left alone until I am ready?"

"Then you'd spend the next three years sulking like a pitiful child."

Yanking on his reins, he halted his mount and then turned to me. The muscle ticking in his jaw and the heated look in his eyes made me want to shrink away from his fury, but I forced myself to hold his stare.

"This is what you do, you know. You find the weakest part of someone, and you attack it until you've shredded them to pieces." My stomach churned at his words, but he had not finished. "And then, when you've decided that *you* are no longer angry, you expect everyone else to just pick up the fragments and move on."

"You hurt me too," I snarled, though now one of my arms was pressing across my torso, almost as if I thought my limb would protect me from whatever blow of his was coming next.

"I know that," Donigan admitted with a sigh. "But the difference is that I didn't mean to. I said something horrible and stupid and felt regret immediately. I even tried to apologize the second it slipped from my lips. You, on the other hand, searched for what you knew would hurt me most and then made the calculated decision to say what you did just to wound me."

He was right, of course, but I didn't have the courage to say as much out loud.

"And I know that is how you are, I just never expected you to be that way with *me*."

He said nothing else before he kicked his mare forward, and I remained silent as I watched him go.

THOUGH THE BUILDINGS of Ferri looked rather rundown in the fading light of the setting sun, the village was still a welcome sight, and I ignored the others as I urged my horse past and approached my father.

"It seems as if all of the other highborn families and the Anointed have arrived already," I said as I lifted my chin to gesture to the lines of brightly coloured tents and banners that glowed under the last bit of orange that remained from the sunset.

"Being the final family to arrive means all eyes will be on us." There was a warning beneath those words, and I swallowed nervously. "Keep to yourself tonight and do not be seen tomorrow. I will tell the others you have caught a fever during our travels and will be resting for a few days."

It would have been a poor excuse for anyone else but given the fact the nobles paid little mind to the bastard of House Baxteel, I doubted anyone would question it. When my father's attention turned to me, I bit my tongue and nodded.

"Your brother's tent will be beside yours; when you leave events, be sure to go to his and stay there until he makes his way out," he explained as if we hadn't done this before.

"And do not be seen by anyone," he warned again.

"But what if they want to name the victors immediately after the event is done like they had tried to do at the last tourney?" I asked. "It is customary to remove your helmet during the awards, and we were nearly caught in the spring."

One dark brow lifted at me. "Are you so certain we will come out triumphant?"

I turned my gaze back to the tents and then lifted one shoulder. "I'm not sure many of these lords or their sons have had as much practice as I have lately."

I knew my father was just as irritated by the lack of action from the other houses. It was the Anointed's duty to protect Elrin; that responsibility was given to us by the Gods themselves. But the lesser noble families had not once offered us help as we dealt with the rising rebellion. Instead, they had hidden themselves away while enjoying the peace we protected, and now we would be expected to put aside any of our ire until the tourney was over.

"I will step in if they decide to award the victors," my father assured me. "I will insist they wait until after the champions have had a chance to make themselves presentable."

"That would save us from having to allow Skileer the option of competing. Gods forbid anyone see him for the fool he is." I had thought that my words were quiet enough that my father wouldn't have heard, but I was wrong. Hauling on his horse's reins, he halted his steed and then lunged for me. My own mount sidestepped away, but it wasn't far enough, and suddenly his large hand was cupping my jaw tightly. Pressing his fingers into the flesh of my face, my father pulled me close and glared at me.

"I allow you a great number of liberties as my bastard, Rígan, but you have forgotten your place too frequently as of late," he growled. "Do not make me be the one to remind you."

"Yes, my lord," I muttered through clenched teeth, and he

tightened his hold for another heartbeat before releasing me so roughly, I nearly toppled off my horse.

Not bothering to waste another moment on me, my father moved towards my brother, though he did not trouble himself with reprimanding Skileer for the smirk he sent my way, and I rubbed at my jaw as they led the group together.

"Are you okay?" Donigan asked softly from behind me, and I realized that I had been so focused on my father's retreat; I hadn't heard the knight approach.

"Fine," I snapped as I glanced at Donigan from over my shoulder. His dark eyes lingered on the skin my father had touched, and I knew there must have been a mark when I saw the way his gaze sharpened.

"I'm fine," I repeated, the ice from our earlier conversation now creeping back into my tone, and Donigan's shoulders fell slightly.

"We just have to get through the next few days, Rígan," he tried to assure me, but I rolled my eyes.

"And what do you think will happen then?" I laughed coldly. "This is my life, Donigan, and you, him, and everyone else never seem to allow me to forget it."

He lowered his head in shame, and I sighed roughly. "There will never be an end to this."

MY TENT WAS NOT NEARLY AS lavish as the other highborns', and I eyed the small area with a wrinkled nose. I knew I should not have expected much, but it was little more than what an errant knight would receive, and I knew it was meant to be a slight against me.

"Oh my," my brother chuckled as he entered what would be my chambers for the next few days. "Are you sure this isn't the servants' quarters, or perhaps it is meant to be for our horses?"

"What is it that you are needing, Skileer?" I snapped.

"Father wanted me to advise you on what events we will be participating in."

"We?" I scoffed with a shake of my head.

Choosing to ignore me, Skileer untied the wineskin from his belt and took a long swig of what I could only assume to be wine or ale. Tilting his head back, he finished the contents, wiped his wet mouth with the back of his hand, and then looked at me once more.

"As always, he thinks we should just consider the joust; he is worried the sword would give us away."

"And as always, he is right," I growled. The sword may have been my best event, had it not been for the fact that I was trying to disguise myself. But given the current arrangement, it would be too close of combat, and we worried my opponent would discover our secret should I even attempt it.

"But this is the final tournament of the year," my brother whined. "At least two events are expected. If we only do one, we won't have a chance at being crowned Grand Champion, and I am tired of always passing up the title."

"There is no we!" My brother's eyes narrowed before he glanced behind him towards the entrance of the tent.

"Lower your fucking voice," he demanded as he took a step towards me.

"The sword is out of the question, Skileer," I insisted, the words now just above a whisper. "It is better to keep our secret than risk our family's name all for the chance at being called the victor of a tourney, you know this."

"We have forfeited the name of champion for too long," he argued. "It is about time we show the other houses our true strength, and being named champion would be an honour for us all." He raised a hand and pointed one long and perfectly manicured finger at me. "You should be grateful to have any part in it."

"You mean *every* part," I growled under my breath while slapping his hand away, and my brother's face hardened with fury.

"Maybe," he murmured. "But even so, no one will ever sing ballads of your glory, sister," he reminded me. "Only mine."

With that he spun on his heel and made his exit, but not before he shot me a sly smile from over his shoulder.

CHAPTER
FOUR

THE WRAP AROUND MY BREASTS PULLED TIGHTLY OVER MY RIBS as I took in a deep breath, and I glanced across the tiltyard towards my opponent before lowering my arm for the lance. Curling my metal-clad fingers around the weapon, I winced at the awkward weight and cursed myself for not practicing over the last few months.

"Are you ready, my lord?" The squire peered up at me, his eyes roaming across the metal that shielded my face, and I gave him a curt nod.

The crowd had gathered, and their shouts and cheers were nearly enough to drown out the pounding of my heartbeat. Taking in another shuddering breath, I tightened my other hand around the leather of the reins while I eyed my competition once more.

My opponent was the eldest Marcer boy, and though his house was small, he had won a good number of jousts last year and would not be easily beat. Knowing this would not be a simple victory, I swallowed roughly against the wave of unease that washed over my body. Sensing my nervousness, my brother's favourite gelding fidgeted beneath me and one of his front hoofs began to paw the ground in irritation. But I didn't have a free hand or the will to soothe him. After all, I was about to force him to charge at a foe who had a high chance of wounding us both with the long lance now grasped in his hand.

"Lords and ladies, may I present our first two competitors," the bard suddenly called out from the royal boxes, and I scanned the noble houses until I found my father's scowl.

"Lord Ricird Marcer." The young man lifted the visor of his helm and raised the lance in their direction, preening under the blushing smiles of the maidens who watched with rapt curiosity. "And his competitor, Lord Skileer Baxteel."

All attention moved to me with far more interest than I had hoped for, and when I lifted my lance, my brother's gelding flew backwards until his front legs were striking the air. Leaning forward, I dug my heels into his belly in an attempt to keep him from rearing again and then turned him in a circle. However, I had been too distracted to notice the waving flag that indicated the joust had begun, and I scrambled to straighten the horse once more in order to push him forward.

"Go," I snarled under my breath while my opponent rushed towards us. "Move, damn you."

Marcer's massive bay mount was covering the ground at an alarming pace, and I was still stuck at my end, kicking at my horse like some green squire.

"Come on, you great beast," I whispered, throwing my hands forward so he would have his head while my calves closed around him, but he still would not go.

"What the hell are you doing?!" a deep voice shouted from behind me, and I glanced over my shoulder to see a hooded figure rush at my horse.

"Move!" he ordered, as if I hadn't been trying to do that very thing. Pressing my heels into the gelding's flesh, I urged my mount onward, but he snorted in protest and then began to hurry backwards.

Seeing my struggle, the stranger closed the distance

between us and lifted a hand. He brought his arm down, his palm striking my horse's flank, and it was enough to finally send the stubborn gelding forward.

"Go! Go!" I barked now that the wind would drown out my voice and then tightened my legs around the animal while we closed the distance between us and Marcer.

Coming to a head, I moved the lance, tucking the end closely to my ribs while the stock came across my body and the point was aimed towards my opponent. However, I had misjudged my approach, and the tip of my lance just missed his shoulder while his crashed into the side of my face, and I felt the end shatter against the metal of my helm.

Struggling to find my balance, I tugged on the reins of my horse and gasped for air while I waited for the ringing in my ears to stop. Once certain I wouldn't make a fool of myself and topple over in my saddle, I spun the gelding on his haunches, straightened my spine once more, and pressed on.

Everything about Ricird's approach was exactly what highborn boys were taught as children. He held his shoulders square and remained focused until the very last moment. I, however, had dropped my chin, too nervous of the impact of the lance to really come at it head-on and that had been why I had missed my mark.

Determined not to make the same mistake again, I held my head high as our horses passed. Moving my lance, I watched with satisfaction as it hit the centre of his chest. Not prepared for the force of the impact, Marcer's shoulders fell back. However, it wasn't until I reached the end of the yard and turned my horse to face him once more that I noticed the man was crumpled on the ground while the crowd suddenly grew quiet. Two squires and the knight marshal ran to him, and I held my breath as we waited.

Unhorsing him would earn me the victory, but as time passed and no one moved, I grew more wary. Winning the joust had been the goal, but I hadn't wanted to seriously injure or maim the boy in the process. But despite my guilt, I highly doubted my father would really mind, especially considering House Marcer was not important in his eyes.

Time seemed to slow; it felt like ages before there was any indication of the seriousness of his injury, and when I heard his scream of pain, I felt my stomach churn. Slowly they lifted his now partially armoured body, and I watched as his right leg dangled at an odd angle before I turned my gaze away.

"Well done, my lord!" the squire from before cheered gleefully as he ran towards me to grab the reins of my horse. "There will be no coming back to the tourney for him!"

Offering him little more than a grunt, I dismounted and shoved past him, making certain my shoulder collided with his roughly as I made my way towards the exit of the tiltyard. However, it would seem that I would not get far, and I froze when my father's voice called from behind me.

"Cool that beast down before you give him any water or grain," he ordered the squire, and I remained still until I felt his hand clap me on the back.

"You did well." My father was pleased, just as I had predicted, and I peered at him through the slits of my visor as he nodded at his fellow lords and ladies who we passed as we made our way through camp. "When we get to the tent, I want you to give your brother your breastplate and plackart."

I stiffened and my stride slowed, but my father had no patience for that and ushered me through the entrance of Skileer's tent. Once protected by the fabric walls, my father tied the flaps shut and spun on his heel to face us once more.

"How did we do?" my brother asked, not bothering to sit up from his bedroll, and my father moved across the space before grabbing at Skileer's tunic. Curling the material in his fingers, he dragged my brother to his feet, and we both watched as he swayed.

"You idiotic fool," my father seethed as he took in the state of my brother. "You couldn't wait one day before indulging yourself?"

"No one is here, no one will know!" Skileer insisted, and fury clouded my father's face before he shoved my brother towards me, and I hurriedly pulled off my helm.

"Are you not embarrassed that *we* are here to see you in such a state?" he sneered as he approached. "Get your sister out of that armour and put it on."

"Why?" he asked, and it was then that I noticed just how glazed his eyes were.

"Because you need to go celebrate your victory, and you cannot do so looking the way you are."

"He's too drunk," I pointed out as my brother struggled with the buckles of my armour, and my nose wrinkled at the smell of his ale-soaked breath. "People will notice."

"We will say he has taken a tonic for the pain from the first blow. That his head ached, and he needed something to nurse the throbbing before he could collect his winnings," my father ordered, and I shrank back from him while the metal of my armour was lifted from my body.

Standing quiet and still, I watched as he helped Skileer with the breastplate, and when he was certain his son looked the part, his stern gaze met mine.

"When all is quiet outside, go to your tent and stay there for the rest of the evening." His eyes narrowed and I lowered my chin to my chest. "Remain silent and unseen as a lady should."

He explained his expectations almost as if I hadn't been doing this well-practiced routine for years, but I still nodded. Certain I understood his instructions, my father placed a hand on my brother's back and steered him out of the tent and into the night so that they could revel in *their* victory.

It was quiet, far quieter than I had been expecting for the first night of the tourney, and I ran my brush through my hair for the dozenth time while I sat on my bedroll beneath the flickering light of the lanterns. My father and brother had already returned from their boasting of their victory and had long since settled in their tents. The rest of our men had scattered throughout the camp as the festivities commenced, though I was certain most were now probably drunk or sleeping, and Donigan had been nowhere to be seen for the entire day.

Realizing I was well and truly alone and unsupervised, I grabbed the cloak I had tossed aside when we had arrived and slid my feet into my boots before lifting the hood to conceal my face. Blowing out the lanterns, I moved to the back of my tent and carefully pulled at the bottom. Loosening the fabric as much as I could, I then lowered myself to the ground. The earth was cool and soft, and the mud would certainly stain my shift, but I didn't care.

Sliding under the canvas, I stayed still for a breath, making certain no one was around before I curled the wool of my cloak around myself and then stood. The tents were backed closely together, leaving only a tight alleyway for me, but with the dimming fires and lack of observers, I would have an easy time of remaining unseen.

Carefully stepping over the stakes and lines, I tried to search between the tents for the bright yellow banner with the pair of snakes. However, although the dwindling light allowed me to travel undetected, it made it difficult to navigate my path, and I had been too distracted in my hunt to notice where I had placed my feet. Catching the toe of my boot on a line, I lifted a hand to press against the tent to my left, and my palm slid across the rough fabric as I struggled to right myself.

"What was that?" a voice called from inside the shelter, and I cursed under my breath when I heard the stranger begin to shuffle towards me on the other side of the wall. Knowing I had little time before I was found out, I scanned the area once more and spotted the yellow that called me to like beacon before I made a run for it.

The night air chilled my skin while I hurried towards the tents, and I shivered as the damp began to seep into my bones. Clinging to my cloak, I curled my covered arms around my torso and then slowed as I finally reached my destination.

Tiptoeing between the structures, I pressed closely to each of them, holding my breath as I tried to listen to who may occupy their space until I found who I was looking for. He was singing softly, his deep voice just a hum really, and I felt my heart race at the sound before I stepped closer.

"Gwain?" I whispered, and I heard his sharp gasp before soft footsteps approached.

"Rígan?" I could make out his silhouette now, and I drummed my fingers against the material. "What are you doing here?"

Rolling my eyes at the disapproval in his voice, I bent low to the ground, searching for a way in.

"Your men need to teach ours how to properly construct tents," I grumbled as I pulled at the fabric, but it would not slacken.

"Step away." His words sent a painful stab of rejection through me, but then I noticed the sharp tip of a blade and I watched as he cut a line down the middle before his hand snuck through the hole and he pulled. Stretching it open, he gestured for me to come forward, and I carefully pressed through the tight passageway.

Now within the shelter of his chambers, Gwain hurriedly wrapped an arm around me and directed my cold nose into the warm skin of his neck while his other hand carded through my hair. "What were you thinking?"

Pulling from his touch, I tilted my head back and peered at his handsome face, taking in his green eyes and auburn hair. Gwain's own gaze roamed across my features before settling on my cheeks, and then his mouth fell into a frown.

"You look absolutely frozen." Grabbing at my hands, he untangled them from my cloak and lifted them to his lips. Cupping them carefully, Gwain pressed the frigid tips of my fingers to his mouth and blew warm air across the skin before kissing each one softly. Certain there was some warmth in them once more, his attention moved to my body, and I watched as the disapproval in his eyes melted into hunger.

"You ran across camp in your shift?" His voice was deep, and the sound sent a fluttering through my belly.

"Yes." One of my brows rose, and my chin lifted in challenge.

"What if someone saw you?" he all but snarled, though his hands were now undoing the metal clasp of the wool cloak that covered me before roughly pushing it from my shoulders.

"I would hope you would have more faith in me than that," I scoffed, but Gwain paid me no mind, he was now totally focused on the laces that sat between my breasts. Undoing the knot with ease, he tugged the fabric down my arms and watched as it fell to the ground.

"What will I do with you?" he whispered softly, and my head lolled back as the tips of his fingers stroked across the now-exposed skin of my chest and then they moved.

Down, and down, and *down*.

He kneeled at my feet, and his hands caressed the back of my left calf before he urged me to lift my foot. Peeling off my boot, he then switched feet and then disposed of the other. Pressing a quick kiss to the skin of my right thigh, Gwain grabbed for the shift that had lain on the earth beneath his knees and studied it for a heartbeat while I panted above him.

Looking up at me, he curled his lips in a sly smile and he lifted the thin material and gently began cleaning the mud that had spattered up my legs. Taking the time to get every droplet, Gwain made certain I was clean and then tossed the sullied fabric towards the foot of his bedroll. Finally finding the strength to move, I lifted a hand and cupped his jaw in my palm, gasping sharply when he took my thumb between his lips and nipped at the pad roughly.

Feeling that familiar warmth pool between my legs, I pressed against his lower lip, dragging it down for a pause and then moved my hand into his thick hair.

"What *do* you want to do with me?" I asked, my voice now low and heated, and his eyes darkened while his mouth shifted into a filthy grin.

"There aren't enough words to accurately describe it all, Rígan."

Curling my fingers, I tipped his head back before bending forward. Pausing just a breath away from his lips, my mouth shifted and the smile now matched his own.

"Then show me."

"WHERE THE FUCK HAVE YOU BEEN?" Donigan's voice came from the dark corner of my tent, and I spun to face him with a scowl before bending to smooth the bottom of the canvas.

"Are we talking again?" I asked as I strode across the space and grabbed the tinder box so I could light the lanterns.

"I know you don't always make the wisest choices, but I never thought you would be so completely reckless," he snapped with a shake of his head. Rolling my eyes, I struck the flint and then dipped a wooden splint into the small flame before transferring it to the wick of a candle. Certain the flame would stay, I blew on the splint and turned to face Donigan once more.

"I was careful." It was not a lie; I had made sure to return to my chambers long before dawn to make certain I would not be spotted. However, I had obviously underestimated Donigan.

"Do you have any idea what happened last night after you decided to go to that fool's bed?" Clenching my jaw, I narrowed my eyes at him, but he ignored my silent warning. "It appears you and your brother do share a trait after all."

"And what would that be?" Donigan's fierce glower faltered at my tone, and I waited as he seemed to gather himself once more.

"He too snuck out in the middle of the night." My stomach twisted at the information, and he nodded when he saw my gaze widen.

"Where did he go?" The words were quiet, but the nervous tremble of my voice was apparent.

"Also in search of someone to warm his bed, I'm guessing. Or at least that had been his destination at first."

Growing annoyed, I strode towards Donigan and squared my shoulders. "You are not this concerned over my brother's choice in bed mate. So, spit it out, what happened?"

Donigan ran a hand through his dark hair and began pacing. "He did end up at the brothel, and when he was turned away from that establishment, he set his sights on the tavern."

"Of course he did." It was no surprise that Skileer would cause us trouble, but I was shocked that he had made it out from under my father's watchful gaze, and on the first night at that.

"He was not the only lord who gathered there," Donigan continued. "It seems most of the highborns were well into their cups by midnight."

"As is customary." I shrugged. Skileer was a drunk, but he

was not alone in that habit. Many of his fellow lords had a tendency to overindulge, and if that was the worst of it, I was not concerned. After all, I was the one who would be participating in the second day of the tourney, not him.

"Your brother's arrogance seems to grow tenfold under the influence of ale," Donigan muttered.

"Unfortunately, I think all men suffer that particular ailment," I replied with a raised brow and crossed my arms over my chest while I waited for him to get on with it.

"Perhaps," he agreed. "But not all of us become stupid enough to challenge a man to the sword."

"What?" I gasped, certain I had heard him wrong.

"He challenged a fellow lord to the event in front of a room full of witnesses; and now they will be expecting him in a few hours."

Reeling, I staggered a step backward while my arm flung to the side to grasp on to the back of a chair. Curling my fingers around the wood, I closed my eyes and tried to put together a plan. However, it would seem that Donigan hadn't finished relaying his story of the night before, and he cleared his throat. Opening my eyes at the sound, I searched his gaze and felt another wave of dread crash into me.

"Who did he challenge?!" I demanded, growing more worried as my knight's face paled and then his expression hardened. "Who did he challenge, Donigan?"

"Reide," he answered. "He challenged Caedell Reide."

CHAPTER
FIVE

"How could you be so stupid?!" I hissed as I tore the furs off my brother, and when he opened one bleary eye with a grunt, I choked down the urge to strike him across his face.

"Godsdamn you, woman! Can't you find someone else to pester?" he growled as he reached for the grey pile at his feet, but I slapped at his hand.

"Caedell Reide?!" I snarled. "Do you have any idea what you have done?!"

"Is that what you're upset about?" he scoffed with a roll of his eyes and then turned away from me.

His casualness about the situation only enraged me further, and when he glanced over his shoulder and noticed my expression, he sighed as if I was the one who was not reacting accordingly.

"Oh, come now, he's just a man, not a God. You have no reason to be so out of wits. I am certain we can beat him."

"We!? There is no we in this, Skileer," I snapped. "How have you still not come to understand that?"

"Mind how you speak to me, sister," Skileer warned as he rolled back over, and I narrowed my eyes down at him.

"You have challenged Caedell Reide in the sword!" I growled. "*I* do not have a chance in hell at winning this."

"Now, don't be so modest," my brother murmured as he sat up from his bedroll. "It doesn't suit you."

"I am not being modest, you idiotic fool!" My voice rose along with my anger, and I watched as his dark eyes shot to the entrance of his tent before the corner of his lips lifted in a smirk.

"That is enough, Rígan." My father's voice was quiet and cold, and I glanced over my shoulder at him in surprise.

"You don't know what he has done," I whispered with a shake of my head, and I pointed a finger in my brother's face. "He would have me face the Heir of House Reide in combat all because he fell into his cups and could not control his pride."

My father's scowl deepened until his face displayed the same fury that was burning under my skin, and I heard my brother shuffle in his bed and then he was stumbling to his feet while my father stared him down.

"You did *what*?" I knew that tone; there would be no talking his way out of this one for Skileer, and I moved aside as my father charged forward.

"I don't see what the problem is." Skileer's eyes darted between my father and me. "She is skilled in combat, and you even said she has had more practice than most! Besides," Skileer muttered. "The sword offers nearly as many points as the joust. We would truly have a chance of being named Grand Champion and bringing glory to our house if we were to win."

"You are right, she has had more practice than *most*," my father agreed, though his voice remained low with rage. "More than any other house."

My brother began to nod vehemently, thinking he had somehow convinced my father that his plan was clever, and I wondered how he missed the coldness in our father's gaze. "Any other house *besides* House Reide."

"They are the other Anointed named by the Huntress and are the only other family south of the northern border who have bothered to fight the rebellion in the name of the Divine Triad," I added through gritted teeth.

"And do you know what they call their heir?" my father asked as he glared at his son, who only shook his head in response. "Of course you don't, why would you bother to pay attention to anything of importance."

"They call him Caedell the Undying," I whispered past the tightness in my throat.

My brother's attention moved to me, and he rolled his eyes at my words. "That sounds like an old wives' tale."

"Tale or not, his reputation precedes him." My father drew my brother's focus once more. "And if the murmurings should be true, then the man is as close to invincible as one could be."

"But he is no older than Rígan." Skileer lifted a hand at me. "How could he possibly be so great?"

"He is two years her junior," my father corrected. "But unlike your sister, he carries his family name."

"And that makes a difference?" Skileer scoffed, and I lifted a hand to rub at my temples in an attempt to will away the pounding behind my eyes.

"It makes a world of difference!" my father barked. "It means he has been raised to lead. He has upheld his family's reputation and has reaped the benefits. He has been trained by the finest of men, sparred with the best soldiers and knights, and he has not been forced to do all of it quietly, away in secret should prying eyes look too closely at him."

"But surely, we should not be so concerned! Rígan must be as skilled as a man two years younger than her, even if she has not had the same options in the light of day." It was no surprise that the only time my brother spoke highly of me was when he needed to weasel his way out from a problem of his own making.

"Even if that were true," I sighed, "there is no possible way that I could be that close in combat with him and not give myself away."

"You will have to find a way." My eyes darted to my father, and my mouth hung open. "There were too many witnesses. To pull out now would be an embarrassment."

Clearing my throat, I struggled to find my voice and swallowed once more before croaking out, "But, Father, what if—"

"Withdrawing is not an option; I will not have the other houses whispering about our cowardice."

"Besides," Skileer chimed in while his gaze caught my own, "even if she does fall to his sword, it's not as if she is your *true* heir."

I was sure I would have flinched from his comment had I not been expecting it. My father, however, did not take the words lightly, and I watched in astonishment as he swung the back of his hand across my brother's mouth.

"She is meant to be you!" he snarled. "What would we do with you should she be seriously injured or killed?"

It was as if Skileer finally realized the seriousness of the situation, and I watched as his face paled.

"You best pray to the Gods, boy, and hope that the Protector hears you." Turning back around, my father scanned me from head to toe before a look of disdain settled over his face.

"And should you make it out of this out alive, we will discuss the punishment suitable for sneaking into that boy's tent last night."

My armour felt twice as heavy as it had the day before, and my vision spun as we approached the sword yards. However, I could scarcely make out the round pen where I would face my opponent. It would seem that word had spread of my brother's challenge, and the crowd looked more than eager to witness the duel between the two Anointed houses of the Huntress.

"Do what is needed," my father murmured quietly, and I tipped my head in question, but remained silent now that we were surrounded by others. "Win by whatever means necessary; this is not a time nor place for honour."

He was wrong, of course, that is exactly what a tournament was meant to show. But I knew that winning was what mattered most to my father, and he did not care how I found my victory.

Unable to respond, I turned ahead once more, not noticing the way that my hands were shaking until I missed the pommel of my sword when I reached for it. Worried someone else may have witnessed my nerves, my eyes bounced across the crowd.

"Edwyn!" a voice called, and I turned to face the man as he strode towards us.

Lord Reide was said to have been a brutal warrior and renowned knight. But looking at him now, it was obvious that time had not been kind to him. What was once a strong and fierce man was now replaced with a middle-aged lord whose bloated belly and deeply lined face reflected none of his great victories.

"I must say, I was rather surprised to hear your son had challenged mine, Edwyn." My father's face hardened at the words, and his dark eyes scanned what was once said to be a childhood friend in blatant distaste.

"I don't see why that would be, Carlel," my father drawled before he roughly clapped a hand against my metal-clad back. "Our houses have always enjoyed a respectable rivalry."

"That may be so," Carlel hummed as he smoothed a hand across his rounded chin. "But I did not expect your son to follow your footsteps. He just doesn't seem the type."

My stomach twisted with unease, but I forced myself to keep still.

"News of his most recent victories on the battlefields against the rebels must not have reached you in Port Huronian" My heart thundered as Carlel's eyes roamed across my helm and visor, and I prayed to the Gods he did not find a hint of whatever it was he was looking for in his assessment.

"Yes, but that is the strange part of it all," the lord sighed. "There are many rumblings of your triumphs, but so few accounts of anyone actually interacting with your son on the battlefield. It is said that he allows his guards and high-ranking men to do the ordering."

My father remained stoic and appeared to be indifferent to the obvious accusation, though I knew it was the well-practiced mask; I could tell by the throbbing vein in his throat.

"Yes, well, you know how battles can be. There is little more than swords and death. Most men lose track of who is who during the chaos, and my son is a strong but quiet leader. He has no need to throw his weight around to prove himself."

Lord Reide said nothing more on the matter and instead turned towards the knight who was now approaching. His helm was tucked beneath one arm while the other rested on the hilt of his blade that was strapped to his waist.

Caedell Reide and I had been close enough in age to come across each other as children, though I was rarely allowed to accompany my father to court in the capital of Wahstand or to Caedell's home in Port Huronian. In fact, the last time we had seen each other had been just weeks after my fifteenth birthday. That had been over a decade ago, and this was not a man I easily recognized.

"Lord Baxteel." My brows furrowed as his voice carried across the space between us when he greeted my father, and I tried to place the familiarity of the sound while observing him closely.

He was tall, perhaps a few inches taller than me, and he was broad in the shoulders, making him seem far more imposing than most men. His jaw was sharp, no longer carrying the fat of childhood, and his distinct amber eyes that I did remember no longer seemed as bright as they had once been. He was handsome, devastatingly so, and I watched as his deep chestnut hair blew in the soft breeze.

"Skileer." His attention had turned to me, and he lifted his left arm in my direction.

Clenching my jaw, I moved to grab at his forearm, as he did the same to me in what was the customary greeting between knights. Praying that my limb felt no different than other men's with the cover of the vambrace, I held my breath as he kept the position for a heartbeat while he seemed to study me the same way his father had.

"I am pleased to see the ale did not have a long-lasting effect on you, sir." His mouth lifted on one side in a mischievous grin. "I was worried you would not find your way out of your bedroll in time to face me."

"He can handle his ale," my father growled, but Caedell's smirk only grew.

"I'm pleased to see it, my lord." My skin may have been damp with sweat beneath all the layers of metal, but I still shivered at the look in the knight's gaze as he took me in. "I have been craving some decent competition. None of the other lads seem to know the difference between one end of their sword from the other."

All eyes turned to me in question, but the Gods must have seen fit to pity me, and I was saved from responding by the sound of the tourney horn, which signified it time we readied ourselves for the event. Lifting his helmet, Caedell glanced at me once more before securing the metal over his head and then he turned for the ring. Remaining rooted in my spot, I watched as he disappeared into the crowd and did not move to follow him until my father roughly pushed me forward.

"What are you standing around for?" he snarled. "Go!"

Stumbling, I trailed behind my opponent while fear's cold, sharp fingers curled around my throat in an unforgiving hold while I entered the sword yards.

Usually, men come out of the tourneys mostly unscathed, and though deaths were rare, it did happen from time to time. But the man before me was called the Undying for a reason. I had heard all about his conquests over the years as he travelled across Elrin and the Barren Sea. At the age of just eight-and-ten he had taken a small fleet of his father's men to Lythnals and the Scattered Islands to stop a group of rebels from destroying the Healer's sanctuary that had been crafted there by the first men of Elrin. The Forefolk had spent decades building the temple for the God of health and longevity, and it was said there were a great many precious and ancient things hidden there.

When Caedell had reached his destination, he was facing at least a hundred men. But by the time he was done with them, the bay of the island was renamed Bloodstone Bay and none of his enemies had escaped with their lives. It was said that even now, six years later, the stones were still darkened from the blood of his adversaries, and I wondered if the soft sand that was currently beneath our feet would meet the same fate as those rocks.

"I promise to give you a chance to show us your impressive skills before I beat you down, Skileer!" Caedell grinned, and the crowd cheered and hollered as we circled each other, but I still said nothing.

"Why so quiet now? You were so very sure of yourself last night!" More noise came from the bodies that surrounded the ring, and Caedell seemed to flourish under the attention. Watching him closely, I waited for him to turn to his audience and then I lunged.

However, he seemed to know I would go for the obvious opening, and he dodged the blow before he spun to face me.

"Now, now," he chided me as we moved once more in a circle, though it was almost as if he prowled across the space, his movements so fluid that they could only be described as feline. "I would have thought better of you, Lord Baxteel. Where is your honour?"

My teeth clenched as I charged again, but he met my blow with his own blade and then slipped out from beneath the attack with more ease than I would have thought possible.

"Where is your patience and cleverness? I've heard so much about it, but it has yet to be seen." He was taunting me, and much to my dismay, it was working. Every failed attack, every miss of my blade, made my irritation grow, and my eyes slid to my father's in the crowd.

"Father dearest does not look too pleased," Caedell taunted, and this time, when our swords kissed, I released the hilt with one hand and slammed it into the uncovered space beneath his arm that was exposed from his defence against my strike.

It wasn't the most painful place, but I made sure to dig my metal-covered knuckles into the groove, and Caedell nearly dropped his sword from the blow.

"You nearly had me there," he chuckled roughly while he shook out his arm before gathering himself once more. "But now I see the kind of fight you are looking for, and I am happy to forgo propriety if that's what you are wanting."

There was something about the way he said the words that had me regretting my decision, and when he came forward, it took every ounce of my strength to hold him off. Blow after blow rained down on me and I panted for air, the heat of my breath making my face damp and uncomfortable in my helm as I defended myself against his onslaught of attacks.

Growing weary, I widened my stance, and when his sword came from above once more, I locked my arms and let his blade rest against mine until his weight was on his toes. And then, when I knew he was changing his balance, I mimicked his move from before and slipped out from under the pressure. Now, without my blade to rest against, he fell forward as I dashed to the side.

Finally getting some relief, I took a steadying breath and then turned to face him, readying myself to finish this once and for all. However, I had not been prepared for the hand he had used to catch himself to come towards my face.

Suddenly the visor of my helm was covered in the sand that was scattered across the ground and my eyes closed from the irritation, leaving me open to his assault. Taking advantage of my blindness, he rammed what felt to be a heel of a boot into my breastplate, and I went tumbling backwards. Sprawled across the ground, I gasped as the wind was pushed from my lungs, and I lifted my sword in hopes of fighting him off. However, it was no use, and the weapon was knocked from my hand instantly.

"Do you yield?" I could feel the tip of Caedell's blade press against the silver that covered my chest, and I took a deep breath while my lashes fluttered as they struggled to clear the grit from my eyes.

"Do you yield?" he asked once more, and though my vision was blurry, I could just make out his form as he bent down next to me.

Hurriedly nodding, I waited for a moment, thinking he had come to my level to offer me a hand in order to help me to my feet. However, instead he lifted his helm from his head and then came close, so close his face was nearly pressed against the steel that covered my own.

"Pity, I thought you would put up more of a fight and show me what a true champion was," he said softly. "Isn't that what you promised to do last night?"

Holding my breath, I remained on my back, and his lips twisted into a sneer. "Though I don't know how you could claim to be such a man when you would have lost your joust had it not been for me."

Stiffening, I turned my head away from him and clenched my eyes shut while I waited for him to rise to his full height once more. Scoffing under his breath, Caedell finally moved, and I swallowed the bile rising up the back of my throat but remained still. And when I was sure he was no longer standing over me, my eyes opened, and I was met with my father's disapproving glare.

CHAPTER
SIX

MY FATHER ALL BUT DRAGGED ME BACK TO OUR TENT, seemingly unaware of the onlookers we passed as they headed to the awards ceremony. When we finally reached our destination, he pushed me through the entrance and then pulled my helm from my head before throwing it at my brother, who was sprawled across the bed.

Not prepared for the impact, the metal collided with my brother's chest, and he grunted in pain before looking at my father with a panic-stricken face.

"What happened?" His attention moved to me, and his eyes narrowed. "Did you fail us?"

When I didn't respond, he pushed further. "I suppose I shouldn't be surprised. As you said, Reide has the breeding; his mother wasn't some kitchen wench who didn't know her place."

Fury burned through me, and I tugged my arm free from my father's grasp before launching myself at Skileer. Swinging, I clipped his jaw with my fist, but before I could get another hit in, strong arms wrapped around my body, and I was hauled away from the cowering man before me.

"Enough!" my father snarled, nearly tossing me to the floor as he shoved me aside.

"She hit me," Skileer whimpered while his hand cupped his jaw, and I rolled my eyes.

"You're lucky she got to you first!" my father bellowed, his dark eyes burning with rage as they bounced between my brother and me. "And if we wouldn't have every eye on us in the camp, I'd give you both a dozen lashes."

Though it had been years, I could still remember his last punishment all too well, and I flinched as his gaze settled on me.

"You disappointed me today, Rígan." The heavy weight of shame forced my head to bow, and I cast my eyes to the ground.

"So that's it then, Reide did beat us? How badly?" Skileer asked, suddenly forgetting his injured face as he scrambled to his feet.

"He wouldn't have had the chance had you not been stupid enough to challenge him!" my father roared, and it was my brother's turn to flinch while he threw his hands in the air in surrender. "You are no better than every other drunken fool, and if you were not my heir…"

There was no reason to finish the threat, we both knew exactly what he would do if we were of no longer any use to him.

"Go back to your tent and get cleaned up," he ordered me before focusing back on my brother. "And you, you do not leave the cover of these four walls until you are sober. We have the feast to attend tonight, and I will be damned if either of you embarrass me again."

"She's going?" my brother scoffed, only to take a step back when my father moved towards him.

"She has been hidden away with a fever and yet, no one has seen her, and we have not sent for a healer. What do you think that means?" Skileer's mouth opened but he had no answer, so my father answered for him. "That means either her fever has broken, or things are far more dire than what we let on. We cannot continue this ploy for much longer, so tonight she will make her appearance, and we will show the other families a united front."

He said nothing more, but lifted a single brow, and I nodded while my brother did the same.

"Good, now get out of my sight, Rígan," he barked. "I don't want to set eyes on you again until tonight."

GLANCING IN THE MIRROR, I took in my reflection while my fingers toyed with the silk skirt of my dress. The deep red colour was not customary for our house, but it complemented my skin, and I flicked the long dark strands of my hair over my shoulder. Admiring the plunging neckline, I traced the gap in the fabric to where it ended only a few inches above my navel and eyed my ample cleavage. Turning to the side, I watched the way the skirt split open to reveal one of my long thick thighs and then swayed back and forth.

Gwain had presented it to me the evening I had snuck into his tent, and I felt my heart race at my reflection. He had gotten it a few months ago when he had visited the southern continent of Osallow, and though it was far more scandalous than any of my other gowns, I felt stunning in it.

Toying with the soft material once more, I tried to picture what his expression would be when he laid eyes on me at the feast, and let the thought ease the anxiety and shame I had been carrying since my father had ordered me away.

"Oh my, that is quite the dress. You are going to send tongues wagging." Spinning, I turned to the entrance of my tent to face my intruder, and she grinned when she saw my startled expression.

"What are you doing here?" I asked once my heart settled in my chest, and then I was crossing the space between us before wrapping my arms around her.

"You didn't think my father would allow us to miss the biggest feast this autumn, did you?" Catiline laughed as her own thin arms embraced me, and I held her tightly for another moment.

Catiline Noorese was the youngest daughter of a lesser house from southern Elrin and had seven siblings who were far more important to her father, especially after the bouts of poor health she had as a child. It had been assumed she would not make it to adulthood, and though her house belonged to the Healer, everyone expected that the God would ignore their prayers and would send her into death's waiting hands.

They had been wrong, of course. The woman, though small, was not as fragile as she appeared, and she had persevered, overcoming whatever challenge the Divine Triad gave her.

"I heard you were bedridden with a fever, but you don't seem to be ill to me." Catiline smiled as her gaze roamed across my face, and I scanned her own petite features. She looked well, her angular dark eyes and pert nose were exactly as I remembered, though her high cheekbones had more colour to them than the last time I had seen her.

"I am feeling much better," I murmured, and then pulled from her embrace to look at her own stunning gown. It was far more modest, the type of dress a highborn lady was expected to wear. The soft orange fabric was flattering on her pale skin while the long length of her black hair was piled high on her head in a neat and tidy twist—another practice most women followed.

"I guessed, especially given that Donigan was not sitting

guard outside your tent." She winked. "There is no way he would have left you to suffer alone."

Catiline and I had known each other for our entire lives, and just like every summer since we were babes, she had been visiting our lands when Donigan had come to us. In fact, she had taken quite a liking to him almost immediately, though was too shy to say as much. Instead, she had kept a distance, too nervous to approach him and he was too oblivious to notice the way she stared. This had continued for the years that followed, though she seemed less enamoured these days, and I wondered if someone else had caught her attention.

"He and I are currently not seeing eye to eye." I shrugged before turning to the mirror to smooth my hair.

"What did you do this time?" I waited until her gaze met mine in the reflection and then I narrowed my own into a glare.

"Why are you assuming I did something, Cat?" Her pretty eyes rolled, and she placed her hands on her hips.

"Because you have a viper's tongue and very little patience." My face hardened, but she did not back down. "Rígan, you know how you can be."

"And how is that?" I snapped, but she did not waver.

"As cold and unforgiving as the Denimoore Mountains."

Much to my dismay, my lips quirked just slightly. "That was your choice of comparison?"

She lifted her little chin and straightened as tall as she could, but even then she only reached my collarbone.

"Well, it works, doesn't it?" she asked and I huffed.

"How would I know? It's not as if neither of us have ever been," I retorted, and she chewed on her lower lip and shrugged.

"Well, they're in the north and I've read about them," she muttered. "So, I stand by my assessment." Not bothering to respond, I instead made certain I looked perfect one last time before moving away from the glass.

"Rígan, what did you do?" she pressed once I stood before her.

"We had a disagreement." I said no more on the matter, but the stubbornness that had kept Catiline alive for all these years despite the odds not being in her favour seemed to rear its ugly head at the worst of times.

"And you said something unkind," she guessed, and I glowered at her.

"As one does in an argument," I pointed out. "And Donigan is not blameless, he said his piece as well." My tone was cool, but she appeared to be indifferent to the chill.

"Yes, that is usually the way of such things," she agreed. "But you are not one to lose. Especially when it comes to a spar of words."

Sighing, I lifted my gaze from her face and looked around the room while she continued. "Though you often forget that the rest of us are not like you."

"You mean you're not cold and unforgiving. Yes, you've said as much already." I noticed the lovely woman tip her head to the side from the corner of my eye.

"Strong," Cat corrected. "You are also stronger than most, and you tend to give more than the rest of us can take."

"What is your point?" I asked while my attention settled back on her, and I studied her face carefully.

"You don't tread lightly, you don't hold back, even when you know the wound you are about to inflict would be lethal, so to speak."

"So, you mean to say that I am expected to take the lashing from others without a blink of an eye because I can, but not retaliate to the same measure?" Her brows furrowed. "Why do I have to cater to those who are weak? Why do I have to watch my words more carefully, why can't they find a way to be stronger? That hardly seems fair. Just because I can handle more cruelty doesn't mean I should have to."

"Rígan," Catiline started, but I lifted a hand to stop her.

"Why do you think I'm strong? How did I become this way?" She had no answer so I pushed on. "Because I had to be, Cat. I had to grow claws, I had to find my venomous tongue and shield myself with the wall of ice, you so easily pointed out, to survive this world and the life I was given."

"Rígan——" Cat whispered but I ignored her.

"If Donigan can't do the same, that is not my fault. Though I'm not surprised to see you come to his aid, you always did have the urge to rescue the sad and wounded, especially if the person in question was Donigan Taith."

Her eyes widened while her face flushed. "I didn't mean——"

"It's fine," I interrupted, I had let things get away from me and had shown her too much, and now I was tucking those pieces of me back inside before a mask of indifference fell over my face. "We are late, you should go."

Turning from her, I grabbed at my fur-lined cloak and covered my shoulders. The sheer sleeves would do little to protect me from the autumn wind, but it did not matter. There was already a sense of numbness covering my skin.

Swallowing roughly, I glanced back at the small woman and gestured for her to exit my tent with a jerk of my head. Ducking her chin, she hid from my piercing gaze, and when the flaps closed behind her, the air left my lungs in a rush.

THE CHATTER WAS SO loud I could scarcely hear the soft sound of the bard singing. But when I stepped into the light, heads turned in my direction and then the talking quieted almost all at once. Lifting my chin, I unclasped my cloak and shrugged the weight of it off my shoulders, and suddenly the hushed voices began once more. And while this time the volume was far quieter, the whispers moved through the crowd in a wave, so obvious I could track its tide. Stepping farther into the feast hall of the manor, I let my audience have their fill.

Attention was not a foreign concept to me. Over the years I had my fair share, and after nearly three decades, I had learned to flourish under it, whether it be bad or good. Currently, it appeared to be a mix of both. Most of the men were watching my every move with wide eyes and open mouths, though some visibly disapproved of my choice of gown. The women, however, were far more favourable and seemed to admire the style.

"Won't you be cold, my lady?" Donigan's voice sounded from my right, and I glanced at him as he offered me an arm.

"On the contrary, ice is in my veins apparently," I replied with a sweet smile while I placed my palm on his forearm, and his face fell in confusion as he led me to our table.

Now within eyesight, my father scanned me from head to toe but said nothing. My brother, however, lowered his cup and curled his lips in disgust.

"What are you wearing?" he whispered while leaning across the table, and I sank into my seat.

"One of your gowns, you can have it back when I'm done," I snapped back, and Donigan choked on his wine from his place beside me. Realizing I had said my retort loud enough for others to hear, I glanced at my father. His expression was hard but rather than reprimanding me, he placed a strong hand on my brother's shoulder.

"She is using her best attribute, as she should," he said as he settled against the back into his chair.

"Notice the other houses." Skileer's attention moved to the other tables and then he looked back to my father. "See the way that they are captivated by her? See the way their thoughts and desires are so easy to read? They either want her, or they envy her."

A feeling of unease curled in my gut, and I silently shifted while I began to regret my choice in gown. Watching every movement of mine, my father lifted his face and peered down at me with those cold and calculating dark eyes.

"She has highborn blood in her veins," he murmured, still observing me closely. However, now it felt more like he was assessing me, as if I was livestock and not his own flesh. "And though it may be diluted, men tend to forget such things when they are in the presence of a woman who looks as she does."

"And that's useful?" Skileer murmured, and my father hummed and then nodded.

"More than you know,"

Grabbing at my cup of wine, I swallowed a large mouthful, and then noticed how tense Donigan was beside me. I could nearly feel his hatred for my father at that moment, and I knew I had to reassure him. Pressing my knee against his own, I took one more swig of my drink.

"I have once again noticed there aren't any banners for the families north of the border, or the Protector's Anointed, my lord," Donigan said casually in an attempt to change the subject now that he knew I was alright, and my father's attention moved to the ceiling where the other sigils hung.

"Yes," he agreed. "But it should not come as a surprise, they do not like to venture far from their dreary lands often, Donigan," he reminded my knight while his eyes roamed across the room.

"Why is that?" Sighing, my father dragged his attention back to my friend, apparently annoyed to have to explain the way of the northern houses once more.

"They are nothing if not recluse. They like to stick to themselves and look down their noses at us." Skileer, who had been busy shovelling mutton into his mouth, stopped his chewing and frowned.

"Down their noses at us? But we are also one of the four Anointed, what right do they have to judge us?" he asked and my father frowned.

"Although we can all follow our lineages for centuries and we were given our duty by the Huntress herself, the Protector's people were the *first* created. They were the very earliest of the Forefolk," my father clarified and then lifted a brow. "I expected you to remember all this."

Skileer had never been one for his lessons, so it was no surprise he did not have a grasp on even the most basic tales of our history.

Donigan, however, hummed under his breath and then nodded. "And then the Huntress's people were made."

"Yes," my father confirmed. "Followed by the Healer's."

Glaring at Donigan, Skileer crossed his arms over his chest. "Yes, yes, we know the rest of that. The great Divine Triad created the Forefolk and then chose their Anointed centuries ago. In return our families promised to keep the peace of Elrin for them."

Rolling my eyes, I readied myself to tune out my brother's voice. However, his next words caught my attention. "But what about the other?"

I frowned as all focus turned to Skileer, and my father narrowed his eyes. "What other?"

Straightening in his seat, my brother swallowed and then glanced at the banners hanging from the ceiling. "What of the Reaper?"

My father froze in his seat, and I watched as my father's expression hardened before he reprimanded him. "We do not speak of him so carelessly."

The God of Death had many tales about him indeed. The most prominent being that though he was the first God, he had later been exiled by the Divine Triad when the people of Elrin turned on him. Of course there was probably a great deal more to it, but it was not appropriate for such a time or place, and my brother paled but still pressed his luck.

"Surely you are not so superstitious—" The bang of my father's palm slamming against the table was finally enough to keep my brother from continuing, and I noticed the onlookers who had turned towards us. Seeming to also realize we had an audience, my father lifted his hand from the wood and used it to smooth his tunic while I offered a charming smile to our spectators.

"Pardon us, my lords," I murmured softly. "It seems my fever has returned, and my father has grown concerned. You'll have to excuse our ruckus; he did not mean to draw your attention with his worry."

It was the best lie I could come up with in a hurry, and to my relief the men nodded their heads and turned away once more. However, now that I was facing the entrance of the room, I noticed the gleam of auburn hair in the far corner. Watching as Gwain made his escape from the feast, I concocted a plan that would allow me to follow.

"I am feeling rather unwell," I croaked out, praying that it would sound as convincing as I meant for it to, and that with my father's short temper, he would not have the patience to fight me. "May I be excused?"

Leaning back in his chair once more, my father glared at me while my brother scowled.

"She just got here; won't that cause more of a scene?" Skileer asked but I ignored him.

"If I may, my lord," Donigan interjected and paid no mind to my brother's glare. "Lady Rígan has been ill since we reached the tourney. Perhaps tonight has been too much for her." He paused to glance at me. "She does look rather pale."

I didn't allow myself to meet his gaze, but I pressed my knee back against his, repeating my gesture of thanks. Looking over me carefully for a pause, my father searched my face and then dismissed me with a wave of his hand.

"Go," he demanded and I stood, readying myself to flee, only to be stopped by his warning tone. "But Rígan, return to your tent. Don't go and do something foolish."

For a moment I wondered if he too had noticed the Heir

of House Dansby leave the feast, but I was sure there was no way he had when he had been so focused on my brother.

"Yes, my lord," I answered, praying he could not see through my deceit. Studying me for another moment, he frowned, and then, when his chin lowered just slightly, I fled.

HIDING the tender ache in my muscles from Gwain was more difficult than I had anticipated, and I sank my teeth into my lower lip to keep from wincing as he lowered his weight onto my body.

"What is it?" His green eyes peered down at me, their emerald colour full of worry as he searched my face, and I lifted a hand to tangle in his lovely hair.

"It's nothing," I promised, but a frown pulled at his mouth. Carefully guiding him back, I sat up and rested my wrists over his shoulders.

"I just worry about my father or brother interrupting us, I suppose." Curling an arm around my hips, Gwain pulled me into his lap and then ran his mouth across the rounded top of my shoulder.

"I wouldn't worry about that," he whispered before pressing a sweet kiss to the side of my neck. "Everyone is still at the feast, and I am sure your father and brother are with the other lords. Apparently, Lord Noorese brought a number of treasures from the south. I can't see your father worrying about your whereabouts when they are so preoccupied, and he won't be letting your brother out of his sight after what happened the last time."

Tilting my head back, I allowed Gwain further access to my skin, and he nuzzled at the space beneath my jaw before humming under his breath and then pulled away.

"Though I must ask, what was your brother thinking? Challenging Caedell Reide to the sword was idiotic," he mumbled with a shake of his head. "However, he did put up a better fight than I thought he would. Or maybe Caedell was just being gracious with him."

It was my turn to tuck my face into the crook of his neck, and I used it as a chance to hide my scowl all while wondering why I still struggled with telling Gwain the truth. It was something I fought with myself over and over again. While I was sure he would understand and support me, every time I prepared myself to let the words slip past my lips, my throat closed, and I felt a prickle of panic spread under my skin.

"You know how he gets when he's drunk, he doesn't think anything through. I doubt *he* even knew what he was doing," I murmured against his skin, and Gwain ran his fingers through my long hair before sweeping the dark strands over one of my shoulders.

"Well, whatever the reason, let's take advantage of the opportunity his stupidity has given us." He moved to lay me back once more, but I pressed my palms against his chest to stop him. Pausing, he frowned again, but I carefully eased him down against the furs of his bed. Offering me a pleased smile when he realized what I wanted, I noticed the way the pink flush spread across his cheeks and then I moved my legs until I was cradling his hips between my thighs.

"And what opportunity is that?" I purred with a raised brow, and Gwain's throat bobbed while his gaze darkened.

"My Gods, you are beautiful." Rolling my eyes, I ran a hand down his chest and then rocked my hips against his, laughing softly when I felt him twitch beneath me.

"Are you going to answer my question, Sir Dansby?" His mouth parted but no words came out, and my grin grew when I slowly sank down onto his length. I had been ready for him since his first touch hours ago, but now I was in no hurry as I circled my hips. Riding him slowly, I watched his pleasure become more evident on his face, and when I was certain he was lost in it, I carefully leaned forward.

"Tell me you're mine," I demanded quietly, suddenly desperate to hear the words and make certain I wasn't alone in the world.

His breathing had grown heavy, and his brows furrowed, but Gwain nodded.

Brushing my lips against his softly, I carefully avoided the scar that ruined the right side of my mouth and then peered up at him through my lashes. Having memorized what it meant when his eyes screwed closed and his chin tilted back, I knew he neared completion.

"Promise?" I whispered, quickening the rhythm of our lovemaking. Grunting in pleasure, Gwain dug his fingers into my hips, and I chased after my own release, easily forgetting my question when euphoria was so nearly in my grasp.

CHAPTER
SEVEN

Losing at the sword had meant there was no chance of us earning the title of champion, and now that my ruse was finished, I was granted permission to watch the rest of the tourney with the other noble ladies. Glancing down at my legs, I took in the pale green colour of my gown. It wasn't a striking contrast in the way the red had been against my skin, but the flare of the skirt flattered my waist, and the neckline showed just enough cleavage to be eye-catching while remaining proper.

Pulling my dark hair over my shoulders, I twisted the strands together until it was weaved neatly down the middle of my back and then I glanced at the mirror. I looked well enough put together, but my face was not at its best. My hooded grey eyes looked bright, but the skin beneath them was dark from lack of sleep, and my full lips seemed to be more prominent somehow, perhaps swollen from the kisses given to me the night before. Examining the plumpness, I noticed the way the flesh made my scar more obvious than I would have liked and I frowned. However, there was nothing to be done for it, so I grabbed my cloak and pulled it to my shoulders before making my way to the yards.

"Rígan!" Cat called as I exited my lodgings, and I turned to see her racing towards me in a very unladylike manner.

Today she wore a pretty light blue gown, though the length seemed to be at least four inches too long and her little fists hitched the hem up so she would not trip.

"Catiline," I greeted, watching as she gasped for air once she reached me. "Are you alright?"

She leaned back to look up at my face, and I frowned as she continued to pant. "I was just going to ask you the same thing."

Grabbing at her arm, I linked it with my own in hopes of offering her some sort of support and eyed her more closely.

"I'm fine," I assured her, though it didn't seem to do the trick and her brows furrowed.

"I didn't see you last night at the feast. I had arrived late but was planning to apologize to you for our conversation in your tent," she explained.

"It's nothing to concern yourself over, it's long forgotten." I could see Catiline didn't believe me, but she nodded anyway.

"I'm glad to hear it," she murmured while she trailed along beside me. "Though given your absence last night, I was worried you may not be able to make it to the joust and I would be stuck sitting alone. Or worse, some old man would feel bold enough to approach and decide to narrate every moment of the event to me."

"So, you chased me down in hopes that I would be your protector?" I snorted and Cat flushed.

"Only if you'll agree to it, and only if you'll truly accept my apology and not shrug it off once more," she insisted, and I rolled my eyes but gestured for her to climb up the stairs before us. Taking the encouragement, she moved up the steps and slid into one of the seats left for the highborn families.

"You know I would not leave you to these men on your own, and you are certainly aware that I would not be here if I hadn't already forgiven you." Sighing in relief, she smiled softly and waited for me to sink into the chair next to hers before leaning forward to peer down the tiltyard.

"Well now that that's settled, who is competing today?" Cat asked, and I followed her gaze towards the large chestnut horse and its rider who carried a purple shield with a grey raven.

"That's the eldest Windester boy. They are a smaller house from the west," I explained. "As for his opponent, let's just hope it's someone other than Reide. I don't need to see his arrogant face after yesterday's loss."

"It would seem that you have rotten luck today," Cat whispered as she looked towards the other end, and I lifted my eyes just in time to see Caedell mount his horse. "But, perhaps the Gods will find it fitting to knock him down a peg or two after his victory against your brother."

"Unfortunately, he's rumoured to be a favourite of theirs," I murmured, studying his face while he asked his squire for his helm. "So, I doubt he will be leaving any of his opponents astride their horses."

"Well, if we will be stuck watching him all day, we should be thankful that he's so handsome," Cat answered, and I watched the way her eyes lingered on the man in question.

"You're wrong," I argued. "I am far more grateful that he has to wear a helmet," I murmured and then grunted softly when Cat nudged me with her elbow.

"Oh, come now, you may dislike him, but there's no need to pretend he isn't nice to look at." Not bothering to respond this time, I sat back in my chair and waited as the young bard ran into the yard with the flag raised and then inhaled sharply as his arm came down.

The Windester boy kicked at his horse, sending the beast into a gallop, and I looked back at his opponent in confusion. Caedell hadn't moved, and even though his horse was pawing the ground impatiently, he seemed unfazed.

Grabbing at my hand, Cat squeezed my fingers and

looked up at me for an answer, but I just shook my head. I had no idea what he was plotting, and I held my breath, waiting for him to do something, anything, before he was eliminated.

But the Heir of House Reide was well versed in the rules of the tournament, and just when I thought he would forfeit the event, he dug his heels into his mount's belly. Moving forward at the cue, Caedell's massive black stallion ate up the damp earth below his hooves in six enormous strides, and then the distance was closed and Caedell lifted his lance with ease. Watching him intently, I saw him aim the weapon with far more precision than his foe, and then, in a great clash, the tip of Caedell's lance collided with the purple shield.

Scrambling to her feet, Cat joined in with the crowd and clapped her hands. "Well done!"

I, however, remained in my seat, examining the young boy to be certain he was uninjured. That is until I heard the soft thud of trotting hoofbeats. Noticing that they seemed to grow louder, I leaned forward to look past Cat and saw that Caedell had taken off his helm and was now approaching us.

"Ladies!" he greeted, choosing to ignore the other maidens who were nearly swooning at his smile, and my expression hardened.

"Lord Reide," Catiline greeted in return, and I glared up at her before moving to stand at her side. "Is there something you need?"

"Not just anything." He smiled. "I would ask for a favour from you, Lady Noorese," he said softly and sweetly, and Cat blushed at the sound much to my annoyance.

"It's customary to ask for those prior to the start of the event, Lord Reide," I growled, and his amber eyes moved to me before his lips shifted into a smirk.

"Is it? I'm surprised you are so knowledgeable about the rules of the event given that you never seem to be a *spectator*." I crossed my arms over my chest and stared down at him.

"I have been unwell since our arrival," I muttered and his brows lifted.

"Have you?" he asked, and I felt Cat stiffen next to me.

"Yes," I answered curtly. "And besides, I do not need to spectate every joust to know the rules. It's common knowledge, sir."

"You don't seem ill to me," Caedell said, ignoring my comment while his eyes scanned me from head to toe, and my brows furrowed.

"Odd, I am feeling rather nauseas just from this conversation." Thrown by my remark, Caedell said nothing, and I fought the smug smile that tugged at the corners of my mouth and then changed the subject. "As I was saying, asking for a favour at the start has a purpose. It keeps your opponent from waiting." Watching as I gestured to the Windester boy, Caedell glanced over his shoulder and then turned back to me with a grin.

"He can wait to lose," he replied and then winked at Cat. Giggling softly, she undid the ribbon in her hair, not caring that I glared at her while she did so.

Lifting his lance, he held it out for her to tie the blue silk around the tip, but his attention remained on me, and I struggled not to fidget under his piercing gaze.

"Good luck, sir," Cat said gently, and he dipped his head in thanks but did not move his focus from my face, and I narrowed my eyes at him.

"You should be on your way now." I waved him off, praying he would leave us be. "We didn't come here to watch you stand around."

"But you did in fact come to watch *me*." It wasn't a question, and my jaw fell slack as he finally turned his horse from us.

"My, he is handsome," Catiline whispered to me, apparently unaware or rather uncaring of my irritation, and I scoffed.

"He's unbearable." Pulling Cat back into her seat, I moved my focus to the others around us who had been watching the interaction with interest, and I glared at them.

"Then go back to praying to the Divine Triad that he gets knocked from his horse." She laughed before rocking her shoulder into my own.

"With any luck, they will hear me," I grumbled. "Maybe he'll even take a blow to that face you find so pretty."

Cat didn't bother to dignify my comment with a response, and as it would turn out, the Gods didn't hear my prayers. That, or they didn't acknowledge them, and Caedell the Undying remained unbeaten.

BEING SURROUNDED by the other Lords of Elrin while keeping my brother under control offered a far better distraction for my father than I could have anticipated, and I took advantage of his absence as often as I could. However, I still had to take precautions. The main one being getting in and out of Gwain's tent undetected, and the easiest way to make certain that happened was to leave as soon as we were finished. Tonight was no different, and I pulled from Gwain's arms before hurriedly dressing and then I crept out of the hidden entrance way he had made the first night.

Now free from the shelter of his tent, I searched the area for any onlookers before racing in the direction of my own quarters. Carefully, I moved through the camp, and then when I rounded the corner, I began to seek out the brown banners of my house. However, they were not where I had expected them to be, and I very quickly realized I had taken a wrong turn in the dark. Spinning in a circle, I tried to find my way back in a panic, and then a voice rumbled from the shadows.

"Lost, are we?" My breath caught in surprise, and I clutched the wool of my cloak closed to hide my shift, but did not turn.

"I thought you were ill. I distinctly remember you saying as much today at the joust. So, imagine my surprise at seeing you running cross camp in the middle of the night, and from what would seem to be Gwain Dansby's tent at that." Closing my eyes, I forced my shoulders to relax and then I faced him.

Caedell Reide's amber eyes were bright in the soft glow that emanated from the torch he held, and I glared at him before lowering my hood.

"You are mistaken, sir," I replied as my chin lifted and a smirk pulled at his mouth.

"Am I? Why don't I go see Sir Dansby for myself? I'm sure I can trace your footsteps right back to his quarters." He gestured with a hand in the direction I had come from, and I narrowed my eyes at him.

"You were right, sir." I tucked some hair behind my ear and then held the back of my hand to my forehead. "My illness always seems to fester with you around, and I fear I am in dire need of some rest. So as much as I would enjoy seeing you make a fool of yourself, I must be off to bed."

Turning on my heel, I began to continue my journey back to my tent. But just as I created a few feet of space between us, Caedell called out.

"I do have to say I am rather surprised you would still crawl into his bed after the gathering last night." He chuckled, and something about the sound made my heart skip in my chest while I nervously took another step away. "After all, despite not being present for the majority of it, it was still a feast to celebrate his betrothal."

The strong gust of wind that blew against me would have been frigid had I been able to feel it. But it was as if I was in a daze, and the world around me seemed to be nothing more than a blur. I stumbled forward, my delicate slipper slid across the damp earth, and I fell. Landing on my knees, I pressed my palms into the mud, and the fine silk of my shift dampened with the wetness from the earth.

Frozen, I blinked down, watching as the muck oozed between my trembling fingers, and then he spoke again, though this time his voice was far closer than it had been. "Good Gods, woman, what has gotten into you?"

One of his strong hands wrapped around my biceps and he pulled until I was sitting back on my heels.

"Are you going to get up?" he asked, and while I understood the words, I couldn't force myself to respond and then he was moving once more.

Still staring at the imprint my palms had left in the mud, I noticed the toe of his boots enter my vision, and then a hand flashed before me and I nearly flinched at the warmth when the calloused skin of his fingers curled under my chin. Tipping my head back, he exposed my face to his golden eyes and then his thumb slid down my cheek.

"Are you actually weeping?" he questioned with a raised brow, and I slapped his hand away when a cold laugh rumbled out of him. "Who would have thought that under all of that haughtiness, the great bastard, Lady Rígan, was just as soft as any other woman. I can't quite believe it."

"What would you know of women?" I seethed before scrambling to my feet, and then I rushed to dry my face with the backs of my dirty hands.

Smiling, Caedell ignored my jab and angled his torch so that he could examine me more clearly. "So, I was right about you and that fool?"

"Leave me be," I snarled while I burned with humiliation, but his grin only grew.

"Hold on a moment," he whispered. "Do you actually care for the man?"

When I did not reply, Caedell shook his head in disbelief. "I would have never anticipated that happening. It is not as if he is your first and I highly doubt he will be the last."

Still, he was met with my silence, but I took a moment to peer up at his face and he rolled his eyes. "Oh, don't look so forlorn. Remember that blacksmith boy you chased around when you were just five-and-ten? I think that was the last time we saw each other. I remember it well because of the beating your father gave you in the town's square. Isn't that what ruined that lovely mouth of yours?"

My scared lower lip trembled, and he shook his head once more. "I've never seen a father look at his child with such hatred." He motioned to the mark that still remained stark against the colour of my mouth.

"And to think, back then you didn't even shed a tear. Not even when you were bloody and bruised and that boy was chased out of the town after being given thirty lashes." Hazy memories I had long since tucked away flashed through my mind, and I swallowed roughly. "And yet here you are, falling apart over some pretty little knight who probably has his next conquest in mind already."

"Watch your tongue!" I growled before striding forward, and then I stood toe to toe with the Heir of House Reide.

"What I don't understand is what makes him so different? I've heard some of the rumours about your other trysts," he murmured. "And even if they have been mildly exaggerated, there's always some seed of truth to the whispers. So, I am quite certain you've enjoyed your fair share of better bed mates."

My cheeks heated but I narrowed my gaze, unwilling to show him the weakness he so obviously sought out. "Odd, I can't say I've heard the same for you."

His grin began to fall.

"Tell me, are you still pining after your father's wife? What must that be like, I wonder?" His face had hardened now, and it was my mouth that was curling. "Do you manage to bed her in his chambers, or does she sneak away to yours when his back is turned? And what of your siblings? I must know, do they call you father or brother?"

Caedell rolled his shoulders and lifted his chin, but his gesture did not give me any pause.

"He must hate you even more than my father hates me. To marry your heir's first love is a kind of betrayal I would never be able to understand."

"You know nothing about me, or my father." His voice lowered, the tone turning into what could only be described as lethal. But it did nothing to chase away the spark of enjoyment I felt at seeing his rage.

"I know more than you think," I chuckled while my head tipped to the side. "I know that the only girl you've ever loved chose him over you without a second thought." Caedell rocked back on his heels, almost as if he had been struck, and I felt another wave of satisfaction fall over me.

But Caedell Reide was not one to surrender so easily, and I watched as his face shifted just slightly.

"Well, now that Dansby has tossed you aside for an *appropriate* match, it looks like you will have first-hand knowledge about that kind of betrayal." The words were soft, just above a whisper, but the quietness did nothing to keep the sharp sting of his words from hitting their mark.

Watching me shiver, Caedell took a step back and then lifted a hand to shoo me away.

"I think we are done here. You should get back to your tent, Lady Baxteel. Your imaginary illness may not have fooled me, but you will catch a fever if you stand out here any longer." His eyes lowered to the neckline of my shift and then fell to the wet fabric that was stuck to the skin of my legs. Then with one final look of disgust, he silently turned back to his tent and left me in the cold.

CHAPTER

EIGHT

There was a commotion coming from the tourney grounds, and I rose from my bedroll and squinted at the entrance of my tent. It was not yet dawn, and I could not make out anything of significance beyond the canvas, but then I heard the thundering of footsteps run past. Wiping at my face, I winced as my fingers pressed over the raw skin beneath my eyes, and then another group raced through our camp.

Grabbing a simple tunic, I pulled the wool over my head before dragging a pair of breeches up my legs. Stepping into my boots, I snatched my cloak from the end of the bed and lifted the hood to conceal my face before ducking through the entrance of my tent.

Now out in the open, I took a deep breath and examined the site. The structures surrounding me were quiet, and for a moment I wondered if I had invented the ruckus in my sleep-hazed mind. However, when I heard more men hurrying towards the end of the tourney grounds, I was certain it hadn't been just a figment of my imagination and decided to follow them.

Moving through the rows of tents, I glanced at the light-

81

ening sky, and now that morning approached, I could see a small group of men crowding in the sword yard.

They were huddled close, their bodies shielding the space from any onlookers. But as I studied them, my confusion shifted to concern. And when the sound of metal clashing and the quiet laughter of the crowd echoed in the air, I hurried over.

Once I neared the rear of the group, I ducked my chin and pressed past the men who watched with rapt interest and then turned my own attention to the spectacle that had caught their notice. However, I had been unprepared for what was before me, and gasped when I saw Caedell Reide in all his glory.

Apparently, the heaviness of our conversation from the night before was long forgotten, and I was once more struck by the way he carried himself.

Even without armour and a helm, he was so sure and calm and moved with a predatory grace that was breathtaking. His rival, however, struggled and flailed about. And had the wave of panic not hit me so sharply, I too would have continued to stand by quietly as the man they called the Undying effortlessly won this battle.

But that was not possible when my family's heir was at the end of his blade.

"Honestly, Skileer, I would have thought you would know to hold your tongue by now. Or was the last loss not enough to teach you that lesson?" Caedell sneered as he danced out of my brother's reach, and I felt my stomach churn while I studied the pair.

"The only lesson I learned is that you're a cheat!" Skileer slurred while he clumsily swung his sword towards his opponent. However, he was not used to the weight of the weapon and toppled over onto his knees. The crowd snickered again while he struggled to get back onto his feet and he spat in our direction.

"A cheat?" Caedell asked with a laugh and then he glanced over his shoulder towards the audience, and for a heartbeat, I could have sworn his burning amber eyes sought out my own.

"You know you are!" my brother growled, drawing my attention back to him, and I watched as he held his blade in front of him in the awkward way one was taught when they first began to learn the sword.

"The only thing I know is that you are a sore loser, Skileer Baxteel," Caedell chided him as he circled my brother like he was prey. "And it is rather unbecoming of a man of your standing."

My brother scowled at his adversary before rushing at him. But it was no use, Caedell slipped out of the way and then lightly tapped my brother on his backside with the flat of his blade.

"Tell me," Caedell chuckled. "What happened to that fire you burned with the last time we faced each other? Where has that admirable opponent gone?"

When my brother snarled in response, Caedell's grin grew. "You should learn to limit yourself, maybe then you would be a worthy competitor. Or maybe you should not challenge others when you are so far into your cups."

My brother bristled but did not respond, and Caedell lifted his blade until the tip was just a foot away from my brother's nose. "After I am finished with you, perhaps that particular lesson will stick."

Lowering his sword, Caedell spun to face us once more and lifted his arms in encouragement until the men who surrounded me cheered him along.

"I don't need to learn anything from the likes of you!" Skileer barked while the flush on his face deepened.

"The likes of me?" Caedell murmured as he turned to his foe again. "You should be honoured to have such an excellent teacher."

"Honour?" Skileer spat the word. "What would you know of honour?" My heart dropped at my brother's tone, and I held my breath as Caedell circled Skileer.

"Your house may be one of the Anointed and your name may be worth something to most, but I know the truth." Panic began to flood my veins, and I prayed that my brother would not be so stupid as to continue. However, it would seem that the Gods could not find it in themselves to pity me, and as I should have predicted, Skileer did not hold his tongue.

"And what truth would that be?" Caedell demanded, and a smug smile pulled at my brother's mouth.

"That you do not know the first thing about honour," Skileer announced proudly. "And as a man who slithers his way between the thighs of his father's wife, you never will."

A hush fell over the crowd that surrounded the sword yards, and my attention frantically bounced between the two men. I, of course, had not been the only one privy to that particular rumour. The whispers had been spreading for years, and though I may have accused him of the very thing just the night before, I had made sure to do so without witnesses. After all, only a fool would be stupid enough to say the words so plainly in front of a crowd, and especially to the man's face—the man they called the Undying.

"What did you say?" Caedell whispered just loud enough for me to hear over the pounding of my heart.

"We all know it to be true," Skileer laughed, not having the wisdom to realize just how precarious the situation had become.

"And do you know what they say about *you*?" The Heir of House Reide snarled, and my breath caught at the words as my chest tightened with anxiety.

What did he mean by that? Did Caedell know what we had spent so long hiding? Was he aware of our ploy? And if he was, would he take this chance to destroy everything?

It would be easy, with just a few words my family and our

reputation would be ruined, we would be the laughingstock of Elrin. Our men and our knights would turn their backs on us. They would decide to follow another house, a stronger house, that had a true heir to lead them. An heir born of two high-born lines that had been chosen by the Gods themselves and who had not been lying to them for the last decade. They would seek out another family that did not have a fool for a leader and a bastard who had been taking his place.

And if that truth came out, and the worst happened, the rebels would see our weakness. They would use the loss of trust between us and our people for their benefit, and the peace we had been struggling to hold on to would be ripped from our fingers. Of that I was certain.

Clenching my teeth, I readied myself for Caedell to expose us, but those eyes caught mine again, and he held my gaze. This time, however, there was something else brewing in the golden colour, and then he turned to Skileer once more.

Whatever game Caedell had been playing was now over. That much was obvious in the way he prowled towards his prey and my brother finally found the sense to be truly afraid. Skileer stuttered back a step, his wide eyes searching the crowd, though I wasn't sure if he was seeking an exit or a saviour. Unfortunately, he would find neither. The men were too engrossed in the duel to let him flee, and I could not come to my brother's rescue. Not this time.

"They say you're a drunk," Caedell sneered. "A waste of flesh. A spoiled child who is in need of a lashing."

Skileer paled as he tried to escape from his foe's pursuit, but Caedell was not having it. "A lashing I would be all too pleased to give."

Cornering my brother, Caedell unleashed his fury, and for a moment my brother was able to fend him off, or at least avoid his blade. But blow after blow came at him and my brother began to weaken under the constant attack. Then, time seemed to slow, and I watched as Skileer slid to his knees while his arm weakly lifted his weapon in hopes of blocking another hit and my fear of witnessing my brother fall victim to Caedell's sword outweighed any concern I had of keeping my presence secret from the crowd.

"Yield!" I screamed, ignoring the heads that turned in my direction. "Yield, you fool!"

Skileer's eyes were panicked as they met mine, and for a moment, Caedell hesitated, waiting just a pause to see if my brother would heed my advice. But Skileer was not only a fool, he was also an arrogant shit, and when he noticed Caedell's hesitation, he swung his sword.

However, the Heir of House Reide had the blood of a swordsman and had won more battles than any other who fought for our Huntress. In return, our Goddess smiled down on him, making certain that he was victorious in all of his pursuits, and I was certain this time would be no different.

Seeing my brother's plan, Caedell crashed his blade against Skileer's and knocked it from his fingers. Then the edge of the great longsword came down once more, and gently kissed the side of Skileer's face.

The blood-curdling scream echoed through the early morning air, and the sound was enough to send the crowd scattering. I remained in my place while I watched Caedell take a step back and roll his shoulders. He then brought the metal to the sleeve of his tunic and cleaned the blood from the silver before glancing down at my brother with a single raised brow.

"He should probably see a healer," he sighed as he turned to me and then scoffed when my brother screamed out again. "Sooner rather than later, or he'll wake everyone."

Looking at my brother, I watched as his fingers clutched at his bloody face as he wailed in pain, and then I looked back at Caedell, my eyes wide in shock at his casualness.

"Well, are you coming to get him, or are we leaving him here to crawl his way back to your tents?" Sheathing his weapon, he gestured for me to come towards them, and suddenly it was as if I had no choice but to obey.

Rushing forward, I grabbed on to the wooden fence and hauled myself over it, and then I fell to my knees next to my brother. It was difficult to make out just how bad the injury was with all the blood and the way his fingers covered his entire face. But I could see the start of the gash that sat between his eyebrows, and my eyes followed it until it ended on his left cheek. It would need to be bandaged and it would leave a mark, but did not appear to be deadly, and I breathed out a sigh of relief.

"Get up," I ordered, but Skileer whimpered in protest, so I tried again. "You have to get up."

"I can't!" he howled while pushing me away with a bloody hand and I grabbed his wrist.

"Get up!" I growled while I pulled on his arm. However, it was no use, he was nothing more than dead weight, and I heard Caedell snicker from behind me.

Hurrying to my feet, I spun on my heel and curled my fingers before swinging at him. Not bothering to avoid my hit, my fist made contact with the sharp edge of his jaw, and he reeled back from the impact.

"What were you thinking?!" I snapped, watching him carefully as he rubbed at the red mark that was blooming against his skin while his lips curled into a roguish grin.

"I did him a favour. It's about time he carries a scar, and he should wear it proudly," he laughed. "He's managed to go too long without one." Ignoring the cries of my brother, I searched Caedell's perfect face and then crossed my arms over my chest.

"I don't see one on you," I pointed out, and Caedell lifted his chin to all but leer at me.

"That is because I am no ordinary man," he bragged, and my lip curled in disgust. "I am a man of legends."

"Or maybe it's because you just pick your enemies well."

He stiffened at that, but when another shriek echoed around us, he glanced past my shoulder and towards my brother.

"My Gods, get him to your father, I can't stand any more of his snivelling." Running a hand through his dark hair, Caedell made his exit from the sword yards, and I turned to Skileer once more with a frown. He was now curled in a ball, his hands still cradling his face while he continued to mutter out nonsense between sobs.

"Skileer, you must get up. I can't carry you," I chided him as I approached him again. But he completely ignored me.

Deciding to take matters into my own hands, I peeled his palms from his cheeks and then stroked his hair carefully, the same way his mother did when he was throwing one of his tantrums. When the motion seemed to soothe him, I did it again, though my nose wrinkled in annoyance.

Finally settled, my brother blinked up at me, and I watched as tears filled his eyes while the crimson rivers continued to coat his skin. "He's ruined my face!"

"And it will only get worse if you sit here in this mud," I explained, praying he would hear me. "If you don't hurry, the scar will be ghastly."

Skileer stiffened at that and then crawled onto his knees before blindly reaching for one of my hands. Grabbing at his fingers, I helped him to his feet and steered us away from the sword yard, noticing that Caedell had remained nearby.

"Give your father my regards and be sure to apologize for the inconvenience." He grinned and then left us to make our way back through camp.

"How did this happen?!" my father roared and I watched the way the healer slunk away from the bed and glanced at me from the corner of his eye. Both of us were well aware of the delicate situation we were in, and I lowered my attention to the ground and swallowed roughly.

"It should heal nicely, my lord. It is really nothing but a scratch," the healer whispered his reassurance, and I glanced up through my lashes, watching as my father turned to the man with a face full of rage.

"Finish what you are doing and go," he ordered, and the healer nodded before wrapping the bandage around my brother's head.

"Now, tell me, how did this happen?" my father repeated while his dark eyes locked on to me, and I tipped my chin to my chest before lowering my gaze to the ground once more.

"I don't know. By the time I got there, he was already engaged in the duel." My father scoffed and turned towards his heir, who was finally quiet. "Had I known, I would have stopped him."

"You should have known!" he snapped, and I clenched my jaw, hating that somehow the responsibility was being put on my shoulders while my father and his son carried none.

"I'm sorry." The words burned my tongue even though I had said them to this man countless times.

"I don't want your apologies or excuses, Rígan." No, the only thing he would want was for me to turn back time and take the sword to my own face. He wouldn't have so much as blinked an eye at that, let alone sit at my bedside. And though I knew that to be true, there was still some tiny sliver of me that yearned for his approval.

"This won't do," my father muttered under his breath, and I peeked up at him. "I cannot have him injured."

"The champion title has already been decided, nothing would have changed that," I offered, but my father just rubbed at his temples.

"That is the least of my concern now," he snapped and then slid a hand into the pocket of his cloak. Grabbing at something, he sighed and then held out the piece of parchment for me to take.

"What is it?" I asked before carefully plucking the missive from my father's grasp.

"We have been summoned by Lord Demys."

"Krayern Demys? The one called Swiftsword?" My father nodded and my brow furrowed. "Why?"

"It seems that he is wanting the other Anointed to come north. Apparently, Synrick of House Moreel is already there."

"Wait, north? As in Denimoore?" He nodded again and I opened the page.

Frowning, I glanced down at the unfamiliar scrawl. "They've never asked us to come to their territories before."

My father rubbed at his jaw and sighed before answering. "That's because they've never sought our counsel before, nor needed our help."

The people of the north were of the Protector, and otherwise known as the Lupines. The name had come from the sigil of their God, the shield with the white wolf. They were a fierce and ancient people who ruled the lands for ages before the next group of Forefolk were born.

"So why do they need us now?" I asked while handing the letter back to him.

"It seems they are having their own issues with some rebel forces. They are asking that we come to them and discuss a way to be done with these lawbreakers once and for all."

"And you will answer their call?" I questioned.

"It may be our only chance to form a true allegiance."

"When do you leave?" I asked.

"I don't," he muttered and then glanced at my brother with a scowl. "You will."

"Me?" He shot me a pointed look and my mouth snapped shut.

"I can't very well send your brother on his own now." He

gestured to Skileer's sleeping face. "Though I'm not sure that would have been wise as it was."

"But—" I began, only for my father to stop me with a scathing glare.

"We have had our own trouble back at home," he explained. "Leaving our lands without a leader for much longer would be a mistake."

"But if I go in your stead, they may see it as an insult," I murmured. "They will be expecting the lord of our family and his rightful heir."

"You are right, they would see it as a slight," he agreed.

My heart thudded in my chest, and my eyes widened but my father didn't seem to notice.

"So, you won't go as just my bastard. I will send a missive informing them that I plan to give you a proper title of some sort." A sudden and shocking warmth bloomed in my chest and my eyes widened. "In the meantime, I will do my best to find a match for you. Should something else happen to your brother, or if this injury were to take a turn, you will need to be married, and if I can do so quickly, there would be no need to fulfill my promise."

I inhaled sharply, but my father continued. "Ideally I will find a man of high enough standing who won't care about your previous interactions with the Dansby boy or any other man for that matter."

The sensation that had just begun to flower under my skin curled in on itself, and I blinked at the stinging in my eyes. Turning my face away, I hoped he would not see my reaction while the bitter pain of his empty words and the hurt of Gwain's betrayal spread beneath my ribs.

"I will write to him now," my father continued as if he was talking to himself. "You will take it with you to show that you are there per my request."

When I didn't answer, he sighed in frustration, and I finally lifted my chin to face him. "This will do you good,

Rígan. It will keep you from wallowing and you can show me your true devotion to our house."

"When do I leave?" I asked, ignoring the shake in my voice.

"At dawn."

CHAPTER
NINE

LIFTING THE SADDLE ONTO MY HORSE, I BLINKED THROUGH the heavy weight of my exhaustion and tightened the girth. Certain the saddle was secure, I scanned the camp. The tourney grounds were quiet, only the group of men my father had decided to send with us were awake, and I made sure they were nearly ready before grabbing the bridle that hung on the fence.

"Whoever decided we should leave by dawn needs a good smack," Donigan grumbled as he sauntered towards me, and I lifted a brow.

"That would be my father, so don't say things like that so loudly, especially with my brother around." Donigan rolled his eyes and then he crossed his arms and studied me for a moment.

"How are you?" We had not truly spoken since our arrival, besides at the feast and when he warned me of Skileer's challenge, and I swallowed down my witty retort before shrugging.

"Fine," I murmured under my breath.

Donigan took a step closer and then lifted a hand to rest on my shoulder, and it took everything in me not to flinch away from his touch. Not because I was repulsed, but because it wounded my pride that he could obviously see the pain I struggled to conceal.

"I am sorry about Dansby." That was enough for me to stop fighting my instincts, and I pulled out from under his fingers. "I wanted to say as much sooner, but you've been rather difficult to find."

"It doesn't matter." Donigan knew better than to push the subject, and his arm that had still been outstretched fell to his side before he glanced over at the party who would be accompanying us in our travels.

"Your father really couldn't spare you any decent men?" I turned to look at the rather sad group. My companions were a mix of green squires and old knights who had long since passed their glory days, and I glared at Donigan.

"He kept all the half-decent ones for his return home." I shrugged.

"But at least you have me." He winked with a grin.

Rolling my eyes, I moved to bridle my horse. "Like I said, he kept all the decent ones for himself."

Ignoring my jab, Donigan grabbed at his mare's reins and then mounted. Settling in his saddle, he looked back to me and I followed his lead. Placing my foot in the stirrup, I hoisted myself up and twisted until I was perched on my horse's back and then arranged the skirts of my dress with a scowl.

"Well, *you* may not have a very high or accurate opinion of me," he scoffed. "But I promise to do my very best to keep your brother and both Caedell and Gwain away from you on the journey."

"What?" I asked with wide eyes, certain I had misheard him.

"It was a suggestion from the lords," he explained. "They are concerned about rebels on the road and decided it was safer if we all travelled together. Especially with Skileer being injured." His attention moved to the tent my brother had been inhabiting and then he lowered his voice to a whisper. "Though it's not as if he was very useful to begin with."

I glanced at my brother, who had finally emerged from his quarters, watching as he shakily hoisted himself onto his horse. His face was still half-covered, and he slouched in the saddle, but at least he hadn't yet started to complain.

"He is going to be a liability should we run into trouble," I agreed. "So, I understand why Caedell is going. He is also part of the Anointed, and his father is in no shape to travel so far north. But why Gwain? He is from a lesser house, and I doubt they were summoned to come along."

"Apparently Caedell extended the invitation." My brow furrowed and I shortened the leather reins in my hands.

"Maybe I will need you after all, if only to keep the peace," I muttered under my breath, and Donigan snorted.

"If you think I will stop you from beating that man black and blue, you can forget it." Glancing at him, I frowned, and his expression grew murderous. "If he so much as looks at you, I will make sure I knock a few of his teeth loose."

"I don't need you to defend me."

"I am well aware of that," he scoffed "But that doesn't mean you don't deserve someone to be ready at your side."

"Have you forgiven me then?" I wondered, and Donigan rolled his eyes.

"Despite what you may think, I wouldn't have held on to my anger for much longer, and now I can direct it at a new target." He grinned while a wave of gratitude crashed into me, and I sighed deeply before reaching a hand out. Resting it on his arm, I waited for Donigan's eyes to meet mine.

"Thank you." If my words surprised him, he didn't show it, and my appreciation grew tenfold.

"You don't need to thank me," he muttered with a shake of his head. "Besides, we can't actually have you showing these men just how well you can defend yourself. It would only bring more questions." Leaning over, Donigan grabbed at the pommel of my sword and pulled the ties that kept it attached to the back of my saddle.

"So, you won't be needing this." He arranged his saddle bags and secured my weapon in place. "It looks like it's time for you to use that pretty little face of yours and play the helpless damsel now."

My nose wrinkled in disgust and Donigan chuckled. "Now, now, none of that. That's not the kind of expression a lady with your looks should wear."

Anticipating my next move, Donigan kicked his horse forward to avoid my slap, and I blushed at the lingering stares of the men who had been watching our interaction from a distance. Narrowing my gaze, I waited until their eyes lowered to the ground and then flicked my hair over my shoulder as I turned my horse on its haunches.

Moving my attention to my brother, I watched him as he slouched over his mount, and rolled my eyes at the sad little whimpers coming from him while his horse pawed the ground impatiently.

"This is going to be a long journey," I murmured to myself and then I noticed a squire grab my brother's steed.

"Are you well, my lord?" the young boy asked, and Skileer spat at him.

"Do I look well, you fucking idiot?" The squire flinched back at the venom in his voice.

"Perhaps you could use some tonic, Skileer?" I suggested, and finally he sat straight, and his uncovered eye narrowed at me.

"Oh, do you think so, sister?" he mocked. "What I actually need is to be back in my bed in Noordeign, or at the very least back in my bedroll here until I am healed. I should not be gallivanting north with the likes of you to meet with the Lupines about problems they can't seem to deal with on their own lands!"

Sighing, I lifted a hand to rub at a temple and glanced at

our men before I tried to placate my brother. "We will stop at the nearest town and be sure to let you rest. I'm sure you will feel better after."

I had meant to appease him, but my suggestion only seemed to make his temper worse. "How dare you presume to order me about like some commoner."

There were snickers from the others, but I did not move my attention from Skileer. "I only meant to suggest—"

"I know what you meant to do," He nudged his heels into his horse and moved in close. "Just because Father isn't here doesn't mean you have a say in anything that will go on. Leave the decisions to me and the other rightful heirs. Your only requirement is to sit there silently and look pretty."

My jaw clenched and I tilted my chin, ready to retort, but he clicked his tongue at me and lifted a finger to point at my face. "That wasn't a *suggestion*, that was an order."

Before I could respond, a voice interrupted us from a few yards away.

"Ah, Donigan, there you are!" Glancing over my shoulder, I spotted a large group of men carrying the gold and green banners and realized it was the Reide party who was joining us.

"Good Gods, man, do you have no respect for the others who are trying to sleep?" my friend chastised the stranger as he approached, and he grinned at Donigan before eyeing me.

"Lady Rígan, this is Fynn Bryne. He is a knight for House Reide." He was not very tall, but what he lacked in height, he made up for in broadness, and I observed his large shoulders and neatly trimmed beard that hugged his jaw. He was good-looking, though burlier than most, and I examined his features, pleased that I would at least have another handsome face to look at while I pretended to be the lady I was not.

"Pleasure." I nodded slightly in greeting, though I felt the corners of my lips curl upwards, and the man's face flushed before he shyly glanced down at his feet.

"Don't try to charm my men, Lady Baxteel." Stiffening, I watched as Caedell pushed his way forward through the group and then he slapped his knight on the back. "And don't try your hand with this one, Fynn, she'll eat you alive."

No one said anything, obviously unsure on how to respond and too uncomfortable to try. But it would seem that Caedell was not done with his goading, and I frowned as his eyes fixated on something behind me.

"Isn't that right, Dansby?" The sound of the name had my breath catching in my throat, and I barely kept myself from turning in my saddle to glance at the man who was most certainly approaching the party.

"Leave her alone, Reide," he growled out as he stopped his horse just a few feet away, but I stared straight ahead, refusing to offer him even the smallest glimpse of my eyes.

"Funny," Caedell said, though his tone did not hold an ounce of humour. "I was going to warn *you* to do the same."

Clearing my throat, I looked to Donigan for some sort of relief from the tension, but he too was glaring at the newcomer.

"Should you not be staying with your *wife*?" my knight snapped, and it took every ounce of my self-control not to flinch at the word.

"We are not married yet," Gwain said, his tone soft and pleading, but I would not give in and instead continued to stare at Donigan.

"I'm not sure that's the excuse you should be sticking with," Donigan growled, and I was very quickly reaching the end of my patience.

"Enough, we don't have time for your bickering!" It was my brother who spoke, obviously irritated as well. However, I was certain his interruption was only because he hated that he was being ignored.

Sighing roughly, I looked to Caedell, and I could just make out Gwain's forlorn face from the corner of my eye. "My brother is right; we need to get going. Are you and your party ready?"

"Just about," he responded with a tip of his head. "We are waiting on one more."

"I'm here!" This time, I couldn't help but turn and glance behind me, and I watched as Cat came trotting up on her pretty little roan mare. Frowning, I looked to the two men who had accompanied her and then to the small carriage that was being pulled along behind the trio.

"Catiline, what are you doing here?" I asked, not understanding why she would be joining us on our journey north. She was noble, but her house was not one who had been called on, and this excursion was no place for a woman of her standing.

"My father is sending some of the relics he found to Lord Demys, and I asked to join so that I could see that they made their journey." Her family's men could have easily done that themselves or had one of us do it, so I wondered why her father would have approved of such a request.

"My father wasn't going to agree," she went on, apparently aware of where my mind had gone. "But then Lord Reide insisted I be allowed to come."

The sharp sting of suspicion grew in my belly, and I narrowed my eyes at Caedell. He, however, grinned at Catiline charmingly and then finally set his attention on me.

Burning amber met cool grey, and I held his stare for a long moment.

"How very kind of him," I muttered, but he seemed unfazed by my wariness and lifted a brow.

"I thought you could use the company. Being surrounded by knights and armed lords would probably be rather uncomfortable for you." He used a hand to gesture to the other men, almost as if he was trying to reinforce his point. "And though you have your brother, I figured you could use another familiar face."

Then his head tipped just slightly to the side. "And I think we would all do well to have such a lovely lady's influence."

"My, not just kind, but thoughtful too. Who would have known?" I muttered, watching as his grin turned smug.

"I'm sorry to see that you're so surprised, Lady Baxteel." Caedell placed a hand on his chest in a mocking manner. "But I'm sure I could be persuaded to show you what other qualities I have. You only need to ask."

Then his attention bounced between Gwain and Donigan. "After all, it would seem that men cannot deny you much of anything."

Donigan stiffened next to me and then reminded Lord Reide of my status. "You are speaking to a highborn lady, my lord."

"A bastard born," my brother corrected sharply. "But a lady nonetheless."

Caedell didn't even look at my brother, and instead chuckled softly while continuing to hold my gaze.

"Trust me, Lord Baxteel, I know exactly *who* I am speaking to."

CHAPTER

TEN

MY BROTHER'S PAINED GROANS AND WHIMPERS ATE AWAY AT MY patience, and every little sound he made almost felt like a blow to my head. Pinching the bridge of my nose, I clenched my eyes shut, and Donigan sighed from his place beside me.

"Why didn't Reide hit him harder? Maybe then we could have been spared from bringing him along," he whispered under his breath, and I laughed softly.

"I assume he thought it was a kindness at the time," I muttered quietly, and glanced at my brother. "I doubt he feels the same now."

"But he doesn't have to deal with it," Donigan pointed out as he glared at the Reide party, who led the rest of us. "They could have at least made Dansby ride alongside him instead, that would have been enjoyable to watch."

I felt my chest twinge at his name, but I commended myself for not seeking out the familiar auburn hair and solid back I had spent countless hours memorizing with my fingers. Luckily for me, Gwain was near the front of our group and far away from me and my knight's wrath. Caedell had been adamant that Gwain ride with them when we had moved through the tourney yards, and though he had tried to protest,

101

an order from the heir of an Anointed was one he had no right to refuse.

"Rígan," my brother called for me, and I twisted to glance at him with wary eyes. "Give me your wineskin."

My brows furrowed, and I looked at the hand he had lifted in my direction. "Where is yours?"

Skileer curled his fingers impatiently at me in response. "I finished it, why else would I be asking?"

My mouth parted in surprise at his answer, and I looked at Donigan. We had not been on the road for more than half a day and my brother had already emptied both of his wineskins. However, knowing better than to chastise him and not wanting to deal with any more of his whining, I reached for my saddle bag. But before I could give it to Skileer, Donigan cleared his throat and then held out his own towards my brother.

"You can have mine, my lord," he offered, but my brother glared at the knight and then turned those dark eyes back to me.

"I don't want yours, Taith," he snapped. "I want my sister's."

Knowing it was not worth the argument, I nodded at my friend reassuringly before moving to retrieve my own once more. Tossing it to my brother, I watched in satisfaction as it bounced against his chest while he struggled to grab a hold of it. He growled in frustration, his lips curling in a snarl before he tugged open the cork with his teeth and took a long sip from the leather sack. However, he didn't swallow the water I had been saving and instead spat it onto the ground.

"What is this?!" he sneered as he threw the brown wineskin back at me, and I clenched my teeth as the water splashed across the front of my gown before falling to the earth. Spooked at the sudden movement, my horse darted forward a step and I pulled on the reins and looked down at the liquid trickling from the opening, watching as it created a tiny river that travelled across the dirt.

"I wanted wine, not water," Skileer barked, and I lifted my eyes to glare at him but was interrupted before I could retaliate.

"Is there something wrong, my lord?" My spine stiffened at the sound of Gwain's voice, and I wondered how much of our argument he had witnessed.

"Nothing that concerns you, Dansby," my brother bit out, and the air around us grew even more tense as the rest of the party stopped to watch the two men with interest.

"Perhaps you would like to rest, my lord?" Donigan suggested in an attempt to deescalate the situation. "There is room in the carriage."

Glancing at him warily, I wondered why he would be so foolish to even suggest it, especially after how badly Skileer had reacted when I had proposed something similar just a few hours prior. However, before my brother could turn his fury on the knight, the men ahead of us parted, and I looked up to see Caedell urging his horse forward. His golden eyes moved from me, to my brother, and back again, and then he halted his massive black stallion between us.

"Is this what I can expect for this entire journey, you two squabbling like children?" My face heated at the implication, while my brother scoffed.

"This is none of your concern, Lord Reide," I muttered quietly, and he lifted a brow in response. Rolling my eyes, I looked to Skileer, praying to the Gods that he would understand my expression and not argue. "My brother is injured, as I'm sure you are aware."

"I am." His mouth lifted slightly, and I wanted to smack the look of pride from his face.

"Then you can understand how taxing this journey may be for him," I continued, though I could feel the glare my brother sent my way.

"That is where you are mistaken, my lady." Caedell shook his head. "I would have no way of understanding that particular issue."

"Is that because your arrogance keeps you from sympathizing with others?" I drawled, not wanting to feed his ego.

Caedell leaned back in his saddle before allowing his eyes to examine my face carefully. It was as if he was searching for something, though I didn't have the slightest idea as to what it could be. But when his stare did not waver after a long pause, I swallowed and turned slightly away. Chuckling to himself, he ran a hand through his hair and leaned towards me.

"No, my lady," he replied in a voice I was sure was meant to sound alluring. However, it only made me bristle, and I glanced at him from the corner of my eye. "It's because unlike your brother, I have never been beat."

Lifting my chin, I swiped my tongue over my marked bottom lip, noticing that his attention had followed the movement, and when his gaze lifted back to my own, I bent towards him in return.

"Yet," I whispered just loud enough for him to hear. "You have not been beaten *yet*. But I look forward to the day that happens. Perhaps if I'm lucky, I will be there to witness such an event."

For a long pause the Heir of House Reide said nothing and then very slowly, he straightened in his saddle and tightened his fingers around the leather reins in his hands. "Yes, maybe you will."

MY NOSE WRINKLED as I examined the small inn, and I heard Donigan sigh roughly as he moved to my side.

"The horses are fed, and the men will be staying outside

the stables," he whispered as he too frowned at our accommodations. "I suppose it is better than nothing, especially now that the weather has begun to turn."

He was right, the shelter the rundown building gave us was better than nothing, but it was certainly not ideal. The floors were filthy, the room stank of ale and sweat, and the patrons who huddled in the corners of the dimly lit space were not the kind of company I would have voluntarily sought out.

"There are about half a dozen rooms," Donigan whispered as he eyed the strangers who were watching us carefully. "Just enough for all of you."

"All of them," I corrected. "I'm assuming you meant the highborn."

"I did."

"I may get a room, but I am not part of that group," I reminded him and then lifted my eyes to the stairs that lead to the chambers. "Make certain that Cat is given the finest chambers."

"I will have her men stationed outside her door." Donigan turned to the exit, but my hand shot out to grab his arm.

"Those guards are old and feeble," I muttered as I studied the small crowd. "They will not do. You will oversee her protection."

"Rígan," he started, but I tightened my grip.

"I am wary of these strangers. Now that we have seen just how far the rebellion has begun to reach, we cannot lower our guard during this journey." His brown eyes darted to the others in the room. "I'm ordering you to look after her tonight, Donigan."

When he nodded, I finally released my hold on him. "See that our men are fed and settled. They are our concern, leave the other lords to do what they will with their own. Once finished, see to Cat."

"And what exactly will you be doing?" he asked, and I rolled my shoulders.

"I am going to hunt." Donigan frowned and glanced at the tavern maid as she began to pass bowls of stew to the men along the far wall.

"How are you going to manage that without being detected?" he whispered, and I lifted a brow.

"Do you really have such little faith in me?" I muttered and his gaze narrowed.

"Fine, but even if you manage to sneak away, how exactly are you going to explain your kill if you're successful?" he asked. "Are you going to suggest it just fell from the sky and say it was a miraculous gift from the Gods?"

"Maybe that would be of help," I chuckled. "A gift such as that could change the poor opinions of the Divine Triad, and perhaps if word spread, it could stop the rebellion altogether," I joked, but Donigan didn't appear amused. Sighing, I pressed in close and waited for his eyes to meet mine.

"I'll be careful," I promised. I could see he was reluctant to concede, but he nodded his head anyway.

SNEAKING AWAY HADN'T BEEN NEARLY AS difficult as I had anticipated. I had excused myself early, blaming the long journey for my exhaustion, and then waited for the men to settle themselves. Once I was sure they were relatively distracted, I changed and slipped out of the window in the small room I was given.

The climb down the side of the building had not been too strenuous and thankfully my room faced towards the long stretch of plains and away from the main road. However, I was still unarmed and needed to creep my way to the stable where the saddles and extra weapons had been stored for the night. That had been a touch more tricky but luckily since Donigan had taken their place, Cat's men were the ones posted there, and as I had suspected, they were easy to get around.

However, it wasn't really until I hid amid the tall, wilted grass of the field that I let myself take in the first easy breath of the day, and I spent a moment watching the snow that had begun to fall. I had not lied when I told Donigan I was going to hunt; the smell of the stew made my stomach roll, and given the state of the inn, I was certain my options for food would be limited.

But even then, my hunger was not what drove me to flee. It was my desperation for an escape. I was frantic to get away from Gwain's solemn face and my brother's looks of contempt. It was the thought of being surrounded by the others, forcing myself to fix the mask that had been slipping while the weight of their eyes and expectations pulled me down. I was being crushed by it all, and yet, I had to pretend otherwise. And while that was a well-practiced skill of mine, even I had my limits.

Feeling that tightening in my chest once more, I shook my head, pulling myself from my thoughts, and took in another deep breath before lowering my body closer to the ground. Now pressed into the frigid mud, I pulled the neckline of my tunic to my chin to hide my chattering teeth while I scanned the space before me. The long stretch of flat land was silent besides the high-pitched whistle the wind made when it blew against me and was absolutely barren.

The summer had been dry, the droughts lengthy and the heat unbearable, but the autumn had only worsened our circumstances. It was as if the Gods had held on to the rain we had so desperately needed throughout the year only to then thrust it onto us all at once as soon as the chill had begun to set in. The heavy downpours had ruined the earth, turning it into a pit of mud that was now freezing as winter approached. Looking at the empty landscape before me, it was obvious that this season would also be one of suffering for many.

After another short while, I saw that my efforts would be in vain, and I pulled myself from the earth and turned back for the small village where I had left my companions. Studying the ragged buildings that seemed even more dreary under the soft dusting of snow and darkening night sky, I carefully made my way back to the old tavern and stood beneath the window of my bedroom before rubbing at my face tiredly.

Coming down had been rather easy. But given the rough state of the stones and rotting wood that made up the side of the inn, it appeared that going up would be more difficult. Knowing I would need both hands free, I placed the bow I had snuck from the stable over my shoulder and gazed up at the wall.

"What are you doing out here? I've been looking for you." A hushed whisper came from my right, and I swallowed roughly before turning to face Gwain.

"I can't see why that would be," I muttered, tugging my cloak closed before lifting my eyes to his face.

"Rígan," he started, only to flinch at the hardness of my stare.

"You no longer have the right to address me in that manner," I snapped, watching the way that same pained look he had been wearing all day returned to his face.

"What would you have me call you then?" he whispered, and despite my anger, I felt my stomach twist at the dejection in his voice.

"I don't want you to call me anything anymore," I retorted, hating that he somehow managed to make me feel guilty for this mess that he had created.

"I don't want it to be this way between us. I never wanted it to be like this." He took a step closer, his hand outstretched towards my face as if he meant to cup my jaw the way he always would when we were together.

I longed to feel it, to feel the touch of his fingers on my skin, to feel the passion that I had so often tried to use to chase away that frigid nothingness that filled me.

But even if he managed to thaw the frost inside my chest, I would be left without the shield of ice and the protection it gave me.

Noticing my hesitation, Gwain took it as an invitation to take another step forward, and my body trembled as that hand neared me. However, just before those fingertips could stroke across the skin of my cheek, a deep voice called out from the darkness that surrounded us.

"I thought I told you to leave her be."

CHAPTER
ELEVEN

Flinching at the warning, Gwain lowered his arm, and we both turned to the man who was approaching us.

"Did you need something, Lord Reide?" Gwain asked as he shifted on his feet. He tried to hide his unease at our visitor's interruption, but I could see just how much Caedell intimidated him.

"The only thing I need from you is to know that you can follow a simple fucking order when I give you one," Caedell growled as he stalked closer, and then he was in front of me, blocking my view as he faced Gwain.

"I am not some guard you can command to do as you please, Reide!" Gwain argued, and I leaned around Caedell to look at him. Gwain stood tall, his chin lifted, and arms crossed over his chest, but his face was ashen, and I noticed the way his gaze slid to mine for a heartbeat before he slowly focused back on the man before him.

"That's where you are wrong," Caedell replied, and those green eyes hardened. "You are a son of a lesser house, you are not one of the Anointed, and you certainly have no rank worth noting in my opinion. You are nothing but another idiotic man reaching for something he has no business concerning himself with."

"You know nothing about my business!" Gwain snapped, and it was then that I noticed the gentle sway in his body. Frowning, I searched for other signs. He was pale with unease, but there was a soft flush creeping along his neck and the way his attention had moved sluggishly between Caedell and me told me he was well into his cups.

"I know what I will do to you if I catch you approaching her again in this state," Caedell barked. "It is a long journey north, and a great number of unfortunate things can occur on our way. Things that would make returning you home to your father and new wife rather impossible."

I swallowed roughly at the threat and watched as Gwain's eyes widened.

"Now get out of my sight," Caedell ordered, and I wondered if Gwain would fight him on it.

Instead, he searched Caedell's face for a long pause and whatever he saw there was enough to send him away. Not moving from where he stood in front of me, Caedell watched as Gwain fled, but when the man had rounded the corner of the inn, he glanced over his shoulder.

"Is this going to be a common occurrence?" he muttered, and I furrowed my brow, not understanding what he meant.

"Is what going to be?" I asked, and he spun on his heel and peered at me through narrowed eyes.

"Saving you," Caedell explained. "Keeping you from making stupid choices."

"Is that what you think you were doing just now?"

"What else would you call this?" One of his brows lifted, and I stiffened.

"I would call it an opportunity for you to throw your weight around," I murmured, while one of my hands motioned to the place where Gwain had just been standing.

"This was nothing more than two fools using me in some sort of measuring contest."

Caedell's mouth curled into a smirk, and he took a step closer. "You think I need to compare myself to Gwain Dansby?"

"Apparently, you do."

"You're mistaken," he said with a shake of his head. "This was me stopping the two of you from making this journey even more difficult for the rest of us. The last thing we need is some lover's quarrel distracting us on the road."

"I beg your pardo—"

Caedell stepped forward again, moving in so closely that I could feel the heat radiating from his body. "I am leading this journey, and I will not have anyone cause unnecessary conflicts. I take my responsibilities seriously, and I expected the same from you."

The accusation was clear, he thought I was nothing more than a mindless lovesick idiot. But of course, how could I be anything else—anything more in his eyes?

"I can promise you there will be no further problems between us," I responded through clenched teeth. "I would hate to make your *duty* more difficult for you to perform."

Leaning back, Caedell crossed his arms over his chest and then slid his eyes from my head to my toes, and back again before his gaze finally held mine.

"I can assure you, Lady Baxteel," His voice had lowered into a deep timbre, and my lips parted at the sound. "There is no *duty* I cannot perform and no contest I won't measure up in, especially against the likes of Dansby."

I could see it for what it was—this was a ploy to unnerve me. He meant to make me flustered, and had I been another highborn lady, I probably would have been far more enchanted by him. But Caedell Reide was not dealing with just another maiden. I too had been taught these tactics in my youth. I had been trained to use my beauty and charm on others, and I would not let him have the upper hand.

Swallowing, I forced my mouth to curve into a sweet smile and then held his gaze and tilted my head. "Is that so, my lord?"

Thinking he was victorious, his grin grew. "It is."

Humming under my breath, I tucked a piece of hair behind my ear and then placed that hand on his chest before shoving him roughly away from me.

"Then I'll be sure to ask for confirmation from your father's wife the next time I see her."

His body stiffened at the words, but I didn't wait for his rebuttal before moving towards the door of the inn, no longer caring about sneaking in now that I had been caught. Standing at the entrance, I turned my chin to my shoulder and glanced back at the man who remained frozen in place.

"Sleep well, Lord Reide," I muttered before ducking through the door.

The inn was quiet and dimly lit now that it was just the fireplace burning in the corner of the room, and I examined the space. The patrons had left their cups and plates scattered across the tables and chairs were knocked over and strewn around the area. Certain I was alone, I pulled my bow from over my head and moved to the stairs. Taking them two at a time, I quickly arrived at the top floor and glanced down the hallway. The doors were shut, the torches were no longer burning, and only Donigan stood on guard outside the room we had given to Cat.

Padding my way towards him, I waited for his eyes to meet mine and then I offered him a small smile. But it was not a gesture he returned.

"What is it?" I asked worriedly. "Did something happen? Was it Skileer?"

"No, nothing like that," he assured me. "What happened with Gwain?"

Sighing in relief, I placed a hand on my chest and then frowned. "Gwain?"

Donigan nodded. "He just came stumbling up the stairs in a fit," he explained. "I think he nearly spat at me when he noticed I was watching him."

"It was nothing," I promised under my breath.

"That seems unlikely," my knight pressed, and I rolled my eyes.

"He tried to speak to me outside. But Caedell stopped him and sent him on his way."

"And here you thought you would go unnoticed," Donigan grumbled. "These men are not your father or brother, and it is also not only your knights who have accompanied us here. You can be sure that they will not just turn a blind eye to your…oddities."

"Oddities?" I scoffed.

"Your choice in clothing, for one," he began.

"Many women choose not to wear gowns all the time, Donigan."

"Not many noble women," he argued. "And that's the least of it."

I noticed his attention moved to the bow in my hand, and I tucked it against my side before offering my next objection to his line of thinking. "Lots of women also hunt in the north."

"Again, not women of your standing, Rígan." He reached for my bow and plucked it from my fingers. "And when you add all of it up, it makes it difficult not to start questioning other things."

"So, what are you saying?" I asked, frustrated that there was no arguing with his logic when he laid it out like that.

"If you want to keep your secret, you need to play the part," he explained. "Stay with Cat, do as she does, and we will make it north without risking any exposure to you and your brother."

"And if we run into trouble?" I whispered roughly, knowing that it was a very real possibility.

"Then trust that I will be there," he answered. "Know that I will not let any harm come to you."

"And what of my brother?" I questioned with a raised brow. "How do we keep him from exposing us?"

"For now, we will continue to exaggerate his injury," Donigan swore. "I will make certain the men are the first to act should trouble find us."

"Do you think we will be able to manage that for the entire trek?" My knight peered down the hallway towards my brother's chambers.

"We don't have much of a choice," he admitted and then turned to face me once more. "Now, with that being said, you should probably head to bed," he instructed before pushing on my shoulder gently. "I will see you in the morning."

Scowling, I glanced at my own bedroom door and then moved my focus to the bow in his hand. Laughing softly, he placed it over his shoulder and shook his head.

"I will hold on to this for now." My frown deepened but I didn't bother arguing, and when he pushed at me once more, I conceded.

THE SLOP of wet oats splashing against the sides of my bowl was even less enticing than the stew had been the night before, but now that I knew that game was limited in the area, I was certain this would be the only option offered. Of course, I could go into our rations, but that would not have been wise considering we did not know how much farther away the next village was, and it had only been one day of travelling.

Poking at the grey mush with my spoon, I tried to pretend

that it was not so dull in colour and the earthy smell wafting from it was just a figment of my imagination.

"I wouldn't if I were you," Cat whispered as she slid onto the bench next to me before pushing the bowl away. "Nothing that looks like that should be eaten."

"I'm not sure we have much choice if we want to fill our bellies," I muttered while eyeing the dish that was now out of reach.

"Here, have some of this." She lowered her eyes to her hands, which were somewhat concealed by the edge of the table, and unfolded a cloth before revealing part of a loaf of bread and some cheese.

"Where did you get this?" I asked, looking up at her face, and she smiled sheepishly.

"That guard of Sir Caedell's gave it to me, the handsome one." Sighing, I rubbed at my eyes and then shook my head.

"Cat, why were you keeping company with the guards?" Catiline may not have been the highest priority to her father, but I was rather certain he had never allowed her to travel alone on a journey like this before, and obviously she was not aware of what was suitable for a true and proper lady. That, or she just chose to ignore such things now that she was no longer under her father's thumb.

"He was with Donigan this morning outside my door when I emerged. He offered it to me so that we would have something else to eat." She glanced at the bowl "Something besides *that*."

"He's sweet on you already," I muttered, and she blushed but shook her head.

"No, not on me." Nudging me with her elbow, she tipped her head towards the front of the inn, and I glanced up at the knights lingering in the doorway. Donigan was there along with Fynn and a third man, and they glanced at us before dipping their chins in unison.

"Cat," I called softly before placing a gentle hand on her

arm. "Did your father not tell you to stay away from the men? Surely, he warned you to keep to yourself, especially since he did not bother to send any maids with you."

"He told me quite the opposite, actually," she admitted quietly while the flush on her cheeks darkened.

"What do you mean?"

"Well, he did warn me to stay away from the guards and most of the men," she confessed. "But he asked that I seek out Caedell as often as possible."

Understanding dawned on me and I felt my jaw slacken. Cat's father was scheming and at the expense of his daughter's reputation. She may not have been quite at Caedell's standing, but she was a highborn lady and should something *inappropriate* happen on the road, the Heir of House Reide probably would marry her if his honour was what it should be. However, there were no lady's maids, no true witnesses or chaperones to keep an eye on them, and in the end, there would be no one to hold him accountable. A fact I was certain her father had overlooked.

"Perhaps we should stick together until we reach Denimoore instead," I suggested and then closed the cloth back over the food she still held in her palm. "And keep this for yourself, you won't be used to the food most taverns and inns serve."

"And you are?" she asked with a furrowed brow before looking at the forgotten bowl.

"I have travelled more than you have and I'm sure I've eaten worse." My nose wrinkled as I eyed the mush. "Though it's hard to remember when exactly."

Laughing softly, Cat linked her arm with my own and then moved her attention to the men who were still watching us.

"Food aside, I think this is going to be a great adventure." She smiled.

TWELVE

"ARE YOU WELL, MY LADY?" FYNN ASKED AS HE APPROACHED, and I glanced at the man, letting my gaze linger on his strong shoulders and thick arms before offering a charming smile.

"I am, and you, sir?" His face flushed and he ran a hand through his hair before dropping his eyes to the toe of his boots.

"Very well." His voice cracked just slightly and that flush deepened when he glanced up at me through his lashes, almost as if he was hoping I wouldn't have noticed his flustered state. Chuckling softly, I turned back to my horse.

"Was the bread and cheese to your liking?" Smoothing my hand across the leather of the saddle, I sighed and then glanced over my shoulder.

"That was very generous of you to share that with Cat. Her stomach will be unfamiliar with tavern food." Fynn's eyes widened, and he looked towards the tavern.

"Oh, that's not—" Lifting a fist, he cleared his throat and then took another step forward. "I meant for her to share it with *you*."

Flicking my hair over my shoulder, I let my eyes roam across his features and then smiled slyly. "Well, I appreciate that, but it wasn't necessary. I'm not as *delicate* as most ladies."

Fynn's flush darkened another shade, the red now reaching the tips of his ears this time, and I lifted my chin and peered at him. He was not like most of the men; he was handsome, that was to be sure, but he lacked the confidence many knights had, or at least pretended to have. He was not what I would have expected, and I found pleasure in watching him shift nervously under my gaze.

"I wanted to be sure you did not go hungry, my lady," he murmured quietly and I rolled my eyes.

"I can assure you, I am more than capable of looking after myself." Donigan was right, I had a part to play, but I would be damned if these men thought I was totally incompetent at doing even the most basic things.

"I just—" he began but then those eyes lifted to glance over my shoulder.

"You heard the lady, sir." Tipping my head to the heavens, I wondered why the Gods felt the need to punish me so early in the day.

"Sir Dansby," Fynn greeted, and I noticed the way he squared his shoulders and pressed his chest forward from the corner of my eye.

"The horses need tending to before we begin our journey, see to them," Gwain ordered sharply, and I heard Fynn's scoff.

"I am not one of your men, sir," Fynn reminded him with a growl, but Gwain paid him no mind.

"You are a knight, and I am a lord, so you will do as I command." Fynn hesitated, his eyes darting to mine in concern, and I wondered if my father had been right in thinking that every person in Elrin knew of our relationship.

"Thank you for the food this morning." I stepped forward and placed a hand on the man's forearm, all while ignoring the gasp that sounded from beside me. "I hope to see you later in the day."

Fynn flushed again before offering me a bow, and then he turned on his heel and headed to the stables. Now that I was left unaccompanied, Gwain took his chance and crowded in beside me.

"You should not be left alone with a rogue like Sir Bryne," he whispered, and I noticed his hand hovered near my shoulder.

"But I would be safe to be alone with the likes of you?" I snapped. "You had no right dismissing him in such a way." Spinning to face him, I slapped his hand away from me, and Gwain stumbled back a step.

"I was just trying to protect you," he argued once he had righted himself.

"No," I disagreed. "After last night, you were trying to throw your weight around with someone who has no choice but to listen. You wanted to mend your pride and impress me." I crossed my arms over my chest and shook my head in disbelief. "As if that could somehow dissuade me from my anger."

"That's not it, Rígan," Gwain whispered, while his green eyes lowered to the ground, and I studied the face I had spent so long learning. He was still just as handsome, but his skin was pale and the darkness under his eyes told me he had not slept well in what was probably days.

"I thought I told you not to address me in that manner." Lifting a hand to rub at his jaw, Gwain frowned and then swallowed roughly.

"My apologies," he murmured.

"Apologies?" I sneered at him, not caring about the desperation his voice held or the way he somehow made himself seem even more pitiful than he had been the night before. "Well, I suppose you do have so much to be sorry for these days."

"I do," he confessed, and my gaze narrowed.

"How could you not tell me?" That had been the worst of

it. Knowing he had taken me into his arms, into his bed, all while conscious of the fact that he would never be mine. And he had not even thought to tell me about his betrothal. It was all a betrayal, but the part that stung the most was the humiliation of it all.

"I didn't want to hurt you," he explained, and I laughed coldly.

"And yet, that is exactly what you did." I didn't think it was possible for his skin to lose any more colour, nevertheless he looked even more pallid than he had just moments ago.

"I had planned to find a way out of it, I promise," he swore, and then those green irises slowly lifted to my own.

"Your promises are no good to me now." Gwain flinched at the words and then wet his lips nervously.

"I know why you doubt me," he began, ignoring my sigh before continuing. "And I know I will have to earn your trust once more. But I promise—"

"Did you not hear me?" I snarled, though my voice broke, and I hated that the sound made his face soften, as if he pitied me.

"I swear on my honour that I will find a way to get out of this match and then I will pledge my loyalty to you and you only." He reached for me, his fingers taking my own before he lifted them so that my palm pressed against the thudding in his chest.

"But that's the problem, Gwain," I laughed coldly before roughly snatching my hand from his. "I no longer have any faith in your honour."

THE CARRIAGE WAS UNPLEASANTLY FULL NOW that both my brother and I accompanied Catiline in its small space, and I felt Cat shift her weight once more as she struggled to get comfortable. Pressing against the wall, I pulled at her arm until she slid into the empty area my movement had offered up and smiled softly at her.

"It shouldn't be much longer now," I promised. "We will stop for the night as soon as we find somewhere suitable."

"There is no chance of that happening," Skileer mumbled from his seat across from us. "There is nothing on this road but poor villages and rundown taverns. I doubt we will find anything fitting for the rest of the journey."

"I don't mind so much," Cat said softly while her dark eyes lifted to mine. "I rather like seeing these little towns and the folk who live there. They are so different from home."

"It's only been a few days, give it time. Soon you'll be longing to return south," Skileer muttered before resting the uninjured side of his face against the wall, and Cat frowned at him.

"Maybe that is true for you, you've spent your life on the road, exploring the lands," Cat replied quietly. "But this is the farthest I've been from our manor."

Skileer seemed to forget that highborn ladies did not have the freedom I did, but he still ignored her excitement and glanced out his own window as we continued to trudge up the rocky road.

"Looks like your prayers have been answered then." My brother glowered at the view. "We have reached another town, and this one is in worse shape than the last."

Listening as orders were barked at the men, I grabbed Cat's hand while we waited, and then the carriage slowed to a halt and the door was being pulled open. Lifting an arm, Donigan waited for Cat to grab a hold of it and then carefully helped her out of the carriage. Watching the pair, I noticed the way the woman smiled at the knight softly, but he did not seem to notice and instead ushered her towards the other guards before reaching for me.

Curling my fingers over his, I gathered my skirts and then moved down the steps before glancing at our audience. The men had gathered around while they waited for us to emerge from our place, and although I hated myself for it, I searched the crowd for Gwain's face.

"He has gone in to inspect the tavern," Donigan whispered as he guided me away from the carriage and then looked towards Skileer, who was ducking through the door.

"Are you faring well, my lord?" our knight asked as my brother stumbled down the stairs.

"Fetch me some wine and something to eat, Taith," he demanded before pressing his palm to the dressings on his face. "And find me the healer. I need more tonic and these blasted bandages changed."

Sighing, Donigan gave my fingers a squeeze and then bowed at my brother before doing as he demanded. Now left without my protector, I moved to Cat's side while we waited for the men to organize themselves. Soon, the horses were led away, and our things were being carried into the tavern, and I watched as Donigan returned with the healer in tow and Caedell following behind.

"Lady Catiline, your room is ready, and I have asked that they have one of the barmaids waiting for you, should you need anything." Caedell grinned at her, before dipping low in a graceful bow. Cat sighed softly, acting as if he had just recited some sonnet rather than offering her what was expected for a lady of her status.

"Thank you, Lord Reide," she responded with a curtsey and then looked at me. "What of Lady Rígan?"

Caedell's amber eyes moved as well, and a brow lifted as he studied me carefully. "I wasn't aware she was used to such luxuries during her travels." It was a slight and most definitely another ploy to get me to react, but I instead tilted my head to the side and smirked, determined to show him how unbothered I was.

"Don't worry about me, sir. I am more than capable of looking after myself."

"Yes," he replied. "So I've been told."

Then his attention shifted to Fynn and then to Gwain before coming back to me. "But should that not be the case, it seems there is more than one person willing to aid your needs, *whatever* they may be."

Everyone's attention focused on Caedell, and I could feel the tension that was falling over the group. Fynn seemed nervous but Gwain looked livid, and I felt Donigan flank to my side.

"I will not tolerate another slight like that against my lady, my lord," he growled, not caring that Caedell was his superior, and I reached a hand out to grab at his arm.

"Ah, it seems there is another to be added to the tally." Caedell grinned before he tilted his head slightly. "Tell me, what do you do to gain such devotion?"

"I suppose it's my charm," I muttered and his smile grew.

"Yes, your appeal is somewhat legendary at this point." Donigan was tense under my hand, and I closed my fingers around his arm tightly in warning before focusing back on the man in front of me.

"Be careful, sir," I warned. "I would hate for you to be the next one to fall victim to it." My eyes roamed across his sharp features and my lips lifted in a sly smile of my own. "Though I can't help but assume that I am not of your taste. There is not enough of a challenge or chase for you, I am all too easy for your pursuit."

Whatever self-assuredness he had slowly slipped away, and I watched as his expression grew grim before he turned on his heel. Pulling from my touch, Donigan moved to follow the Heir of House Reide, but it was my brother who stopped him this time.

"Leave it," Skileer growled. "Let him insult her, defending

her honour is obviously a waste of time, and we have better things to do."

Glowering at my brother, Donigan watched as he ordered the healer to follow him to his room, and then he glanced at me. Lowering my chin, I gave Donigan the okay to trail after the pair and felt Cat reach for the hand that had been holding on to the knight.

"I now see why you dislike Sir Reide so much," she whispered while her dark gaze searched my face. "How could he speak to you in such a way?"

"Don't fret, Cat," I reassured her. "Words can only wield the power you give them, and I refuse to give his any."

Catiline nodded but her face still showed her worry, and I squeezed her fingers before tugging her forward.

"Now, let's go see what this tavern has to offer." I smiled, hoping to ease her concern. "You were so desperate to explore the villages, wouldn't you rather ignore men like Sir Reide and instead enjoy this adventure of yours?"

My words seemed to have the effect I had hoped for, and I pushed past the group of men, ignoring Gwain's longing stare and Fynn's blush as we made our way towards the entrance of our lodgings for the night.

CHAPTER

THIRTEEN

THE PATRONS IN THIS PARTICULAR ESTABLISHMENT WERE FAR less interested in us than the last crowd had been, and I searched the room from my seat in the darkened corner. There were small groups of men gathered around tables. Some were laughing and goading each other, others were quietly sipping on their drinks, but overall, they paid us no mind as we settled in.

"It certainly smells better in here," Cat observed as she lifted the overflowing cup of ale and then stared at it with curiosity.

"That's because no one has vomited on the floor yet," I grumbled and then I focused on her, watching as she brought the cup to her mouth before poking her tongue out to taste the foam that settled on top. Her little nose wrinkled but she stabbed at the white froth again before wetting her lips.

"Is it meant to taste so bitter? Almost like…" She trailed off with a furrowed brow as she searched for the right word, and I lifted my own drink and took a long swig before wiping my face with the back of my hand.

"Piss?" I asked and Cat frowned but nodded. "It's an acquired taste, it will take some getting used to."

"I never truly learned to like wine either," she admitted with a sigh, and then she clenched her eyes shut and tipped her head back before gulping down the contents of her cup. Unable to look away, I noticed the small rivers of ale leaking past the rim before they raced down the edge of her chin, and my brow lifted when I saw the mess she was making on the front of her gown.

"If you drink it fast enough, you can look past the taste," Cat croaked out once she had finished, and then she covered her mouth and her eyes widened while her cheeks swelled with a burp.

"I'm not sure that is the way to go about it, Cat," I laughed softly, noticing the way her pale skin had begun to pinken. "Why not stick to water for now?"

Catiline pouted at the suggestion before motioning to the barmaid for another serving of drink. "I don't want to be the only one not partaking."

Placing a gentle hand on her shoulder, I pushed my cup away for good measure. "I can forfeit ale for the night, it's not a hardship in the least."

Sighing, Cat looked at me from the corner of her eye and then to the maid who wore a sour expression as she carried a tray in our direction. Stopping at our table, the older woman unloaded the dishes onto the wooden table and then gave a sloppy curtsey before going on her way.

"What will we do with all of these then?" she asked worriedly, and I glanced at the strangers who sat around the room.

"Give them to the villagers before the rest of our men get here and take them for themselves," I advised. "We do not need our protectors falling into their cups, or worse, my brother."

Standing from her chair, she collected the goblets in her arms and then all but skipped away. Keeping a watchful eye on her, I followed her movements around the room as she went from table to table until her hands were empty, and I noticed the way the strangers smiled and thanked her politely. None showed any animosity or nervousness towards her, and she seemed to almost blossom from their kindness.

"What is she doing?" Donigan asked as he approached the table, and I looked up at him only for my attention to be pulled back to the crowd when a noisy folk song started.

I hadn't even noticed the ensemble that had been hidden away amongst the others, but now the room began to cheer, and tables were being pushed aside. Startled by the flurry of movement, I stood from my chair and watched as one of the men clutched at Cat's hand before leading her to the space that had been cleared. She looked over at me nervously for just a pause before her partner was directing her attention back to him and then towards their feet.

He was a small fellow, and was certainly old enough to be her grandfather, so I deemed him to be no threat and instead sat back down to watch her try to learn the jig he was apparently determined to teach her. Studying his nimble feet, Cat tried to imitate him to no avail, and when she nearly fell over, she tossed her head back with a laugh.

"I thought ladies were meant to be masters of dancing," Donigan murmured quietly and I shrugged.

"This is not the kind of dancing they teach young noble girls," I explained before turning to observe the pair once more. Flustered but obviously committed to learning the pattern her feet were meant to move in, she watched the man again and again, taking one step at a time.

"Well, it doesn't look as if she will need to master their way any longer, she has a saviour coming." My brows furrowed, and I stood once more to see to whom Donigan meant.

Tapping the man on the shoulder, Caedell interrupted the two and then bent in half in an extravagant bow before pressing a kiss to the hand Cat had placed in his own. Waiting until she slid into his arms, he straightened his spine and then began to lead her in a much more sophisticated dance.

"They do make a striking pair," Donigan remarked under his breath, but there wasn't an ounce of jealousy in the words, and I wondered if he really was still blind to Cat's lingering affection for him.

"Don't give her any more ideas," I snapped and Donigan's brows lifted in surprise. "Her father encouraged her to seek out his company during our travels."

"How very ambitious of him," Donigan drawled mockingly and I nodded.

"I have begun to try and sway her away from the idea. Caedell is impulsive, and rash, and he has quite the reputation."

"Something you can understand, I'm sure." My head whipped towards him, and Donigan pressed his lips together before lowering his chin.

"We just rekindled our friendship," I growled in warning. "I would hate for you to make the same mistake again, Sir Taith."

"I only meant you share some of the same qualities; I was not agreeing with the reputation bit," he whispered sheepishly.

"Then perhaps you should choose your words more wisely," I suggested with a cold tone, and he swallowed nervously.

"Of course, my lady." He nodded. "My apologies."

Deciding not to linger on the conversation, I focused back on the two, who were spinning across the floor. Donigan was right, they did seem to complement each other, but I would be damned before I allowed Caedell to sink his claws into someone as innocent and good as Catiline.

Noticing the shy smile that was painted across Cat's mouth and the way her face was stained pink, I knew I had to do something. Striding across the floor, I waited until they swayed towards me and then I caught the underside of Cat's arm before glaring at her partner.

"Donigan is in need of your presence," I whispered to Cat and Caedell rolled his eyes.

"What would a lowly born knight need from her?" Caedell laughed as he held my stare. "If you were jealous, just say as much. It is better than embarrassing yourself with such a poor excuse for interrupting."

"I should go make certain he is okay," Cat interjected before she hurried to Donigan's side, and Caedell watched her with a surprised expression.

"How very dutiful she is, and for just a simple knight. Tell me, is she always so eager to be at his beck and call?" he wondered out loud, and my jaw clenched at his words.

"Don't talk about her in that way," I barked, and those bright amber eyes slid back to my face before he took a step closer and then his arm was curling behind my back.

"What are you doing?" I questioned while pressing away from him, but his hold was unwavering, and his arm felt like an iron bar against my spine.

"If you have the gall to cut in, you can at least do me the courtesy of dancing with me so that I don't look as if I have been abandoned for another."

"Shouldn't you be familiar with that feeling?" I pressed, smiling smugly when I heard his gasp. However, the shock of my words did not last long, and within a heartbeat he was pulling me close to his chest before placing his lips next to my ear.

"Say what you will, lash out while you can," he growled. "But know this, Rígan Baxteel, despite your insults and taunts, I see through you, and I know what lingers beneath the surface."

Shoving me away, Caedell strode across the floor, and I crossed my arms around my torso while I struggled to fight off the chill that began to seep into my chest.

My head was pounding from my lack of sleep and too much ale, and I kicked at the furs that covered my legs before sitting up in my bed. The commotion was still at its height downstairs, and though I had decided to retire early, the others had continued to enjoy the festivities. Well, everyone besides Caedell and me.

Growling in frustration, I turned to look down at the lumpy bed below me and then pounded my fists against the wool beneath the surface in hopes of smoothing it out. Yet still, even after my beating, the bed remained unbearable, and I instead tugged the pelts from their place and spread them across the floor. Moving to the ground, I curled on my side and brought my knees to my chest before closing my eyes again while wishing for slumber to take me into its arms. However, just as that heaviness began to caress my consciousness, I heard the sound of a muffled scream come from outside my window. It was quiet, just barely there, and nearly impossible to hear over the ruckus happening downstairs. But when my skin prickled and my stomach tightened, I knew I was not mistaken.

Crawling to the window, I grabbed at the sill and lifted onto my knees to peer at the ground below. There was no one there, no stranger or passerby. But still the empty roads and quietness of the air only added to my unease. Searching the dark for some sign of threat, I waited while my heart began to pound in my chest, and it was then that I saw it. It was just a flicker of movement coming from behind another building, but it was enough for my eyes to remain locked on the spot, and then I noticed the flapping material of a cloak. The intruder was not nearly as stealthy as he needed to be to go unnoticed, and now that I had spotted him, I could see he was not alone.

Lowering myself back onto the floor, I crept to the door and hurried from my room. Running to the railing that lined the upper floor, I curled my fingers around the wood and peered down to space below. The crowd was still enthralled in their dancing and drinking, and it would be nearly impossible to get their attention.

"What in the name of the Huntress are you doing out here?!" Caedell snarled while one of his large hands seized my right arm and then he roughly hauled me away from the bannister. "Are you trying to make more of a mockery of what is left of your reputation?"

Pulling free from his grasp, I glared at him. "What are you talking about? And since when have you ever cared about my reputation?"

Caedell's eyes were dark and heated, and I felt the scorch of them on my skin as they roamed across my face, down the length of my neck, and then to my breasts, which were barely concealed by the light shift I wore.

Realizing the mistake I had made in my panic to find help, I pinched at the hem that ended at my knee in an attempt to lengthen the material. However, that only ended up stretching the soft silk tightly against the full curve of my chest, and Caedell's jaw clenched before he hurriedly unbuckled the cloak that adorned his shoulders. Swinging it around so that the weight fell heavily over me instead, he pulled it closed across my front and then backed me into the wall. Placing a palm next to my head, he leaned in close and caged me there with his own body.

"I know you love attention and have little regard for propriety, but I would have thought even *you* would know better than to parade around in front of a group of strangers and guardsmen in something so revealing!" he seethed.

Narrowing my eyes, I pushed the green wool from my

shoulders, displaying the front of my body once more. "If it was attention I was seeking, I would have found another shift far more fetching."

Lifting a hand, I ran the backs of my fingers down the centre of my chest until they hit the lace of the neckline. "Though judging by the stares I have received from your men and the rest of our party over the last few days, I'm sure a burlap sack would work just as well at this point."

Refusing to follow my fingers on their path, Caedell's eyes remained locked on my own, though I noticed the way his throat bobbed. "If attention wasn't what you were looking for, why are you out here?"

"There is someone outside." Caedell's brows furrowed in confusion, so I continued. "I heard a scream, and when I looked out the window, I saw a small party hiding amongst the shadows."

"What kind of scream?" Caedell asked, and I tipped my head to the side.

"What do you mean? Is there more than one kind?" The pointed look Caedell gave me was enough for me to understand what he had meant, and I rolled my eyes.

"No." I shook my head. "This sounded like it came from a man and it was not one of pleasure," I assured him, and he finally pushed off the wall and took a step back.

"So, there are some rogues outside up to no good. What would you have me do?" he questioned, and my jaw slackened.

"Do your duty and seek them out!" I answered as I closed the space between us once more and he rolled his eyes.

"Am I to waste my time with every single miscreant you come across?" I couldn't believe what I was hearing and was too stunned to answer, even when Caedell ran a hand over his face in frustration.

"If they are no threat to us, I will not go looking for trouble," he explained as if I was a child and not someone two years his senior. "And we do not have the time to be distracted at every turn, so stop looking for problems when there are none."

"But what if they are a threat?" I implored while my hands waved through the air in frustration. I could see Caedell's doubt; he did not see any significance in what I had witnessed, and my irritation would have reached a boiling point if it wasn't for the fact that at that very moment the door of the tavern was torn from its hinges and then went crashing to the floor.

FOURTEEN

Chaos erupted from the scene below, and the panicked screams were enough to finally send Caedell into action. Turning from me, he reached behind him and took a hold of my hip and then guided me back until I was pressed against the wall once again. Grabbing at the dagger on his belt, he unsheathed the weapon and moved his grasp from my body to one of my arms and then slid his fingers down the flesh of my forearm until he captured my hand. Twisting slightly, he placed the weapon in my palm and looked over his shoulder.

"Remain here until this is settled," he ordered, and when my mouth parted, he shook his head with a growl. "I can't be worried about you while I am dealing with this. Don't be a fool, stay here."

"What of Cat!?" I called as he stormed away from me.

"I will see to her safety!" By now he had reached the middle of the stairs, and I watched as he grabbed on to the railing before hauling himself over. Landing on the ground gracefully, he had somehow managed to unsheathe his sword, and I slid away from the wall just as he began to cut down the men who had forced their way into the room.

Initially, when I had first noticed the group outside, I had thought there had only been a handful of men. But it was obvious this group was far larger than I had assumed, and though we would have been evenly matched, the panicked townsfolk made it more difficult for our party to gain an upper hand without injuring one of the innocents.

Scanning the room below, I searched for my friends and breathed a sigh of relief when I located Donigan. He was masterfully beating back two men on his own, and my eyes lingered for a pause, making certain he was uninjured before moving on from his form. Cat, however, was not so easily spotted, and panic flooded my veins when I realized I couldn't find her. Rushing forward, I leaned over the bannister while my eyes darted across the room. She was a small thing, but her dark hair and pale skin should have been easy to locate. However, when I still hadn't found her after my third time searching the room, I knew I needed to get down there.

Rushing down the steep wooden steps, I curled my fingers around the hilt of the dagger and pressed my way through the crowd while I scoured the area for my friend. Guards and men were scattered across the tavern, their shouts and the sound of metal clashing was loud enough to make my ears ring, and I dodged as many as I could while I began shouting for my companion.

"Cat!?" I screamed, turning this way and that while the commotion worsened all around me. But when she didn't answer, I pressed my way to the other end of the inn.

"Just where the fuck do you think you're going?!" The metal clasp of the cloak was suddenly pressed sharply against the tender flesh of my throat, and I was being dragged backwards until I was sprawled across one of the tables. Blinking up at the man above me in a daze, I turned my head away from the stench of his breath and he chuckled.

"My, my, you are a pretty thing," he murmured as he bent closer towards my face, and I lifted a knee to strike at his groin. However, he twisted away just in time to avoid the impact, obviously well practiced in this particular scenario, and when I swung the weapon towards him, he grabbed my wrist. "What is a lady doing with a blade like this?"

One of his meaty hands moved to uncurl my fingers from the weapon, and I held my breath as his focus turned to the blade. Certain he was thoroughly distracted, I shot upwards and my head collided with his own. There was a great burst of blood from his nose and the pain was enough to send him staggering backwards.

"You bitch!" he shouted, his yellow teeth now a crimson colour as the blood continued to pour, and his dark eyes hardened with determination. But I was already two steps ahead of him, and when he reached for my neck, I spun away from his grasp.

Not prepared for me to move so swiftly, his hand moved to catch himself on the table, and I lifted the dagger I had managed to keep a hold of, and brought it down, aiming the tip of the blade towards the knuckles that were covered by the bulging blue veins. The metal sank through the skin and pierced the wood below easily, and the man tossed his head back with a howl of pain. Ignoring his cries, I grabbed the sword that was dangling from the tips of his other fingers.

"Keep that there and don't move," I ordered him, laughing softly at his whimpering. "When this is finished, I have a few other pieces of you I would like to maim before I send you to the Gods."

Moving my free hand to the clasp of the cloak, I undid the metal, shrugging out from under its weight and then I was dashing across the room. One by one our attackers were cut down and yet I still could not find my friend, and my stomach twisted with worry as I moved from one corner of the tavern to the other.

Pressing my back against the farthest wall from the door, I took in the madness, and then I saw a flash of black hair. She was there, tucked beneath the stairs, seemingly unharmed but obviously shaken. Breathing a sigh of relief, I smiled to myself for just a pause and then I saw him. He was a beast of a man, easily half a foot taller than I, and though his face was covered by a silver mask, I knew he had set his sights on Cat by the way he was slithering towards her.

Pushing away from the wall, I tightened my hold on the sword and ran towards the pair, listening to my heartbeat pound as I closed the distance between us. However, it would seem that I would not have the upper hand, despite the element of surprise. Just as I neared the two of them, the spine of the man straightened and then he was looking over his shoulder.

His face may have been concealed, but his eyes were visible, and the terrifying look in his gaze made my stride falter and then my bare feet were sliding across the blood that was now covering most of the stone floor. Turning to me, the man slammed his own blade down onto mine while his other hand curled into a fist and he rammed it into my ribs. Gasping for air, I bent in half and the stranger took the opportunity to twist my long strands of hair in his fingers and then he tugged my face towards the ceiling.

"Just what kind of highborns did we stumble across?" He chuckled as he examined my features. "I've never seen a woman try to wield a blade like a man."

"That's because you've never seen a woman like me," I snarled and then I collected the saliva in my mouth and spat it onto the metal. Though I could not see his face, I recognized the rage burning in his eyes, and the hand in my hair tightened as he dragged me towards his body.

"Even if that was true, you will break just as easily as all the rest," he growled, not bothering to wipe the spittle from the steel before he was tossing me onto the floor. Landing painfully on my exposed knees, I scrambled across the damp stone in an attempt to get some distance from him. But it was no use, his long strides ate up any space I created, and then a heavy boot was pressing into my back before I was crushed against the ground. Struggling for air, I turned my head to the side and peered up at him from the corner of my eye.

"Don't tell me that was all the fight you have in you!" He laughed before applying more pressure to my spine and I cried out.

"Get off of her!" Cat screamed, and I watched in panic as she launched herself onto my attacker's back before clawing at his covered face and bare neck. Surprised by her sudden bravery, the man stumbled back, relieving me of his weight, and I hurried to my feet before facing him once more. He, however, did not seem fazed by Cat's assault, and he reached over his shoulder to pluck the flailing woman off of him with more ease than was natural. I felt my body tingle with fear, and his gaze caught mine again before he tossed Cat aside.

"When I'm done with you, I will make sure to take my time with your friend," he swore before lifting the back of his massive hand to his throat and he wiped at the streaks of red that had been left there. However, now that the rivers of blood were gone, I could clearly see the skin of his throat once more, his perfectly *unmarked* skin that held no evidence of Catiline's attack.

"That's not possible," I whispered to myself as he stalked towards me while sheathing his weapon, and he chuckled again when he noticed the way I began to tremble in panic.

"You don't even understand the realm of possibilities this world has to offer," he claimed and then he dashed towards me.

Curling a hand around my neck, he effortlessly lifted me from the ground and slammed me into the nearest wall. My eyes fluttered shut at the impact, and I took in a staggering breath before I began to struggle. Raising my arms, I scratched at him in an attempt to loosen his hold, but he just applied more pressure to my windpipe and then tore his mask from his face before capturing one of my wrists. Lifting it above my head, he pressed the joint into the wall and watched my face as my mouth opened in pain before nuzzling his nose against my temple.

"I wasn't sure what you were when I saw you racing through the room in this scrap of fabric," he muttered against my skin. "But you certainly smell like no whore I've ever encountered before."

He inhaled deeply and then hummed. "No, certainly not a whore. You have noble blood in these veins, and I am going to enjoy spilling every drop."

His tongue darted out from between his lips, and he licked up the side of my cheek while blackness began to creep into my vision as the air in my lungs was snuffed out.

"It is not her blood that will spill tonight, you bastard!" a voice shouted from someplace nearby, and I was jostled just slightly before I heard an odd gurgle, and then I was falling to the floor in a heap.

Unable to catch myself, my body hit the ground sharply, but the pain was enough to awaken me from my dazed state, and I clutched at my throat while I began to cough. Shaking my head in an attempt to finish clearing the haze from my mind, I glanced up at my saviour, and Gwain softly called out my name before falling to his knees before me.

"Are you alright?" he asked, his hands lifting towards me but remaining a few inches away while he waited for some indication that it was okay to touch me.

"He—he—" I stuttered out, lifting a shaking finger to point at the unmasked man who was slumped on the floor with his throat slit, and Gwain nodded.

Whatever hurt and betrayal I had been consumed with since the tourney no longer thrummed through my veins, and I looked at him while I choked on a sob. Grabbing at his hand, I let him pull me to his chest, and he nestled my face into the crook of his neck while he rocked us softly.

"I'm here now," he whispered. "I'm here. It's alright now, he can't hurt you."

But it was if Gwain's words breathed some sort of life into my assailant, and a great gasp came from his body. Turning my chin to my shoulder, I noticed that the stranger was moving, and I watched as one of his massive hands lifted to the gash on his neck that now appeared to be nearly closed.

Gwain froze under me. "How is that poss—"

I didn't wait for him to finish his question before I was lunging off of his lap to grab at the man's sword that was still at his side. Pulling it from its leather cover, I linked my fingers together and clutched the hilt between my palms. Lifting the great blade above my head, I waited until those dark eyes widened at me. And when I was sure he realized what was about to happen, I brought down the weapon with as much force as I could muster. Thrusting the blade into the flesh of his cheek, I pulled the metal free and did it again, this time aiming at his temple and then I repeated the process over and over until there was nothing left that resembled the face of a man. However, unwilling to risk the chance of his somehow healing from this as well, I turned the sword and brought the edge across his neck, making certain his head was no longer attached before I tossed the blade away.

Falling backwards against the wall, I quivered with shock, and Gwain stared down at my victim for a long pause before eyeing my blood-soaked shift. As he took in the carnage I had created, his skin paled but then a hand was cupping my shoulder and urging me to turn around.

Kneeling before me, Donigan grabbed at my upper arms and he began to speak, but his words were really just a quiet hum to my ears, and my eyes moved back to the man before us. Growing desperate, Donigan began to shake me gently, hoping to pull me from my frozen state, but I kept my gaze fixated on the stranger's chest while I waited for another sign of life. And while I knew it shouldn't be possible, I had witnessed the man somehow come back from the brink of death just a moment ago, and I was certain it had not been a trick of my imagination.

No, it was no illusion.

It was something far more sinister.

CHAPTER

FIFTEEN

Luckily, our losses were minimal—only one of Cat's men had not made it through the confrontation. Our attackers, however, were far less fortunate, and though I was frustrated that none had lived for us to question, I was glad the threat was gone. Glancing around the room, I studied the evidence of our encounter while Gwain carefully palpated my wrist and then he lifted a damp cloth to clean the dried blood from my fingers.

"It is not broken, but it will be tender for a few days," he murmured, and I turned my attention back to his handsome face.

"I wasn't aware you had become a healer." I had meant for the words to be teasing, but they sounded cold, even to my own ears, and his frown deepened.

"I've seen a few injuries in my days," he claimed while he took my other arm in his grasp and began to wipe down that limb as well.

Muttering softly to himself, he continued his work while I instead looked to Cat, who was being seen by her own healer. She looked shaken and paler than usual, but I could not see any serious injuries on her, and I sighed in relief. Slouching into the chair I sat on, I tipped my head back and closed my eyes, only to be startled by the sudden weight of wool being placed on my shoulders.

"You lost this," Caedell said before his gaze moved to Gwain, and the man stiffened under our visitor's attention. "How does she fare, Dansby?"

"Bruised but whole," Gwain sighed, not bothering to look up from the hand he held, though I noticed the way his fingers paused in their ministrations and then he plucked at the green material of Caedell's cloak and flicked it over my shoulder.

"And the blood?" Caedell inquired as his amber eyes examined the once cream-coloured shift that was now a deep maroon.

"Not hers," Gwain replied, though the quiet sound did not hide the shakiness of his words. Ignoring his puzzling reaction, I chose to watch Caedell, and I noticed the way his brows lifted to his hairline in surprise.

"Looks as if we have a shewolf amongst us." His eyes slid to my own, and I held his stare even when his expression hardened. "But tell me, where is your brother?"

Pulling my attention from him, I glanced around the tavern, searching for Skileer but to no avail. Scowling, I drew away from Gwain's touch and stood from my seat, hating that I hadn't even thought to look for my brother until now.

"Has no one seen him?" I questioned as I spun back towards Caedell in panic. He, however, did not look concerned in the least and crossed his arms over his broad chest.

"No one has seen him at all this evening," he answered. "Not even after our visitors kicked down the door and began their attack," Caedell pointed out, his tone feigning innocence, though I could clearly hear the accusation.

"My brother is no turncoat, if that is what you are implying, Sir Reide," I snapped, praying that I sounded more certain than I felt.

Lifting his chin, Caedell straightened and then peered at me from down his nose. "I never accused him of being such a thing."

Pressing my lips into a thin line, I clutched at the cloak he had placed over my shoulders and then fled from my place and headed to the stairs. Rushing up them, I sprinted down the hall towards the bedroom I knew had been given to Skileer, and I pounded my fist against the wooden door. But when no answer came, I repeated the motion before pressing my ear to the surface in an attempt to detect movement coming from the other side.

"Skileer!?" I hissed, slapping my palm against the barrier in frustration once more, and finally, I heard rustling.

"My lady." The healer who had accompanied my brother into the inn when we arrived greeted me, and my brows furrowed when he wedged the door just wide enough for me to see his ashen face.

"Where is my brother?" I snapped, lifting onto my toes to glance over his head.

"He is resting, my lady," the man whispered while his eyes turned down to the floor, and I clenched my jaw.

"Resting?" I repeated the word, letting the sound roll of my tongue before I narrowed my gaze at him.

"Yes, my lady." He nodded hurriedly and then pressed the edge of the door tighter against the side of his face, as if that would keep me from prying for more information.

"I think it's best that you move aside, sir." I took a step forward and braced my hand on the wood next to his temple.

"I cannot do that," he replied, and my lip curled in a snarl, and I moved until my nose was just a hair away from his own.

"You can move aside on your own," I warned. "Or I can force you to. The choice is yours."

"I'm sorry, my lady, but your empty threats have no power here," the man argued, but then his gaze lifted, and his eyes widened.

"You heard my lady," Donigan snapped as he pressed in close behind me. "Move aside or I will cut you down myself and save her the trouble."

I could see his hesitation, almost as if he was trying to quickly formulate another plan. But I had reached the edge of my patience and used as much strength as I could muster to press on his shoulder while I shoved him aside. Unprepared for the power behind my touch, the healer stumbled back, nearly falling to the floor as I passed him, and I heard the door slam behind me.

Glancing over my shoulder, I watched as Donigan leaned against the slab of wood with his arms crossed while he peered down at the man on the floor in challenge. And that challenge was clear—make a wrong move and he would make certain that the man did not live to see another day. After all, healers were easy to come by, and we did not need one who questioned me. I turned to the bed once more, my feet padding quietly to the side of the mattress, and I looked down at my brother.

"Skileer?" I asked, grabbing at his shoulder before giving him a rough shake, but he did not stir.

"What is wrong with him?" Donigan demanded, and the healer slowly pulled himself to his feet before wringing his hands together.

"As I said, he is resting." Glaring back at the man, I frowned and then placed my hand on my brother's throat. His pulse was even and relaxed, but still he did not awaken, and I spun on my heel and stalked towards the healer.

"That is not just resting," I snarled. "What did you do to him?!"

The man's eyes bounced from Donigan and then back to me nervously, and I took another step closer while my knight closed in from behind. Growing panicked, the healer raced to the table next to the bed and picked up a vial.

"A fever overcame him suddenly," the man explained. "He was in need of a tonic, which I happily supplied."

"And this tonic left him in this state?" Donigan scoffed, not believing his words.

"It did, sir," the healer insisted.

"And just when did this fever overtake him?" I drawled. "Before or after the pounding on the door downstairs had begun?"

"You'll have to forgive me, my lady, I can't seem to recall," the healer mumbled.

Snorting, Donigan shook his head. "Yes, I'm sure."

"Just how long will he be *indisposed*?" I demanded as I looked at my brother's prone state.

"Hours," the man answered. "At least until dawn."

Running a hand over my face, I stepped past the healer and came to Donigan's side. Keeping his eye on the man, he leaned towards me so I could whisper in his ear without a chance of being overheard.

"Whether we believe it or not, we need to tell the others," I instructed my knight. "They must be made aware of his illness, even if it has to be exaggerated so that his courage does not come into question."

Dipping his head, Donigan hummed his agreement. "And what of the healer?"

My head turned to my shoulder, and I studied the man for a pause. "Loyalty has a heavy price, see that he takes our offer." My attention moved to the healer, and I studied him closely before continuing. "Willingly or not."

THE NASTY BRUISE on Cat's face was prominent against the pale colour of her skin, and I lifted my fingers to stroke across the blemish carefully.

"Is it very painful?" I asked worriedly, and she batted my hand away with a roll of her eyes.

"It is nothing," she assured me while her dark eyes lowered to the deep purple marks that littered my throat. "Yours is much worse."

Though that may have been true, I had grown a tolerance for pain over the years, and I seriously doubted Cat had ever been injured in such a way. Settling in my seat once more, I lowered my hand and lifted the cup of tea before taking a sip, though my attention didn't waver from her face.

"Honestly, Rígan, I'm alright," she promised with a smile. "I'm just a little sad it will fade, and I will have nothing to show for my efforts of trying to stop that beast from harming you, even as pathetic as those efforts may have been."

"They were not pathetic!" I countered. "If not for you, things would have been far worse."

"I'm just sorry I couldn't do more," Cat admitted softly. "I didn't know what else to do, and he just seemed to be so strong."

Catiline was right, but she probably wasn't aware of just how *unnaturally* strong he had been. It still plagued my mind, the memories of him taking that gasping breath, the way he had easily tossed me around, and the speed in which he had moved. At the time I had wondered if it was just the fear and adrenaline pumping through my veins that made it feel as if my attacker was something more, but now that it was all over, I knew there was something not right about the man.

Reaching for her hand, I held it in my own. "You did everything you could, and your bravery and quick thinking saved me." Her cheeks pinked and I smiled. "I owe you my life, my friend."

"I think you exaggerate, but I'll take your thanks anyway,"

she giggled and then squeezed my fingers. "However, if we are going to discuss bravery, we need to talk about yours."

Tilting my head to the side, I waited for her to explain. "You came for me, sword in hand and ready to cut him down. I may not know much about the art of battles or fighting, but even I could tell that holding a blade was not foreign to you."

I was caught, and there was no point in denying it, though I tried to remain as vague as possible. "I have had some practice, that is true."

"How much practice?" Cat pressed.

Sighing, I rubbed at one of my temples. "More than most noble women."

Pulling her hand from mine, Catiline crossed her arms and narrowed her eyes at me.

"More than all, you mean," she muttered quietly. "Noble ladies don't get the opportunities to learn those kinds of skills, Rígan."

"Bastards do," I snapped, and her arms slowly lowered to her sides. "I suppose it is one of the only benefits to being illegitimate."

Cat seemed to be at a loss for words, so I lifted my tea once more and finished it while a silence fell over us. Catiline, on the other hand, studied the table while her fingers traced the grooves and indents, and I watched as her attention focused on a gouge that seemed new. Wondering if it was from the night before, I lifted my head to glance around the room that had been soaked with blood and bodies just a few hours prior.

The dead had been disposed of and the gore that covered the stone floors was gone as well. Anyone who walked into the tavern now would have no idea about the incidents that had happened the night prior, and then I remembered Cat's loss.

"I am sorry about your guard," I said softly, and Catiline's eyes moved from the table to look at me before she shrugged.

"Uther had served my father for a long time," she replied,

but I noticed the way her lips ticked up at the corners, almost as if she was trying to keep herself from grinning.

"Catiline! Why are you smiling?!" I demanded, shocked that she would have such a reaction.

"I am sorry he is dead," she clarified. "But I would be lying if I said the man wasn't a cunt." My mouth fell open at her choice of words, and she rolled her eyes at my scandalized expression.

"Oh please, Rígan, I have heard you say far worse," Cat grumbled and I laughed in response.

"Be that as it may, I never thought I would hear such crudity from you." Waving her hand in the air as if to shoo the conversation away, she then twisted to face me more fully and inched closer.

"I have a question to ask you. Or rather a favour." My brows furrowed in concern, and I swallowed nervously while I shifted towards her.

"What is it?" Catiline sighed and then glanced around the room for eavesdroppers, though it was pointless. Most of the men were outside preparing for our departure, and my brother remained upstairs, though he was finally conscious this morning. The others who stayed with us had settled around a table at the opposite end of the room, obviously uninterested in partaking in any conversation between Cat and me.

"Would you teach me?" she whispered, and I blinked at her, not understanding what she meant.

"Teach you to be crude?" I asked. "I rather think you are on your way to mastering that skill given your last comment."

Rolling her eyes, Cat shook her head and then wet her lips nervously, and my eyes traced the purple bruising on her face.

"No, would you teach me how to handle a sword? Would you teach me how to fight?" My stomach twisted painfully, and I moved back and straightened my spine.

"Cat, I may have some practice, but I am not knowledgeable enough to teach you," I lied and her face fell. "Besides, just as you said, it's not something noble women do."

"But we are on the road, away from our fathers and court," Cat whispered. "And no one needs to know, it could be between us."

She made an excellent point, and although I worried what consequences would come from me teaching her anything to do with handling a blade and what questions would be asked if others found out, I could not argue with her logic or fault her for her desire.

"I am not the right person to ask, Cat." Her lips pouted but she nodded, and I sighed at her pitiful expression. "But I may know someone who could help."

Immediately her face brightened, and she glanced around the room with keen interest. "Who?"

"I make no promises," I began, praying that she actually heard me. "But I will ask Donigan." Her cheeks pinkened at the mention of my knight, and I barely held back my snicker.

"Do you think he will agree?" Her voice was hopeful and the way her dark eyes shined told me she was rather happy with my choice.

"As I said, I can't make any promises, but I will ask." Cat clapped her hands together excitedly, and I grabbed at them before pressing them into her lap. "But these skills you learn would only be used should you need to protect yourself, Catiline. It's not something you will boast about or show anyone else."

She began to nod her head earnestly, but I tightened my hold on her hands and narrowed my eyes. "I'm serious, don't go looking for trouble and do not tell anyone. If word got out, there would be serious consequences for Donigan and for me."

"I understand," Cat swore.

"Very well," I sighed roughly. "We will start tomorrow."

CHAPTER

SIXTEEN

"No, no, no." Donigan shook his head in frustration, and Cat looked at me with an annoyed expression. "You can't just go around thrusting your blade forward like that whilst stumbling about! It will be knocked from your hands within seconds, and you will be sprawled in the dirt."

"I'm sorry, but this whole footwork nonsense is rather boring," Cat groaned as she fell back into first position, and I placed a hand over my mouth to muffle my laugh.

"Knowing how to keep your feet under you is the most important thing you can learn when it comes to protecting yourself. Without it, you will never win a fight," Donigan explained before glancing in my direction, and I shrugged.

"She's just excited, forgive her for her impatience." I grinned, but my knight just shook his head before turning his attention back to the woman before him.

"Well, this will make for a long lesson," he muttered under his breath, and I looked to the setting sun.

"One we will not have time to finish," I called from my place a few yards away before pointing to the sky. "They will be expecting us back at camp any minute now. Our ruse of going for a leisurely walk will not seem believable if we are gone for much longer."

Closing the distance between them, Donigan snatched the blade from Cat's hands and sheathed it once more before buckling it to his belt. Now that the lesson was over, I walked to Cat and linked our arms together before steering us in the direction of camp.

The road between villages had grown longer now that we were farther north, and we had been too exhausted to continue our search for one. Deciding instead to set up camp amongst the heavy forest, I had invited Cat to take a walk with me while the rest of the party had opted to stay behind.

"It is a good thing that none of the other men have any interest in accompanying us for such a womanly activity." Cat sighed as we strolled through the forest, and I nodded as I examined the thick curtain of green cedars that surrounded us.

"Though it seems as if they are preoccupied anyhow," she whispered. Turning to look at her, I watched as she gestured to the group who had now come into view, and I frowned as Skileer shoved at Caedell's chest.

"What is it you are implying, Caedell?" my brother snarled as we neared, and I rushed to his side, grabbing at his arm in warning, though I'm sure it looked like the action of support to the others.

"You are mistaken, I was not implying anything," Caedell swore, but the smirk pulling at his mouth told me otherwise. "I was just asking out of concern."

"Concern," my brother spat. "What a farce!"

"Skileer, perhaps it is best if you retire for the evening," I suggested. My brother stiffened beneath my hand, and he pulled from my touch before shoving me away so roughly, I nearly fell to the ground. Cat gasped from behind me and Donigan swiftly hurried to my side, but it was Caedell's reaction that surprised me.

Those burning amber eyes narrowed with anger, and he reached forward, grabbing at the back of my brother's tunic before hauling him away from me. Certain there was space between us, Caedell moved to shield me from Skileer, and I watched the way his shoulders seemed to quiver with rage while his fingers curled into fists at his sides.

"You overstep," Caedell warned, his voice low and dangerous, and I glanced past him to examine Skileer's face.

The eye that was free from the bandages was wide with surprise, and he looked at Caedell and then to me before shaking his head in disbelief.

"A lifetime of devotion to one woman and you throw it all away for this?" He lifted a hand to gesture at me, and I scowled. "I knew you were skilled, sister, but I had no idea you had quite so much power."

My face heated at his insinuation, and I glared at him. However, Caedell remained stoic where he stood and, to my shock, did not deny anything, but rather came to my defence once more.

"Watch your tongue, Skileer," Caedell seethed, still not moving from his place in front of me, and my brother seemed to take a pause to determine what his next action should be. Thankfully, his cowardice won out, and with one last lingering stare in my direction, he fled to his tent.

Now that the entertainment was done, the men who had lingered slowly crept away, though I could hear their soft whispers, and Donigan carefully ushered Cat past me and towards the row of shelters. However, I remained, not moving until Caedell un-balled his fists and then, when he took a step away, I grabbed at his shoulder.

"What do you think you were doing!?" I growled, pulling at him until he faced me. "You had no right to step in."

"No right?" he repeated. "I stepped in for your benefit."

"I didn't ask that of you," I disputed. "Nor did I need you to."

"He has no business putting his hands on you for coming to his aide," Caedell barked. "Where is his decency?"

"It was a shove, Sir Reide," I reasoned. "It caused no harm to me, and you know how taxing this journey has been for him given the state he is in, given the state *you* put him in."

I had years of practice in making excuses for my brother, and I crossed my arms over my chest while Caedell searched my face carefully.

"Oh yes, how very taxing indeed," Caedell scoffed before finally moving his gaze to look at my brother's lodgings. "I am rather surprised to hear you defend him."

"Why is that?" I snapped. "He is my brother, my flesh and blood."

"Because he is so undeserving of it," Caedell muttered before those amber orbs were back on me, and they roamed my face once more and then settled on the scar that marked my mouth. The one my father had given me, the one Caedell had seen me receive all those years ago.

Keeping his focus on the mark, Caedell ran his hands through his hair and then turned from me before pausing to whisper. "They both are."

Not knowing how to respond, I swallowed nervously and then bowed my head in embarrassment, waiting until the sound of his footfalls faded before running to my own tent.

"YOU DON'T THINK any other bandits will find us here, do you?" Cat whispered nervously from her bedroll, and I sighed before turning over to face her.

"No, sweeting," I reassured her. "They were nothing more than a group of common outlaws searching a village for money or treasure. We just happened to be there at the wrong time, it was purely coincidence."

It was a lie, and I think she knew that, but if it eased her worry, then it was worth telling.

"Donigan said the same," she said softly. "He said that there were no signs that they were part of the rebel forces, and there are probably no others they left behind who may come looking for us."

Chewing on my lower lip, I pulled myself from my bed and crawled across the space between us until I was at her side. "See, so there is nothing to fear," I promised. "And tomorrow we will continue on our journey, and we will be in Denimoore within a fortnight."

"Only if you, Skileer, and Caedell keep from killing each other," she grumbled and then faced me, and I could just make out her features in the darkness of the tent.

"Well, that I cannot guarantee," I muttered, and she playfully shoved at my shoulder.

"I am sorry your brother touched you like that," she said softly, and I sighed, frustrated that the topic was being broached once more.

"You have nothing to be sorry for, he was the one who did it," I replied. "And it was nothing, Cat, I promise. Skileer is angry and he hates being cooped up. Once he is healed and has the freedom he longs for, all will be well."

"Your father also treats you poorly," she pointed out. Turning onto my back, I placed my hands over my belly and blinked up at the ceiling while wondering how many others discussed my family's matters behind our backs.

"Such is the life of a bastard, Cat," I reminded her. "But I am far more fortunate than most."

"It still doesn't make it right," she argued before yawning, and I placed a gentle hand on her shoulder until she nodded off.

However, sleep would not come to me so easily, and I

peered up at the space above me for another long while before deciding to get up. Creeping around the tight area of the tent, I gathered my gown and pulled it over my shift before snatching my cloak and boots. Now dressed for the cold northern weather, I ducked through the entrance and stepped into the night.

The fire was still burning a few feet from camp, and I studied the back of the man who sat in front of it and watched the warm glow reflect off the auburn colour of his hair. Sneaking towards him, I placed a gentle hand on his back and noticed the way he jumped. Frowning, I fell to the earth beside him.

"I didn't mean to startle you, I thought you would know it was me," I muttered, and his throat bobbed as he swallowed, and then he gave me a half-hearted smile.

"I was lost in thought, I guess." My brows pinched, but he ignored my expression and shifted until he had put another few inches of space between us, and I felt my stomach twist at the realization.

"What has you so distracted?" I questioned before dipping my head so that he would meet my eyes. His emerald irises were unreadable, and he only held my stare for a heartbeat before he lifted his attention to the flames in front of us.

"Why did your brother say that about you and Caedell?" Confused, I blinked at him, but when I didn't answer, he continued. "About you changing his devotion, about your *skill.*"

Sitting straight, I lifted my chin and narrowed my gaze. "What is it that you are asking me, Gwain?"

"I think that is obvious," he snapped, and I reeled back as if he had struck me.

"If either of us deserves to have their loyalty questioned, it's *you*," I reminded him, and Gwain's face fell before his eyes closed. "As for my brother, you know why he says the things he does. It's to get a rise out of those around him. I, however, never expected you to be so foolish as to believe anything he utters."

"Can you blame me?" The words were spoken so softly I could barely make them out over the crackle of the fire. But as quiet as they were, they still left me wounded.

"What does that mean?" I retorted while pulling myself farther away from him.

Lifting his hands, he rubbed at his face for a moment and then turned to look at me. "I feel like I don't even know you, Rígan."

"And just when did you come to this realization?" I demanded, not understanding how he could utter such a thing.

For a pause, he said nothing but instead focused on the flames again. However, I could not allow his silence to continue. "When did you decide such a thing?"

"That night," he croaked out. "That night when you went after that man. The look on your face…the brutality of it all." My mouth parted in shock, and I was certain I had misheard him.

"He was trying to kill me, Gwain. What would you have had me do?" I asked, not knowing how he could blame me for my actions for that night. Especially when my life had been in danger.

"I know that, but I was there, I would have protected you," he argued.

"So this is about your pride. You're upset that I didn't let you come to my rescue?"

"No, that's not it." He shook his head, and I scrambled to my feet in sudden understanding, and I felt that chill creep in, the one that seemed to follow me no matter how far I ran from it.

"You were frightened of me." Gwain had the decency to look embarrassed at my words, but still, he did not deny them.

"That was not you, Rígan," he countered. "That woman, *she* was not the woman I know, the woman I love."

Curling my lips in a snarl, I looked down at him and finally saw the truth of *him* for myself. "It seems you are in fact correct, Sir Dansby, you do not know me at all."

SEVENTEEN

THE LOOMING FOREST THAT SURROUNDED THE VILLAGE OF Noorde Point was intimidating and mighty, and I ducked my head to watch out the window as the trees passed by. Cat also seemed just as impressed by the scenery as she studied the woods from her side, and then she suddenly reached for my hand.

"This village looks more promising." She smiled and I nodded, ignoring Skileer's scoff that sounded from beside me.

Noorde Point was not a prominent village, but it was well put together unlike the others. It also seemed that the people of the town were more accommodating as well, and I eyed the line of residents who had gathered for our welcome.

Suddenly, the door opened, pulling me from my musings, and Donigan once again helped Cat and me out of the carriage. Not bothering to wait for my brother, he flocked behind us, and I noticed that Gwain kept as much distance as he could.

"Lord Reide! We have been expecting you. Lord Demys sent word that you would be arriving any day now!" An older man greeted the leader of our group as he hurried towards us, and I eyed him warily as he bent himself in half in a rather dramatic bow. Urging him to stand with a flick of his fingers, Caedell glanced around the area.

"You have no gate, sir," he pointed out and the man nodded. "Nor guards or outpost—"

"Roy," the man interrupted, and despite Caedell's seething look, he placed a hand on his chest and continued his own introduction. "Henri Roy."

"I don't believe I asked," Caedell bit out and then gestured to the road we had just travelled. "You have no defence at the ready."

Lifting his face, Henri too glanced in the direction Caedell had been focused on and then patted his fingers against his chest nervously. "Yes, well, we are a small village with few visitors. We've never had the need for such things. Though we do have a bell tower—"

One dark brow lifted at the man, and Caedell rolled his shoulders before interjecting. "There may be a day where you do have such needs, and you will be unprepared," Caedell warned, but then dropped the subject to introduce the rest of the men before focusing on us.

"This is Lady Noorese and Lady Baxteel. See that they have everything they need before supper." Offering a half-hearted curtsey, I did my best to ignore the stranger's gawking, and a throat cleared when the man made no move to signify that he had heard the Heir of House Reide.

Henri's lashes fluttered at the sound, almost as if he was coming out of a daze. Glaring at him, I studied the way the colour drained from his face when he noticed my hostility.

"Of course, my lord," he squeaked, and then lifted an arm towards a large building. "This way, my ladies."

Although the town was better kept, the inn looked the same as all the rest, and we followed the man through the entrance and up the stairs to the rooms we would be occupying for the night. Slamming the door of my chambers behind Henri, I turned to examine the room. The bed appeared comfortable, and the space was warm from the fire burning in the corner. However, the heat did not seem to reach my flesh, and I curled my arms around myself before crossing the floor to the wash basin.

Taking the time to clean my arms and legs, I waited for the guards to bring my trunk to my room and then sifted through the clothes folded within the wooden chest before choosing a deep blue gown. It was one of my favourites, one I usually only wore on special occasions, and while this night should have been of no importance, I couldn't help but long for the confidence this gown gave me. Deciding that now was as good as any time to wear it, I quickly changed out of my simple frock and pulled the extravagant fabric over my head.

Smoothing my hands over the soft skirt, I undid my long dark hair from its neat braid and combed my fingers through the strands before stepping into a more formal pair of silk slippers.

"Lady Rígan?" a voice called from my door, and I turned towards the entrance and beckoned my visitor to enter the chambers.

"Sir Fynn." My brows rose in surprise, and I noticed the way his ears reddened while his eyes roamed across the deep blue colour of my dress. "What can I do for you?"

"Supper is ready, everyone else is waiting," he replied, and I tilted my head.

"And you were sent to fetch me?" I asked as I closed the space between us, and then smiled when that blush crept down the length of his thick neck. "Or is it instead that you offered?"

The purr of my voice left him speechless, and though flirting with him would not ease the hurt from what had transpired between Gwain and me the night before, it was an excellent distraction.

"I offered, my lady," he confirmed, and I reached out a

hand to place on his arm and then waited until he tucked it into the crook of his elbow before gesturing towards the door.

"Then lead the way." He was right, the rest of our party had gathered in the common room, with the exception of my brother, and I glanced at the closed doors that lined the hall, wondering which one he hid behind now.

"Have you seen my brother?" I asked as we made our way down the stairs, and the knight nodded.

"He has taken to his bed, he is still feeling rather unwell it would seem." I was absolutely certain he was fine, but at least this lie would keep him out of trouble and away from Caedell for the night.

Noticing our descent down the steps, Cat stood from her chair and hurried to me with a smile. Her bruise was not as dark in colour but was still a striking contrast against her pale skin and was only heightened by the pretty lavender gown she wore. Frowning at the sight of it, I reached for her hand once I stood before her and squeezed her fingers.

"Does your healer not have anything to aid its recovery?" I whispered as she led us to our table, and she nudged me in the ribs with her elbow.

"Would you stop with that?" she growled, and my mouth fell open at her annoyed tone. "I am not as fragile as you keep trying to make me out to be. So enough of your fussing. Treat me as you would want to be treated."

Catiline was right, I had been coddling her, and if I had been in her place, I would have absolutely hated it.

"I'm sorry, Cat," I replied softly, and waited for her to sit before I did the same. "I won't do it again."

Seeming to be happy enough with my apology, she nodded and then her fingers pinched at the skirts of my dress. "This is lovely, you look stunning."

Rolling my eyes, I swatted at her hand. "It is nothing," I muttered under my breath, but the smirk pulling at her lips told me she thought otherwise.

"It's a good thing you chose to wear it," she giggled before lifting her chin to gesture to my right. "It would seem the ladies of the town have all flocked to the inn to see our men for themselves. Unfortunately for them, there will be no competing for Gwain's attention when you look like this. Though, I doubt that they would be of little contest, with or without that gown."

Glancing at the women who whispered amongst each other, I watched the way they stared at our party, though they seemed particularly interested in Donigan and Gwain. Lifting the goblet of wine to my lips, I took a long drink from it, letting the bitter liquid find its way down my throat while I prayed that it would ease the unnerving twist in my belly.

It wasn't jealousy. No, that emotion I was familiar with after decades of watching my brother thrive while I was hidden away until my father found a use for me. This was something deeper, something sadder, and it made my chest tighten when I noticed the way Gwain seemed to enjoy the ladies' attention as he smiled at them shyly and then offered a few a seat at his table.

Also noticing Gwain's reaction, Cat scowled at the man. "What is he doing?"

Lifting her own cup, I pressed it to her chest until she took a hold of it and then placed a finger under her jaw and directed her attention back to me.

"Pay them little mind, Cat," I ordered. "Most men are vapid creatures, and we have no use for such beings."

"What are you two whispering about?" Donigan asked as he and Fynn headed towards us, and I felt Cat shift in her seat as my knight's eyes caught hers.

"The disappointment that only men can bring," Cat murmured before she sipped her drink, and Fynn looked to Donigan nervously.

"I thought you said the ladies were a safer option when it

came to choosing our dining partners," he said, and I studied the pair of them.

"I never said safer, I said preferred," Donigan retorted before falling into the chair across from me.

"Worry not, sir, our annoyance is not directed at you—at least not yet," Cat reassured Fynn and then gestured to the other empty seat in encouragement.

"Who is it directed at then?" Donigan asked while his eyes roamed across the room, and then he stiffened.

"That pathetic bastard." I flinched at the insult before I could stop myself, and Cat inhaled sharply while Donigan bowed his head. "Apologies, my lady."

I narrowed my gaze at him but said nothing else and instead raised my cup to my mouth. The men, however, kept a watchful eye on Gwain, and when my knight slammed his fist on the table, I looked back in my previous lover's direction.

Those deep green irises caught mine, and he pressed his lips into a thin line before turning to the woman who had slid closer to him. She was a pretty thing, with dark hair and eyes like most of the northerners, and her skin flushed charmingly when Gwain whispered something.

"He has no shame," Fynn gasped, but I remained silent.

"We ought to drag him out onto the street and put him in the stocks," Donigan added, and I leaned back into my chair before carefully setting my goblet back onto the table.

"You will do no such thing; we will not feed into his game or add to the rumours about me," I finally snapped, and Cat's brows furrowed. "It would be my reputation tarnished should either of you make a scene, and there is no reason for it, there is nothing to defend. Gwain may be betrothed to another, but he is not yet married. You know how this works, he may do as he pleases."

The men did not respond, but Cat's frown deepened with worry. "But what about you? What about your honour?"

"Don't concern yourself with something no one else holds

any value in, Cat," I advised. "Besides, despite the rumours, there is nothing between Sir Dansby and me."

I would have thought by now the words would feel more believable. Especially considering how many times I had said them over the last two years. But the lie sounded just as feeble as always. Not to mention the fact that the people surrounding me had obviously seen the familiarity between Gwain and me for themselves. Thankfully, however, no one in my current company protested, and I sighed before giving Donigan a pointed look. "There is no reason for any of you to bother with him."

Saying nothing more on the matter, they turned the conversation towards a new topic, though I was not able to focus on their discussion and instead watched Gwain interact with his newly acquainted friend.

"Would you like some more wine?" Cat asked, stirring me from my observation, and I moved my attention to the empty glass sitting before me with a frown.

Normally the idea of losing myself in my cups would be tempting, but the bitterness in my mouth and the uncomfortable feeling in my belly kept me from nodding. Instead, I stood from my seat. Following my lead, both Donigan and Fynn rose as well and shared a look between each other before Cat reached across the table to grab at my knight's arm. Urging him to sit down once more, she glanced up at me in concern.

"I think I will check on my brother and then head to bed," I announced to the three of them, but this time it was me who Cat was grasping for.

"Are you sure?" she asked softly as her fingers curled around my wrist, and I noticed the way her dark eyes darted in Gwain's direction.

"I am." Pulling from her hold, I turned on my heel.

I felt eyes on me as I moved through the room, and it became more apparent that the others were watching my every move when the whispering grew as I passed by. It was almost as if they had been waiting all night for something to talk about. However, I was sure that this time they were not discussing my pretty dresses or striking face. No, they gossiped because they were hoping to see what mockery I would make of my family's name. They were interested in witnessing what reaction a simple man could pull from me because of my hurt and anger at being slighted so publicly.

Taking a breath, I straightened to my full height and even then, lifted my chin. If I was going to be forced to endure their gawking, I would be sure to do so while looking down on them all.

"A shewolf indeed," Caedell murmured as I reached the top of the stairs, and I spun to face him.

The grimy light-coloured walls of the tavern did nothing to alter his attractiveness. If anything, the flickering light of the torches that lined the hallway only seemed to illuminate his dark hair and the sharp features of his face in a most alluring way.

"What do you mean by that?" I demanded, only to realize I had fallen for his trap when he lifted a brow and smirked at my irritation.

"Isn't it obvious?" He gestured to me with a wave of his hand, and I crossed my arms over my chest. "I saw the way you just prowled across that room, ready to rip the throat out of your prey should they cross you. It truly was a sight to behold."

"And just who have you deemed as my prey?" I questioned, watching him with wary eyes as he closed the distance between us. However, he didn't stop at me but instead moved to the top of the stairs and looked down at the others.

"I would reason that everyone falls under that category," Caedell answered, though I noticed the way his attention stilled on Gwain. "But particularly those who do not see the wolf that hides below the sheep's wool. They will be surprised when you finally drop your disguise and show them what lies beneath."

Something about the way he said it made my breath catch and Caedell seemed to notice my reaction, though his eyes were turned away from me.

"Did I strike a nerve?" he asked softly and my mouth parted, but my tongue felt heavy. Running the tip of it over the back of my teeth, I tried to come up with an answer that would not expose me to more of his mocking. But it was then that I heard it, the sound of a bell chiming in the distance.

"What is that?" I whispered with a frown, and Caedell looked towards the south end of the tavern with a furrowed brow.

"That, my lady, is our warning," he answered before curling his long fingers around the pommel of his weapon that was strapped to his hip. "It appears that the day has come where they do in fact need more than a bell tower."

CHAPTER

EIGHTEEN

THE TAVERN BECAME SILENT AS THE BELL CONTINUED TO CHIME in the distance, and I could feel the fear cover the crowd like a fog as the last toll rang out before there was nothing but silence. Looking at Caedell worriedly, I watched the way he stared at the wall for a pause and then suddenly his breath left him in a great rush, and he was hurrying down the stairs.

Not understanding, I ran to the end of the hall where a window overlooked the front of the tavern and pressed one hand against the cracking wood of the sill while the other slid across the brown grit that covered the glass. I couldn't make out anyone or anything that would pose a threat, but there was a strange flapping noise, the sound similar to the one our banners made when they stood strong against a great gust of wind.

"What is it, my lord? More visitors?" I heard Donigan shout, and I watched him rise from his seat. Clutching at his shoulder, Caedell gestured to Cat while whispering in his ear and I frowned.

Whatever he said was enough for my knight to grab Cat by her arm and haul her from her chair before dragging her away from the table, all while ignoring her protests. Not

169

understanding what would cause Donigan to handle her in such a rough manner, I moved to the stairs, only to be stopped by Fynn as he peered up at me from the last step.

"It's best you get to your room, my lady," the man instructed, but my attention had already moved on from him and back to the Heir of House Reide as he ordered the crowd about.

"What is happening?" my brother's voice called from down the hall, and I glanced over my shoulder at him.

"I have no idea," I answered honestly as I strode to his side. Scowling at me, Skileer lifted a hand to his freshly bandaged face and then glanced at the scene below.

"Reide, what is the meaning of th—" My brother's words became a garbled mess as a great shriek sounded from outside the walls, and then the room around us shook as something collided with the building.

Skileer grasped at my shoulder to steady himself, his visible eye looking to the roof, and it was then that I noticed the great pouring of dust coming from above. Lifting my arm, I pressed my face into the crook of my elbow and pulled Skileer back towards the wall.

"Get her out of sight!" Caedell roared from his spot below, but Skileer was still staring overhead and remained frozen. Growling in frustration, I snatched my brother's hand and tugged him towards the stairs. However, just as we neared the steps, the sound of wood shattering echoed around us, and I glanced up, watching as a massive hooked claw dug its way into the ceiling above before pulling on the feeble structure.

Slowly the corner of the roof was peeled away, and the cloudless night sky became exposed. Gazing up at the stars twinkling in the dark abyss, I held my breath, waiting for the creature to expose itself.

"What in the Gods' names is that!?" Skileer cried as an enormous bright yellow eye blinked down at us through the hole it had created, and I felt bile rise in the back of my throat. It was a massive thing; its eye alone was the size of my head, and I watched the way its pupil seemed to lock on to me before it dilated.

"Damn it, Baxteel!" Caedell shouted once more while ushering some of the crowd under the tables. "Get her away from there!"

But my brother couldn't hear him, he was too focused on the black scaled snout that was now attempting to wedge itself into the gap of the roof while its teeth bared and snapped in frustration.

"Skileer, we need to go!" I ordered, shoving at him roughly in hopes of bringing him to his senses. But he was already swaying on his feet as the giant teeth clamped down on to another one of the beams above us before tugging once more.

"Move!" I shouted, turning away from the beast in a panic while I searched for the nearest room. Grabbing on to my brother's tunic, I dragged him with me as I ran down the hall and then slammed open the door before hauling Skileer into the dark chamber. Ushering him onto the bed while I gasped for breath, I listened to the chaos. I could hear the shouting and Caedell barking out orders from downstairs, but the sound of the creature and its destruction had ceased.

Placing a hand on my chest, I willed my heart to slow while I searched the room for anything that would be of use should the need arise. The chambers were obviously unoccupied, but I still checked under the bed and in the closet for any hidden blades or tools.

"What was that?" Skileer whimpered as he brought his knees to his chest. I turned to him with a frown.

"I can't say for certain, but whatever it is, it seems to have left us for now," I whispered and then crossed the room to glance out the window. Certain there was nothing there, I focused on the dresser that leaned against the wall beside the glass and pulled open the top drawer.

I sighed in relief, my fingers stroking across the leather

sheath of a small dagger that had been left behind, and then I looked at my brother from over my shoulder. Noticing the blade, Skileer crawled across the bed and grabbed at my free hand.

"We need to get out of here!" he cried. "While the others are distracted, we should leave and go back home."

Ripping my fingers from his grasp, I shoved at his shoulder roughly. "Are you daft? We can't leave this place now and certainly not on our own."

"But the beast may come back!" he argued and I scoffed.

"Or it may wait for someone foolish enough to break free of the group and try and run!" I spat. "For once in your life will you be the man you should be and forget your cowardice?"

"How dare you!" my brother snarled as he rose from the bed. Apparently, my insult was enough to distract him from his fear, and he rushed towards me before grabbing at my shoulders and pinning me to the dresser. "How dare you speak to me that way!"

"Get your hands off me," I growled while I pressed the covered dagger into his belly. It wouldn't harm him, but the threat was clear, and he and I both knew who would come out of this brawl victorious should it escalate to that point. As predicted, Skileer glanced down at the leather while his throat bobbed and then he took a step back.

"Father will have your head when I tell—" But the rest of his warning was interrupted when that great ear-piercing shriek sounded once more, and then the wall in which I stood in front of was suddenly nothing but splinters as the monster collided with it. Scrambling with panic, Skileer tripped over his own feet, and I watched as his bandaged face rammed into the bedpost. Clutching at his head, he wailed in pain, and I clambered across the pieces of broken wood to get to him.

However, just as my fingers roamed across the soft fabric of his tunic, the sound of mighty wings returned, and I looked behind me to see that the moonlight, which had been pouring into the room, had been replaced by the massive black scaled body. Fear rocked through me at the sight, and I unsheathed my dagger before turning to face my foe.

It was unlike anything I had ever seen before. Its body was that of a serpent's, though it had six legs armed with claws that were half the length of my forearm. Its long muzzle was pointed at the end, and its wings looked like those belonging to a bat. The most unnerving part, however, was its bright yellow eyes that once again seemed to be utterly and completely fixated on me.

"Get back, Skileer!" I ordered as my attention followed the monster's movements while it tried to claw its way into the room. Taking one step away and then another, I moved until I was next to my brother, and then I curled a fist into his sleeve and ushered him to the door, not once moving my focus from the beast.

"Go!" I screamed once we reached the exit, but Skileer was struggling with the handle, and he whimpered as he tugged on the brass.

"It won't open!" Glancing down at the metal his hands had curled around, I watched as he heaved and heaved to no avail, and that was when the beast made its move.

Using the tail I had not accounted for, the monster wrapped the long length of scaled muscle around one of my calves and jerked my leg backwards. Crashing down onto my belly, I was then pulled across the ground, through the pieces of scattered wood and debris. Twisting in its grasp, I flipped over and searched for some way to stop the creature from taking me into its clutches.

But it was no use, the monster was too strong, and the fabric of my gown snagged on the uneven wooden floor as I was dragged across the room. Suddenly reaching the gaping hole left in the wall, a set of claws curled over my shoulders, and the tips sank into my back. Gasping in pain, I thrashed against its hold, but the more I moved the tighter its grip became until it was nearly impossible to breathe, and then I was being lifted.

Letting my head loll, I looked to my brother for help, praying to the Divine Triad that he would be there, ready to save me. But my pleas went unanswered, and I realized that he was still cowering against the door, watching wide-eyed as the creature took me away.

CHAPTER
NINETEEN

THE BLOOD DRIPPING FROM MY BACK WAS WARM IN comparison to the cold night air, and I took in a ragged breath as the wings above me sent gusts of wind in my direction, only chilling me further. I could still hear the screams coming from the tavern, the panicked wails and shouts of my name. But their cries for me were in vain; the beast had caught its prey, and there would be no stopping it now.

Watching as more distance came between me and my comrades, I lifted my arm towards them in a silent goodbye, and it was then that I noticed the white of my knuckles as they tightened around the gleaming silver blade. I somehow managed to not drop the dagger I had found, and I blinked twice before moving the weapon towards my face so that I could study it closely. It truly was a little thing, nothing more than a kitchen knife really, and most likely would do little damage to the amour of scales that covered the monster, but I knew I had to try.

Lifting my hand, I swung down at the claw that held me with as much force as I could muster. However, not even half an inch of the blade sank into the beat's flesh, and I tugged on the handle to withdraw the weapon before attempting again.

Over and over, I cut at the foot that was wrapped around me, but it went unnoticed, and my strength was beginning to waver. Dislodging the weapon once more, I lifted myself in its grasp, whimpering in pain as the flesh of my shoulder tore around the claws and then I raised my arm in an attempt to cut at its belly instead. However, there was still half a dozen feet between the tip of metal and its scales, and I felt a tear leak from my eye before the wind snatched it from my cheek.

Turning my head in the direction in which the droplet disappeared, I observed the massive wing that came down to block my view for a pause, and it was then that I noticed that the soft skin that seemed nearly translucent under the moonlight, and my eyes followed the lines of veins. The pattern was unusual, almost as if they were a replica of the constellations above. And when the wing lowered once more, I couldn't stop myself from reaching my free hand out to trace the tiny marks with the tips of my fingers. The surface of the flesh was cool and smooth, almost like leather, and I watched as it pulled from my touch only to return once more as the monster continued to fly above the lands of Elrin.

Falling into a dream-like state, I repeated the action of touching the flesh each time the wing lowered, and then suddenly the idea came to me. Bringing my hand to where the other lay against my chest, I carefully moved my fingers over the handle that was trapped within my grasp. It was risky, my limbs had gone numb from the cold and my nervousness made them tremble, but this was my last option. Carefully exchanging the weapon between hands, I held my breath as my right set of fingers grasped the dagger, and I extended my arm once more. Angling the blade, I traced the end of the metal along the thin tissue, following the same pattern I had been tracking, and then, I cut.

The first slice went unnoticed, but I watched the way the wind made the edges of the wound flap as air rushed through the opening and then I did it again. However, this cut alerted the monster to my plan, and the claw that was curled around my shoulder tightened its grasp.

Gasping, I blinked back tears and forced myself to ignore the pain in my shoulder as I reached for the thin flesh once more, slicing my way through the wing again. A great shriek suddenly sounded from above, and the monster fell to the side. The wounds were not enough to be deadly, but they were sufficient in throwing the creature off balance, and the more air that passed through the holes, the harder the beast struggled to remain airborne.

Grabbing on to the talons that surrounded me, I pressed my palm against the scales and lifted my body as much as I could while I stabbed higher along the wing. With one last great effort, I slashed a cut nearly a foot long through the monster's flesh, and when the skin gave way, I knew I had succeeded.

It was nearly impossible to breathe as we plummeted to the ground. But when I noticed the tops of the northern trees had begun to pass us in a flurry of green, I stopped trying to fill my lungs with air and instead closed my eyes and prayed to the Gods that they would see me home.

THIS IS NOT what death was meant to feel like, of that I was certain, and I sank my teeth into my lower lip to keep from groaning out while I fought to open my eyes. For a moment, I was worried the impact had somehow managed to blind me. But when my sight adjusted, I realized I could in fact make out a sliver of cloudless sky through the thick treetops. The soft glow of the sun that trickled between the branches told me it was dawn.

Now sure I was in fact alive, I carefully wiggled my toes

first, then my fingers, and when I was confident that I could feel each limb, I turned my neck and glanced to my left.

The soft snow around me was covered in pine needles and tree branches, and I could see where the beast had landed given the indentation it had left in the earth. However, that was the only piece of evidence remaining, and for a moment I wondered where it had gone and why it had left me behind. But those thoughts did not have much time to linger in my mind, especially not when the cold began to seep through my gown and into my aching bones.

Gritting my teeth to keep them from chattering, I braced my hands against the ground and pulled my torso up from the forest floor. Though even with my clenched jaw I was still unable to keep the cry of pain from leaving my mouth. Closing my eyes against the wave of nausea that rocked through me, I lifted a trembling hand to reach behind me and traced the wounds that littered my back. They weren't as deep as I had been anticipating, but they throbbed, and I pulled my hand away to inspect the red coating the calloused tips of my fingers.

"Just a little blood," I told myself while my head bowed, and then I sighed, thanking the Gods that it somehow wasn't worse, especially when it should have been.

After all, I had not only miraculously survived the capture from the beast, but also a fall from the stars and was left with little more than a few punctures and a tender body. It was truly a blessing from my Gods indeed.

However, I knew my luck would eventually reach its end, and I could not remain in the open and vulnerable for much longer. Gathering my courage, I pulled myself to my knees and then unsteadily to my feet.

The first thing to do would be to find shelter and to build a fire. Without one I would succumb to the elements eventually, and it was already a miracle I had lasted as long as I did. Hunting was not a priority; I had eaten not long ago and could go a few days, but I did need to fashion some sort of weapon. The northern forests were not just unforgiving because of their climate, they were also the home to the beasts of Elrin, and those animals were not likely to pass up the opportunity to take down such easy prey. Curling my arms around my torso to ward off the breeze that somehow seemed to find its way through the thick cover of trees, I moved across the snow.

The white that blanketed the woods had begun to melt under the light of the sun, and had I not been certain this forest would be my final resting place, the soft glow bouncing off the snow and the crystal-like droplets coming from the branches would have been a sight to behold. However, the mere pause I had already taken was all I could afford to spend appreciating the picturesque sight, and now I needed to get to work.

Moving through the thick brush, I searched for a place that would offer me adequate cover, all while hating that each footstep only reminded me just how numb my toes had gone. The fine silk of my slippers absorbed more moisture than they shielded me from, and soon the skin would be purple. I needed to find a way to warm up before it got to that point or else there would be no saving them.

But as time went on, I grew weary and more desperate. Knowing I needed to hurry, I began to sprint through the forest, no longer taking care to watch where my feet went as I travelled over the wet terrain, and that had been my mistake. Too focused on covering ground in a hurry, the sole of one of my shoes slipped across the slush and I was flat on my back, sliding down the steep incline at a rapid speed.

Wincing as the uneven ground scratched against my already injured shoulders, I curled my fingers into claws, hoping that I would be able to sink my nails into the snow to slow my descent. But they were no use against the momentum of my fall, and down I went. My pretty gown was torn to shreds as I glided across the forest floor, and I glanced down at my feet in fear, noticing that my journey was about to end. Ahead of me was a cliff, and though I couldn't see the ground yet, I was certain the drop would be significant.

Knowing I had to find a way to stop myself from going over the edge, I flipped onto my belly and dug my toes into the drifts while I scrambled to find something to grab on to. However, the branches I managed to grasp were either torn from the ground, their roots weak from the cold, or my hands slipped down the length of them, leaving splinters in their wake as they slithered from my hold.

Glancing over my shoulder, I checked to see how close I was to the end that neared and then I noticed a small sapling to my right. Knowing that this would likely be my last chance, I lunged for the tiny tree and used both hands to grab a hold of the trunk that was no thicker than the hilt of a longsword. However, the dainty thing was far stronger than I would have thought, and even though my grip was heavy, it only bowed slightly under the pressure but remained in its place.

"Thank the Gods," I whispered to myself now that I was stationary and luckily a mere few feet from the edge of the cliff. Catching my breath, I carefully rose onto my knees, still clinging to the sapling as I did so, and then I glanced below.

The cliff offered a small ledge, one wide enough for me to sit on, and I slowly uncurled my hands from the bark. Then, using my heels and fingers to dig into the snow, I inched my way closer to the edge. Peering down, I noticed that there was space below the lip I sat on, and it would offer me some protection from the cold as well as a solid wall to place against my back. Having that would mean I would only need to be aware of the surroundings I would face head-on, and it would also allow me to build a fire that would last, should the weather turn for the worst. Now the only issue was finding a way down.

Searching the face of the bluff, I looked for an option that would save me from breaking a limb, or worse. The area to the left of the edge I currently sat on was less steep and had a few crevices I could use to climb down. Sighing, I lowered my eyes to my feet, taking in the sad state of the silk that covered them, and then plucked at the remaining fabric of my gown. The bottom of the lovely blue material was torn and soaking wet and would do little to protect me. However, the bodice was mostly intact and there was enough to the middle of the skirt that it could cover my legs if I curled them to my chest. Looking back at what would be my way down, I slid across the rough stone and then placed my foot into one of the cracks before lowering myself down.

It seemed to take ages to get to the bottom of the wall, and by the time I dropped to the ground, my entire body shook in exhaustion and my knees buckled beneath me. Falling onto the earth in a heap, I placed my forehead against the wet slush and blinked down at the murky grey mix of dirt and melting snow.

"You've nearly done it, Rígan," I mumbled. "Almost done now."

It was the same mantra I would mutter under my breath on the battlefields. The same words I told myself in secret when my father ordered me to take my brother's place, or when I had to stand before my peers and their judging eyes. Or when my heart ached from the bitterness of it all.

"You're almost done now, soon you can rest," I promised before staggering to my feet once more.

My legs were weak, but I ignored their trembling and searched the area for the things needed to build a fire. Thankfully there was a pile of leaves beneath the lip of the cliff; obviously the autumn wind had trapped them there and the overhang kept the snow from covering them. There was also a plethora of pine needles, which would work for kindling, but finding dry wood would be difficult. Locating a large tree close by, I noticed several dead branches and pulled them from the trunk before bringing them to my knee. Using my joint, I cracked the wood in half and inspected the state of them.

"Thank you, Huntress," I sighed, bowing my head in gratitude before hurrying to the place I would call camp for the night and then got to work.

The fire took time to light. I was not practiced in starting one without flint, and by the time the branches caught, the sun was setting. However, I couldn't find it in myself to be frustrated; I was too cold and exhausted to feel anything but thankful that I had managed to survive as long as I had. Curling my legs to my chest, I pulled the torn fabric over my limbs and watched as the orange flames danced before me.

I don't know how long I sat there, or when my eyes had closed, but slowly the warmth of the fire lulled me into a relaxed state. Bending my head back, I rested it against the cool rock behind me while my skin thawed. However, just as I began to allow my body to sag against the stone, I heard a crack come from the darkness that was now creeping through the trees and my eyes snapped open as I searched the area before me.

To the average maiden, there would be nothing amiss, but as someone who had spent many years being a hunter, I knew there were eyes on me. Pressing my spine against the cliff, I ignored the way the jagged wall irritated my injuries, and I glanced at the fire longingly. I knew I should put it out now before whatever was near followed the flickering light. However, before I could get the chance, I heard my visitor approach and I rose to my feet, grabbing at one of the branches I had put aside before pressing the end into the flames. Certain it had caught, I held it in front of me the way I would wield a weapon and then I waited.

"And so, the shewolf lives."

CHAPTER
TWENTY

Gasping, I swung my head towards the voice and watched as Caedell appeared from the shadows of the forest. His amber eyes were bright against the reflection of the flames I held in his direction, and I noticed the way they surveyed the state of my dress before he lifted a brow.

"What are you doing here?" I whispered roughly.

"Well, I thought that was rather obvious," he drawled as he moved towards me, and I looked around the dark woods before my wide eyes sought him out once more.

"You came after me?"

"You're surprised." It was a statement, not a question, and it caused him to pause in his pursuit and then he crossed his arms over his chest while the muscles of his jaw ticked.

"How did you find me?" He ignored my question and closed the distance between us before snatching my makeshift torch from my fingers. Angling it towards my body, he curled his free hand under my chin and lifted my face for his inspection.

"How badly are you injured?" he asked as he pushed my hair back over my shoulders, and I hissed when the strands pulled at the drying blood on my back. Cursing under his breath, Caedell cupped one of my arms, but I pulled from his touch and glared at him.

"What are you doing?" I demanded. "Do not manhandle me!"

"Good Gods, woman, must you bite at every hand that offers you help?" he growled in return while I lifted my chin in defiance.

"I didn't ask you for anything of the sort!" I snarled back only to watch him roll his eyes before shaking his head in disbelief.

"Even now you fight me when instead you should be thankful that I came to your aid."

"I'm not some damsel," I declared, hating the way his attention lingered on my torn gown and trembling legs.

"Trust me, I am well aware of that." Caedell moved past me to put the burning branch back into the fire and then squatted down next to the flame before lifting his palms towards the warmth. "Come over here before you freeze."

I bristled at his order, but the aching cold had returned, and I knew I could not stand to be away from the fire for much longer now that the temperature had dropped for the night. Walking to the opposite side of the flames, I sank to the ground and pressed my knees to my chest before wrapping my arms around my calves.

"Will you tell me how you fare now? Or must I find a way to pull it out of you?" Lifting my eyes, I searched his face, watching the way the bright blaze illuminated his handsome features.

"Minor wounds on my back and a chill, but otherwise I'm fine," I murmured softly while the wood crackled from the heat.

"Good," Caedell answered. "We will have to rest here tonight before finding our way back to the road."

For a long pause neither of us said anything, though I could still feel his gaze on me, and I shifted back towards the stone wall before glancing at him from the corner of my eye.

"How did you find me?" I asked again, and Caedell moved, sliding across the ground until he was only a foot away before answering.

"Valkhags are horrid creatures, but they are predictable," Caedell stated with a shrug. "As soon as I knew you had been snatched, I found a horse and did my best to follow you. At first it was difficult, valkhags are predators of the night, and though they are not the fastest beasts, they are usually quite good at concealing themselves."

Caedell rolled his shoulders, his golden eyes flickering to mine for a moment before focusing back on the fire. "Luckily for me, this particular monster was just an adolescent and not as practiced in the way they usually hunt, it seems. That, and the fact that you somehow managed to maim it."

He paused and I noticed the way his lips quirked. "Though if I am being honest, when I saw it fall from the sky, I was certain I would not be returning with you alive."

Leaning back, Caedell brought a knee up towards his chest and rested an arm on it. "Thankfully that isn't the case. Now I won't have to listen to the others' insistent moaning when we return."

"What of the others? Are they okay?" I asked, terrified of what Caedell would tell me.

"Your brother suffered a blow to the head though is no worse for wear," he explained with a scowl. "Your men will still be surly with me for ordering them to continue on while I searched for you, especially Taith. Otherwise, everyone is fine. You are the only one who managed to find themselves in a valkhag's clutches."

"How lucky for me," I grumbled.

"They usually do not attack villages, nor are they typically so determined to get into a building. However, once they lock on to their prey, there is no swaying them." I remembered the way the creature's eye had focused onto me as it tore open the roof of the tavern, and I shivered at the memory.

"So, you followed the creature on horseback and then…?" I trailed off, waiting for him to continue.

"The northern forests are full of hills and drops; it is not safe for a horse, and I did not feel like falling to my death in pursuit of someone like Rígan Baxteel." My spine stiffened at his words, and I scoffed.

"Right, because who would want to die trying to save a bastard?" It was Caedell's turn to freeze, and he glared at me.

"That is not what I meant, and you know it," he argued. "Do not put words into my mouth or make me carry the burden of your insecurities. It is not your status that makes you so intolerable."

"Oh, I'm the one who is intolerable?" I narrowed my gaze at him. "How lovely it must be to see the world in such a way, to be so lost in your own delusion."

"What are you implying?" Caedell questioned, his amber eyes burning hotter than the flames before us.

"You are the one who is unbearably condescending," I seethed. "Even now your arrogance astounds me."

"My arrogance?" he repeated. "Are you sure you did not hit your head? You certainly seem to be out of sorts." My jaw went slack at his words, but Caedell continued.

"I am not the one who has yet to show a sliver of gratitude to the man who came to your aid and saved you from certain death." My mouth snapped shut, and I turned my face away in shame.

"We have not yet survived the night. As far as I'm concerned, we may both die here in this Godsforsaken forest and then I will have nothing to thank you for," I grumbled.

"That is unlikely for me," Caedell argued.

Turning, I glowered at him as he shifted until he was lying

back against the wall, and he then crossed his legs at the ankles before lifting his arms behind his head. He looked completely at ease, and I eyed his wool cloaking longingly before tucking my knees as close to my chest as possible. "You, however, have much worse odds. Especially with that chill you've caught."

"I'm fine!" I barked, though given the chattering of my teeth and Caedell's smirk, I was certain my words were not convincing.

"I suppose I have no choice but to believe you," he murmured and then closed his eyes. "But wake me should you change your mind."

Admitting I needed help was difficult on the best of days. But asking Caedell Reide for anything was not something I would do willingly. Instead, I buried my face into my knees and glared at the dark forest while large flakes of snow began to fall.

"GODSDAMN IT! You are more stubborn than you are daft!" Caedell snarled while my body was jostled around, and I shivered before I buried my face into the warmth that was pressed against my cheek. "Fuck, you're freezing!"

Frowning at being woken up, I nestled my nose into the soft skin and then my lashes flickered open. I could hear that the fire was still burning, but pale flesh was the only thing visible given how closely I had nuzzled into Caedell, and I heard his swift inhale when I burrowed farther into his neck.

"You're going to be livid with yourself once you thaw," Caedell murmured quietly, and my brows pinched as I grumbled in irritation but then pressed closer to his body, hoping to absorb some of the heat he offered. "Easy now, let me get this cloak around us before you go and get cross with me once more."

He moved again, but it wasn't until his thick arms banded around my waist that consciousness really crept in. Placing my palms against his muscled chest, I lifted my head and pushed at him.

"What are you doing?" I croaked, the grogginess making my voice thick and slow, and Caedell rolled his eyes and then grabbed at one of my legs.

Gasping at the boldness of his actions, I glanced down at his hand and watched as it curved over the thickness of my thigh. Caedell, however, growled under his breath before he rucked up the end of my skirt. Now free from the fabric, he sank the tips of his fingers into the plush flesh, and my breath caught at the heat of his touch. Ignoring me, he pulled on the limb until it was arranged to sit on one side of his hips and then repeated the process with the other leg.

When I realized I was straddling him, my cheeks heated and those amber eyes studied me carefully before he chuckled under his breath. "Is that a blush I see? Don't tell me you've traded your fangs in for modesty."

Clenching my jaw, I curled my fingers into his tunic, and he laughed again when he felt the bite of my nails. "There she is, the fearsome creature of the north."

"Are you always so brazen with highborn ladies?" I growled, and Caedell lifted a brow.

"I thought you were certain of my experience or lack thereof?" he prodded. "Besides, we've already established what exactly you are, and it is not a lady of any sort."

Before I could think better of it, one of my hands lifted to wrap around his throat, and I leaned my weight on that arm. Feeling the flesh of my palm press into his jugular, I moved until my nose was just a hair away from his own.

"You forget yourself, Reide," I whispered.

"No, I don't forget anything," he argued. "I just wanted to

see how much it would take for you to remove the wool, shewolf. I was getting bored of you playing pretend."

"And now that you've pushed me to that point?" I could feel his pulse beneath my fingers, and I smirked as the rate quickened.

"I will admit it is a sight to behold. I can see the appeal, I suppose," Caedell said softly while a hand curled into my hair, and he tugged on the blood-coated strands until my chin was tipped towards the overhang of the cliff. "However, now is not the time to press this particular issue and test one's charm."

"You are the one who took liberties," I gasped, wincing at the way the torn flesh of my shoulders stung now that my back was arched.

"Liberties? I would hardly call it as much. And anyway, I was trying to keep you warm, not seduce you," he said before letting go of my hair to rearrange the cloak that had fallen to my waist.

Now free to look down at his face once more, I lowered my eyes to our position with a pointed glare. "You would have me believe you were being chivalrous, that you were trying to help me?"

"It's the truth, not an excuse," he muttered. "There is no other reason for my actions, I'm not interested in anything else."

The sting of his rejection was unsuspected, and my brows furrowed before my lips lifted in a cruel smile. "Is it because I haven't fucked your father?"

I heard his sharp inhale, but he did not miss a beat with his answer. "Even my father would not overlook your sullied blood." I recoiled as if he struck me, but he paid me no mind. "Besides, you like your lovers to be weak. I don't think you would know what to do with a true man."

"A true man?" I scoffed, and Caedell nodded.

"Dansby puts on a good show, but you and I both know he

is a timid thing. I don't understand how he's held your attention for so long."

"He is nothing of the sort," I argued feebly as I glared down at him, but Caedell shook his head in disbelief before throwing an arm out to the side, pulling the cloak from us once more.

"Then where is he?" he demanded, and I glanced around the blackness of the forest before swallowing roughly. "Where is your knight? Why is he not here?"

"You said you ordered them to remain with the others and continue north." The words were soft, weak even, and I hated it.

"And he listened, doesn't that tell you something?" I frowned and Caedell leaned back against the stone once more before lifting the wool to drape around us again. "If the woman I loved was taken from me, nothing would keep me from going after her. No order—no man—would keep me from finding a way to save her, and Dansby didn't even so much as utter a single word in disagreement."

"Behaving in such a rash way is foolishness, not evidence of one's love," I growled, and Caedell's brows rose.

"I've always been of the opinion that rashness and love often go hand in hand," he said. "Matters of the heart make even the most sensible men reckless."

"If that's what you think, perhaps you don't know enough men."

Caedell shook his head, and his eyes lingered on my face. "Or maybe you don't know enough about love."

Unable to form words, I slumped my shoulders, and I lowered my eyes to the collar of Caedell's tunic. Sighing roughly, he fidgeted with the wool cover for a moment and then guided me forward until I was pressed against his front once more.

"Sleep," he ordered. "We will have a long journey

tomorrow and you will have to keep up, I will not be dragging your unconscious body around."

Whatever scathing response I had on the tip of my tongue was immediately forgotten as warmth seeped into my bones and I was pulled under the spell of sleep.

TWENTY-ONE

"We are lucky it is only the start of winter and that it has been unusually mild." Crossing my arms over my chest, I wiggled my toes against the soaking silk of my slippers and then glowered at the man ahead of me.

"Mild is it?" I mocked, and he glanced over his shoulder at me.

"Yes, and it would seem that your Gods continue to take pity on you." He lifted a hand towards the morning sun. "Had the weather been like it usually is at this time of year, there would have been no saving you from the elements."

"So, I owe my life to you and the Gods? Is that it? Did I have no part in me staying alive?" I sneered, but Caedell continued walking, not bothering to answer me.

Following behind, I grabbed at the heavy wool he had lent me, and I pulled the cloak closed around my torso while I continued to trail after the Heir of House Reide. Studying his back as we made our way through the trees, I wondered if I could find a way to push him down one of the steep hills and be rid of him, though I would probably be better off taking his boots and weapons from him first. However, given the state of me and the fact I was unarmed, I doubted I would win in a brawl against him.

Actually, I was sure of it. I already knew what it was to fight him, and it was not something I was eager to experience again in the near future, even if he had gotten on my very last nerve.

"It looks like we've nearly made it." Quickening my stride, I hurried to his side and glanced at the clearing of trees.

"That is the road?" I asked doubtfully, and Caedell rolled his eyes.

"The Gods' Passage is not well maintained this far north, surely you were aware of that." Catching his gaze, I scowled, and he scoffed softly. "You are part of an Anointed family, and you are a northerner, you have been farther than Noordeign, haven't you?"

Looking back towards the rather sad path, I shrugged. "There's been no reason to be."

"My, what comforts you must enjoy," he murmured. "Never having to leave the manor, never having to travel through the northern wilderness. No wonder my father cannot stomach your family. What a disappointment you all are."

Lunging forward, I grabbed at his shoulder and hauled on him until he fully spun to face me. "What did you just say?"

"I think you heard me just fine," he snapped before shrugging out from my touch. "My family has been doing our duty. Surely you have heard the stories."

"Oh yes, tales of your adventures have been very grand indeed," I fumed. "But while you've been out gallivanting across the Barren Sea and enjoying your great quests, *my* family—my brother—has been here, keeping the rebellion under control."

Caedell's jaw clenched, and his amber eyes searched my face. "Your brother has been leading your men? Skileer, the great son of House Baxteel, has been responsible for commanding your forces?"

Lifting my chin, I held his stare. "He has."

"I didn't think he had it in him," Caedell chuckled. "He plays the fool well; I would have never imagined he could really be such a man, such a grand leader."

"That is because he has the integrity not to boast about his victories. I'm sure that is something you couldn't understand."

Not taking the bait, Caedell continued. "And his triumphs have been truly remarkable. We are fortunate to have him guarding Elrin, I suppose."

"We are," I agreed, thankful that the words did not come out as begrudgingly as they felt.

Eyeing me closely, Caedell stood tall and imposing, and I forced myself not to fidget under his glare. "Yes, I understand my father's disappointment now, *you* are not at all what I hoped you'd be."

Frowning, I waited for him to explain, but instead he carried on down the path, and I watched him for a moment, wondering what he could have meant.

"WHERE ARE WE?" I whispered as my body shivered from the evening breeze, and Caedell glanced around the small village with a furrowed brow.

"Your guess is as good as mine," he muttered quietly as he marched down the narrow road that had forked out from the Gods' Passage.

"I thought the great and mighty Heir of House Reide was a vast traveller," I grumbled while we made our way through the town, and Caedell stopped to look back at me.

"A vast traveller who does not frequent small mining villages when he is rather busy keeping the duty that was given to him by the Gods," he retorted and I rolled my eyes.

"You are not the only heir of an Anointed, you do not need to remind me of your responsibilities at every chance." Choosing not to respond, he turned on his heel, and I crossed my arms over my chest before trailing after him.

The village was quiet, its people already tucked away for the night, and I took in the tiny buildings and bare streets with a wrinkled nose.

"Get that look off of your face," Caedell barked as he stopped in front of what looked to be an inn. "Should anyone see you, the townsfolk will not take kindly to such an expression."

"Why should I care what they think?" I muttered under my breath, disregarding the warning glare Caedell sent my way.

"Perhaps you should not care what they think, but maybe you could consider how they may feel?"

"Why?" I asked with a furrowed brow.

"Because it may offend them." Caedell ran a hand through his dark hair, and my frown deepened.

"I don't waste my time worrying about what may offend the common folk." His amber eyes searched my face and then he pounded his fist against the heavy wood of the front door.

"If you refuse to heed my warning, the least you can do is keep your mouth shut and your opinions to yourself," he ordered as the door creaked open and a massive burly man stepped through the threshold.

The stranger was half a foot taller than Caedell and had dark hair and a long thick beard that nearly reached the place his navel would sit on his bloated belly. His face was hard, and his eyes were wary as he scanned us from head to toe, and I noticed the way his attention lingered on the ripped skirt of my gown.

"We don't take the likes of you lot in this establishment. I suggest you carry on your way and find accommodations elsewhere." He stepped back through the entrance while one of his thick hands grabbed at the handle to push the door closed. But before it could click shut, Caedell hurried forward and wedged one of his boots into the narrow opening.

"My apologies for disrupting you at such a late hour." Caedell placed his hand over his chest and then lowered his head. "We are just looking for a warm place to rest for the night. We promise not to be any trouble and will be on our way by dawn."

"Did you not hear me? We do not offer rooms to men and their…companions." His brown eyes darted to me and then lowered to my bare legs again before narrowing at Caedell in accusation. "We are not that kind of place, and you would be wise to continue on."

"I understand how this appears," Caedell replied softly, his tone far more warm and soothing than I had ever heard it. "But I can assure you, sir, you are mistaken. You see, my wife and I ran into some trouble on our way north—"

"Your wife?" the man interrupted, and I had just enough time to snap my jaw closed before his doubtful gaze met mine.

"Yes, I know that it does not look that way, but you will have to forgive her appearance, she was snatched by a valkhag," Caedell murmured as one of his hands lifted to cradle my face in his palm, and I fought the urge to smack his fingers away from me. Instead, I took a deep breath and let him stroke his thumb across my cool cheek before I nuzzled into the warmth of his calloused skin. "It took me hours to find her in the woods. Thankfully the creature released her, but she did not make it unscathed."

His touch disappeared from my flesh, and my eyes flickered open at the loss before I noticed that he had moved to cup a shoulder. Following his direction, I turned my back to the pair and felt Caedell lift the heavy wool in order to show the man the evidence of my injuries.

"Good Gods! It's a Huntress's miracle that you found her alive!" he gasped and Caedell hummed softly.

"I understand your hesitancy, but we would be so very grateful if you could find a place for us, just for the night." Turning my head, I searched Caedell's face. His handsome features had somehow softened into something far less intimidating, and his eyes were so sincere I wondered how often he used this tactic to get his own way.

"I suppose we could find a room for you tonight," the man relented, and Caedell offered him an earnest grin.

"And a bath perhaps?" I pressed with a raised brow, ignoring the elbow Caedell subtly sent into my ribs.

"Hauling water up the stairs at this hour—"

"Would be expected by any other guest you house," I interjected, and the man glowered at me before looking at my companion.

"Please excuse my wife's manners, sir." Caedell glared at me again before turning back to our host. "It has been a long journey and I fear the chill has gotten to her."

"Of course," he answered, though his voice sounded unsure. However, obviously against his better judgement, the man moved back from the door and opened it wide before gesturing for us to come forward. "I will do my best to have a bath drawn for you both. While the water heats, perhaps you and your wife would like something to eat."

"That would be most appreciated." Caedell nodded and then pressed a searing hand to my lower back and pushed me through the entrance. "Isn't that right, wife?"

Narrowing my gaze, I waited for those amber eyes of his to meet my own. "Yes, *dearest.*"

It may have been a term of endearment, but given the way Caedell's throat bobbed, I was certain he saw what was lingering just beneath the surface.

A shewolf indeed.

CHAPTER
TWENTY-TWO

THE ALE AND RABBIT STEW HAD BEEN ENOUGH TO SATISFY MY hunger, and I sighed in my seat, ignoring the lingering stares of the maid who was filling the tub while Caedell slurped at his meal.

"Must you make so much noise?" I snapped, watching as he lifted the spoon of broth to his mouth.

"Is it annoying you, *dearest*?" he asked with a tilt of his head before he swallowed another mouthful, and I glowered at him.

"How long have you two been married now?" the maid asked, and I jumped in surprise, not noticing that she had left the tub to approach us with another bowl of stew for Caedell.

"It's *very* recent," I replied, hoping my clipped tone would send her on her way. However, the older woman just placed a hand on her hip and looked between us with a fond smile.

"Well, I sense you will have many happy years together. You seem like quite a match, both handsome and I dare say very well suited indeed." Rolling my eyes, I turned slightly in my seat to face her more fully.

"How amazing your talent is that you can see such a thing

after only the smallest of interactions." I lifted a brow and the woman flushed before her lips parted.

"You'll have to ignore my wife; she can be rather temperamental when we have not had much time *alone*," Caedell whispered to her with a wink. "I can assure you she will be much more agreeable by morning."

It was my face now that was heating, and I spun to glare at Caedell. He, however, paid me no mind and took the fresh bowl of stew in his hands before forgoing the spoon altogether and lifting the dish to his mouth.

Clearing her throat, the maid lingered at my side. "Well then, shall I help you with your…gown, my lady?"

Looking down at the ragged state of my dress, I toyed with the frayed ends of the skirt and then lifted an arm to stroke my fingers across the torn fabric on my back with a wince.

"There is no need," Caedell muttered, and for the first time since she had joined us in our room, his voice held no warmth for the woman. "I will assist her, you may go."

The maid's brows furrowed at his dismissal, but she did not move and instead sought out my gaze. "Sir, I would be happy to aid your wife—"

"You may go," he repeated, and the woman offered a clumsy curtsey and then fled from the room.

"My dress may not be totally intact, but it will still be a challenge to remove on my own." I scowled at my companion before glancing at the closed door where the maid had disappeared.

"I thought I had been clear; you won't be removing it on your own," he answered as he stood from his seat and then rounded the table in my direction.

"You think you are going to aid me?" I asked with a scoff before rising to my feet and lifting my hands in front of my body to stop him from coming any closer.

"You wanted a bath," Caedell reminded me, pausing in his pursuit.

"And you sent the maid away before I was even ready," I argued.

"I did that to protect us. The last thing we needed was for her to witness any more of your hostility." He crossed his arms over his chest and stared me down. "How much longer do you think they would believe our little story with your behaviour?"

"My behaviour?" I repeated with a scoff.

"You became nearly feral over a simple comment from the woman," he murmured and I rolled my eyes.

"I was nothing of the sort."

Clicking his tongue, Caedell tsked at me softly. "Perhaps that wildness runs so deeply in your veins, you no longer see it for what it is." His eyes glanced at the shredded gown. "At least now the disguise is gone, and you look the part."

I smoothed my palms over the skirt, my nose wrinkling at the filth that transferred onto my skin, and then I eyed the tub that had been filled. There was no scent of rose or lavender, no oils or petals added to the water, but the steam was enticing and the aching in my muscles and dirt on my skin made me long to sink into it.

"Fine," I growled before spinning around.

"Fine?" Caedell laughed. "Is that how you ask me for a favour?"

"Would you just get on with it?" I seethed while glaring at him from over my shoulder.

"My, is this the charm that has inspired so much gossip across Elrin?" He laughed again. "It's no wonder your reputation precedes you when you order a man about in such a way."

My anger grew, but Caedell didn't look the least bit ashamed and instead moved close. Holding my head high, I turned my face away once more and waited for him to begin. Bracing myself for the soft tugging that would indicate the laces were being loosened, I waited with bated breath. However, the sensation didn't come.

Sighing in annoyance, I glared at the wall before me. "Shall I call for the maid—"

My words broke with a sharp inhale as I felt the warmth of his fingers trail across the back of my neck, and my skin tingled as he carefully collected my long hair before lifting it over a shoulder.

"We will need to tend to these wounds," he murmured, and I could feel that one of his hands had begun to trace the torn bloodstained fabric.

"Are they very bad?" I whispered while my eyes lowered to the floor.

"The bleeding has stopped," he answered while his other hand fingered the edge of the fabric at the top of my spine. "But they will need to be cleaned and bandaged, I think."

Humming under my breath in agreement, I remained still while he finished his examination. Then those massive palms cupped my shoulders. The heat of his touch seeped into my body while he lowered his mouth near my ear, and the sensation of his breath caressing my flesh made my lashes flutter closed.

"I am going to begin," he warned, but I was not jostled the way I normally would have been. No, Caedell was meticulously careful in his work, so much so that I hadn't realized he had completed the task until the bodice of my dress loosened and I pressed my arm across my bust to keep the material from falling to my feet.

Taking a step back, he cleared his throat, and I fought a shiver as he moved about the room. "I will go ask the innkeeper if he has any bandages and salve."

Focusing on the wall once more, I finally whispered my gratitude, "Thank you."

If Caedell was shocked by my subdued behaviour, he didn't make it known, and instead I listened to his footfalls as he crossed the room and exited our chambers.

Now that I was alone, I took a few minutes to catch my

breath and then allowed the fabric to fall. Free from its weight, I tiptoed my way to the tub and lifted a foot over the side. Dipping my toes into the water, I tested the temperature and glanced around the room in search of some sort of soap. Realizing there was none to be found, I sighed before readying myself to enter it fully.

"To no one's surprise, their supplies are lacking. But I brought what I could and even found you an apple tar—" Yelping in alarm at Caedell's sudden appearance, I wrapped my arms around my body and scowled at the man.

"Are you daft?! Why did you come barging in here?!"

For a pause Caedell did not move, and the tart that sat precariously on top of the pile of supplies tumbled to the floor. The dull sound of the dessert crumbling on the wood was enough to pull him from his daze and he gave his head a little shake. Suddenly, a mask of boredom fell over his face and his eyes met mine. Swallowing roughly, I searched his features, and had I not noticed the soft flush that crept down the skin of his neck, I would have assumed my nakedness did not faze him in the slightest.

"Getting you supplies, or did you forget already?" he asked as he stepped over the ruined pastry. "Perhaps the valkhag injured your head?" Spluttering, I watched as he placed the items on the table and then turned to me once more.

"Well, are you getting in the bath or not?" He lifted a hand towards the tub, and my jaw went slack as he began to step out of his boots and remove his belt.

"What are you doing!?" I snapped as he rolled the sleeves of his tunic to his elbows, taking time to fold the fabric back carefully. I noticed the length of his fingers and then the shape of his muscular forearms as more of his skin was bared to me.

"Do you plan on cleaning the wounds yourself?" One of his brows lifted but his gaze did not lower from my face.

"A man of decency would not assume to be so bold," I

growled. "And he certainly would not think that a noble woman would be so willing to bathe in his company."

"You know nothing of my decency," Caedell rebutted. "And we've already established how I see you."

My patience wavered at his words, and I took a deep breath. "Be that as it may, I am still of an Anointed family and you—"

"*I* am trying to help you," he interrupted. "If you would prefer that I find the maid, I will do so."

"It would be far more appropriate," I muttered.

"Appropriate maybe," he agreed. "But I doubt her fingers are as skilled as mine."

My jaw fell slack at his words and before I could stop myself, my attention moved to the long digits I had been admiring before. The same ones that had managed to thaw my skin and undo my laces with more gentleness than I would have thought possible.

Lifting a hand, he brought it in front of his face and wiggled his fingers before catching my eye. "They've had a great deal of practice."

Swallowing, I snapped my mouth shut, lifted my chin, and lowered my arms, fully prepared to call his bluff. "Have they now? I'm surprised to hear as much."

Confidence had never been a quality I lacked, and though I was well aware I looked nothing like his fair Lady Ceara, I was determined to not allow Caedell Reide to shake me any more than he already had. Letting my hands dangle at my sides, I stood tall, not caring that I was now fully exposed while Caedell's throat bobbed before his lips parted.

"And why is that?" he asked, his voice hoarser than it had been and the corners of my mouth curled at my victory.

"Well, rumours of your faithfulness have been rather extraordinary," I said as I finally sank into the water with a moan of approval. "Though considering the current circumstances, perhaps I put too much weight to them."

"And what do you know about my circumstances?" His footfalls were heavy as he approached, and when I heard him settle behind me, I closed my eyes, hoping to look more relaxed than I felt.

In truth, I knew very little. The Lady Ceara Reide was a beauty, only a year younger than myself, and from what I could remember from our very few insignificant meetings, she had more charm and wit than most noble women. She had also been from a lesser family, but that hadn't stopped them from growing an attachment to each other at a very young age.

"You two have been together since you were children, and you were both rather devoted." I felt pressure on the back of my neck, and he urged me forward so that my back was exposed for his inspection.

"*Devoted*, what an odd choice of word," he muttered before his hands dipped into the water near my shoulder. Cupping it, he poured the liquid over the torn flesh carefully before wiping away the dried blood, and I hissed at the sharp sting.

"Is that not what you would call it?" I asked through gritted teeth while he repeated the motion.

"I suppose you could say I have been," he answered. "Devoted, that is."

"But not her," I continued. Of course, that made sense, she had married his father after all, and given the handful of children she had since produced, I doubted the marriage between her and the Lord of House Reide had been chaste. Though there had been rumours that their offspring shared more qualities with Caedell than his father.

"She has had to make difficult decisions. We all have." Snorting, I rolled my eyes and I noticed he had stilled.

"Is that what you tell yourself?" I wondered while I waited for him to continue with his work. "Surely you don't believe that."

The pressure of Caedell's touch increased, and when the

tips of his fingers prodded at my injuries, I shrugged away from him before turning to glower at him.

Lowering his hands back into the water, he hung his head slightly, and he rolled his shoulders before clearing his throat. "That was not well done of me, I am sorry."

"I thought you said your fingers were skilled," I reminded him while my eyes narrowed in accusation.

"Perhaps I overestimated my talents." He shrugged. "I have had much practice. I have cleaned and stitched a great many wounds on my men."

"Is that what you were alluding to?!" I growled and his chin lifted. Those amber irises were light with humour, but he still tilted his head in feigned confusion.

"What else could I have meant?" Then his eyes widened, and he shook his head in disbelief. "You didn't think I was talking about—"

"I thought nothing of the sort," I snapped while my face heated and I spun back around while ignoring his snort. However, when I heard no movement, I lifted a hand to gesture to my back before ordering, "Well then, get on with it."

"As the shewolf commands," he chuckled quietly, and I clenched my jaw shut and held my breath as he began.

TWENTY-THREE

"T HEY AREN'T AS DEEP AS I ORIGINALLY THOUGHT," C AEDELL said softly as he applied the salve, and I shivered at the cool temperature of the ointment.

"Well, that is something, I suppose," I murmured, and Caedell hummed under his breath before he stood. I looked over my shoulder at him, watching as he moved to return the items to the table.

"I am finished," he announced. "I will step out and let you dress."

"A bit past that point, aren't we?" I asked with a scoff before rising from the tub. Caedell froze, his spine was straight and his shoulders stiff while the sound of water sloshing echoed in the room around us.

Stepping over the rim, I reached for the long piece of linen, which had been left on the floor. Dabbing at my damp skin, I dried myself as best as I could before snatching the shift the maid had left behind for me. Pulling the fabric over my head, I frowned at the length of it. Generally, they would come to just below my knees, but this one was obviously intended for a woman far shorter than myself, and the hem barely reached the middle of my thigh.

"You can turn around now, I am decent," I said while my fingers ran through my wet hair.

Glancing at me, Caedell quickly spun back to face the table once more and whispered something under his breath.

"What was that?" I demanded. I was certain I could stomach whatever insult he had decided to murmur to himself and was also unwilling to allow him such cowardice as to say the words without facing me.

"It was nothing," he sighed before rubbing a hand over his jaw, and I bristled.

"Nothing?" I scoffed. "If that is true, why not repeat it?"

He turned to me again, his burning eyes met my own, and I watched the way he squared his shoulders as if he was preparing to face a foe. "I said that I disagree, you are anything but."

There was a deepness in his voice that had a warmth blooming across my cheeks. Straightening to my full height, I ignored the way the fabric of the shift tugged tightly on the roundness of my hips and fullness of my chest.

Eyeing me carefully, Caedell scowled and then his gaze darted to the far end of the room.

"What is it now?" I asked while I strode towards him. "Do you have something else to add?"

Running a hand through his dark hair, he tipped his head up to the ceiling as if he was seeking out the Gods themselves, and then he looked back to me. "Just get in the bed."

For a moment I was certain I had misheard him. Surely, he would not have the audacity to order me in such a way and about such a thing. However, as time went on, we remained rooted in our places and then one of his arms lifted and he pointed a long finger towards the bed.

"Go" was all he muttered, and my jaw clenched at his command.

"How dare you speak to me—"

"I am done with this game, my lady," Caedell interrupted. "This back and forth and the constant hurled insults—"

Frowning at him, I took my chance to interject this time. "Insults which are being hurled by *both* of us."

"Yes, fine," he agreed with a sigh. "But be that as it may, I am exhausted, and I am ready for sleep. So, you can either get in the bed, or you can stand there for the rest of the evening, I no longer care."

Shocked, I watched as he crossed the room and folded down the furs before I found my words. "Wait, do you mean to take the bed as well?"

The very idea seemed unthinkable. I had, of course, spent hours in a bed with company, that was not new to me. But it had always been during sex or while we settled from our throes of passion. I had never just slept next to a man for the purpose of rest, nor had I stayed for the entire night.

"Well, I certainly am not going to spend the night on the floor," he drawled, and I glanced around the chambers.

"But then we will have to share," I pointed out and he chuckled under his breath before giving me a pointed look over his shoulder.

"How very observant of you, Lady Baxteel." Narrowing my eyes at him, I watched as he lifted a hand over his head and gathered his tunic in a fist before tugging on it. Following the fabric with my eyes, I studied the expanse of his back, watching the way the muscles moved beneath his skin as he pulled himself free from the fabric.

"Now will you be joining me, or do you plan on continuing with your gawking?" He hadn't even so much as glanced at me, and my mouth parted in surprise at being caught.

"I thought you were concerned about decency," I reminded him.

"And as you so clearly pointed out, we are past that point," he murmured before sliding onto the mattress. "Do not tell me you are shy now, not after such a show of confidence."

He was right, I had no reason to now be nervous after I had stood before him so proudly while being nude. But lying next to him, sleeping beside him—that was something else entirely.

"You lay against my chest and slept under my cloak just last night," Caedell whispered as he waited for me to make a decision, and I wondered if he somehow had the ability to see into my mind.

"That was different," I argued weakly, wincing at the hoarseness of my voice.

"I don't see how," Caedell muttered with a raised brow.

"I was cold and wounded, and I wasn't even aware it was happening until you had already taken the liberty to arrange me on your lap," I growled before crossing my arms, and Caedell's eyes lowered to the hem of the nightgown for just an instant before he cleared his throat.

"And yet there were no complaints." His lips curled into a smirk. "Especially when you were nuzzling against me like a pliant little kitten."

Heat filled my face, and I had no retort to his point. After all, it was true, but I had certainly not been in the right mind at the time and now, I regretted my actions. Especially since I was sure Caedell would not soon let me forget them.

"Fine, move over," I demanded, but he made no effort to follow my instructions and instead glanced at the other side.

"Must you fight me on everything?" I growled in annoyance, but he remained unbothered by my temper and just pulled down the furs beside him.

"You will take this side," he replied and I set my jaw while remaining in place. Sighing at my stubbornness, Caedell stood from the bed and approached me with determined strides. Wrapping an arm behind me, he pressed his palm against the small of my back and then bent at the waist. Not understanding what he was doing, I stiffened under his touch only to squeal when he swept my legs out from under me and lifted me into his arms. Cradling me close to his chest, he walked to the side of the bed he had deemed mine and then, without warning, dropped me clumsily onto the surface.

"I will sleep closest to the door," he declared as he peered down at my shocked face. "Now can we not agree on a truce for the night so that we might both get a good night's sleep?"

The plushness of the mattress beneath me was surprising, and my eyes flickered down to the soft pelts he had folded back before he cleared his throat.

"What do you say?" he asked and I sighed roughly.

"Fine, but only for tonight." Rolling his eyes, Caedell rounded the bed once more and slid into his space before blowing out the candles that had been placed on the nightstand.

"I would expect nothing less," he muttered in the darkness, and I fell onto my side, hugging the edge of the bed while I waited for his breathing to even out.

MOVEMENT from my side pulled me from the dreamless sleep and my lashes fluttered open when I heard a pained groan echo throughout the room. Frowning, I held my breath, waiting to see what was the cause of such a noise while I lay as still as possible.

"No," Caedell gasped while his legs thrashed beneath the covers. "No!"

It was an agonizing sound. His voice broke over the word as if it was being forced out of him, and I turned my head to my shoulder to gaze at him. The room was dark, but the ill-fitting shutters on the window allowed just enough moonlight to slip in that I could make out his features. Caedell was sprawled on his back and now that his share of the blankets had been pushed to his waist, I could see the way his bare chest rapidly rose and fell as if he couldn't bring enough air into his lungs.

Turning to him, I rose onto my elbow and waited, hoping that he would calm, and I could go back to sleep. However, whatever was plaguing his dreams only worsened, and the sound of his pained whimper made my gut twist sharply.

"Sir Reide," I whispered before I turned to him fully, waiting for him to stir.

"Please!" he cried out as his body rolled towards me, and I frowned at the grimace painted across his face. "Please, no!"

Glancing at the door nervously, I prayed that the others staying in the inn could not hear his pleading and then I inched closer.

"Sir Reide," I called out louder this time, but my voice only seemed to disturb him further, and his thrashing continued with far more vigour.

Not knowing what else to do, I closed the rest of the space between us and placed a careful hand against his chest. The muscle beneath my palm was impressive, far firmer than I had been expecting, and had his skin not been slick with sweat, I would have taken more time to admire his build. Instead, I grew more concerned and pressed my hand against his racing heart in an attempt to jostle him from sleep.

"Sir Reide, you must wake—" Suddenly I was on my back and the hand that had reached for him pinned was on the pillow next to my head while Caedell's heaving form loomed over my body. Recognizing the sudden threat, my body instinctively bucked beneath him, and it was then that I realized he had straddled my hips, effectively keeping me trapped under his weight.

Caedell must have felt my struggle, because the pressure on my captured fingers tightened, and I blinked up at him, watching the panic in his face as his unfocused eyes searched my own. Worried that he was still lost in his nightmare, I took a deep breath and forced my body to relax while I waited for him to come to.

"Caedell," I tried once more, doing my very best to make my voice as soothing as possible. "It's me. It's Rígan."

Caedell panted as his gaze finally seemed to truly acknowledge my own, and I lifted my free hand to cup the sharp angle of his jaw, praying that my touch would not aggravate him further. Much to my surprise, however, he turned into my palm, nuzzling the flesh for just a moment before clarity crept into those golden eyes. Then he suddenly threw himself back towards the end of the bed. Sitting up, I watched him closely, the way I would a spooked animal, and Caedell ran a hand over his face before he bowed his head.

"My apologies," he whispered, and I rose onto my knees, unsure of what else I should do.

"Are you alright?" I asked while I studied him closely. I noticed the way his breath still came in gasps and how his fingers had twisted into the fur below his knees.

"Fine," he replied sharply, and then he was sliding from the mattress to stand at the end of the bed. "I shall spend the rest of the night on the floor."

"There is no need for that," I tried to assure him, but he wasn't hearing it. Frustrated that he chose to ignore me, I lunged forward, grabbing at one of his wrists to stop him from crossing the room. "Come back to bed."

Caedell's face lifted, and I swallowed roughly before clearing my throat, and then I let my hand slide down until our fingers were tangled together. "You will need rest for tomorrow's journey and sleeping on the cold floor will keep you from being at your best." Pulling on his hand, I repeated my command. "Come back to bed, Caedell."

For a moment he did nothing but search my eyes, and then he took one step forward, then another, and I moved back, making space for him to join me once more. Following me onto the bed, he settled against his pillow, and I followed suit.

We lay facing each other, neither of us speaking, and my feet shuffled under the covers. Seeming to notice my unease, Caedell sighed, and my eyes moved to his at the sound.

"What?" I demanded when I noticed the way he examined my face closely.

"Tell me something," he answered softly, the words almost sounding like a plea, and my brows furrowed. "Distract me."

Not knowing how to do such a thing, my attention roamed around the dark room. However, I was unable to come up with something to say and my toes twitched again while Caedell shifted closer.

"You used to be a good storyteller," he murmured softly. "Though the occasion was rare, I remember the way the rest of us would gather around you when you came to court."

"What are you talking about?" Caedell wet his lips and then ran his fingertips across the narrow space between us. Watching his hand smooth over the mattress, I waited.

"When our fathers were busy conducting business or discussing plans of the future, we would be shuffled into the feast halls or libraries."

"Yes." I nodded.

"You often took on the role of entertainer, especially with the younger children who were overlooked. I remember the way Cat would cling to your skirts."

"I suppose so."

"There was one time you convinced everyone that the south wing in Wahstand was haunted by a headless knight."

My lips quirked at the memory, and I chuckled under my breath. Noticing my reaction, Caedell stopped his fidgeting and I glanced down at his fingers.

"Your brother had been unusually cruel to you that day," he whispered. "And you didn't tell another story for the rest of your stay." The smile that had been pulling at my mouth was replaced with a frown, and he cleared his throat. "The night before your departure, Synrick and I teased him, we told him we were sure he was just afraid of the ghost and that is why he made you stop."

Shuffling, I pressed in close, not realizing that my hand had overlapped his own.

"We dared Skileer to wander the halls that night," Caedell continued. "Synrick had rushed ahead and hid in one of the empty suits of armour. At the time he was so small, he didn't need the helm to cover his face. The top of his head hit just the middle of the breastplate."

"Then what happened?"

"Well, your brother made it halfway down the corridor before he noticed the headless man," Caedell laughed. "When he finally saw him, he wet himself and ran back to his room in tears."

My own soft giggles joined his, and the fingers beneath mine splayed open and then our hands were intertwined. Tightening his hold, he took in a deep breath, and I watched the way his lashes fluttered closed. Now left with silence, my own eyes grew heavy, and as the last sliver of consciousness left me, I realized I had not withdrawn from his touch.

CHAPTER

TWENTY-FOUR

"M'LADY?" A SOFT VOICE CAME FROM THE DOOR, AND I LIFTED my head to glance at the window in confusion before I reached behind me and across the mattress. The space at my side was empty, and the room was silent besides the sound of my movement under the furs. Frowning, I turned over and looked around for any sign of Caedell, and when I found none, I pulled myself from the warmth of the bed and padded across the cool floor.

"M'lady?" the stranger called again, and I rolled my eyes before heaving on the handle of the door. Startled by my sudden appearance, the young maid stumbled a step backwards and then hurriedly curtseyed while lowering her gaze to the floor.

"What do you need?" I asked while I lifted my chin to peer down the hallway, and when she stood, she too glanced over her shoulder uncertainly before facing me once more.

"Your husband asked me to bring you these." For a pause, I stared at her with a bewildered expression, and then I remembered the lie Caedell had spun and snatched the clothing and boots from her hands.

"Do you need my assistance?" the girl asked as she shifted

215

from one foot to the other, and I shook my head before looking down the hallway once more.

"Where is…" I struggled with the title Caedell had given himself and cleared my throat. "Where is my husband?"

"I'm sorry, I do not know," the girl said softly. "He just instructed that I bring you these and then see that you broke your fast."

"Did he say when he would be back?" I questioned while ignoring that twinge of panic at the idea that he had abandoned me here on my own.

"He did not, m'lady." Sighing roughly, I pulled the clothing closer to my chest and then stepped back to close the door.

Moving forward, the girl placed her palm on the wood to keep me from shutting it. "What about your tea? The cook also prepared some bread and cheese for you. Your husband also requested we bring you an apple tart."

Noticing the tray that had been placed on the floor next to her, I wrinkled my nose. "I am fine, you may leave me."

"Are you sure? Your husband was rather adamant that you eat." Her face softened and she smiled shyly. "He seems very concerned for your well-being. He obviously cares very much for you, you are very fortunate."

One of my brows rose before I could stop it, and she studied me in confusion. Smoothing a hand over my face, I sighed again. "Oh yes, he's very doting. Almost to the point of exasperation one might say."

The maid offered me a nervous grin, unsure if she was meant to laugh at my words or take them to heart. But instead of wasting more time worrying herself with the right reaction, she glanced around the hall in search of an escape. Taking pity on her, I bent to grab the cup of tea and a piece of bread, I backed farther into the room. "You may go."

Scurrying from my gaze, she fled towards the stairs, and I kicked the door shut once she was out of sight and then glared at the unmade bed. Now alone, I wondered where my *husband* had gone off to so early in the morning, and if it had to do with what had transpired the night before.

He had been so distressed and had seemed so pained. Had I not been there to see for myself that the cause of his turmoil had only been his dreams, I would have assumed he was being tortured. Though perhaps he was. My own imaginings had often been responsible for much of my heartache, I could relate to the agony that they could bring to one's self.

Pulling myself from my thoughts, I stripped from the too small of shift and carefully dressed for the day, doing my best not to aggravate the healing wounds any further. Once clothed, I noted that the green gown was much more my size and made from a thick fabric and the boots and warm wool stockings were also far hardier than I expected. Moving my focus to my hair, I collected the strands and braided them down my back before hurrying from the chambers. The inn was empty besides the maid who was now sweeping the floor and the man from the previous night who was sipping his tea in the far corner, and I glanced around the room with a scowl.

"He went to fetch a few things for your journey, my lady," the gruff voice of the man in the corner called, and I peered over my shoulder at him. "It seems he is in a hurry to get you home."

Home, that was not our destination despite how much I longed for it at that moment. But no, the call for us to come to Denimoore was still imperative, and given that Caedell was the heir of an Anointed family, we could not ignore it. If anything, we needed to make haste given our delay, and I wondered how far the rest of our party had managed to get.

"Thank you," I muttered to the innkeeper before moving towards the entrance.

"Are you not best to wait for his return?" he asked, standing from his chair. "It is rather nasty out and I'm sure he would prefer you stay here until he can escort you himself."

"I can assure you, sir, I am not that delicate," I replied with a tight smile and narrowed eyes, and he shrank away from my attention before catching himself.

He ran his hands over his rounded belly, his attention roaming across the room, and then he huffed. "Well then, I suppose if you are sure, there is no stopping you." Picking up a cloak that had been folded on the table next to him, he walked towards me with his hand outstretched.

"He is at the smithy. I think he hopes in procuring you a horse or two, though we do not have many to go around. He will have to pay a pretty penny if he wants something sound enough to ride."

"I'm sure he will manage," I murmured before taking the offered cloak. Flicking it open, I watched as the fabric floated in the air and then twisted my arms so that I could lay it over my shoulders. "Did he find a way to settle with you for our stay?"

The man's mouth lifted into a large grin, and he nodded his head. "When I first saw the pair of you, I was certain the Gods were testing my charity. I had no hope that I would see even a silver for your stay." He paused, eyeing me closely. "Especially considering the state *you* were in."

My brows lifted and the man grabbed something from behind his back and then showed me his hand, and I noticed a pile of gold coins in his palm. "Your husband was more than generous though, and it would seem that my act of compassion has paid off."

There was something about the way he said the words that made me study his face. His expression was one of wonder, but there was more to it, something suspicious, and I took a step back before offering a quick curtsey.

"Yes, well, I am glad to hear it, but I should be on my way," I muttered. "Thank you again for your hospitality."

He said something under his breath in response as I stepped through the door of the inn, but I could not make out the words over the whistle of the northern wind that blew a flurry of snow against me. Tugging the hood of my cloak over my head, I glanced down the narrow street in search of the smithy. Thankfully there were only half a dozen buildings to choose from. Turning left, I began my trek and was grateful for the boots that shielded my feet from the snow that had begun to collect on the ground.

"Good Gods, where is that man?" I growled as I moved farther down the road, stomping my way through the storm.

"Cursing at the Gods already? It's a bit early for all the anger, is it not?" his voice called, and I lifted my chin to glare at him.

He stood before me, his plain black jerkin accentuating his broad shoulders while his cloak blew behind him, and yet, his hair seemed to somehow remain stylishly tousled even though the wind continued to grow in strength.

He looked like a knight from our songs and stories, and by Gods, I hated him for it.

"Why did you not wake me this morning?" I snarled as I closed the distance between us. "You should not have left me alone in that place!"

Rolling his eyes, he pressed a hand against my back and steered me into the smithy with a sigh. The heat from the fires struck me the moment I stepped through the doorway, and I pressed back against the far wall, dazed from the rapid change in temperature. The whistling from outside could still be heard past the wooden walls, but the fire burning in the centre of the room illuminated the space while keeping the chill at bay, and I observed the weapons and tools scattered around the area.

"Here you go, sir," the blacksmith grumbled as he came from the back room, and he lifted a long silver blade in Caedell's direction. My brows furrowed in confusion while I watched the Heir of House Reide take the weapon from the stranger before sliding a gold coin into his soot-covered hand.

"Thank you." Caedell's head dipped in acknowledgement,

but the man did not see it, he was too busy glancing at me from the corner of his eye. Squaring my shoulders, I peered at the stranger with a clenched jaw, making certain to show him just how unwelcome his gawking was.

"If you value your teeth, I suggest you stop staring at my *wife*." The words were just barely above a whisper, but the sound still made a shiver run down my spine despite the heat from the hearth, and then man's attention shifted to Caedell before his lips parted in shock.

"My apologies, sir," he spluttered out before wincing at the sound of Caedell sheathing his newly purchased weapon.

"It is not me you owe an apology to," Caedell replied while gesturing. "You will ask her for forgiveness."

Not understanding why he needed to press the issue, I frowned. But Caedell was still watching the blacksmith closely, waiting for him to follow the command.

"Forgive me, my lady," the man said weakly, and my focus bounced between the two, noticing the way Caedell's spine remained straight, and his head held high. It was the same look he had given me during our duel. It was the expression that had warned me he was prepared to beat me into the dirt. And though the blacksmith had never faced him as an adversary, he recognized the expression for what it was and bent at the waist while keeping his eyes on the ground.

"Well, dearest, what do you think? Shall you excuse him?" Caedell asked as he turned to me with a raised brow. Studying his face, I noticed that his eyes remained dark with displeasure, and I hurriedly nodded, no longer wanting to participate in whatever this was. "How lucky for you, she's not usually one to be so amiable."

"We should be leaving," I murmured with a tip of my head, directing his attention to the exit. Nodding, Caedell turned from the smith and guided me through the door and into the cold once more.

He remained silent as he directed me around the corner

of the building, and I followed in stride, glanced at the stable yards ahead of us, and noticed a young girl. She was no older than nine and was marching through the snow while leading a large bay horse towards us. Knowing I should not say anything about what had just transpired in front of a child who may repeat my words, I stayed quiet and watched as Caedell moved to greet her.

"Thank you, my good lady." He bowed dramatically, and the girl grinned with a pinkened face.

"Did you get the blade I told you about!?" she asked, her voice cracking in excitement, and Caedell nodded before turning his hip towards the wide-eyed girl so that she may see that the blade was strapped on the opposite side of his other weapon.

"It was a very good choice indeed," Caedell whispered, and though I thought it would be impossible, the girl's smile grew.

"It is my favourite one!"

"You have very good taste then." The child preened under the praise and Caedell winked at her. "I will be honoured to carry it on our journey."

My head spun at Caedell's sudden change in temperament. In fact, I wasn't certain I understood anything about the man. He was anything but predictable.

"Now tell me, what is this noble steed's name?" Caedell requested, taking the reins from the child.

"We call him Billie," she said, and I noticed the shakiness in her voice. "He's older, but he's a good horse and he won't put a foot wrong! I swear it!" The girl's attachment to the animal was obvious, and I could see that she was beside herself at the idea of us taking him.

"I am sorry your father has sold him." Caedell placed a gentle hand on the child's shoulder. "But I promise we will take very good care of him."

"Do you think you will return him some day?" Her

hopeful brown eyes peered up at Caedell, but my companion shook his head sadly.

"I cannot say for certain that we will ever return to your village," Caedell explained honestly. "But I promise I will often tell him the story of the girl who loved him so much she was willing to take ten lashes just to keep him."

My breath caught in my throat, and I studied the girl carefully. Her long damp eyelashes caught the large flakes of snow before she blinked them away and her lower lip trembled. Patting the lass on the back reassuringly, Caedell then turned to the horse and slid his boot into the stirrup before mounting the animal. Settling in the saddle, he looked to the child and gestured for her to bring the block over.

The girl's breath hitched but she quickly fetched the steps and placed them in front of me. Watching the way her gaze remained downcast, I bent at the knees and placed my fingers beneath her chin before directing her face towards mine.

"Thank you for sharing your friend with us, we will take the very best care of him," I whispered before reaching for the hood of her cloak. Lifting it, I covered her head in hopes of keeping her pretty black hair from dampening any further from the snow.

Biting at her lower lip, she inhaled sharply and then offered me a clumsy but earnest curtsey. "You're welcome, m'lady."

Smiling softly, I turned to Caedell and stepped onto the wood before taking his hand. Helping me mount the horse, he waited until I settled behind the saddle and then urged the horse into a canter. Quickly we passed through the village and once we had entered the cover of the forest, I leaned forward so that Caedell may hear me over the wind.

"Are you going to explain what happened this morning?" I asked and he pulled on the reins, slowing the horse to a walk before glancing at me from over his shoulder.

"Whatever do you mean?" he murmured, and I rolled my eyes.

"First you arose without waking me and didn't so much as tell me where you were going. Then your behaviour with the blacksmith—"

Caedell growled under his breath and looked forward once more. "I didn't like the way he was looking at you."

"He was harmless," I scoffed, but Caedell did not seem to share my sentiment.

"I could practically hear the vile things he was thinking," he snapped. "He had no shame and should conduct himself with more integrity."

Rolling my eyes, I leaned away from him. "So you were protecting my honour then?"

Caedell said nothing, but I noticed the way his fingers fidgeted with the leather reins and the gelding below us tossed his head at the tension on his mouth.

Choosing to move on from the subject, I cleared my throat. "And the girl?"

"What about the girl?" he replied softly.

"You seemed to take a keen liking to her," I pointed out, unable to hide my surprise at that discovery.

"She was a sweet child and did not deserve to be treated so poorly by her father," Caedell explained. "Perhaps that is why my patience was so thin with the man. He had threatened the little lass for her tears just minutes before you came to find me and then had the gall to stare at you in that way."

"And you take the time to comfort every child after they have been threatened to be punished by a parent?" He flinched at the question and my brow furrowed.

"I would not call a lashing a punishment."

Sighing, I straightened my shoulders. "I think my father would disagree."

"Your father is not one I would seek approval from when it came to parenting and discipline. It is a beastly practice and one that should not be tolerated. No child deserves such cruelty," he muttered before he turned towards me, but he only met my eyes for a heartbeat and then I was faced with his back again. "Besides, she was different."

"Different," I repeated. "Different how?"

Kicking his heels into the horse's barrel, he pushed our mount into a gallop, and I tucked my chin, burrowing my face into his shoulder to keep the snow from blowing against my cheeks. Certain he had chosen to ignore my last question, I readied myself for a journey filled with silence, however after a few moments, I felt Caedell stiffen, and then he said something that would haunt me for the rest of the ride.

"She reminded me…" He paused, and his voice became so soft, I should not have been able to hear it over the gusts raging against us. "She reminded me of you."

TWENTY-FIVE

WE TRAVELLED AT A STEADY PACE FOR HOURS, AND I DID MY very best to remain as still as possible on the horse's back. However, my hips ached from sitting on the animal without the comfort of a saddle while its gait jostled me around. I also struggled not to rest against Caedell and forced myself to keep my chest from brushing against him, which did not ease my discomfort.

Slowing the gelding into a steady trot, he guided the horse off of the pathway and into a nearby thicket before halting. Swinging his leg over the horse's neck, he slid from the saddle and then turned to me with an open palm. Looking down at the long length of his fingers, I raised a brow and then dismounted. Landing on the ground, I winced at the sharp sting vibrating through my limbs from the impact, and my knees buckled. Scrambling, I grabbed at Caedell's shoulder to keep myself from crumbling to the snow.

"Are you not accustomed to being on horseback?" he grumbled before glancing down at the fingers that still remained on him, and I snatched my hand back.

"I am," I bit out. "I am an avid rider, but I usually have a saddle and a creature that doesn't have such an uncomfortable gait."

"I apologize for my choice in steed," Caedell scoffed. "Next time I will be sure to find a beast of impeccable breeding so that you may have a more enjoyable ride. Though perhaps you would have preferred to walk?"

I understood his unspoken words; he thought I was being ungrateful, and though he may have had a point, the weary exhaustion settling into my bones kept me from fixing my attitude.

"Why did you have us stop here?" I asked as I glanced around the darkening forest, and Caedell turned to the horse and began untying the saddlebags.

"It is a good place to camp for the night," he explained, and I snorted. "You disagree?"

Tipping my chin, I took in the tall trees and thick bush that was covered in a blanket of snow and then crossed my arms. "It offers us some concealment, but it certainly is not ideal."

"And you believe you could find a superior place?" He laughed under his breath with a shake of his head, and I bristled at the sound.

"I do, and we should continue until we find such a spot," I pressed, and he stopped what he was doing to glare at me.

"You think you know better than me?" he demanded as if the idea itself was unimaginable.

"I think you do not give me enough credit."

"What credit is there to give?" he asked with a raised brow. "You may have done well after the valkhag snatched you, but I am certain that that was a one-off. After all, what would *you* truly know about surviving in the wilderness?"

"More than you think."

"Really?" There was something sly in his expression that made me very much feel as if I had been cornered by a fox.

"You don't know everything about me," I grumbled as I

reached past his shoulder to grab at one of the leather bags. I was no longer interested in arguing about our location now that it felt as if I had been caught.

"I disagree," Caedell murmured as he plucked the bag from my fingers. "I would wager I know you quite well."

"Then you are sorely mistaken," I seethed, watching as he tied the horse for the night and then wandered a few feet away before crouching down to the ground. Eyeing him carefully, I wrapped the wool of my cloak across my body with a frown.

"I know that the girl you used to be was rather sweet," Caedell continued as he unpacked the bag. "Though I wonder when she disappeared, and just how far beneath the surface she lingers."

"She does not linger," I whispered. "She is gone, she is as good as dead and has been for some time." The words settled around us heavily, and Caedell's brows furrowed while he searched my face for a long moment.

"That is a shame, I quite liked her."

"I can't see why, no one else had any use for her." There it was, the blatant truth that I had learned to live with. My father, my brother, and the rest of the world had taken what *sweetness* I had and twisted it into something else entirely. And now when I looked in the mirror, I no longer saw a hint of the girl he mentioned.

"Do you remember when my family came to your lands for the first time?" Caedell asked, pausing in what he was doing to see if I would acknowledge what he spoke of.

"It was just after your mother had died; you were no older than seven," I answered. "You had also fallen off your pony and broken your arm on the road, only days before your arrival if I am not mistaken."

"Yes, that's right." Standing, Caedell lowered his chin and studied the ground beneath his feet. "And do you remember much of our visit?"

I thought back, trying to remember if something of significance had happened. But I could not recollect anything that might stand out from his time in Noordeign, especially since it was nearly two decades ago.

"I do," he murmured. "I remember how you snuck me the last apple tart, despite them being your favourite, because you knew my father had decided I was not to have any after my tears on the journey there. I also recall you spending your days with me in the yards. You told me legends about the forest that surrounded the manor and about the ghost of the woman who haunted the lake there."

"They were just old wives' tales," I muttered under my breath. "Fables the servants used to whisper about."

"Be that as it may, you eased a young boy's heartache," Caedell replied. "It was the first time I had felt anything but sadness in those months after my mother was taken from me. And soon your stories became my favourite part about travelling when I was a lad. I was always disappointed when your father left you at home."

"It was a long time ago," I sighed before lifting my chin, and I waited until his gaze met mine. "Those memories hold no importance now; I am no longer that child nor are you."

"Perhaps not," he agreed. "But I could not help but reminisce."

"Because the blacksmith's girl?" Caedell shrugged, and I was at a loss as to what to say. I had never expected Caedell to ponder on the moments we had spent together as children, nor had I ever thought that he would still hold on to such memories. Not when things had changed so drastically for the both of us.

"Well, we should make camp for the night, should we not?" I asked in hopes of directing his attention elsewhere.

"I thought you found this spot disagreeable," Caedell retorted and I turned to grab the other saddlebag he had left on the ground next to our horse and then strode past him, making certain that my shoulder collided with his as I made my way to the place he had begun to unpack the items.

"I am too tired to care any longer," I growled. "I will start on the fire and you can take first watch."

THE SOUND of hooves crushing the icy layer that covered the snow around us dragged me from my slumber, but I was not truly awake until a warm hand covered my mouth and my eyes shot open as I began to flail. Grabbing at my wrists, Caedell urged me onto my back, and when my gaze met his, he placed a finger to his mouth. Certain I would not make a noise, he guided me up and then ushered me to my feet, and I followed as quietly as I could.

Keeping one of my hands in his grasp, he reached for the hood of my cloak and lifted it over my head before gesturing to our horse, who had begun to paw nervously as our visitors closed the distance.

"Take him east," Caedell instructed under his breath. "The woods will thin, and you will be back on the Gods' Passage."

My brows furrowed. "I'm not leaving you."

Growling under his breath, Caedell tightened his hold on my fingers and dragged me closer to the gelding. "Get on the horse, Rígan."

It was odd that my mind focused on the fact that it was the first time he had ever addressed me by just my name, and had he not continued to pull me along, I would have pondered on why I had such an odd reaction to it. Instead, however, I ripped my hand from his and shook my head while taking a step back. "No."

"We do not have time to argue about this," he whispered, and I moved another step away.

"Then stop with your protests and listen to me," I urged. "I am not leaving you here alone."

I could see the fight building in his eyes, but the hoofbeats that had awoken me sounded much closer, and Caedell froze and then swung his head towards the noise while we listened to their approach.

"Find shelter and get out of sight," he hissed as he pointed towards a bush that would offer me enough cover that I would not be easily seen. "Go."

"But I can help you," I argued, and when he remained silent, my eyes lowered to the sword strapped to his hip. "At least let me be armed should I need to defend myself. You do have two after all."

Noticing where my gaze had moved to, he curled a hand around the pommel while he searched my face hesitantly. It was a valid argument, and I could see the moment he decided to relent, and sighed in relief when he pulled the steel from its sheath. Placing the handle into my hand, he pushed on my shoulder with the other.

"Fine, but hide while I try to deter them from making a poor decision," he whispered, and when he saw my doubtful face, he exhaled. "You standing there armed may only provoke them further." With that, he pushed at my shoulder once more, though this one was stronger than the last, and I stumbled forward.

"And if they decide not to turn the other cheek?" I asked as I glanced back at him. "What if they choose violence instead of talking?"

"Am I correct in assuming you know how to use that?" Caedell gestured to the blade in my hand, and I looked down at it before jerking my head in a single nod.

"Then should it come to that point, wait for my signal," he

murmured and gestured to the bushes once more. "Go now, hurry."

Lowering myself to the ground, I pressed through the narrow space between branches and then turned to watch and held my breath while I waited. Caedell had snuffed the fire out with a boot and was now looking to the west, and it was then that I noticed the changes in his posture. He was no longer tight with worry but looked rather at ease given the situation, though I noticed his hand was now resting on the hilt of his remaining blade.

"If you were hoping for the element of surprise, I am sorry to say you have failed rather miserably," he called out, his voice sounding more carefree than it had any right to, and I observed the figures as they moved through the trees.

"We do not need surprise when we have you so outnumbered." It was a gruff voice, but one I knew, and my jaw slackened when the innkeeper stepped forward.

"I must say, I am rather surprised to see you again so soon, sir," Caedell replied, and though I could not see it, I was certain his lips had curled into that arrogant smirk I loathed. "Did you need something else or was it your greed that sent you after us?"

I still could not make out the faces of the other men, but I could count three of them, and each appeared to be armed. Shifting slightly so that I may get a better look at our visitors, I hadn't noticed that one of the branches was snagged on the wool of my hood and when I tipped my head, the bush rustled with the movement. Caedell and the innkeeper were still speaking, but one of the other men stepped to the side so that he could peer in my direction, and I froze, praying to the Protector that I had not been found out already.

"And just where is your lovely little wife?" The innkeeper's voice drew my attention back to the conversation, and I watched Caedell as he pulled his sword free from his hip at the mention of me. Lifting a brow, I wondered how he meant to dissuade them from fighting if he was in fact the one to draw his weapon first.

"Lovely, yes," one of the others interjected as he too readied his blade. "But little she is not. I saw her this morning making her way through the town. She is rather striking even with that snarling expression she wore."

The others murmured their agreement as they began their pursuit towards Caedell, and I pulled my hood from my head before balancing on the balls of my feet. Not realizing the hidden threat, they closed the distance, and Caedell prepared himself for combat before his head turned just slightly, and he glanced at me from the corner of his eye.

"If you leave now, you will be saved from her wrath," he advised. "For she is even more fearsome than you can imagine."

Caedell's voice no longer sounded at ease, and I rose just slightly, ready and waiting for the right moment.

"Oh, we are not afraid of her." The innkeeper laughed, and Caedell lifted his chin and then gave me that Godsdamn smirk, dimples and all. Tossing me a wink for good measure, I took that for all the sign I needed, and he laughed under his breath before issuing a final warning.

"You should be."

TWENTY-SIX

Caedell was well practiced in the art of battle, and I didn't need to so much as give him an alert to my movement in order for him to dance out of my way. Unprepared for the other armed body, the men floundered for a moment, and Caedell took the opening and lunged for the innkeeper. I, however, turned my sights to the man who had taken such an interest in me and prowled towards him.

"Is this the way of it then?" he asked with a wide grin as his eyes roamed across my body before he used his free hand to motion at my weapon. "I am to face off with the pretty wife?"

"I'm afraid so." My mouth curled as well, and the man hesitated for a moment at the sight of my smirk and then shook his head as if he was gathering his wits.

"Well then, I will do my very best to be gentle with you," he purred, and my grin grew as I closed the distance between us.

"That's a shame," I laughed coldly. "My tastes have always been keen for something a little rougher."

Without another word, I brought my sword down onto his own and the force of my attack seemed to take him by surprise. Leaning forward, I placed my face just a hair away from the crossing blades, and noticed the way the heat from my breath fogged the steel before I moved my attention. Holding the man's gaze, I shifted my expression until it matched the snarl I had donned just this morning. It was the very same look he had mentioned observing.

"Do you still think I am rather striking, sir?" I bit out, and when he blinked at me in confusion, I used a foot to swipe his feet out from beneath him.

However, it would seem that the impact of him hitting the ground was enough to jolt his companion into action and he leapt towards me. Thrown by his attack, I narrowly missed the blade aimed at my shoulder and my rage grew.

Spinning on my heel, I rushed at my new advisory. Unprepared for my speed or the wrath he had been warned about, the man stumbled back, and his blade fell from his fingers.

"Please," he whimpered as he lifted his hands in surrender. "Please, m'lady."

"Begging for mercy already?" I scoffed before I kicked his blade away. "What a disappointment, I would have thought you would have more fight in you."

"I meant you no harm, m'lady," he whispered while his gaze darted to his other two friends who were swinging at Caedell unsuccessfully.

"I've never heard a rebel say such a thing," I snarked with a raised brow. "Usually your kind have one goal in mind, and it is most certainly to maim those you deem an advisory."

"I am not a rebel, m'lady."

"No? Then tell me, what are you?" My eyes scanned him from head to toe, taking in the worn boots and the raggedy breeches with a frown. If I was honest, there was no way of telling which side the people of Elrin took these days. Only the Anointed carried banners that incorporated the sigils of our Gods, the nobles had their own of course. But lesser born men had no emblems whatsoever. So, the rebellion forces went unnoticed until they gathered for a battle and their leader, the High Commander, was yet to be identified by any of us.

"I am not a rebel," the man whimpered. "I am just a baker."

"A baker?" I repeated, and he hurriedly nodded. "A baker who armed himself and his party and then followed a couple into the woods. Now tell me, why would you do such a thing if you aren't part of the uprising and if you truly meant no *harm*?"

Pulling himself from the ground with a grunt, the first man moved to stand on trembling legs, and I looked back at him with a glare.

"Because you have gold, more gold than we have seen in years!" he growled, and I lifted my blade to point at him, though he made no move to do the same with his own weapon.

"And that alone gives you the right to hunt us down like animals?"

"If it means keeping our village fed through winter!" he exclaimed, and I scowled at them both. "Is it not better to sacrifice two lives rather than letting dozens starve or freeze?"

The sound of metal clashing ceased from behind me, and I glanced at Caedell from over my shoulder, noticing immediately that he too had unarmed his foes. Meeting my eyes, he searched my face and then scanned my body before turning to the innkeeper, who was currently sitting on the snow while clutching his leg. There was a deep red oozing between his thick fingers, and the fourth man was cupping his nose while his chest heaved with every breath.

"You meant to take our gold so that you may save your fellow townsfolk?" Caedell asked, his tone skeptical as his attention moved between the four men.

"We have nothing left to trade with the neighbouring villages," the innkeeper admitted. "Our crops were meagre this season and pelts have been hard to come by now that winter has set in. Without gold, we have nothing of value."

"The Gods have truly forsaken us all," the baker added, and I frowned as I examined his face. However, it would seem that Caedell was not nearly as doubtful as I was and I heard the clinking of coins before he spoke.

"Take it." The air left my lungs in a gasp and my attention lifted to his face for only a pause before I noticed where his fingers had moved to.

"You cannot be serious." I snapped, but he ignored me.

"Sir?" the innkeeper asked, his eyes bouncing between the two of us, and Caedell walked towards him while he plucked at the pouch that was tied to his belt. Pulling the laces, he tossed the coin purse into the air, caught it smoothly, and then held it out to the man.

"Take it," he repeated, but just as the man's bloodied fingers reached for the leather, Caedell snatched it back. "But first you must promise me two things."

The innkeeper eyed him suspiciously, but nodded nonetheless.

"You must promise to never attempt this type of trickery again," he scolded. "The Gods may have forsaken us, but it does not mean we must always turn our backs on each other."

"I promise," he grunted. "And the other?"

"See that the blacksmith's girl is taken care of," Caedell demanded. "You are not to let that father of hers raise a hand to her. See that she is fed and clothed."

All four nodded in agreement, but I approached the innkeeper with a narrowed gaze and towered above him as he remained on the ground.

"If we are giving you our gold"—my narrowed eyes slid to Caedell for a pause before returning to the man—"I have my own guarantee I would like you to give me."

"And what might that be?" he asked with a tilt of his head, and Caedell crowded in behind me as if he was preparing himself to step in should I disregard the truce he had just established.

"You will give us one of your horses and take ours in replacement." Glancing at the bay gelding who remained where Caedell had tied him, the innkeeper studied the horse for a pause and then his attention lifted to my face once more in confusion. "When you arrive back home, you will return him to the girl."

The man's bewildered eyes moved to his friends, but once again they nodded, and I took a step back and then spun to face Caedell. His brows were lifted, and I bristled at his look of surprise.

"Hurry them along before I forget my sudden good nature and change my mind," I snapped, and he snorted softly before rolling his eyes.

"You heard her, lads," Caedell sighed. "You best get going."

Not having to tell them twice, the three rushed to the innkeeper and helped him to his feet. He was unsteady but they managed to aid him along, and Caedell collected their forgotten blades before following behind them.

Keeping a watchful eye on the group, I tightened my fingers around the hilt of my sword, worried that they may try something at the last moment. Thankfully, however, they seemed to know a losing battle when they saw it and instead exchanged the horses without so much as a whisper before disappearing into the night.

Left alone with me once more, Caedell led the smaller chestnut mare through the trees, and I scowled at the animal.

"They may be starving, but this horse certainly is not," I muttered. "We will be lucky if we can even manage to get it to trot with such a massive belly and that horrid conformation."

Glancing at the mare, he leaned to the side to look at its barrel and then shrugged. "You are the one who decided to trade our steed, which I must admit still shocks me. I didn't think the small interaction with the girl affected *you* so much."

"I didn't do it for her," I argued. "I just thought that the exchange could only result in us gaining a better mount. I didn't think we could possibly be stuck with something worse."

Brushing past me, he guided the mare along, and I scowled at him as he mounted the animal. "Well, if you are that displeased with our circumstance, the offer for you to walk is still an option."

"A good man should never suggest such a thing," I grumbled while glaring at the hand he offered me. "I would think you of all people would know that, especially considering who you are."

"So now not only do you have opinions on my circumstances and decency, but you also believe I should be good?"

"You are one of the Anointed, something so simple should be paramount."

Curling his fingers in a gesture for me to hurry along, he waited, and I placed my foot in the stirrup and then allowed him to guide me behind the saddle. Certain I was settled, Caedell gathered the reins and peered back at me from over his shoulder. "Perhaps you too are sorely mistaken for also thinking you truly know *me*."

TWENTY-SEVEN

Concerned that the men may decide to break their word and return with even more companions, we had decided to continue our journey through the night. However, now my head lolled while I struggled to keep my eyes open despite the sunlight that had begun to lighten the sky, and I wondered if we had been overly cautious.

"We will stop here for a few hours," Caedell said over his shoulder, and I blinked through the haze of exhaustion and then glanced around. It looked exactly the same as the other spot had. In fact every inch of this Godsdamned forest looked similar, and I glowered at the green trees and the white snow that glittered under the golden morning sun.

"How far are we from Denimoore at this point?" I croaked as Caedell dismounted.

"I would wager another day at least," he replied. "And that is if we ride faster than we have been and do not come across any more surprises on the road."

"Do you think that is likely?" I wondered before blinking down at him in question while he held a hand out for me to take.

Sighing in annoyance, he reached for my forearm closest to him and curled his fingers around my wrist before tugging on me gently. Much to my dismay, my body sagged under his touch, and I slipped from the mare's back before I could catch myself.

"Easy there," Caedell murmured as I fell against him, my legs buckling under the weight of the rest of my body, and I pressed my palms against his firm chest before pulling my head back to look at him with a scowl.

"I'm fine," I bit out, though I couldn't seem to gather enough energy to pull from his arms, and Caedell rolled his eyes but did not release me from his hold.

"You are dead on your feet."

"I can't even feel my feet at this point," I growled before glancing down at my boots. My legs were trembling and the skin of my thighs, though covered by the wool of my dress and stockings, stung from the cold.

"We'll find shelter and start a fire." Caedell glanced around, and I took the opportunity to finally shove away from him.

"We could rest beneath those trees. I can break some of the branches to lie on the ground to keep the furs dry." I glanced at a space just to our left. The forest had only grown more dense as we continued north, but there was a small space between two evergreens where the snow did not seem as deep, and it would be easy to sit and curl up between the trunks while a fire blazed at our feet.

"Think you can manage that?" Caedell asked skeptically, and I stiffened at the doubt in his voice.

"What do you mean by that?" I demanded. "Surely you see that I am not just some useless damsel by now."

"Yes, I am well aware of that," he drawled, and then narrowed his gaze. "But you are being purposely obtuse. Though I can't understand if you're doing it to annoy me or if that part just happens to be a coincidence."

"Obtuse?" I spat out the word.

"You just said you can scarcely feel your feet," he reminded me. "Which is why I asked if you could achieve such a task. I wanted to make certain that I would not find you toppled over in the snow when I returned with kindling."

"I can assure you, that will not happen," I swore, and Caedell rolled his eyes.

"Because I would never be that fortunate? Or because you live purely out of spite at this point?" He chuckled softly, but I did not see the humour in his words.

"Spite can offer far more strength than you can imagine. It can allow even the weakest of beings to persevere under the worst conditions," I muttered under my breath.

"Speaking from experience, I take it," Caedell guessed. "I suppose that means I will be stuck with you for the rest of a journey despite your frozen toes."

"Would that be such a hardship for you, sir? I thought you liked me?" I remarked with a frown while crossing my arms.

"No, I said I liked you when we were children, before you grew into this." One of his hands gestured from my boots to my face, and I clenched my jaw. However, I couldn't help but notice the flush creeping into his cheeks, though perhaps the pink was from the chill of the northern air rather than my reminder of his previous confession.

"Yes, what is it you call me again?" I tilted my head. "A shewolf?"

"You certainly have the nature of one," Caedell agreed with a quirked brow, and I rolled my eyes.

"I didn't hear you complaining when you needed help," I pointed out, and he scoffed with a shake of his head as he began to untack our horse.

"Let us be clear, I never actually really needed your help. But yes, I can admit that you are quite the thing to behold."

"Rather fearsome as well," I continued, enjoying the way

he avoided eye contact, and now I was certain it was a blush that coloured his strong cheekbones. "Or did I mishear you?"

"I did say as much," Caedell confirmed, and my head tilted just slightly as I examined him.

"And yet I get the feeling *you* do not fear me." His fingers stilled on the buckles of the saddle bags, but he said nothing in return, so I pressed the issue. "Truly? Not even a little?"

Caedell still had not moved, and when the silence grew uncomfortable, I cleared my throat. "I shall get to work."

Brushing past him, I snatched at one of the bedrolls that was tied to the saddle and then carefully reached for his belt. Stiffening, Caedell glanced over his shoulder at me, and I held his stare while my fingers curled around the hilt of the dagger sheathed beside one of his longswords.

"I will be taking this," I whispered before drawing the blade from its place, and when he remained still, I smirked. "For the branches, of course."

Swallowing, he dipped his chin in acknowledgement, and I put some space between us, though my smile grew. "And here I thought you were not frightened of me."

Not waiting for his answer, I spun on my heel and got to work, though I was certain I could feel his eyes on me.

Caedell had taken first watch while I dozed in the morning sun, and by the time he had woken me, it was nearing late afternoon. Sighing in annoyance, I shifted towards the warmth of the fire and then glanced at the man from the corner of my eye.

His usual meticulously put together appearance was slightly dishevelled. His hair was less tame than normal, most likely due to him running his long fingers through the dark strands, and his fine tunic was dirty, and his jerkin was partially undone. His striking features were still unbearably handsome, but his skin appeared ashen and the dark circles under his eyes were worrisome.

"You should take your turn to rest now," I suggested and rolled my eyes at his quiet grunt in disagreement. "I am being quite serious. You look ghastly."

Turning to look at me, he waited until our gazes met and then lifted a single brow. "That is not even in the realm of possibilities."

"My Gods, you are full of yourself," I snapped, and his lips curled in a smirk though his amber irises remained dull with exhaustion.

"That may be, but I do not hear you actually disagreeing with the statement." Choosing to ignore his point, I pressed my knees to my chest and reached for the dagger I had placed on the fur beside me before I had fallen asleep.

"You do still think travelling at night is the wisest option, correct?" I asked.

"Journeying in the dark is not ideal, that is to be sure," he muttered quietly. "But the daylight means we can relax more easily. We are less likely to be taken by surprise and our fires won't be as noticeable."

Nodding, I hummed my agreement while my eyes scanned the bright forest. "Then would you please just take this time to rest? Even just to give me a break from all of your squawking?" I grumbled before squaring my shoulders in preparation for his stubbornness. "We still have a few hours of sun left and you should take advantage of it before we continue on. Make the most of the opportunity while I take my turn in keeping watch."

Caedell's mouth parted in what would have been an argument, but I lifted a hand to interrupt and shook my head. "I will wake you should there be a need."

His gaze narrowed with suspicion while his jaw clenched,

and I exhaled roughly before gesturing to the pelts beneath us with my unarmed hand and then lifted the other to show him the blade.

"Should a rabbit attack, I will be ready, otherwise I will make sure to alert you to any other threat." Shuffling down onto the furs, Caedell crossed his legs at the ankles and placed both hands behind his head but did not close his eyes.

"You will wake me as soon as the sun sets." It wasn't a question but rather an order, and I scowled at him.

"When was it decided that you will be the one to give commands?" I seethed.

"The moment I had to rescue you from your own demise," Caedell responded just before his long lashes fluttered closed.

"That is not what happened," I disputed, but he lifted a hand from behind his head to wave me off before getting comfortable once more then laughed softly.

"Now who is the one doing all the squawking?" Snapping my jaw shut, I glared at him but remained silent while the fire crackled before us.

Caedell must have been far more exhausted than he let on. Within moments his breathing had evened out and the harshness of his features softened. It was as if sleep had gifted him a few more years of youth, and for the first time since the tourney, I could see the boy who had followed me around Noordeign all those years ago.

Resting my chin on my knees, I turned my focus to the flames as they danced in the wind and then lifted my attention to the dusting of sparks that burst from the burning wood as it cracked in half. Noticing the way the bright orange flecks twirled through the air before turning black, I lifted my fingers towards them, trying to catch the ash in my palm. However, the breeze blew them farther away, and they instead fluttered down until they rested against the white snow for just a heartbeat and then disappeared altogether.

Time seemed to drag as Caedell slept, and I lost interest in watching the sparks and shifted for the dozenth time in an attempt to get comfortable while the shadows of the forest grew. However, as I moved to settle on my knees, a pained groan echoed from beside me and my head turned to my companion.

The peaceful expression that had been painted across his face had changed into something more worrisome, and I watched the way his brows furrowed before his lips parted and he moaned again. It was a sound I had heard before, and I was certain I knew what was coming next.

Just as I predicted, that high-pitched whimper broke from Caedell, and I felt my stomach churn at the painful sound before I inched closer to him. Lifting my hands, I let them hover over his shoulder, unsure if I should wake him or not, and I frowned as his head tossed from one side to the other.

"No!" he called out while his fingers grabbed at the fur below him, and I scanned him from head to toe with worry.

"Caedell," I whispered, hoping that somehow, he would hear me. But my voice did nothing to soothe him, and I lowered my fingers towards his body as I readied myself to jostle him awake.

However, just as I was about to make contact, a strange sensation pulsed through my body, and I shivered at the feel of it before my eyes lifted to the trees. Frowning, I noticed that the heavy branches had stilled and the forest itself was silent besides my uneven breaths and Caedell's whimpers of pain. Turning my head, I scanned the area only to jump when Caedell began to beg once more.

"Please, no!" he cried out, and the mare, who had been tied a few yards, neighed before she began to swing her hindquarters back and forth in agitation.

"Please!" Caedell sobbed once more, and my chest constricted at the sound. Leaning over him, I grasped his shoulders, curling my fingers into his jerkin until they were pressing into the muscle beneath the fabric, and then I shook him.

"Wake up!" I shouted, but the words were drowned out by the shrill whinny coming from the mare, and I looked back at the horse just in time to see its body crumple to the ground in a heap while crimson splattered across the white snow.

CHAPTER

TWENTY-EIGHT

Twisting away from Caedell, I fell onto my backside and stared at the horse, watching as its body was jostled just slightly, and it was then I heard the low growls that were accompanied by slurping and chewing. Not moving my gaze, I stretched my fingers out across the furs, searching blindly for the dagger I had tossed aside while my other hand grabbed at the collar of Caedell's tunic.

"Do not make any sudden movement," he whispered, his body already stiff beneath my touch, and my eyes darted to his face. Watching him, I held my breath as he glanced at the carcass of our horse and then those burning amber irises met mine. "Are you still armed?"

Nodding, I looked down at my hand that was curled around the hilt of the dagger, noticing the way my knuckles had turned as white as the snow surrounding us.

"Good," he murmured. "I am going to sit up very slowly. Do not move from where you are but turn your focus onto our visitor."

Doing as he instructed, I looked up through my lashes to study the body of our mount once more but still could not see what kind of animal it was that had found us. Growing more

247

uneasy as time passed, I clenched my jaw and tried to swallow down the burning bile creeping up the back of my throat while Caedell finally managed to lift his torso from the ground without being detected.

Now that we were shoulder to shoulder, I peered at him from the corner of my eye. "What is it?"

His face was troubled, his furrowed brow and the ticking muscle of his jaw told me as much, and I waited for him to answer with bated breath.

"I can't say for certain," he said softly, and then I watched as his gaze widened and heard his sharp inhale. "No, that's not possible."

Frowning, I glanced back at the carcass and then noticed two bright burning orbs floating amongst the shadows of the forest, and for a moment I couldn't comprehend what it was I was seeing. At least not until the glowing circles flickered, and it was then that I realized the shining circles were in fact eyes.

Bright burning eyes blinking at us, and yet, there was nothing else that even resembled a face.

"Get up!" Scrambling to his feet, Caedell reached down and hauled me upright and pulled me to his side, obviously no longer concerned about sudden movements.

Curling my fingers into his cloak, I noticed the way he trembled beneath my touch, and I peered back at the monster, wondering what kind of being could make the great Heir of House Reide quiver so.

"What is it?" I whispered again while my eyes squinted as I struggled to make out its shape amongst the creeping darkness of the forest.

He bent his arm, his fingers grasping at my hand that clutched at him, and he urged me back one step, then another all while keeping his attention on the monster. "It's a gloomhor."

Frowning, I tightened my hold on the long length of his fingers, and he ushered me back again, creating more space between us and the beast. The eyes that had seemingly been focused on our bodies floated higher in the air, and then there was a strange clicking noise.

"We need to run," Caedell muttered, but I could scarcely hear him over the pounding of my heart that echoed in my ears. Digging his fingers into my hand, Caedell glanced at me from over his shoulder. "Did you hear me? We need to run."

The gloomhor made that clicking noise again, and my attention shifted back towards it only to see a row of triangular crimson-coloured teeth that were now being bared in what may have been the most terrifying smile I had ever seen. However, despite the chilling sight, it seemed as if its gaze was searching, and when it repeated the noise, I realized it was calling out—almost like it was having difficulty locating us.

"Keep your dagger ready, back away slowly," Caedell ordered softly. "When I give you the go-ahead, I want you to run as fast as you can towards what is left of the sunlight and do not look back."

My skin had broken out in bumps, and I glanced at the remaining golden hues that filtered through the trees behind us and then swallowed past the tightness of my throat. "And what will you do?"

"I will run the opposite way in hopes of luring it away," he answered, sounding far more confident than should have been possible given the way his palm shook against mine.

"We would be better to face it together," I argued as my eyes glanced at the soft rays that just kissed the edges of our heels.

"We are no match, and there is no time to bicker about it," he snapped. "A gloomhor only travels in the cover of darkness and we are quickly running out of light. Once the sun is gone, we will be easy prey."

"And what exactly do you think is going to happen if we split up?" I growled. "If there is no defeating it together, we certainly should not try to on our own."

"I am not attempting to defeat it," he muttered. "I am hoping to give one of us a chance at surviving! Now go!"

"But Caedell—" He moved to snatch his hand away from mine, but my hold remained firm.

"Rígan, our time is running out!" he snarled before finally pulling his fingers from my grasp. "Go east, I will circle around and try to meet you back on the road. But should I not be successful with this plan, continue north. It will take days to reach Denimoore on foot, but there is no other option at this point. You must go on."

"And if I am faced with the gloomhor?" I asked as I began to distance myself from the Heir of House Reide.

"It is a creature of the Reaper," he whispered, and I noticed that the beast had continued to gaze in our direction but had not moved from behind the horse's body that was now barely visible as the shadows of the forest crept forward. "It is made of darkness, and should it find you, there will be little you can do to stop it from consuming you whole."

The words were enough to shake me from my stupor, and I held the dagger in front of me before my eyes sought his one last time. "We will meet on the Gods' Passage and then continue on our journey."

My voice shook with nervousness, but Caedell dipped his head in a nod. "I will see you soon."

It was an empty promise, but I had already wasted too much time to try to push for a more honest farewell.

"Now go, Rígan." Spinning on my heel, I sprinted towards the fading orange that had begun to disappear through the branches.

Slipping and sliding across the snow, I reached out for the trees as I passed, hoping to steady myself as I crossed the slick terrain. However, it would seem that the forest itself was determined to keep me as it's captive. Each time I braced my hands against the rough bark of the trunks, the branches lunged for me in return, snagging the fabric of my wool cloak or scratching at the skin of my cheeks. Wincing at the sharp sting as another cut my temple before tangling in my hair, I curled my fingers around the wood and pulled it free from my locks before continuing on my path.

My heart thundered in my chest, my lungs burned as I gasped for air, and my tongue tasted of metal, almost as if blood had replaced the bile that had been creeping up the back of my throat. The muscles in my thighs had also begun to tighten in protest as I ran, but the last bit of lingering light kept me focused on the task at hand.

"Gods protect me," I wheezed as the heel of my boot slipped across a particularly icy patch of earth, and the momentum I had forced me to scramble forward onto my hands while my ankle twisted painfully and the healing wounds that littered the skin of my back stretched with a stinging burn.

Hissing in pain, I remained on my hands and knees and glanced over my shoulder towards the limb that throbbed in pain. Sinking my teeth into my lower lip, I wiggled my toes under the leather of my boot, testing the extent of the injury before pushing myself to stand on my good foot. Certain I had balance, I then lowered the other to the ground and carefully increased my weight onto it. It ached as I pressed forward, but it was not nearly as bad as some of my other injuries had been in the past, and I was sure I could ignore the tenderness for the time being. Especially since the last remaining glow of dusk had begun to disappear.

"Damn Anointed fools!" I growled under my breath as I took another careful step forward.

Had it not been for our call to come north, I would not be in this Godsforsaken forest alone, cold, and injured. Had I not been forced to accompany my useless brother, I would be on my way home, nursing my anger and bitterness towards him, my father, Gwain, and all the other unfairness I had been subjected to in my short life. Instead, I was stranded amongst the trees while Caedell Reide took it upon himself to play hero and I was left to flee like some powerless damsel.

Had I been gifted a different fate, perhaps I would not have minded the loss of control or the lack of power. That or I wouldn't have known any different. But being helpless had never been an option I could afford, and I scowled at the snow beneath my feet. Allowing myself to wallow for a pause, I took in a deep breath, then another, and then I swallowed down my disappointment and hurried my pace.

The shadows had only continued to deepen around me as I staggered through the snow, and I pulled my cloak around me tightly as I searched for the path that would eventually lead to Denimoore. However, there was nothing distinctive about the area around me, and I wondered how much land I had covered since parting from Caedell.

"Surely it must be near," I whispered to myself as my brows furrowed, and then a shiver ran down my spine and I glanced over my shoulder.

The looming trees stood tall and proud, but the space between the trunks was nearly black now, and when I noticed how still the air had become, I knew there was something amongst the darkness that watched me. Forcing myself forward, I scanned the area once more and hurried on my way.

The light that I had been chasing had finally been snuffed out by the night sky, and now I had no choice but to run, my ankle and anger be damned. Keeping the dagger at the ready, I ran as fast as I could, though my stride was clumsy as the tender joint throbbed in pain. However, the worry coursing through my veins was enough for me to overlook the ache, and I instead did my best to only put weight on the ball of my foot in hopes that it would ease some of the discomfort.

That is until I heard that odd clicking noise echo from behind me, and I gasped at the sound before sparing a second to look over my shoulder. There were no glowing eyes, but it called out again, and this time it sounded much closer than it had before.

"Dear Protector, stand with me now," I whispered, praying that the God would hear my words and would find some way to shield me from the creature.

However, no sense of security fell over me, and instead the cold feeling of fear raked across my skin like sharpened fingers and its claws seared into my flesh until I felt nothing but panic. Unable to stop myself, I began to run as fast as I could, no longer caring that my ankle was bruised and swollen or that the injuries across my back stung more painfully with every stride. No, nothing mattered besides escaping the predator that was in the midst of its hunt.

But in the end, I was nothing more than wounded prey, and as my hunter finally caught the back of my cloak between its clutches and hauled me onto the forest floor, I was sure I had met my death. The Gods had not sought to answer my prayers; they did not care that I was of Anointed blood or that I had spent my life honouring them. In the end I was just another mortal who had found her life cut short and all my sacrifices would amount to nothing. In the end I would amount to nothing.

Yet despite that, I did not want my final moments to be one of surrender. Instead, I closed my eyes and lifted my armed hand before swinging my dagger, determined to fight until the last breath of life left in my lungs while the darkness of night finally consumed me.

CHAPTER

TWENTY-NINE

S TRUGGLING BENEATH THE BEAST'S WEIGHT, I FLAILED AND swung my blade, though I could not bring myself to open my eyes and face my foe. It was cowardly of me perhaps, but I refused to have the eerily glowing orbs be the last thing I saw before I met the Gods. However, being blind meant my attacks were clumsy, and my captor easily grabbed my wrist and pinned it above my head. Pressing my knuckles into the snow, its fingers tightened their hold.

Digging my heels into the earth, I bucked beneath its solid weight in an attempt to dislodge it from its place over me, but its grip on my arm strengthened in retaliation, and then it shifted until it was pressing against my chest, taking the air from my lungs with the movement. Clenching my jaw, I began to kick my legs, but it did little to deter the beast and instead it only forced me farther into the snow. On another day, I may have been an admirable adversary, but the strength and resilience I had always prided myself on having seemed to be far more fleeting than I would have thought imaginable.

"Stop, Rígan." A sharp gasp left my lips and my lashes fluttered open. The dark made it nearly impossible to make out the face above me, but as I squinted and my eyes adjusted, I recognized his auburn hair and pale skin.

"Gwain?" I whispered doubtfully as I went still beneath him, wondering if this was an illusion of some sort, if I was imagining him, or perhaps I was already dead and this was what had been waiting for me.

"It's me," he replied, bringing his face closer to my own so that I could see his eyes. I searched his features for a pause before exhaling roughly, and then I went slack beneath him. Releasing my wrist, he planted his palm next to my head and used his other hand to smooth back my hair carefully.

"Are you hurt?" he asked while the backs of his fingers ran across my cheek, and I nearly tipped my face towards the familiar touch, only stopping myself when I finally noticed the dampness soaking through the sleeve of the arm that was still lying above my head. Moving it from its place, I wedged it between our bodies and pushed at him.

"Nothing more than a few bruises and a tender ankle," I muttered as he stood, and then he held out a hand for me to take. Scoffing, I slapped it away and scrambled to my feet on my own. Now that my heart began to slow and the fear had somewhat cleared from my mind, I caught my breath, and then scanned the trees. However, there was not another soul to be found, and as time dragged on, I felt the fear I had for my own life shift to a new worry.

"Where is Caedell?" I demanded, though my eyes did not stop roaming across the blackness in hopes of spotting the Heir of House Reide when he finally emerged from the shadows.

"Caedell?" Gwain repeated before stepping closer to me, and my gaze begrudgingly lifted to his face.

"He did not find you first and send you back for me?" I whispered as I searched his expression.

Gwain's brows furrowed, and then he twisted to look back in the direction I had come from before placing a hand on my back. "Rígan, I haven't seen Caedell since he left the tavern," he admitted. "I had thought he may have turned for home, or perhaps gone to Denimoore on his own in hopes of finding glory once more. But I never truly believed he would…"

Gwain trailed off as he ushered me forward, but I pulled away from his touch before I crossed my arms and peered at him through narrowed eyes. "Did not believe what? That he would come find me?"

Running a hand over his face, Gwain exhaled roughly and then glanced at me with a pointed look. "Can you fault me for assuming such a thing? It is not as if Caedell Reide is known for being gallant. He is nothing more than a——"

"Careful, Gwain," I warned. "You are speaking of an Anointed."

Gwain flinched at my cautioning but moved close once more. However, when I avoided his pursuit, he frowned and then shoved past me. Quickening his stride, he ignored the way I faltered behind as my injured limb struggled to keep up with his hurried pace.

"That may be so," he called back. "And the great Heir of House Reide may be many things, but selfless he is not."

"I do not think you are in a position to cast judgement on anyone, especially not on the *only* man who came to my aid," I growled in reply.

Stopping suddenly, Gwain spun on his heel and threw his arms out at his sides. "You say that as if you believe I did not want to take his place. Like I did not long to be the one to go after you."

"I think the only thing you've ever truly longed for is a good supper and a woman of higher status to warm your bed," I snarled.

"Surely you do not believe that," Gwain scoffed, and I shook my head in disagreement. "That's not true, you know it's not. I love you, Rígan."

Those sweet words may have warmed my heart once, but

now they were little more than the winter winds that blew against our bodies. They caressed my being but did not leave a mark. Sensing my mistrust, he closed the distance between us, and then he waited until my gaze met his.

"I love you," he repeated as if saying the words would make me really believe them to be true. As if they would somehow matter more if he whispered them over and over again. "And I am here now, isn't that enough?"

"You are here, but how did you find me?" I asked with a narrowed gaze, and Gwain frowned before his attention moved to the trees, and I pressed the issue. "Where are the others? I wager you did not venture too far from them."

As it would turn out, I did not need his answer. I could now see the orange flickering flames of the torches, and if I listened closely, I could just make out the sound of the horses. Marching on, I ignored Gwain's whisper of my name and hurried towards my men.

"Halt!" one of the guards shouted, and the other knights drew their swords. Bursting through the trees, I felt my breath catch in relief and then I lifted my hands in the air. Stepping into the light, I prayed they would have the good sense to think before acting rashly.

"It is me," I called. "It is Lady Baxteel." At the sound of my voice, the door of the carriage swung open, and Cat flew from its shelter, though I noticed a dagger was clutched in her right hand.

"Oh, thank the Gods!" she cried as she launched herself at me, but I leaned away from her armed hand and took a step back. Noticing my hesitation, her attention moved to the blade in her grasp and then she tossed the weapon onto the snow before hurling herself at me once more. "I've been so worried!"

Ignoring the throbbing in my ankle and the sharp sting coming from the skin under her hands that pressed across my back, I returned her embrace for just a quick pause and then pulled from her touch.

"Are you well?" I asked before noticing movement from over her shoulder, and my eyes caught Donigan's as he roughly pushed past the other men to get to me.

"Rígan, a beast of the sky snatched *you* from the tavern and somehow, by the grace of the Gods, you survived that ordeal only to then endure living in the northern forest for days on your own." Her hands grabbed at my own fingers desperately. "*We* are fine, stop fretting over us," she commanded and then turned her head to follow my gaze towards my knight before moving aside for him.

Given that we were being watched closely, he had to remain a few feet away for propriety's sake. However, I did notice the way he searched every inch of me for any obvious sign of injury before bowing at the waist in greeting.

"Lady Rígan," he said softly as he straightened once more, and I stepped forward to place my hand on his armour-clad shoulder.

"I am so very glad to see you both," I murmured before glancing around the party who had gathered around us. "But where is my brother?"

"He is resting," Cat growled before casting a glare towards the carriage. "Apparently, he can sleep through anything."

"Is he well?" I demanded as my attention moved between my friend and my guard.

"He is fine," Donigan assured me. "He has been recovering well."

"If you asked me, I'd say it's been at a rather leisurely pace," Cat added before crossing her arms over her chest, and my brow lifted at her soured expression while Donigan spoke up.

"Although he is not overly concerned, the healer has been certain to keep him as comfortable as possible with tonics." Cat scoffed but my knight continued. "However, it seems that with such a frequent dose of medicine, it has kept Lord Baxteel rather indisposed. He has spent most of his time resting *away* from the others. The healer did ask if he should refuse your brother's request for more, but I assured him to give my lord whatever is necessary to keep him at *ease*."

The pointed look was easy to decipher—Donigan was pleased by this choice, and I understood. The extent of Skileer's injuries may have been embellished, but the chosen treatment had kept him from causing any disturbance.

I sighed in relief, my shoulders sagged, and I winced when my ankle throbbed under the shift in my weight.

"What is wrong?" Donigan demanded, obviously noticing my distress, but I lifted a hand to wave him off.

"It's nothing of concern," I promised, "and now that I know you are all safe and well, we have something more pressing to focus on."

Donigan frowned, but I lifted my chin and smoothed my expression. "I need you to gather some men to accompany me in my search for Lord Reide."

"Lord Reide?" he repeated with a furrowed brow, and I nodded and glanced at the men who surrounded us.

"He was with me just before sundown," I explained to the party. "We had been travelling together after he had found me in the forest. We had been set to journey to Denimoore. However, we were separated when a gloomhor—"

Cat's sharp gasp pulled my focus to her face, and I noticed the way her eyes had widened before she worriedly glanced at my knight. Donigan too seemed troubled by my words, but he said nothing and instead lifted his attention to scan the trees that towered over us.

Ignoring the sudden uneasiness pressing on my chest, I continued. "Given that it's nearly impossible to navigate this place in the dark, I would suggest at least three or four men —" Cat began to frantically shake her head.

"You cannot possibly be considering venturing back out there if what you are saying is true!" she argued.

"Of course I am," I retorted. "I will not leave him on his own if I have the means to find him."

"But Rígan, a gloomhor is not a typical beast, it is something far more dangerous," Cat cautioned, and I narrowed my gaze at her before squaring my shoulders.

"Even more reason to make haste," I reasoned. "And the longer we stand here debating the issue, the more time we waste."

"Ríga—" My glare slid to Donigan, and his mouth shut when he realized his mistake at addressing me in such a way.

"I will not leave him to fend for himself," I explained. "Not only did he come to my aid, but Caedell Reide is also an Anointed, and I expect the rest of you to remember that."

"We have not forgotten—" Cat began, but I lifted a hand to stop her.

"These men have a duty," I reminded her. "They are to serve the Gods and their chosen. That is what they swore to, and should they ignore the call—*this* call—then their word, their promise, and their honour means nothing."

A tense silence fell over the group, and I let my attention roam across the faces of the party, watching as each of the men shrank back from my cold stare.

"My lady, if I may?" a voice called, and I glanced up to see Fynn move to Donigan's side. "While I appreciate your concern for my lord, and I share that sentiment, perhaps Lady Cat is correct. Gloomhors are beasts of legends. No mortal has faced such a creature and come out of the fight victorious."

"Odd," I scoffed before I scanned him from head to toe, and he fidgeted under my gaze. "I did not take you for a coward, sir."

I could see the red flush cover his face even with the soft

light coming from the flickering torches, and he looked at his comrades in disbelief.

"It is not cowardice that stops me, my lady," he whispered, and I tipped my chin and peered at him.

"Then it's desertion of your lord," I snarled before looking at Donigan. "If you will not accompany me, give me your sword and armour and I will trade you my gown."

My knight's jaw clenched at my suggestion, but his focus moved to the snow beneath our feet. "It is not that we do not want to search for Lord Reide. It's that this forest is no place for a highborn *lady*."

I bristled the insult and crossed my arms over my chest. "And yet I have spent these last few days amongst those very trees, sir," I barked. "I am more familiar with this forest than any of the rest of you!"

"Yes, that may be so," Fynn began carefully while he kept his head bowed. "But I am certain my lord would not have you risking your life to find him."

Cat hurried to my side before placing a gentle hand on my arm. "They are right, Rígan," she said softly. "You have been through a great ordeal and would be best to remain here and be examined by the healer. Perhaps when the sun rises, we can send a small party to search for Lord Reide."

"It may be too late by then!" I cried, and Donigan's wide eyes lifted to my face at the desperation in my voice. Realizing how panicked I sounded, I wrapped my arms around my torso and took in a deep breath. "He came for me. He came for me when no one else did, and without him I am not sure I would have survived."

Swallowing roughly, I looked at my knight and begged him to understand the debt that weighed so heavily on my shoulders. "I owe him my life. If something has happened to him…"

I paused, fighting down the bitter taste creeping up the back of my throat at the thought of Caedell lying out there in the dark, injured, or worse. However, now that I had spoken the words out loud, the image would not leave my mind, and I sought for some inkling of understanding in Donigan's dark gaze.

But there was none to be found, as his attention had moved to the space just over my shoulder, and my brows furrowed.

"My, my, I had no idea you cared so much, shewolf."

CHAPTER

THIRTY

THOSE BURNING AMBER EYES ONLY SEEMED TO BLAZE BRIGHTER under the orange hue of the torches, and my lips parted as he held my stare. The men, however, were not transfixed, and the group that surrounded me scattered all at once to race towards their lord.

Hands clapped against his back while the less familiar men kept a distance from his body but asked after his well-being. But Caedell paid them no mind, as his attention was still trapped on me.

"It would seem that you were worried for nothing," Cat whispered from her place at my side, and the sound of her soft voice was enough to stir me from the daze I had been put under. Blinking, I lowered my focus and immediately noticed the dark brow she had lifted in question. "Though given the way he is watching you, it appears that you were not alone in your concern."

My cheeks heated at her suggestion, and I was about to argue when I heard footsteps approaching.

"You survived," Caedell drawled, and those burning irises sent an unfamiliar warmth across my skin as he examined every inch of me.

263

Crossing my arms over my chest, I rolled my eyes while trying to ignore my body's odd reaction. "You sound surprised, sir."

"Had it been any other maiden, I would be," he chuckled. "But I know better than to discount your stubbornness. Or was it that spite you mentioned that kept you going?"

"I think I would call it skill in this particular circumstance," I corrected under my breath.

"And how did you manage it, my lord?" Cat asked from her place beside me. "How did you survive a gloomhor?"

Caedell finally looked away from my face and turned his attention to my friend before offering her a blinding smile that had me bristling. "It may have been luck, or the Gods..." He trailed off, and Catiline sighed softly at the timbre of his voice.

Caedell's grin grew at her reaction. "Or perhaps it was the desire to see your lovely face just one more time."

My friend giggled quietly, and I pressed my tongue to my cheek and rolled my shoulders before interrupting the two of them. "Well, if you two are finished with your flirting, I'd very much like some wine and perhaps a tonic or two."

Shifting to glance at me, Cat placed a hand on my arm and frowned. "Oh, Rígan, of course, I should have sent for the healer already."

Caedell said nothing, but I noticed the way his posture seemed to stiffen. Peeking at his face, I examined his furrowed brow and how the golden colour of his eyes burned even brighter while tension filled his face.

"Did something more happen? Tell me, are you unwell?" he asked, and the sharpness of his tone made my throat dry. Swallowing roughly, I narrowed my gaze at him.

"I'm fine," I replied, but Cat wrapped one of her small arms around my waist and glanced down at my feet as I tried to take the weight off my aching ankle that throbbed painfully now that the adrenaline had fully left my body.

"She's not bearing much weight on this foot of hers,

though she continues to try." Caedell's focus lowered to the ground, and his frown deepened. Ready to wave off their concern, I cleared my throat again. But whatever words that had been sitting on the tip of my tongue were forgotten, and a high-pitched squeak took their place as Caedell curled his strong arm under my knees. Sweeping me up into his arms, he cradled me against his chest, and I grabbed at his shoulder in surprise.

"What are you doing!?" I snapped, but the ridiculous man ignored me and set his sights on my friend.

"I will take her to the carriage, tell the healer to meet us there." Cat blinked up at us with an open mouth, and I blushed at the wonder on her face before pressing my hand against Caedell's chest while I began to struggle in his hold.

"Would you put me down?!" I growled. "I am perfectly capable of walking there myself."

Jostling me slightly, Caedell tightened his hold but paid my words no mind and instead kept his attention on my friend. "Tell him to bring some salve as well."

"Salve?" Cat repeated in question.

"For her back." Cat looked even more puzzled, and my cheeks burned fiercely while I glared at the man who now held me captive. "Tell him her wounds will need to be cleaned again. I had done a decent enough job, but looking at the state of her, I fear they have been sullied once more."

"Cleaned again?" Cat seemed unable to do anything but echo the words Caedell spoke, and I moved my hand to the nape of his neck and curled my fingers into the hair before giving the soft strands a sharp tug.

"Would you please stop talking," I seethed. "Your words have implications, and I do not need anyone thinking something improper happened between us."

Chuckling softly under his breath, Caedell arched his head back into my touch while his tongue darted out to lick his lips and then he spun on his heel. Heading in the direction of the carriage, he ignored the lingering stares of the men who surrounded us.

"I think we are well past that point, shewolf." His voice rumbled out of him, and I could feel the words vibrate against the side of my body that was pressing into his torso.

Glancing at the group of eager onlookers, I flushed hotly once more. "Well, if you would just let me walk——"

"Trust me," he interrupted, "it's not my carrying you or my comments that will have sent their imaginations wild. In fact, I think they were already jumping to conclusions long before I touched you and I refuse to take the blame for their assumptions——whatever those may be."

"If you're not responsible, then who is?" I demanded as he gracefully moved across the snow, and I couldn't help but notice the heat radiating from his body as the icy winter winds blew against us.

"Well, shewolf," he murmured softly, "when one is willing to risk their life for someone else, it usually means *something*." Stiffening at his words, I clenched my jaw and then shifted as far away from his chest as I could, the cold be damned.

"I assure you, sir." I swallowed again before I forced the words from my lips. "It meant nothing."

THE SOFT LIGHT of the morning sun filled the carriage, and I glared at my brother's sleeping face and watched the way his head bobbed at every bounce while his snores continued. Cat, who had also been snoozing, curled into my side before she groaned under her breath, and I felt her press closer into my shoulder.

"Can we not find some way to shut him up?" she growled quietly, and I snorted.

"We could shove him out the door," I suggested, and she sighed before blinking open a bleary eye.

"Don't tempt me," she grumbled. "At least I have you back. Now I won't have to deal with him on my own."

"Has he caused much trouble?" I asked with a frown before peeking at the cotton that still covered half of my brother's head.

"Not truly," Catiline admitted, "but he's certainly not an ideal companion for such a long journey. Especially one where we are stuck in close quarters."

"I always thought you were rather fond of him," I admitted quietly, and Cat hauled herself away from my body before she tiredly rubbed at her face.

"I'm fond of his face," she corrected, and I shook my head in disbelief. "You can't blame me, he is awfully handsome, even if he ruins it every time he opens his mouth."

"Has he offended you in some way?" I demanded, praying to the Gods my brother had been on the best of his behaviour while I had been gone.

"I think he has offended everyone he has spoken to recently," Cat replied. "He is terribly…"

She trailed off and I leaned away so that I could look at her more easily. "Terribly?"

Her dark eyes slid to my brother, and she watched him for a pause, waiting until another snore rumbled from his lips before she smoothed her hands over her skirts and then ducked her chin.

"He just is not what I imagined, I suppose." Cat shrugged and she looked at me for a heartbeat before lowering her eyes to the floor of the carriage. "I know I haven't spent much time with him, at least not since we were young children, but I *have* heard of his conquests and victories. He is highly regarded; he is an Anointed and one who has been said to be rather valiant. Many say he is going to be the end of the rebellion."

"Do they?" I murmured under my breath, and Cat nodded before grabbing at my hand.

"He is a hero, a true and honourable man," she continued. "Don't think I don't understand that. It's just, he has not been——"

"What, Cat?" I shifted so that I faced her more fully and peered down at her. "What has he done?"

"He was not at all worried for you, Rígan." Her eyes closed as if she was bracing herself for my reaction.

"Is that all?" I laughed dryly. "That is not a surprise to me in the least."

"But he is your brother!" Cat snapped, and then her attention darted to Skileer and we waited to see if her outburst disturbed him from his slumber. But when his head lolled to the side and another grunt echoed around the small space, Cat sighed and cleared her throat.

"He has been unkind to the men, impatient with Donigan and the healer." She crossed her arms over her chest and pressed back against the seat. "He demands more and more tonic and has spent almost every hour sleeping or so influenced by the medicines that he forgets all propriety completely."

"Propriety?" I repeated and then rage burned through my veins so swiftly, I struggled to breathe. "Has he crossed a line with you?"

"No," Cat assured me. "He has done little else but ignore me."

"That is a blessing, trust me," I whispered, and Cat nodded her head.

"I can see that now, though I will admit, my feelings were hurt for the first while." I said nothing and instead watched Skileer once more.

"But, Rígan," she murmured, "I am sorry for what I said at the tourney."

My brows furrowed, and I glanced at her from the corner of my eye in question.

"If I had a brother and father like yours, I don't think I would be nearly as good as you are. I should not have said the things I did."

Her admission made an uncomfortable tension fill my chest, and I shifted away from her, hoping the space I created would chill the feeling blooming beneath my ribs.

"You should try and rest some more," I said coolly. "We still have a way to go before we arrive and I do not think the rest of the journey will be any easier."

Her dark eyes searched my face for a long pause and her mouth pulled down at the corners, but she said nothing and instead lifted her legs and curled them under herself before resting her head against the wall and closing her eyes.

CHAPTER

THIRTY-ONE

THE SKY WAS HEAVY WITH DARK CLOUDS, AND I BLINKED UP AT the snowflakes that fluttered from the mass of grey before turning to the men who were now busying themselves with constructing our lodgings for the night. Watching them, I noticed that every member of the party was armed and ready and then my attention moved to the small figure standing just at the edge of the clearing.

Cat's arms were wrapped around her torso as she shifted from foot to foot, and I frowned at her ashen complexion. For the first time since we had been reunited at the tourney, she looked like that sickly child I had grown up with, and I crossed the distance between us.

"Are you alright?" I asked softly once I reached her side, and her dark angular eyes met mine.

"Fine." Her tone was clipped and my frown deepened.

"What has put you in such a state?" I pressed when I noticed the way her fingers trembled as she tugged on the wool of her cloak.

"I'm not in a state," she murmured, and had I not been worried by the ghastly colour of her face, I would have been impressed by her stern expression.

"Are you feeling ill?" Our rations had been rather bland and were not enough to fill our bellies, but no else seemed to be affected the way she was.

"I'm fine," Catiline repeated but the words were even less convincing this time around.

"Our lodgings will be ready shortly, then you can rest."

Cat sank her teeth into her lower lip and the hands that clutched at her cloak pulled the material tighter across her body. She did not seem to be comforted by my comment, and I gently bumped my hip against her.

"Catiline, what is it?" Cat swallowed as she glanced around and then suddenly her eyes lowered to the ground and it was at that moment that I noticed Caedell approaching.

"It will be dark soon," she said under her breath, and I looked at our visitor from the corner of my eye.

"Is that what worries you?" I asked just as Caedell stopped at our sides, and his brow furrowed when he noticed my friend's expression.

"How can you not be after everything you both have been through?"

"You have no need to worry, my lady, we are all well-armed," Caedell interrupted as he rested his hand on the pommel of his weapon, and Cat sighed softly.

"If what you faced truly was a gloomhor, a sword will be useless." Caedell's lips quirked at the corners, but he nodded.

"I am aware of that." He lifted a hand and placed it carefully on Cat's shoulder. "But we have a few dozen torches and we are as prepared as we can be. Besides, we were easy prey when we were journeying through the woods alone, a creature is not likely to attack a party as large as this."

Cat did not look reassured, and I narrowed my eyes at the fingers that remained on her being. Cat, however, did not seem to mind such familiarity between them, and I pressed my lips into a thin line.

"Perhaps you are in need of a distraction?" Caedell suggested while ignoring my glare.

"What exactly is it you are suggesting, sir?" I hissed through clenched teeth, and suddenly the limb I had been fixated on disappeared from Cat's shoulder and moved to hang limply at his side.

"Only something you can offer, my lady." My brows furrowed, and Cat lifted her chin to glance at Caedell's face. "And it is something I have found myself *longing* for."

"And what would that be, Lord Caedell?" Cat asked as she searched his expression, but those burning amber irises were still locked on me.

"A story, of course," he answered with a blinding smile. "I'm not sure if you recall, but your friend here has always been an excellent storyteller."

"Yes, I remember," Cat said quietly as she peered up at me with a thoughtful expression.

"And here I thought I was the only one who reminisced about those days." My cheeks heated as he continued with his staring, and I glanced at the other men of the camp.

"Well, the memories are all you'll have," I murmured. "Those days have long since passed. And even if that were not the case, this is not the time or place for such a thing."

"Nonsense," Caedell argued. "There has never been a better time."

Cat looked uncertain as she chewed on her lower lip, but then she reached for my wrist. "Perhaps Lord Caedell is right. It has been so long since I've heard any of your tales and it's been a trying day, we could all surely use a diversion."

Pleased with his victory, Caedell clapped his hands together. "Then it is decided," he said as he gestured towards the tents with a sweeping arm. "Shall we gather around a fire?"

My lips parted with my argument, but Cat tangled our

fingers together and began to tug me along, and I wondered how I ended up in this position.

"Maybe you could start with the one about the lady of the lake who waited a hundred years for her love," Cat suggested softly.

Caedell hummed in agreement. "I do remember that being one of your favourites when we were young, Lady Catiline."

The pair led me to a small fire that sat in the centre of our site, and I noticed Fynn and Donigan were already standing next to the flames that danced with the northern breeze. Lifting their heads in our direction when they heard the sound of our footsteps, they then bowed in greeting and Cat blushed prettily.

Grateful to see some colour return to her face, I decided not to point out her sudden change in attitude and instead lowered myself onto the furs that had been spread across the snow. Falling into the space next to me, Catiline pressed in close, and we waited as Caedell settled in his place across from us. The glow of the fire highlighted his features, and for a moment, I studied the shadow of dark hair that covered his strong jaw and the way the orange flickering light brightened the gold colour of his eyes.

"Well?" Caedell grinned while one of his brows lifted, and I realized I had been silent for too long. Feeling my cheeks burn again now that I had been caught gawking, I swallowed roughly and turned my attention to Cat.

"Which one was it that you wanted to hear again?" Her dark eyes brightened with excitement, and I snorted at the eager expression on her face. However, before she could even get the words out to answer my question, Caedell spoke.

"'The Lady of the Lake.'" His voice was soft, barely audible over the crackle of the fire, and I peered at him from across the flames while my lips curled at the corners.

"Is that one of your favourites too? I had no idea you

enjoyed such romantic tales," I chuckled softly. However, when Caedell did not deny it, my laughter stopped abruptly, and I realized he was watching me with wide eyes.

"What is going on?" Jumping at the sudden interruption, I cleared my throat and straightened my spine before I turned to look at my brother.

"Rígan was just about to start one of her stories," Cat explained nervously, and Skileer's gaze narrowed as he peered down his nose at me.

"You cannot be serious," Skileer sneered.

"It has been a long journey and I think we could all use a lift in our spirits," Cat whispered and then leaned into my side as she shrank away from my brother's wrath.

"Those tales are for children," Skileer scoffed. "And while you may need coddling, Lady Catiline, the rest of us have better things to do than to gather around my sister as if she is someone of importance and listen to her spew out fables and nonsense."

"Is your dislike for her stories or the fact that she is on the receiving end of our attention, Skileer?" Caedell asked in a low tone. "Because I seem to remember a time when you did not think the stories she told were just nonsense."

My brother stiffened at the words, and I watched as Caedell rose to his feet.

"Perhaps you should spend your evening elsewhere before it's too late. I would hate for you to have an incident like the one you had when we were children." Skileer bristled at Caedell's suggestion, but said nothing.

"You remember what I'm speaking of, don't you?" Caedell pushed. "That time when you wet yourself—"

"Get up," my brother demanded with a flick of his fingers, and Cat stiffened next to me. "Get up, Rígan. I won't tell you again."

"Skileer—" I began, but my brother reached down and grabbed at my arm before hauling me to my feet. However, the force of his touch made my injured leg slip, and I winced at the throbbing pain in my ankle. However, my brother ignored my obvious distress and pulled me in close.

"Haven't you caused us enough trouble on this journey?" Skileer seethed.

"I've done nothing," I murmured under my breath while I leaned away from him.

"Nothing? Is that what you think?" he demanded. "You have single-handedly delayed our journey by days. You have been nothing but a burden to the rest of us, and we are all tired of dealing with you."

Rage curled in my gut, but I noticed that the others in the camp had paused what they were doing so that they could watch us. Not wanting to escalate this further, especially with such a large audience, I pried my arm from his grasp and took a clumsy step backwards.

"They just wanted to hear a story, Skileer," I tried to reason with him, but his attention had lifted to Caedell, and I glanced back to see he was still glaring at my brother.

"The shewolf is right, it was just something to pass the time," Caedell said, though the tension in his face told me he was not as unbothered as he was pretending it be. "There is no need to be so upset over it."

"She does not need you coming to her defence, Reide," Skileer snapped and Caedell scoffed.

"You're right, she wouldn't if you would just piss off and leave her be. But I suppose you need to have someone to torment, you always have enjoyed targeting those who can't fight back." That had been the wrong thing to say, I could see it in the way my brother curled his fingers into tight fists, and I grabbed at one of his wrists before he could make a rash decision.

However, my brother snarled at my touch and pulled away from me before spitting at my feet. Crossing my arms around my torso, I waited with bated breath for him to say or do something else. Instead, he raked his cold gaze down the length of my body and then turned his focus to Caedell.

"Enjoy your stories from the *bastard*," he seethed, and I flinched at the name as he pushed past me.

Even though he no longer stood before me, my brother's heavy presence had snuffed out any ease I had felt, and my eyes caught Cat's.

"He is right, they are just nonsense," I said coolly. "Perhaps one of the guards can find you a book or something to help you pass the time."

Spinning on my heel, I took in a deep breath and ignored my knight's look of concern as I began my trek to my tent. However, I had only made it a few strides before long fingers were curling around my arm, and then Caedell turned me to face him once more.

"Don't," he demanded. "Don't let him do this."

"Do what?"

"Let him affect you like this. Don't give him that power." I rolled my eyes and shook my head.

"I'm not letting him do anything," I argued before snatching my arm from his grasp. "This was not my idea in the first place, and he wasn't wrong, those stories are for children."

"Fuck the stories," Caedell growled. "That is not what I am talking about. You were enjoying yourself, you were almost…"

"What?" I snapped. "I was what?"

"You. You were almost *you* again." He had said the words softly, but they still sent me reeling.

"I need to go," I whispered under my breath, and Caedell's brows furrowed.

"No, stay——" I shook my head while my eyes lifted from his face, and then I caught the dark stare of my knight and I felt a wave of embarrassment at the sight of him assessing us closely.

"I need to rest, perhaps I will see you later." With my dismissal, I turned my back on Caedell once more and ducked into the shelter of my tent.

"How are you?" Donigan asked as he approached, and I glanced over my shoulder at him. I had managed to remain hidden away until nightfall, however Cat had all but begged me to come eat with her. Once we had finished our rather pathetic supper of dried bread and an apple, I had moved to stand near one of the fires that burned at the end of the camp and away from the others.

"Fine," I replied before facing the flames once more, and I heard his rough sigh and then the sound of his feet crushing the snow beneath him. Stiffening, I waited until he stood shoulder to shoulder with me and then tipped my chin and hardened my expression, praying he would see the signs that I wished to be alone.

"The healer says you should be resting, especially after aggravating your injury with Skileer earlier." The fire crackled before us, and I watched the way the orange flames swayed.

"The healer should worry himself with someone who wants to hear his opinion."

"You might not want to listen, but perhaps—" Lifting my hand, I indicated for him to stop speaking, and then I turned my head to glare at him.

"I do not need any more fussing over a bruised ankle and a few scratches," I growled and Donigan's brows lifted.

"Rígan," he began, but I scoffed before facing the fire once more.

"I am not frail or feeble," I snarled. "I can ride, I can walk, and I certainly do not need to be coddled any longer."

"You've been through a great ordeal," Donigan tried again, his voice calm and quiet, and the soothing tone made me want to throw my fist into his jaw.

"And I've been through worse," I reminded him, and he frowned before glancing over his shoulder at the men who huddled around the small fires that littered across the small clearing.

Thankfully the winds had died down as the night wore on, and the snow was no deeper than a foot or so, which meant our journey could continue at a decent pace in the morning and I was eager to get going.

"They don't know that." Blinking, I stared at Donigan in confusion, and he took a step closer before lowering his voice. "To them you are another highborn lady who should not be so calm considering what she has been subject to. Ladies are not usually so stoic."

Rolling my eyes, I laughed under my breath. "Any man who says such a thing has never spent enough time with a woman."

"I just meant they are not raised to be so accustomed to the things you've seen. Things like death and creatures and blood and then with your brother today—"

"I think you'll find a woman is far more familiar with blood than any man would be," I interrupted. "We are not so weak; we deserve more credit than that. Catiline certainly does if what she told me about your training sessions are true."

Donigan lifted a hand to rub at the back of his neck, and I noticed the flush that covered his cheeks. "She has been a quick student; I will give her that."

"She told me she has even landed a few hits." Donigan nodded and I was thrilled I had managed to steer the conversation in a new direction. "Tell me though, how have you managed to continue your sparring?"

My knight glanced around once more and pressed close.

"Most of these men are easy to get by, but Fynn was not so effortlessly fooled. In the end we had to disclose our lessons to him. Thankfully he didn't question our reasoning and has actually been rather helpful with teaching Lady Cat."

My brows lifted in surprise. "He has a few sisters himself, and he has apparently trained them in such things as well."

Turning from my knight, I searched the party for the handsome soldier. Finding him at the far end of the camp, I noticed he was seated next to Caedell, and I watched the pair whisper amongst themselves.

However, it was as if I had called *his* name, like he had somehow heard me summon him from my mind, and the Heir of House Reide lifted his head while those amber eyes caught mine. Unable to look away, I held his stare until Donigan cursed under his breath and then moved in front of me, effectively breaking the connection.

"Why does he keep gazing at you like that?" my knight demanded and I frowned at him.

"Men look at me all the time, Donigan."

My knight shook his head. "Not that way."

"What way?" I asked, and he glowered at me.

"The same way he looked at you earlier when he followed you to your tent," Donigan muttered. "I'm not sure I can describe it."

He may not have been able to describe it, but when I glanced over his shoulder and met those burning irises once more, I understood.

Caedell Reide was not just watching me. It was so much more than that. It was as if he was peeling back the layers, like he was slicing away the icy armour made up of the anger and hurt before lifting the skin and bones until he got to the very heart of me. Those amber eyes were pulling me apart at the seams until I was bare and raw.

I knew then that he didn't just look at me, he *saw* me.

And I hated it.

CHAPTER

THIRTY-TWO

On any other day, the solid wooden walls of the carriage would have felt like a prison. However, it was much more preferred over having to face Caedell in the light of day, and I gladly took my place within its shelter and away from his knowing gaze. Cat, of course, had been thrilled that I had decided to remain next to her, and thankfully, Skileer had continued to be so inebriated from the tonic, he was rarely a problem.

Glaring at him now, I watched the way he uncorked the small vial given to him despite the healer's objections and frowned as he tipped his head back before hurriedly swallowing the liquid.

"Perhaps you should limit yourself today, brother," I suggested, and Cat stiffened next to me while she prepared herself for his rebuttal.

As she predicted, my brother turned his half-covered face in my direction and narrowed his visible eye. "Perhaps you should keep your mouth shut and leave me be."

"The healer said—"

"That fat old goat knows nothing," Skileer seethed. "And

280

when we return home, I will see to it that he has his title stripped from him."

"He worries for your well-being, Skileer," I tried to reason, but my brother straightened in his seat and pointed one long finger at my face.

"You think I'm a fool," he accused. "But I am not. I know what you all are plotting."

Curling a small hand around my forearm, Cat glanced at me worriedly, and I placed my fingers over hers before softening my expression in hopes of placating my brother's temper.

"Skileer, no one is plotting anything," I assured him. "It is the tonic that is making you feel so unnerved."

"Don't lie!" my brother shouted before throwing the glass vial at me forcefully, and Cat gasped as she ducked out of the way.

Thankfully, given the state of him, his aim was off, and the bottle shattered against the wall next to my head rather than against my face, and I watched as the small fragments scattered across the skirts of my gown. Looking at the shards, I admired the way they glistened under the soft light streaming through the slats of the window coverings, and then I brushed them from my lap.

Too lost in my observation, I hadn't noticed that we had stopped moving until the door of the carriage was wrenched open and Donigan appeared. Glancing around the space with frantic eyes, his attention bounced between the three of us before focusing on the broken vial that now covered the floor.

"Is everything alright?" he asked quietly, though I could hear the rage brewing just beneath the surface.

"It is none of your concern, Taith!" my brother snapped, and my knight glowered at him before moving his attention to me.

"Everything is fine," I muttered, though I could still feel the tension wafting off of Catiline as she remained stiff and quiet next to me. Moving his eyes to my friend, my knight examined her closely, taking in her shaken state.

"Lady Catiline?" he asked, and Cat turned slightly to look at him. "Are you well?"

Her dark gaze lifted to my face, and I felt badly for how affected she was from my brother's outburst. Squeezing the fingers that still lay beneath my own, I offered her as much comfort as I could without upsetting Skileer any further, and she inhaled swiftly before peering at Donigan.

"We are fine, sir," she whispered.

"Are you certain? We heard—" Donigan began to press, but Cat's mouth lifted in a half-hearted smile.

"Nothing more than an accident," she promised, and a heavy wave of guilt slammed into me at the lie she told.

"Well," Donigan began while his attention moved to me once more, and I forced myself not to shrink under his accusatory gaze. "Be sure to watch your step, I don't want you to hurt yourself."

Lifting a hand, he offered it to Cat, and she frowned at him in confusion. "Are we stopping?" she asked.

Moving, I reached to open the wooden shutter and squinted at the blinding light that flooded into the carriage before my jaw went slack at the sight before me.

The tall stone walls and pristine lakes of our home in Noordeign were impressive, but the structure before me put our palace to shame. The castle stood high and imposing, elevated above the town that sat at its base, though even its magnificent towers were dwarfed by the enormous mountains that surrounded us. Ducking my head, I peered up at the building and watched the way the sunlight bounced off the large glass windows that littered the wall overlooking the village.

"Holy Gods," Cat gasped as she took Donigan's hand before allowing him to guide her out of the door and down the steps. Moving to follow behind, I began to stand, but my brother leaned forward and shoved at my shoulder. Pushing me back into my seat, he then slammed the door shut and locked it.

"What are you—"

"I want you to listen, Rígan," he snarled as he closed the space between us, ignoring the glass that broke beneath his feet as he crouched before me. "I am not blind; I see your schemes for what they are."

"I truly have no idea what you are speaking of. There are no schemes, Skileer," I argued while rubbing a hand over my face. However, my brother snatched my wrist and pulled me forward until we were nearly nose to nose.

Staring into his uncovered eye, I tugged my arm free from his grasp and placed my palm on his chest, not pushing him away, but keeping it pressed firmly against him.

"There are no schemes," I repeated.

"So, you think I'm stupid then? As if I haven't noticed what has happened?" he whispered. "You think I'm not aware of the way the men have started to watch you?"

"That is hardly my fault," I scoffed. "Men are easily turned by a pretty face."

Skileer shook his head and then grabbed at me, holding my jaw firmly between his fingers. "If it was just your body they wanted, I would hardly care. But the way they talk about you now—"

"Talk about me?" My brows furrowed, and my brother's eye narrowed.

"The *shewolf*," Skileer hissed, and I stiffened at the venom in his voice. "That's what he calls you, is it not?"

"Skileer," I began, but his hold tightened.

"The great Heir of House Reide," he sneered. "Seems rather besotted with you and you him."

"You are imagining things," I whispered, but he laughed coldly.

"I told you I was no fool," he argued. "So imagine my surprise to see you once again forget your place."

"My place?" Skileer nodded, and I pushed at his body, though he remained unmoved. "And where would that be?"

"In my shadow," Skileer answered. "In the dark, alone and forgotten until I have a use for you. That is your place in this family, that is your fate in this world, bastard."

My brother pushed my head back before roughly releasing me from his touch. Straightening to his full height, he smoothed his hands down the front of his tunic. Certain the fabric was free of wrinkles, he ran his fingers through his dark hair and then the tips lingered on the wrap covering half of his face.

"And if that simple fact is too difficult for you to remember," he growled, "then perhaps you will recall that Caedell Reide is responsible for this."

My brother pulled at the white cloth and slowly it began to unravel until his entire face was finally bared, and I felt the air leave my lungs as I gazed up at him. His once perfect and pristine skin no longer existed. Now an ugly gash ran across his sharp features, from temple to jaw, marring the entire side of his face.

"I will be marked for the rest of my life, and he is to blame!" he shouted. "Do you not understand what that means?"

When I said nothing, my brother shook his head in disbelief and crossed his arms over his chest. "My father's blood runs through your very veins, Baxteel blood, and any attack on your family is an attack on you too. Or have you simply chosen to ignore what we stand for? Duty, family, and honour."

"I know the words of House Baxteel," I snapped. "You do not have to repeat them to me." Skileer's expression became furious, but I held his gaze.

"To the world, you are nothing, Rígan," he bit out, and I

winced at his words. "You are the result of a poorly chosen tryst on our father's part and yet he has raised you as his own. He has fed you, clothed you, and given you far more than you deserve. Far more than any other bastard would receive from an Anointed lord."

My jaw clenched shut, and I let my eyes drift from my brother's face and instead stared blankly at the wall behind him.

"So perhaps before you decide to do something stupid, you will think of all we have done for you and listen when I say that Caedell Reide is not someone to be trusted, Rígan."

Moving, Skileer reached for the lock before pressing open the door and then he ducked out of the carriage. Falling back against the wall, I sank into the seat and sighed roughly before glancing at the door where Donigan appeared once more.

"My lady?" he said softly, and his unspoken question hung in the air while he examined my face.

"All is well," I replied, but when I saw the disbelief flicker across his face, I tipped my chin as I cooled my expression. "My brother was just reminding me of my loyalties and duty."

"To whom?" my knight asked while his brows furrowed.

"To the only ones who matter," I explained, and when his frown deepened, I glanced back out at the window and peered up at the castle before me. "To my family."

A GROUP of guards had been waiting at the city limits for us to arrive, but I paid them no mind when I had stepped out of the carriage and followed dutifully behind my brother as he joined Caedell at the head of our party. In fact, I had done my best to ignore everyone as they peered at me curiously. That is until their lingering stares became too much for me to bear, and I finally turned my head and glared back. Startled by the rage in my eyes, the men ducked away from my piercing gaze and kept their distance as we made our journey through the village of Denimoore.

"Lord Krayern was expecting you days ago," the head guard muttered as he guided us towards the castle, and I took a moment to observe him. He was massive, taller than the rest of us, and his shoulders were imposing despite being covered by his long black hair, and his skin was a rich golden colour. He would have been rather handsome if it was not for his gruff expression and the way his dark eyes examined our every move.

"We would have been here earlier had we not run into some trouble on the road," Caedell replied, and the stranger slowed his pace while a dark brow lifted in question.

"The journey north is not for the meek." Caedell shrugged, and the man chuckled softly under his breath.

"Well, it certainly is not an easy feat for southerners such as yourselves." Skileer scoffed at the words and the stranger frowned at him.

"We are the Huntress's Anointed; we are familiar with the north," my brother growled. "We *are* the north."

The man's lips quirked as he struggled not to smirk. "I am not so certain I would call Noordeign the north, sir."

"My lord," my brother corrected sharply, not caring that the man was a head taller and nearly twice the width of him. In fact, every guard seemed to tower over us, which was not easily done considering Caedell and myself were well above the average height of most men.

"My apologies, *my lord*." He stopped to bow at the waist with an exaggerated flourish, and my fists clenched at his mocking.

"Tell me," Caedell interrupted, and I was grateful for the change of subject. "Are you aware that both valkhags and gloomhors live in your forests?"

"Why would we not be?" the man answered. "The forests are dense and full of creatures most are not even aware exist. Though you speak as if you have done more than just heard of them."

"I would say so, wouldn't you, shewolf?" Caedell, who stood to the left of me, caught my eye, and I bristled at the name while my brother glared at us.

Moving his focus to me, the guard let his attention lower to my boots and then slowly dragged his dark gaze up the length of my body until our eyes locked. However, his golden skin did not pale or flush the way most men's did when they were caught gawking. Instead, his lips lifted into a smirk, and he held strong despite my scowl.

"Shewolf?" he asked. "What a peculiar choice in name."

"Careful," Caedell warned, and though his tone sounded light-hearted, there was something lying beneath it that made me nearly desperate to look at him. "It was not given without cause."

"Then tell me, my lady, do you bite?" the man leered with far more confidence than he should have, and the group around us seemed to still, though a quiet inhale came from beside me. However, I remained unbothered, and when another moment passed with no reaction from me, the stranger began to finally squirm.

"As Lord Reide said"—I smirked—"I'd be careful."

The man's attention darted to Caedell, but I took a step closer, not caring that I had to tilt my chin. And when he glanced down at me, I let my attention lower to the tan skin of his throat.

"Because when I do bite, I always go for the jugular."

THIRTY-THREE

If the outside of Denimoore's castle was impressive, it was nothing compared to the lavish halls within the stone walls. Tipping my chin up, I took in the impossibly high ceilings and the banners that hung throughout the corridors. The silver thread of the protector's sigil stood strong against the purple fabric, and I studied the shield with the wolf's head for a pause before moving on to the massive piece of white cloth that caught my eye.

"It's a rather new idea," the guard from before murmured next to me, and I jumped at the sudden interruption before glaring up at him. "But it was decided by our Grand Elder that carrying a banner that unites us all may improve our efforts to stop this rebellion."

Lifting my attention once more, I studied the combination of the golden emblems. The Protector's shield offered a clean and crisp background for the Healer's setting sun and half moon that sat in the centre of the space while the Huntress's antlers curled just beneath them.

"Do they truly think it will make much difference?" my brother drawled, and I glanced at his scarred face before returning my attention back to the sigil of the Divine Triad.

"You're skeptical," the man murmured, and I shifted on my feet before looking over my shoulder.

The Heir of House Reide lingered at the back of the group, and I noticed the way he examined the white and gold for a moment before his eyes met mine. During our time together, I had seen a number of expressions painted across his handsome face. Frustration, arrogance, even relief would have been recognizable, but this look was not one I understood.

"I don't see how something so insignificant could hold such power," Skileer rebutted. "It's just fabric and thread. That is not going to make our men, nor our efforts, any more valiant."

The guard's mouth opened to respond, but a deep voice spoke out instead. "It's not the banner itself, it's what it stands for and the faith that it inspires." Turning my head, I peered at the newcomer. "Besides, even the smallest of things can change the course of our fate."

The man was tall, nearly the same height as the head guard, but was dressed in much more finery, and I frowned as I watched as his long legs carried him across the space between us. Reaching the guard, he slapped a massive hand against his armoured back. But then newcomer's hazel eyes quickly turned to Caedell, and the rest of the party moved aside so that the pair could study each other.

"I see you made it in one piece, Caed. And here I thought you had been lost to the wilderness."

"You should know better than that," Caedell chuckled in response. "I won't be so easily defeated."

"A shame," the man responded, and my jaw clenched while my eyes narrowed at him. "I hate sharing the title of the most handsome lord in Elrin."

Scoffing, Caedell crossed his arms over his chest and then shook his head. "We have never shared that title; it has always belonged to me and me alone."

The two moved at the same time, meeting in the middle while they gripped each other's arms in greeting. Now huddled close, they spoke quietly and then the man's attention lifted and slid to my brother, scanning him from head to toe. I noticed the way his brows furrowed and then his gaze moved to me.

"We were not expecting to have both heirs of House Baxteel in our halls," he said as he examined my face, and I saw my brother move from the corner of my eye.

"Well then, it is a good thing you have the honour of hosting only *one*," Skileer sneered as he brushed past me. Extending a hand towards the man, my brother waited, but the dark-haired man squared his shoulders and glared at him before turning to me once more.

"Lady Rígan, I have not had the pleasure," he said softly as he approached, and I watched as he curled an arm across his body before bending at the waist. Ignoring the glare Skileer sent my way, I offered a curtsey in return, and the man straightened once more.

"You are Lord Krayern Demys I assume," I murmured, and his lips lifted into a warm grin that only made him even more handsome, and I was certain I could hear Cat swoon from somewhere behind me.

"The one and only," he chuckled. "I do hope my brother was not too grating during your trip through the village."

"Your brother?" I turned my chin to glance at the guard and took in the similarities between the two. They shared the same golden complexion and dark features, but so did the rest of the guards. The knight was also dressed in simple silver armour, not at all what I would expect a highborn to wear.

"Aarik, why did you not introduce yourself?" Krayern demanded as he turned to glare at his brother.

"I did as you asked me to, I escorted them to the castle," Aarik argued. "Besides, what does it matter, they are not here to see me."

Rolling his eyes, Krayern turned to Caedell. "And you did not think to do it?"

Caedell shrugged and glanced between the two brothers. "I was just following his lead."

"Well then, allow me to do it myself before you are escorted to your chambers." Lifting a hand in the knight's direction, he waited for his brother to step forward. "This is Aarik of House Demys, my older brother."

THE SOUND of our footsteps echoed as we made our way through the great stone halls, and I glanced up at Aarik from the corner of my eye as he showed me to my room. He, on the other hand, stared straight ahead, not bothering to acknowledge me in any way as we journeyed through the corridors.

"These are your chambers, Lady Rígan." He lifted a hand and gestured to the door in front of us before waving to the other that was just a yard or two down the hall. "And this one will be yours."

Cat's gaze followed the direction of his fingers and then glanced around. "And the others, where will they be staying?"

The men had not bothered to accompany us and instead chose to relocate to the council room while Cat and I rested. Apparently, we were too delicate to be part of any discussion, or perhaps they just simply did not see any value in what we might have to say.

"Lord Baxteel will be staying next to his sister and Lord Caedell and Lord Dansby will have a room at the very end of the hall," Aarik explained.

"And Sir Donigan?" Cat asked, only to flush prettily at the knight's lifted brow. "And the other men, of course."

"Do you always concern yourself with your guards' whereabouts?" Aarik inquired, and Cat tucked a piece of her dark hair behind her ear before tipping her chin up, though it did little for her, her head still only came to the middle of his chest.

"I want to be sure that we will be protected by those we trust," she explained, and I was impressed by how steady her voice was as she addressed the enormous man.

"Protected from what?" Aarik questioned as his gaze moved back and forth between us. "What dangers do you think lurk in the halls of the Protector's Anointed?"

"You mean your brother's halls, correct?" I asked with a pointed look, and he scowled at me. "Because you are not the Anointed, your brother is."

"Is that what all your gawking was about?" Crossing my arms over my chest, I schooled my expression.

He was a stranger, that was true. I knew many of the greater houses, but the Protector's Anointed remained a mystery. So perhaps I had no right to expect them to be forthcoming upon our first meeting. However, there was something about his lack of introduction that made me suspicious.

"Why did you not tell us who you were?" Aarik rolled his eyes at the words, but I ignored it. "And why are you not titled?"

"I am titled," he replied.

"But not as heir," I argued. "I may not know much about your house, but I knew of your brother. However, I had no idea you even existed until today."

"That should hardly come as a surprise to you," Aarik interjected

"And why is that?" I demanded.

"Look at who your family is." Straightening my spine, I glared up at him. "It's not as if House Baxteel places any value on those they deem irrelevant. It's not as if they care for anyone other than themselves."

Perhaps if it hadn't been such a slight against my family's

honour, I would have agreed with him. But this man and his brother had remained tucked away in the north, not so much as bothering to send aid or even a letter until they were asking us to come to them. So, he had no right to have such an opinion.

"That is hardly true, we are the Huntress's Anointed," I quarrelled. "And we are spending every effort we have to fight the rebellion that threatens our people. So, tell me how exactly anyone could possibly come to such a conclusion?"

"*You* are not an Anointed, your brother is." Aarik seemed smug about the fact that he could repeat my words. "And I am fairly certain that the only reason why he has answered any call to fight is because the rebellion threatens the power he obviously holds so very dear, not because he is interested in anyone else's well-being."

"His reasonings are his own, but that doesn't take away from the fact that he has indeed answered the call, as you put it," I growled. "But tell me, where have you and your brother been while we did so? I have not seen either of you on the battlefields."

"You seem to know a lot about these battlefields," he drawled as he peered down his nose at me.

"I know that my brother has continued to put his life in danger to stop the rebels and their uprising," I snapped.

"Oh yes, your brother seems to be quite the hero indeed," Aarik chuckled dryly, and I stiffened at the sound.

Sensing the rage that was coursing through my veins, Cat placed her delicate fingers on my arm and pressed in close to my side.

"Rígan, perhaps we should go clean up and rest before dinner as Lord Krayern suggested," she advised. "It has been a long and hard journey for us both, and it's been a while since I have been able to enjoy the comforts of a warm bath."

Glancing down at her, I took in the pleading look she gave

me and then shrugged out from under her touch before agreeing. "Very well."

"Wonderful," she sighed while placing a hand over her chest. "Thank you, Sir Aarik, for showing us the way."

"My pleasure," he murmured, though his eyes had not lifted from my face, and he did not at all look as if he enjoyed even a second of our company.

"We shall see you at supper," Cat said softly, smiling while dismissing the man, and I watched as he strode down the hall before looking back to her.

"Not even half a day and you are already picking fights." She shook her head in disbelief, and I glowered. "I suppose it's a good thing Caedell warned them about your temper, I fear you are living up to the name shewolf."

THIRTY-FOUR

"ARE YOU NOT HUNGRY, MY LADY?" KRAYERN ASKED AS HE looked at me from his place at the head of the table, and I met his stare over the rim of my wineglass.

"Not really," I replied once I had finished what was in my cup, and then I reached for Cat's glass, which had remained untouched.

"Odd, I've heard that you can be particularly ravenous." Scowling, I froze with my arm outstretched and stared at the man.

"I'm not sure I know what you speak of." Krayern smirked and sipped his own drink.

"Well, I just figured you would have worked up an appetite during your time with Caedell." My fingers stroked against the cold stem of the cup, and I noticed the others around me had also stilled.

"Krayern," Caedell warned from his place across from me, and my eyes darted to his face for just an instant before I turned back to the man at the head of the table.

"I'm just asking." The Lord of Denimoore shrugged. "It must have been a *vigorous* and exhausting few days for the two of you. And then to continue the journey through the cold, surely your hunger has not yet been satiated."

"I can assure you, my lord," I replied coolly, "I am fine."

Krayern looked at his friend. "So Caedell was sure to keep you satisfied then?"

A choking noise came from Gwain's direction, but I did not move my focus from the man who was now grinning at me smugly.

"I actually found the previsions were quite generous," Cat spoke up, her voice soft and innocent, but when no one acknowledged her, she sank back into her chair and leaned in my direction. "We are talking about food, aren't we?"

Not answering her, I finally snatched her wine from its place and took a long sip and then lowered the cup back to the table before addressing Krayern. "I am more than capable of seeing that my needs are met on my own, my lord."

"How very efficient of you." His brows lifted at Caedell. "Tell me—"

"That is enough, Krayern," Caedell snapped again while one of his hands slammed down onto the table and the dishes rattled at the impact.

"My, you have quite the temper over a few innocent questions," he pouted at his friend. "Seems like an overreaction to me. You were never so sensitive before, but I suppose perhaps you have changed."

That unreadable expression was back on Caedell's face. The one from the hall with the banners, and I watched his throat bob while he swallowed.

"I thought we had been summoned to discuss important matters," Skileer muttered. My attention moved to him, and I noticed my brother's glare from over Cat's head. "My sister is not a priority."

"Have we not discussed the rebellion enough for the night?" It was Gwain who replied to Skileer. "Surely there is not much more to say on the matter for now."

Since the subject had changed, my interest was piqued, and I looked around the table. Donigan and the other knights had not been invited to dinner, and since my friend had not had a chance to speak to me before we gathered for the meal, I was still in the dark as to what had been said while I was in my room.

"What was discussed?" I asked, and every man besides Caedell seemed to share a look amongst themselves. The Heir of House Reide, however, glanced at me with a weary face.

"Nothing that you need to worry yourself over," Gwain promised, and I rolled my eyes at his earnest expression.

"As part of the Anointed—"

"Which you are not. So, you have no right to ask such a thing," Skileer seethed, and the atmosphere in the room became tense once more.

"Skileer," Gwain muttered softly, but his mouth snapped shut at the glower my brother sent his way.

Knowing I could not argue with others around, I had no choice but to keep my questions to myself. Lowering my eyes to the food on my plate, I clenched my jaw and tried to soothe my annoyance.

"Lord Baxteel," Krayern called from his seat. "Your father sent you both to Denimoore as his kin, and I would remind you of the missive he had you bring along. The one that said he plans on giving your sister a true title."

Skileer's jaw hung open, but the man was not finished. "And while war is not a topic I would usually discuss with the fairer sex, I will not have you speak to her in such a way."

Someone coming to my defence was rare and may have even been welcome on another occasion. But this man had just spent the last few minutes trying to embarrass me and I did not want nor need his help.

"Is that where the line is for you?" I snapped while my head tilted in question, and Krayern's hazel eyes widened at the sharpness of my tone. "You may tease me, you may imply distasteful scenarios that were not veiled in the least, mind you, but it is my brother who oversteps?"

The lord seemed to be at a loss for words, and I decided then to take my leave. Placing my palms on the table, I stood from my seat, ignoring the way the chair scraped across the stone floor, and lifted my chin.

"If you'll excuse me, I think I will return to my room." Cat reached for my wrist, but I dodged her touch and exited the great hall with my head held high.

LYING IN THE SOFT BED, I stared up at the canopy above me and sighed for what felt like the dozenth time before I turned on my side to peer at the large panel of glass. The moon was covered by a thick sheet of clouds that also blanketed the tips of the mighty mountains, and I watched as large snowflakes fluttered down from the grey sky.

It was quiet, peaceful even, and yet it was as if every muscle under my skin was drawn tight like a bow string. Pulling myself up, I leaned against the headboard and then moved the furs from my body. I had hoped that once I was free from their weight, I would lose the tension I was carrying. But despite the cool air that stroked the bare skin of my legs, I continued to feel unnerved and irritated.

Swinging my feet over the side of the bed, I pressed my toes into the pelt that lay across the floor and stood before stretching my arms over my head. Still, I did not feel better, and I moved towards the window so that I may look at the scene below. The small, picturesque village was dark and quiet, its townsfolk tucked away from the snow and wind, and I scanned the area for a long pause, taking in the roads and buildings before I sighed again.

"Perhaps a sleep tonic," I muttered to myself before I glanced at the heavy wood door of my room and then looked around for the robe I had discarded. Not finding it immediately, I settled for the furs that lay atop my bed and pulled them from their place before swinging them over my shoulders. Clutching the corners with one hand, I pressed the other arm out from under their weight and moved to the door. Slowly and carefully, I tugged on the handle, hoping that if I opened the door gently, it would not wake anyone else, and then I leaned forward and peered around the wood.

The hall was dark and empty, and I frowned when I realized that neither Donigan nor any of our other men were stationed outside our rooms. Stepping into the corridor, I waited for a pause. All was quiet and the other doors were firmly closed, thus leaving me to find my way to the healer on my own, I supposed.

Extending one leg out, I carefully placed my toes onto the rug that lay in the middle of the hall. Testing to see if material would quiet my footfalls, I then stepped out from the doorway and searched the corridor. For a pause, I just stood there while I tried to remember which way I had come from dinner. However, at that point I had been so angry, I hadn't been unable to pay attention to anything. By the time I found a serving boy, I nearly brought him to tears when I shouted at him to lead me back to my chambers. Now it seemed that I was paying the price for my temper.

Clutching the furs in my fist, I pulled at their weight until they came farther down my shoulders and then decided to go to the left. I moved as quietly as possible, taking my time to make sure I would not disturb anyone from their sleep as I passed their rooms and then finally made it to the last door of the hall.

However, just as I went to round the corner, I heard something. Freezing where I stood, I held my breath and waited. It was there again, a thud of some sort, and I looked at the door, trying to remember whose room it was. While I did so, silence fell over me again, but that only lasted a moment before a deep groan echoed from the room, and my eyes widened when I realized who it was who occupied those chambers.

Despite assuring myself I no longer cared about him, white, hot, seething rage burned through me, and before I could stop myself, I was grabbing for the handle and pressing open the door. I was ready to confront him, no longer giving a damn about waking the others. But it wasn't Gwain in the bed, and that deep groan I had heard in the hall had shifted into the pained whimpers I was familiar with.

Watching for a moment, I studied the way Caedell thrashed and clawed at the blankets and pillows. His hands were grabbing at anything they could reach, and his lean, muscular torso was naked and shined under the moonlight that poured into his room. His face was twisted in a devastating grimace, and the sight of it made my stomach drop.

He was in pain, and from what, I still had no idea.

"Don't!" he gasped, his voice shattering on the word, and the sound pulled me from my shock.

Stepping into the room, I quickly shut the door and then hurried to his side. However, when my thighs brushed against the edge of the mattress, I realized I had no idea what to do. I had tried waking him from these dreams before, and it had always been a struggle, and those nightmares had not seemed to be nearly as horrific as the current one that held him captive.

"Please!" he cried while his hand lifted from the furs to reach into the air. Noticing some dried blood on his knuckles, I frowned. However, before I could get a closer look, his long fingers stretched and strained, appearing frantic to grab on to something that wasn't there.

Placing a knee onto the bed, I let go of my fur cloak and grabbed on to his hand before interlocking our fingers. His grip was tight, painfully so, but I held on and brought our hands to my chest while I leaned over him.

For a moment, my touch seemed to pacify his pain, but that didn't last long, and when his lower lip began to tremble, I shifted farther onto the bed until both my knees brushed against his waist. His skin was scalding and damp, and I used my free hand to push the blankets farther down his legs.

"Not her," he sobbed. "Not her. Please, Ceara."

That was a first. I had heard his begging before, and his cries, but he had never mentioned *her* before.

Helpless, I glanced around the room, praying that a solution would come to me. However, it would seem that I would not have time to give it much thought, as Caedell had begun to thrash once more, and his voice rose in volume. Before I could think better of it, I shifted down the bed until my body was pressed to his side, and then I used my free hand to stroke his hair back from his face, the way I imagined his lover would do.

"It's alright," I whispered while my fingertips traced the lines between his furrowed brows. "Everything is okay."

His movements had settled, but I could see the flutter of his pulse just under his jaw and the rate of his breathing was still rapid. Moving closer, I folded one of my legs over his thigh in hopes that the weight would bring him ease rather than fear, and then ran my fingers through his damp hair.

For a moment I thought it had worked. Though his expression remained wounded, his struggling had ceased, and I was sure the worst of it was over. But what I had witnessed would only be the calm before the storm.

Just as I began to put distance between us, Caedell's back bowed and he tugged on my hand so sharply the force of his pull sent me sprawling across him.

Surprised by the unexpected action, I had pulled my fingers free from his and now both of my palms were pressed against his chest. Blinking down at his wide amber eyes, I felt my breath hitch and my long hair fell around us like a curtain.

Panting, Caedell stared up at me in a daze, almost as if he couldn't truly believe I was there. Slowly lifting a hand, he tucked some of the strands behind my ear before cupping my jaw softly. His fingers were warm and gentle, and his thumb stroked back and forth over my cheek.

"You're here," he whispered in awe, and while I was sure those words were not meant for me, the sound of the relief in his voice made my chest ache.

Parting my lips, I ran my tongue over the tender flesh as I tried to form a coherent sentence. But the action caught Caedell's attention, and I noticed the way he focused on my mouth while the amber irises darkened.

Surging forward, he brought his head up from the pillow at the same time he tilted my face just slightly and then he brushed his lips against mine.

It was the barest of kisses, more like a test rather than a true kiss. But it must have given him the answer he was looking for, because suddenly his hand slid up my jaw, past my ear, and into my hair. Splaying his fingers, he let them tangle in the dark brown waves and then dragged my face to his while his other arm banded over my waist until I was flush against him.

This time when our mouths touched, it was an all-consuming inferno that I felt down to my bones. The power and heat of it made my eyes shut and pushed every thought from my mind. Lost in the way he tugged my lower lip with his teeth, or how he groaned into my mouth when I flicked my tongue against his own, I hadn't noticed he was moving me until it was my back against the bed and he was leaning across my body.

Then, he was pulling away, slowly though, like he loathed to be parted from me, and I fought to catch my breath as he settled at my side. Turning to face him, I surveyed the way he seemed to sink into the mattress while he fought to keep his eyes open.

"Stay?" he murmured quietly as his lashes fluttered closed, and had he not grabbed my hand and placed it on the pillow next to his face, I was certain I would have thought I misheard him.

However, he finally seemed at ease, his face was relaxed, and his breathing was even. I, on the other hand, was reeling. My skin burned under his fingers, and my heart was still pounding beneath my ribs. But most distracting of all was that sharp stinging knowledge that he had thought I was her, the woman he had called out for. He believed I was Ceara.

No time hath she to sport and play:
A charmed web she weaves alway.
A curse is on her, if she stay
Her weaving, either night or day,
To look down to Camelot.
She knows not what the curse may be;
Therefore she weaveth steadily,
Therefore no other care hath she,
The Lady of Shalott.

She lives with little joy or fear.
Over the water, running near,
The sheepbell tinkles in her ear.
Before her hangs a mirror clear,
Reflecting tower'd Camelot.
And as the mazy web she whirls,
She sees the surly village churls,
And the red cloaks of market girls
Pass onward from Shalott.

Sometimes a troop of damsels glad,
An abbot on an ambling pad,
Sometimes a curly shepherd lad,
Or long-hair'd page in crimson clad,
Goes by to tower'd Camelot:
And sometimes thro' the mirror blue
The knights come riding two and two:
She hath no loyal knight and true,
The Lady of Shalott.

But in her web she still delights
To weave the mirror's magic sights,
For often thro' the silent nights
A funeral, with plumes and lights
And music, came from Camelot:
Or when the moon was overhead
Came two young lovers lately wed;
'I am half sick of shadows,' said
The Lady of Shalott.

"THE LADY OF SHALLOT" PART II
BY LORD ALFRED TENNYSON (1832)

PART TWO

PART TWO

CHAPTER
THIRTY-FIVE

The creaking sound of the door opening woke me from my deep sleep, and I glanced over my shoulder to see the shocked face of a young maid at the door. Lifting onto my elbow, I met her gaze with my own bleary eyes, and then my head swung to my right and I saw that Caedell was still slumbering soundly at my side.

For the second time, I had lain next to him for an *entire* night and not once had I woken. Lost in that realization, I remained frozen and I was unsure what to do. But then the woman cleared her throat and broke the daze I had been under.

"Apologies, m'lady." She rushed to give me a clumsy curtsey before scurrying from the room and then the door was closing behind her. Untangling my fingers from Caedell's, I flew from the warmth of the bed, stumbling over the pelt I had brought with me the night before, and I chased after her into the hallway.

Snatching at her arm, I spun her to face me. Unable to stop herself, the girl gazed up at my face nervously while she swallowed, and I tightened my hold on her wrist while glaring down at her. "You saw nothing."

Her sharp inhale was noticeable given how close we were, and her attention darted around the hall as she searched for an escape. I, however, was unwilling to release her until I was certain that I would not hear the other maids gossiping about what she had witnessed, and I bent my knees so I could look directly into her face.

"You saw nothing," I repeated, my voice quiet, but threatening.

"Yes, m'lady," she croaked out, but I still wasn't convinced that I believed her.

"Should I hear any whispers about this, I will know it came from you," I explained. "And no one, not your friends, not your lord, not even the Gods themselves, will save you from my wrath."

Uncurling my fingers, I pushed her arm towards her and gestured with my chin towards the end of the hall. Pressing her hand to her chest, she spun on her heel and fled without another word. Taking in a deep breath, I watched the hem of her skirts disappear around the corner.

"Rígan?" Donigan's voice called from the other end of the corridor, and I stiffened at the sound before glaring over my shoulder at him.

"Where the fuck have you been?" I demanded when I noticed that he was fastening his sword to his hip and his appearance looked rather dishevelled.

Hurrying his strides, he closed the distance between us and then lifted a hand to rub at the back of his neck. "I—"

"You were not here. You were not where you should have been," I snarled. "Did you forget you have a duty to me and my house or do you just not care?"

"Rígan," he started, but I reached forward and curled my fingers around the edge of his breastplate and pulled him close.

"Don't you dare address me in such a place where anyone

could be listening," I hissed, and Donigan's face went slack with surprise. "You should have been here."

His dark brows furrowed, and he searched my face for a long moment. "What has happened?"

"Nothing," I growled and then I released my hold on him before crossing my arms over my chest.

"No, someone has hurt you." My teeth clenched together at his assumption, and his eyes moved around the hall, searching for the culprit. "What happened? Was it Skileer?"

"No one has hurt me," I argued, and my knight leaned back to get a better look at my face before tilting his head.

"Well, at the very least, someone has offended you." Rolling my shoulders, I lowered my arms and forced myself to relax my posture. It was then that Donigan's attention wavered and drifted lower. However, after only a quick second, his eyes were lifting to the ceiling and a bright pink flush marred his face. Confused by his reaction, I looked down to follow the path his gaze had just taken and gasped.

The shift I had chosen was thin, and given the chill of the air, I realized there was no way of hiding just how fine the material was. Not to mention the hem reached an inch or so above my knee and the white colour was translucent in the right light. Light much like the morning sun that was now shining through the window behind my knight. And when I noticed the way the rays cast their glow on the front of my body, I realized why the maid had been scandalized.

"I shall head back to my chambers," I muttered while moving my arms to cover me. Donigan, however, straightened, and his eyes, which had still been aimed up at the ceiling, found mine in concern.

"*Back* to your chambers?" he asked as he looked to the door behind me. "Where exactly are you coming from?"

It was my turn to stutter over an answer, and I turned towards the solid wood plank at my back. "I—"

"Why are you out here?" I peeked at him nervously and

saw the moment it dawned on him. He shook his head, his gaze turning disappointed. "It was Gwain, wasn't it?"

"Gwain?" I scoffed, but my knight had only begun his lecture.

"I had hoped you were done with that, with *him*." Donigan ran a hand over his face and turned to glower at the door that must have belonged to the man in question.

"I should run him through." Moving before I could stop him, Donigan began to stride down the hall, and I rushed after him, grabbing at his metal-clad arm before hauling him backwards.

"You will do no such thing!" I growled as I pulled him farther and farther away from Gwain's chambers.

"He deserves nothing less after everything!" Donigan barked. "After everything he has done and then what he said last night."

My hand went slack on his arm, and I blinked at him in confusion. "Last night?"

"That fool had the audacity to make some sort of claim on you after you had gone to bed!" Shocked by the words, I let my palm slide from the metal of his armour and I waited until he faced me.

"What?" I whispered, and my knight nodded with a grave expression.

"I don't know exactly what was said," he explained. "We had been dismissed from the room, but Aarik remained."

"And what did Aarik say?" I demanded sharply.

"He told me that Gwain had made some sort of comment about you. Aarik thinks he did so in hope of gaining favour from the other lords." He looked troubled as he examined me closely. "Almost as if he thought the others would be impressed by him if they knew about your…relationship."

My jaw hung as I gazed at my friend, and he exhaled roughly. "Are you really that surprised? It's not as if he has any other victories to boast about."

"So, he used me to gain their admiration?" I whispered, and my chest tightened at the words.

"He tried," Donigan corrected. "But it seems it did not go accordingly."

Frowning, I searched my knight's face. "How so? Did Skileer—"

"Not Skileer," he interjected. "Caedell."

Running my fingers through my hair, I let my gaze roam across the hallway, and when my eyes landed on the door I had left just minutes ago, I swallowed. "What did he do?"

"Apparently Lord Dansby may not be joining us for some days." When I shot my knight an impatient glare, he continued. "Not after the beating Caedell gave him."

"Beating?" My mind thought back to the wounds on Caedell's knuckles, and my eyes widened.

"Aarik says Gwain was lucky that Krayern stopped Caedell from going any further, though apparently Skileer did nothing but watch." That detail did not surprise me, but Donigan was not finished. "Caedell, however, was adamant that he should cut out Gwain's tongue."

"And Aarik did not tell you exactly what was said? He did not say what warranted such a reaction?" I wondered, and my knight shook his head.

"He would not repeat it," Donigan muttered angrily.

"At least one of the Demys brothers has some decency," I grumbled, and it was Donigan's turn to frown in confusion. "Krayern spent a bit of time at dinner implying that Caedell and I may have been inappropriate with each other while we were travelling together."

"No wonder Gwain decided to make a fool out of himself." Annoyed at the excuse, I scowled at him.

"If that's all it takes for a man to disregard someone they are meant to care for, then men are fools," I hissed, and he raised a dark brow at me.

"Certainly the ones you chose are," he agreed. "So,

considering that fact, I have no idea how you could believe Caedell is a better option." My gaze widened at his implication, and he crossed his arms over his armoured chest.

"Caedell? Caedell is not an option, and I have never thought otherwise!" I argued, but he just rolled his eyes.

"Then how do you know which room is his, and why do you keep looking at his door?" Caught, I felt my face flush, and Donigan sighed roughly and then reached past me. Grabbing at the brass handle, he pressed it open and ushered me back into my chambers.

"And you think men are the fools?" Before I could even defend myself, or deny him once more, Donigan closed the door with a firm click, and I glared at the wood all while telling myself he was mistaken.

CAT WAS NEARLY QUIVERING with excitement as we were guided through the halls, and had yet to notice or mention my solemn attitude. Thankfully the lady's maid who led our tour also ignored my mood, though I couldn't help but wonder if that was more to do with my threats to her fellow staff member and less because she was being polite.

"And this is the library," the woman said softly as she gestured to the open doors before us.

Cat clapped her hands together and pressed them to her chest as she gasped at the sight. The room was impressive, with its elevated ceiling, tall windows that faced the mountains, pretty blue chairs, and large tapestry that hung in the corner of the room. However, none of it, not even the rows and rows of books, held any interest to me now, especially when I knew the men had gathered once more to discuss the uprising.

"Oh, how wonderful," I drawled sarcastically, ignoring the sharp poke to my ribs from Cat's elbow. "But tell me, where is it that the men have assembled?"

"My lady?" the maid asked uncertainly, and I scowled at her.

"Surely you know where their meeting is being held, correct?" She glanced at Cat for a pause, almost as if she was hoping my friend would intervene. But Catiline remained silent. "Are you going to answer me?"

"They are in the council room, my lady," she whispered, and my eyes flickered back to the library for a moment before I glanced down the hall.

"And where would I find such a room?" Her face clouded with confusion, and I exhaled roughly in annoyance. "If you won't lead me there, the least you could do is tell me where to go."

"The council room is for the men, my lady," she replied nervously. "I have been instructed to bring you both here. Soon we will be serving tea."

She said that as if it was meant to dissuade me from leaving, and I chuckled softly. "I have no interest in books or tea," I snapped. "So, I will ask you again, where will I find the council room?"

Cat was chewing at her lower lip anxiously while her dark eyes bore into the side of my face. I, however, had not looked away from the servant, and when I saw her shoulders sag under the weight of my glare, I knew I had won.

"Take a right at the end of the hall and follow the red rug until you reach the portrait of the Protector," she explained with a shaky voice. "The council room will be just around the corner from there."

Pleased to have gotten my answer, I gave the woman a nod of thanks and then placed my hand on Cat's delicate back before turning to her. "Enjoy your books and tea, I will come find you after."

"Are you sure you would not rather stay?" Her dark eyes were pleading, but I shook my head.

"I may not have a say in anything they decide," I admitted more to myself than her, "but I would at least like to be privy to the decisions they make."

"What if your attendance upsets Skileer?" she asked worriedly.

"Don't worry about that," I reassured her. "I can handle my brother."

Cat did not look convinced, and given my brother's behaviour during our journey, I could hardly blame her. However, having Skileer in that room, knowing he was there without someone to oversee him, was far more terrifying than his temper.

"I will find you after," I promised again with a soft smile, and she frowned as she watched me turn away. However, just as I reached the end of the hall, Cat called out for me, and I glanced over my shoulder at her in question.

Watching as her lips curled up in a sly smile, I held my breath. "Say hello to Caedell. I'm sure *he* will at least be pleased to see you."

My cheeks heated and my brow furrowed, but I said nothing in response. I couldn't even if I wanted to—her words had temporarily thrown me. But as I moved through the halls, a tiny part of my being that was tucked away in the very depths of my chest hoped, just maybe, she would be right.

THIRTY-SIX

"You are the one who summoned us here!" My brother's infuriated voice rang out, and I quickened my stride as I neared the room.

The grand double doors were just slightly ajar, but I stopped as I reached them and then peeked through the crack. Krayern, who was sitting at a large round table, glared at my brother while Skileer paced back and forth, and I shifted my head to look at the other end of the space. Donigan had been right, Gwain was nowhere to be seen, but I could see the side of Caedell's face, and I studied him closely as I tried to understand his expression.

"Yes, I did," answered the Lord of Denimoore. "But that does not give you any authority here."

"We are equals; my voice counts for something!" Skileer wailed as he flung his arms out at his sides like a child throwing a tantrum would.

"Is that what you think?" Caedell asked, his tone low and deep, and I felt my skin prickle at the sound while the air rushed from my lungs.

"We are all part of the Anointed," Skileer proclaimed,

though his voice cracked nervously, and I winced at his weakness.

"We are, but that does not equate to us all having even sway when it comes to these types of decisions." It was a voice I recognized but couldn't place, and I carefully moved again so that I may get a better look at the part of the room I could not easily observe.

He was shorter than the others, and lean. His skin was a rich brown, his hair was black and was pieced together in long thick twists that nearly reached his waist. Scanning his face, I took note of his full lips, high cheekbones, and slightly angular dark eyes. He was handsome, undeniably so, and when I sensed a warmth that reminded me so much of Catiline, I realized this was the grown version of a boy who I had not seen in nearly a decade.

Synrick was the Heir of House Moorel. They were the Healer's Anointed and watched over the southern province of Elrin. They were a wise group and would choose peace and tranquillity over conflict. Synrick had those same characteristics. He was shy and quiet but no less clever, and I remembered him having the patience of the Healer himself even from a young age.

"You should have no sway, Synrick," my brother growled. "You are the Anointed of the Healer, what would you know about fighting a war?"

"Standing here, I would say he's the smartest of you all," a woman chimed in, and my forehead nearly collided with the door when I heard her.

Shifting again, I searched the room for her. She was tucked in the corner, holding a wineglass against her chest while she seemed to study the men. She had golden skin and black hair, and though I could only see her side profile, I could tell that she bore a striking resemblance to Aarik.

"Mother," Krayern sighed as he rubbed his face tiredly. "We already know your stance on this."

"Good, then I won't have to repeat myself," she snapped back.

"Lady Demys, if I may," Caedell began, but I heard her interrupt him with a rough scoff.

"The last time you used my title, you were six and ten, Caedell Reide," the woman muttered. "Don't bother with that tactic or any other attempt at charm, it will not get you far."

"Dyani," Caedell started again. "The rebellion is showing no signs of stopping. Deciding to go about it in that manner will escalate the issue. I beg you to reconsider."

"And when have you ever chosen to take a gentle hand to things, Caedell the Undying?" A silence fell over the room, and my teeth sank into my lower lip, running over the scar that marked the corner of the flesh while I waited for someone else to speak up.

"While I do agree with you, Dyani, Caedell is not wrong for wanting to preserve the lives of our people," Synrick said softly, and it was my brother now who laughed.

"These rebels are not our people," he growled. "They are bandits, they are criminals, and they are polluting the rest of Elrin with their notions! They are a plague that must be eliminated before it poisons more."

"What do you say, Aarik?" Krayern asked as he glanced at his brother, who stood with his back to the rest while he gazed out the window.

"I think Skileer is right." My brother preened at the words, and my nose wrinkled at his pleased smile. "We must not be soft with those who question us and who want to destroy the peace we have been charged in keeping."

"The Gods gave us the duty to maintain the harmony they created," Dyani agreed. "We cannot fail them."

"So we are all in agreement then?" Krayern asked as he peered at his comrades. Both Synrick and Skileer nodded, but Caedell was no longer looking at them. No, his gaze had moved, and those deep amber eyes were locked on my own.

"I think I would like to hear from the shewolf." It seemed as if the room had gone silent—though I couldn't be certain, because now that I had been caught, all I could hear was the pounding of my heart.

Pushing away from the wood, I straightened to my full height as I prepared for a confrontation. And when the doors swung open, I was face to face with my brother's furious glare.

"What are you doing here?!" he demanded as he reached for me, but I slapped his hand away and took a step back.

"Do not touch me," I snarled, and that rage that had been burning in his dark eyes only grew.

"I will do as I damn well please." His hand curled around my biceps, and he hauled me along behind him and into the room.

Rising abruptly from his seat, Caedell watched as my brother pulled me towards the table and then a gloved hand was reaching forward. Grabbing at my brother's wrist, he twisted the joint until Skileer cried out and his fingers lifted from me.

"She told you not to touch her," Caedell warned, and Skileer's wide gaze bounced between us for just a moment before that rage returned.

Sensing that he was not the only one observing us closely, I stepped aside to put some distance between us and then turned my chin to meet the striking silver gaze of the Lady of Denimoore.

"So, you are the one Caedell calls shewolf," she murmured as she searched my face, and then she was moving, circling me slowly, as if she was taking note of every detail. "A stunning thing to be sure, far too striking to be a true Baxteel, but I will be honest, I am rather disappointed that I do not see the fearsome creature I have been warned about."

"Give her time, she will show you her fangs sooner or later," her younger son chuckled softly. "Then you won't be able to see anything else."

Snapping my head in his direction, I narrowed my eyes at Krayern, and watched as he lifted his palms in surrender before his mother hummed softly.

"Ah, there she is," Dyani whispered.

"And who are you?" I growled as I swung my attention back to her and crossed my arms over my chest.

"Oh, sweeting, don't insult both of our intelligence by pretending like you have not been eavesdropping behind that door for the last few moments." Flushing, I knew I was caught, but I did not soften, and her brow lifted. "I am Dyani, Lady of Denimoore. Now are you going to properly introduce yourself or must I rely solely on the second-hand knowledge I have been given?"

"Rígan," I bit out begrudgingly, and she nodded before stepping close. Lifting a hand, she gestured to the chairs before me, and Synrick, Skileer, and Krayern took it as a sign to find their own seats while Aarik remained by the window.

"You may sit now, Caedell," Dyani drawled as she addressed the man who lingered at my side. "Your shewolf is no longer in need of your hovering."

The sound of the heavy wooden chairs scraping over the stone floor echoed through the grand room, and I took a moment to observe the walls that encased us. Just like every other part of this castle, the space was stunning. The walls were tall and imposing, and the tapestries that fluttered above were vibrant with colour as they hung from the vaulted ceiling. The table was massive, its rounded edge smooth and worn, and our seats, with their high backs and thick arm rests, were really more like thrones.

Sinking into the plush cushion, I let my arms rest on the table and peered at the men. None of them seemed the least bit surprised to see me, though Synrick took a moment to study me, and I shifted under his gaze.

"I was under the impression this meeting was for men

only," I murmured as my eyes glanced at Dyani for a moment, and my brother scoffed and then narrowed his gaze.

"It is for the Anointed and people of significance," he corrected. "Not bastards."

One would think the term would no longer carry any weight given how often I was reminded of my deficient lineage. However, I was not immune to the sting the word brought me, and I clenched my jaw at the sensation.

"Aarik," Dyani called out, her voice a welcome interruption. "Do you have something to say about that?"

All heads turned to the man in question, though Skileer and I seemed to be the only ones confused. Glaring at my brother, Aarik crossed the space between them and stood behind his chair. Now that he was blocking the sun that poured in through the glass, his massive frame cast a shadow over Skileer, and I frowned.

Not sensing the turn the energy in the room had taken, my brother leaned back and laughed as he looked to his comrades. "Why would he?"

Those dark eyes turned dangerous as they peered down at the top of my brother's head, and I stiffened at the sight as I tried to think of a way I could deescalate the situation. Lifting her cup to her mouth, Dyani smiled and then sipped at her wine.

"We do not take kindly to such prejudices here," Aarik snapped, and finally my brother had the sense to see that he had made a mistake with his words.

"Prejudices?" Skileer murmured as he looked around the table.

"You are aware that Aarik is not the Lord of Denimoore, correct?" Dyani asked as she lowered the glass to the table and then placed her hands on her lap delicately. She appeared to be every inch of a proper highborn lady. Her posture was flawless, her long purple gown was stunning, and she looked like a queen sitting next to me. But there was something menacing about the way she stared at my brother, and I was unable to move my attention from her as she inspected him thoroughly.

"I am," Skileer croaked out.

"Then considering he is my first-born, you must have gathered the reason why he does not hold that title." I had questioned the very thing our first night but had somehow been blind to the obvious answer until that moment.

Aarik Demys was not a true heir; he was a bastard. A bastard who was still given power and a title and held importance to those around him. Aarik Demys was the very thing I loathed, and yet, he had everything I had ever wanted.

CHAPTER

THIRTY-SEVEN

Skileer continued to gawk at the woman before him, as if he couldn't fathom what she had just said, and the others around me were tense while they waited for someone to break the awkwardness.

"But you look so much alike," Skileer sputtered out, and I wished the Gods would open the earth beneath my chair so that I may be swallowed up and taken from this room.

"He is my son," Dyani murmured, and the confusion on my brother's face grew.

"But he's a bastard." It took everything in me not to cover my face in embarrassment, and the rest of the men looked just as uncomfortable.

Lifting a brow, Lady Demys nodded. "Yes, he is my offspring, he is from my womb."

"Then you lay with another, someone other than your husband." Lifting a hand towards her chest, the woman plucked at the delicate gold chain that lay around her neck and began to fiddle with the shield-shaped charm that hung from the thread of metal.

"I did," Dyani confirmed. "Would you like to know how many? Or perhaps you would be more interested in the details, such as how big their cocks were and how adequate they had been at the act.”

One of her sons exhaled loudly, though I couldn't be sure which one, and Synrick seemed to choke on his own spit and then began to pound at his chest with a closed fist. Caedell, however, was the most unnerved of the group, which was surprising, and I took note of the flush covering not only his cheeks, but his neck as well.

“But you are of an Anointed family,” Skileer stammered as his eyes darted around the room while he sought out assistance from one of us. “You are the Lady of Denimoore, you can't do that.”

“I think you'll find I already have,” Dyani pointed out as she crossed her legs before leaning forward onto the table. “Here, we do not hold the same notions as you and your father. We do not punish a child for things they cannot control, and we do not ridicule those who sometimes find love outside of marriage.”

Looking at Krayern, she smiled softly and then moved her attention back to my brother. “I did as was expected of me. I married a man of noble blood, one of the Gods' favourites, no less, and I cared for my husband. But before him, I had found love, and something that comes from such a powerful bond should not be admonished.”

Aarik shifted uneasily behind my brother and my gaze lifted to his. I never knew my mother; I didn't know if my father had even truly cared for her, let alone loved her. Although, considering I was regarded as a mark on my family's name, I could only assume that love did not play a part in my creation, and I realized I had found another reason to be envious of Aarik.

“Now,” Dyani said as she leaned against the back of her chair once more while her fingers continued to fiddle with the necklace. “Shall we get back to the topic at hand, or was anyone else looking to discuss their previous bed mates?”

"We shouldn't have wasted so much time talking about this to begin with," Aarik growled as he finally moved to the empty chair that was to the left of his brother, and when he sat down, I glanced around the table.

"What was being decided?" I asked while doing my best to ignore the murderous glare from my brother.

"The rebel forces have grown over the last few months and with their numbers comes more and more territory at risk," Krayern explained. "We have had a dozen raids just in the north alone this season."

"But you've managed to keep them at bay." Aarik nodded at me.

"For now," he agreed. "But the winter will be difficult, many will go hungry, and they will be looking for someone to blame."

"Which gives them all the more reason to join the uprising," Krayern added. "They not only believe that the Gods are at fault, but that we share the responsibility as well."

"It's more than that," Synrick sighed as he rubbed at his temples. "The very core of the rebellion revolves around the desire to abolish our houses and the other nobles. They think if they dismantle the Gods' chosen, if they destroy us and create dissent amongst those who are faithful, then they will take power away from the Divine Triad. But now I worry they are hoping to have another take their place."

"It is said that the High Commander is a devoted servant to the Reaper, despite all the God has done to the people of Elrin in the past," Krayern whispered, and both Caedell and I tensed at the name.

"What?" Skileer asked as he looked between Synrick and Krayern. "What has he done?"

"The first and forgotten God was one of vast power," the Healer's Anointed explained. "He began his torment of the Forefolk because he was displeased by their love for the Divine Triad and their resentment towards him. He was ruthless and unmerciful, and it took nearly two hundred years and *all* three Gods to shut him away."

The room had gone silent at Synrick's words, but he continued. "At that time, the people of Elrin had been thrilled to see him leave after suffering so long under his reign. And with him gone, the tragedies that had nearly brought Elrin to its knees went with him. The Forefolk began to live long and pleasant lives once more."

"But, you think he has returned?" I asked worriedly. "And that the High Commander worships him?"

"I can't say for certain, as I mentioned we have only heard quiet rumblings," Synrick said softly.

"Did Ceara have any news, Caed? I know it would not be current given that it arrived this morning and it would have taken a fortnight to reach us. But did she say anything about what was happening in Port Huronian? Was there any word of rebel forces or information on what was occurring across the rest of the provinces?" Krayern asked, and my heart fell to my stomach at the name.

Keeping my head straight, I took in a quiet breath and then peeked at Caedell. His face was unreadable, but I did notice the muscle in his jaw twitch.

"She said nothing of consequence," he murmured through clenched teeth, and I swallowed past the tightness in my throat.

"So there is no *actual* true proof," I croaked out, hoping that my words would chase the heaviness in my chest away, and Synrick hummed softly and then offered me a weak smile.

"As I said, we know nothing with absolute certainty," he explained while his dark eyes moved around the room. "However, there have always been whispers that a part of the God still lingers in this world despite his absence."

"And you think these rebels may have found something?" I questioned.

"Even if they have not," Krayern interjected, and I took

in his weary expression, "it is more than just gossip. I think that they have begun to worship him once more in hopes that he may be merciful to those suffering."

The uprising had grown stronger than any of us had anticipated, that was to be sure. However, I was not ready to just assume that they had completely turned their backs on the Divine Triad only to fall to their knees for another God, and a forgotten one at that.

"But what they fail to remember," Dyani whispered from her place on the chair, "is that he is not a God of prosperity, but of destruction. He will not aid them, and they will burn the world to ash if they find a way to bring him to power once more."

"And so you have decided…?" I trailed off in hopes someone would have a solution to a problem that now seemed far worse than I could have ever imagined.

"We will meet these traitors with the wrath of the Divine Triad," Aarik growled as he slammed one of his massive palms against the solid wood surface of the table. "Once we are free from those who would cross our Gods, Elrin will flourish again."

"That, however, may take the power of every noble house." Krayern sighed. "And I am not sure they'll be eager or willing to answer our call."

Turning, I sought out the gaze of the Lord of Denimoore. "From what we have seen, these men are nothing more than common folk, surely we do not need every noble force to deal with this."

"They are no longer just common folk though." Synrick exhaled roughly as he sank into his chair, almost as if the heaviness of the world was slowly weighing down onto his shoulders, and I frowned at him in confusion.

"There are reports that some of the higher ranked are not common at all. It appears that some of our own have deceived us." Synrick wiped a hand down his tired face before clearing his throat. "It is also said that some may even possess magic."

"Magic?" Skileer scoffed as he stood abruptly from his chair. "What kind of magic?"

"The kind that would keep an army from failing," Caedell answered with a low voice. "The kind that would ensure his soldiers would outlive us all."

Sneering, my brother rolled his eyes and lifted a hand to wave the words away. "There is no such power."

I could not blame him for his disbelief; it would have seemed impossible to me as well if I hadn't witnessed the power for myself. Picturing the hulking man from the tavern, I remembered the way those bloody jagged edges of his wound began to close and the sound of his gasping breath. I remembered the strength that had coursed through his veins as he had tossed me aside and the speed at which he moved.

That man had not been ordinary. I knew that the moment I set eyes on him, and now I understood why.

"We need to end this rebellion at all costs," I whispered, and all eyes turned to me. "We must do it and we must do so now. They need to be stopped before more have the chance to acquire this magic."

BY THE END of the meeting there had been a missive sent out for every noble house of Elrin, and despite my brother's protests, I had been allowed to stay until they adjourned. It was an odd thing, the feeling of being treated as if I was nearly their equal, and though it was apparent that Skileer hated it, for the first time in a long time, it felt as if some of those jagged edges inside me had been smoothed. However, knowing that it would not last, I reminded myself of what my life would be once again when we left this room and its occupants.

Pinching the skirt of my gown between my thumb and index finger, I smoothed my pads across the soft fabric and watched as Krayern moved towards the door. Turning when he reached the entrance, he glanced at his friend who remained in his seat and grinned slyly.

"Will I be seeing you two for supper?" he asked while he lifted a brow at Caedell.

"If it will be a repeat of last night, I feel I will have no choice but to decline," Caedell growled as he glared at the man from over his shoulder. But Krayern did not look the least bit worried, and he slid his gaze to me.

"It does not seem as if my little bit of teasing caused any harm that could not be repaired." With a tilt of his head, he eyed the space between our chairs and then crossed his arms over his chest. "Or rather, has not *already* been repaired. I knew she was made up of hardier stuff, it's no wonder you—"

Standing from his seat, Caedell spun on his heel and pointed one long gloved finger at the door. "Leave, damn you!"

Snickering, Krayern fled, and I blinked at the now-empty doorway for a long moment before seeking out those amber eyes. Caedell looked tired, his complexion was dull, and the skin beneath the golden-coloured irises was nearing a dark purple. When I had left him this morning, he had seemed at ease. But now I couldn't help but wonder how long and how often those nightmares had plagued his sleep and what was their cause.

"Are you alright?" I asked, unsure of how else to go about starting this conversation.

"Fine," he answered with a clipped tone, and I glowered at him.

"You don't seem it," I pointed out rather snidely. "Or look it for that matter."

Moving around the heavy wood bulk of his seat, Caedell looked as if he was about to go to the door, but then he stilled and one of his gloved hands rose, curling those long fingers over the back of the chair. I noticed the way the leather stretched over his knuckles while he hung his head with a rough exhale.

"It is nothing," he whispered, and I angled myself in his direction in an attempt to get a better look at him.

Perhaps if he saw my face, saw that I was not truly trying to mock him but rather was genuinely concerned, he would tell me what was wrong. Maybe he would give me a hint of some sort, some small indication as to what he had been thinking of the night before when he had pinned me to his bed. Or rather *who* he was really thinking of.

I had been sure this morning that it had been a mistake on his part. That he had been panicked and terrified by his dreams and truly thought I was *her*. But after Catiline's comment and the way he seemed to linger by my side today, I wondered if I had jumped to the wrong conclusion despite the fact that *she* had written to him.

And maybe, against all odds and any logic, he felt it too, that peculiar lingering warmth—that spark of heat that seemed to pass between us when we were close.

"Caedell, I would not speak of it to any others," I promised while I tried to gather the courage to be honest with the man before me. "I have suffered through things similar; I know how it can feel—"

"Don't," he snapped. "Don't act as if you have any idea of what I have to suffer through." His hand tightened its hold on the wood, and I was sure the leather of his glove would split at its seams.

"It is nothing," he repeated. "Last night was *nothing*."

Perhaps they would not be the only stitches to rip open.

"But—" Caedell pushed away from the chair and crossed his arms over his chest while he peered down at me with a smug grin, though the look in his eyes didn't seem to match the rest of his expression.

"You have a habit of being misguided when it comes to those who welcome you into their bed." Ice curled in my gut, and my nails scratched at the arm rests beneath my fingers. "And you continue to think it is more than what it is, that you have more significance than what you do. Gwain has been proof enough of that."

I was rendered speechless, too caught up in the sharpness of his words to do anything but allow him to cut me further. "So, believe me when I say last night was nothing. And for you to think otherwise just proves how foolish you can be."

THIRTY-EIGHT

I HAD NOT LEFT MY CHAMBERS SINCE I HAD RETURNED FROM the council room and even ignored Cat when she had softly knocked on my door. I had heard the worry in her voice as she called for me, obviously aware something had gone amiss during the meeting, though I was certain she had thought it was due to my brother and not because of Caedell's cold dismissal. Too embarrassed to tell her the true reason, I had remained silent and waited for her to leave me be.

Now perched in the chair that sat before the vanity, I glanced at the looking glass and took in my reflection. The exhaustion I had seen on Caedell's face earlier matched my own, and I frowned at the state of my appearance. The sharp features were there, of course, the high cheekbones and piercing eyes, but the impenetrable mask I had grown fond of seemed weak at best. Unnerved by the fragility of the woman looking back at me, I turned to my trunk and pulled out warmer clothes. While dining with the others may have been out of the question, there was no reason why I had to sulk alone in my darkened room, and I was certain I would feel more like myself if I could just have the chance to escape the stone walls of the castle. Changing quickly, I rushed to the door and tugged it open.

However, unlike last night when I had ventured off on my own, the halls were brightened by the torch light, and I was, in fact, not alone. The man who stood guard across the hall lifted his wary eyes to me as I stepped out into the corridor, and I folded my cloak over my arm before addressing him.

"Good evening," I said coolly. "Where is Donigan?"

Swallowing, the man glanced down the long corridor before facing me once more. "I believe he is taking his supper with the other men, my lady."

"Which men?" I asked with a narrowed gaze.

"Lord Caedell and Lord Krayern insisted he dine with them tonight."

"And you were ordered to be stationed here," I concluded. "Odd, considering it is just me, you would think they would have preferred to have you elsewhere."

"Actually, I think that's exactly why they put me here," the man answered, but when my expression hardened, he hurriedly bowed at the waist before trying his explanation once more. "I mean my lords did not wish for you to be alone."

"Well, as considerate as that may be, I wish nothing more than to be left alone. So, you may go."

The man did not seem surprised by my dismissal but rather appeared to be gathering his courage to argue. I, on the other hand, was quickly losing patience, and when his lips parted to speak again, I lifted a hand.

"Do not bother, you have been cleared from whatever task they gave you." But the man still made no move to leave. "While I admire your dedication, I must advise you that quarrelling with me is not for the faint of heart, and I am convinced you do not have what it takes, so be smart, and leave. Now."

"You may go, Ryckard," a voice called from down the hall, and I looked at Aarik as he strode towards us.

The guard before me sagged in relief at the sight of his lord and offered me a clumsy bow before nearly racing down the hall.

"Going somewhere?" Aarik asked as he closed the distance between us, and I examined his massive armoured body before I tipped my head back to peer up at him.

"Just going out for some fresh air," I muttered as I pulled my cloak from my arm and flicked it in the air. Certain it was free of the folds, I swung it over my back and tucked it around me.

"On your own?" he asked.

"I am fully capable of doing as much," I retorted, and the man frowned.

"Yes, you often seem to be left to your own devices," Aarik remarked dryly. "Somehow always evading our staff or your guards, no matter how much they might protest."

"Well, you seem to have distracted my guards this time," I snapped. "I haven't seen much of them since our arrival. And as for your staff, well, you just saw how their attentiveness can easily be diverted if you take the right approach."

"I had heard reports of a certain woman taking pleasure in frightening our servants," Aarik muttered. "But I did not think I would witness such a thing for myself. It seems I will have to exchange the ones arranged to be in your service for those with a little more nerve."

"Good luck," I laughed softly, and the man scowled but changed the subject.

"It was fresh air you were looking for?" he inquired with a raised brow. "Wouldn't you rather I escort you to supper?"

Swallowing, I shrugged and then glanced down the hall behind him. "It would seem that I am not particularly hungry this evening."

"Yes," he mumbled. "I also seem to lose my appetite when

I am forced into close proximity with your brother and that other lord—Dansby, I think his name is."

Narrowing my eyes, I searched his handsome face. "I don't know what you are implying."

"You do," Aarik argued. "I now know you are too clever to pretend otherwise, but I won't push you on it." Stepping to the side, he lifted an arm towards the hall, and I gazed down the long length of his limb but did not move.

"Well, are you making your escape or not?" he demanded.

"And what will you do if I go ahead?" Pulling at his own cloak until it covered his metal-clad shoulders, he then lifted the hood so that it concealed his long black hair and shielded his face.

"Accompany you, of course." My scowl deepened and he rolled his eyes. "You may long for privacy, but certainly you understand that I would never allow you outside of these castle walls without an escort."

"I would be just fine," I argued.

"I don't doubt that," he replied. "But my honour still commands that I do not leave a noble unattended."

"I am not a noble. Not a true one anyway." The words lacked their usual bite, and when I saw the look of pity that crossed Aarik's face, my body stiffened.

"You can think what you want," Aarik sighed. "And you can call yourself whatever name you see fit. Lady, Rígan, *bastard*, shewolf—I don't care."

"But?" I asked, sensing that he was far from finished whatever pretty speech he had conjured in that head of his.

"But," he started once more, "I do know that even the fiercest of creatures feel pain, no matter how well they try to hide it."

I remained silent, and Aarik took a step forward. "And looking at you now, I can see that you don't need air, you need a place to lick your wounds."

"So what? You wish to watch me, to mock me?" I snarled.

"I wish to grant you the peace to do so while keeping you safe from those who can't understand and who would see this momentary softness as a failing."

"And you?" I whispered. "Do you understand?"

Aarik peered down at me for a long moment and then his chin lowered in a single nod. "I understand better than most."

"So, your brother is the heir, but you are still titled?" I asked as we strolled across the snow-covered yards, and Aarik glanced at me.

"I didn't think there would be talking," he drawled. "Had I known, I wouldn't have agreed to this."

"Are you going to answer my question?" Resting his forearm on the pommel of his weapon, Aarik stopped walking and tipped his head up towards the evening sky.

"My brother is the heir of the Anointed. His father was a Demys while our mother was from a smaller house," he explained.

"But a noble one," I added, and he hummed softly.

"Yes, a noble one." Raising my own eyes to the wall of grey clouds, I searched for a sliver of dark blue while deciding on my next inquiry.

"Did you know your father?" While it may have been the easiest one to answer, it was also the one I had been longing to hear since learning of his parentage.

"He died while my mother carried me," Aarik said softly. "But I've been told he was a good and kind man and he loved my mother very much."

"And Krayern's father?"

Frowning, Aarik looked at me from the corner of his eye. "What of him?"

"Was he kind to you?" I wondered out loud.

"The kindest," he confirmed. "He was the kindest of men, and when we lost him, it felt as if I had said goodbye to my true father."

"But Krayern was still made heir," I reminded him.

"Because *he is* the heir, nothing could change that. He has Demys blood, and I do not. Unlike you, I have no claim for an Anointed title."

Turning to face him, I shook my head. "I have no claim."

"You are a Baxteel," Aarik argued. "Your father sired you; you are an Anointed and the oldest at that."

"But by mother's lineage—"

"Doesn't truly matter in the grand scheme of things," Aarik argued. "She may not have been noble, which could mean fighting for your right to a title may be difficult, but it's not impossible. Besides, your father assured us that is his plan anyway."

I knew that was incorrect; my father would never truly give me such power, but I was too embarrassed to share as much.

"Now that I have answered your questions, I have one of my own." Taking a deep breath, I straightened to my full height and readied myself for whatever it was that he wanted to know.

"What is between you and Caedell?" The air I had just pulled into my lungs was knocked from me at the name, and I felt my jaw go slack as I stared at him.

"*Caedell?*" I choked out, and Aarik snorted.

"You look as if I just hit you over the head with the handle of my sword," he laughed, and I blinked through the daze of my surprise and then snapped my mouth shut.

"I don't have the slightest idea as to what you are talking about." I wrapped my arms around my torso as a particularly strong gust of wind blew against us and then watched as the power of the blast sent the cover of snow at our feet up into the air, creating a wall of white.

"You do, Rígan," Aarik continued as he examined my face, and I glared at him from the corner of my eye. "There is no use denying it."

"We travelled together," I reasoned, though pitifully.

"Yes." Aarik nodded. "And?"

"We have known each other for years, our entire lives really." Lifting his hands in exasperation, he gave me a pointed stare, and I rolled my eyes. "It goes no deeper than that, I assure you."

"For you," he said softly. "It goes no deeper than that for *you*."

Confused, I furrowed my brows. "What?"

"Is it because of that Gwain fool?" Aarik continued as if I hadn't said a word. "I don't know why Caedell insisted he come; he is useless and not at all what you should want in a man. I could not believe he would talk about anyone, much less a woman of your standing in such a way—"

"What?" I repeated, and Aarik froze before covering his mouth with a fist, as if he thought the action would somehow take the words back. I, however, was not fixated on his retelling of Gwain's poor behaviour despite Aarik thinking otherwise.

"What did you mean, *for me*?" I demanded, and when he did not reply for a moment, I closed the distance between us. "What did you mean, Aarik?"

"It is rather obvious where Caedell's feelings lie," Aarik said with a shrug, and I had never wanted to hit a man so badly over such a simple gesture before.

"You're wrong, Ca—" Aarik lifted a hand, stopping me mid-sentence while he glared.

"Don't try to tell me what I know, what I have seen with my own eyes." His voice was low and firm, and I bristled at the tone.

"Well, you do not *know* me," I snarled. "And you obviously do not know Caedell."

"There is something more than just history between the two of you," Aarik quarrelled. "It is obvious."

"The only thing between Caedell and me is our mutual aversion for one another," I snapped. "Implying anything more is not only wrong, it is *foolish*."

Aarik glowered at me, but I ignored him and spun on my heel. "I think I have had enough fresh air for the night," I muttered. "Good night, Sir Aarik."

CHAPTER
THIRTY-NINE

"I am surprised to see you in here," Catiline remarked as she entered the library. She had tried to make it sound as if she was not bothered, but the way her small frame curled in on itself as she crossed the room to pluck a book from the shelves told me otherwise. And had that not been all the proof I needed, the fact that she chose to sit in the chair farthest from my own made it all the more clear.

She was upset. For missing dinner, unlikely, but for ignoring her last night when she had obviously been worried, most certainly. Knowing I had to apologize was annoying, but more so because I had still not come up with an adequate excuse for my behaviour.

"I thought we could spend some time reading together," I offered softly, and she snorted before lifting the book to cover her face.

"I suppose yesterday's meeting must not have been as interesting as you had thought it would be if you are willing to miss today's in favour of sitting here with me." It was meant to be a barb, but I slammed my book shut and rose from my seat.

"They're meeting again?" I asked sharply. "Today? Right now?"

341

Closing her own book, she placed it on her lap. "Oh, did they not tell you? I suppose they did not see the need."

"Alright, Cat," I murmured. "I realize that you are upset by my ignoring you yesterday."

"Not just you," she snapped as she rose from her chair before tossing the book onto the cushion. "And not just yesterday!"

Thrown by the harshness of her voice, I blinked at my well-mannered friend and then closed my mouth as she ran her palms over the pretty pink fabric of her gown. Her lower lip wobbled while her eyes roamed the room, and I waited a long moment before attempting to address her.

"Cat," I said softly, though I remained where I stood in hopes that the space would ease her, especially when I noticed the tears filling her lovely eyes. "You're crying, what is going on?"

"I'm not crying," she sniffed, and I lifted a brow. "I'm just angry and frustrated and I cannot stop my eyes from watering when that happens."

"Alright," I soothed, but she curled her fingers into tiny fists and stomped one of her little feet.

"I'm not!" she barked, and I ran my top teeth over the scar of my bottom lip while I watched her wipe at her cheeks angrily. "These are not tears! These are symptoms of anger—my anger!"

"Alright," I said once more, but Cat was not pacified, and she lifted a hand to point a finger at me.

"My anger at you!" she shouted, as if it had not been clear. Deciding that perhaps it would be better to sit while she collected her thoughts, I placed a hand behind me and felt for my chair before sinking into the cushion, all while keeping my eyes on my friend.

"Anger at me for ignoring you?" I clarified, and she nodded before pressing her palms against her eyes and then sniffed again. "But I'm not the only one?"

Lowering her arms, she glared at me in question, and I shrugged. "You said it was not just me who ignored you, so I must not be the only one you are angry at."

"No," she conceded. "But you are the only one here and the only one I can shout at," Cat admitted with a solemn tone, and I frowned.

"And that is well deserved, isn't it?" I asked before exhaling roughly. "I have not been very fair to you since we've arrived."

She shook her head, and I stood once more and crossed the room. "I am sorry that I did not speak to you last night, and I am sorry I abandoned you to go to the meeting. But it was important."

"I don't doubt that. I just wished I was able to have been a part of it," Cat replied, and I ran my hand through my hair.

"It was only for the Anointed, Cat." My friend's expression hardened once more, and I lifted a brow in question.

"When you say things like that, when you make it clear that I am not like the rest, I can't help but wonder if you see the similarities." Not understanding, I frowned, and she shook her head gently. "You treat me as if I am beneath you, as if I am not as worthy because I am not of Anointed blood. The same way others cast you aside because of your parentage."

Guilty weighed heavily on my shoulders, and I wet my lips while I studied the deep blue hem of my dress. She was right, I had behaved just like those I loathed. Maybe not to the same degree, but certainly more poorly than she deserved, and I was ashamed.

"Cat," I started, my voice weak with sorrow. "I am so sorry."

Wiping her nose with the back of her hand in the most unladylike fashion, she cleared her throat and then shrugged. "I know my place in the world, I just wish I didn't need to be reminded of it so often."

"No." I shook my head. "You are far more worthy than

that. I should have been aware of how you felt. I feel stupid for not noticing it earlier."

"You have your own worries," she whispered, and I cupped her shoulder.

"That doesn't excuse it," I argued and then softly squeezed the joint beneath my palm. "Come with me."

She blinked up at me in confusion. "Come with you? Where?"

"To the council room," I explained. "The decisions they are making in there will affect the rest of us, and I think you and I should have some knowledge as to what they decide."

"But I don't know anything about battles and war," Cat reminded me, and I tried to act indifferent to her statement.

"Nor do I, really." Linking our arms together, I pulled her along and then paused at the doorway before we crossed through the threshold.

"But you must make me one promise." Leaning away from me, she looked up into my face with a kind expression, and I prayed she noted just how serious I was. "Do not speak to Caedell about me. Do not engage with him in any way that would include me, and please do not make any remarks on how we act around each other, especially the way I behave around him from now on."

"Did something happen yesterday?" Catline asked. "Is that why you would not let me into your room?"

Not knowing any other way to answer her question, I nodded.

She frowned, her eyes searching mine. "What did he do?"

I lifted my attention to focus straight ahead and then began to lead her from the library before I answered.

"He reminded me of *my* place in the world."

THIS TIME I did not hide behind the doors like a coward, and instead grabbed at the brass handles and pushed them both open before stepping into the room with my head held high. Cat, who began to lose her nerve after we had put a mere few feet between us and the library, trailed behind nervously, and I grabbed at her hand and led her to an empty chair while the rest watched.

Skileer was seething, Gwain's bruised and battered face was hard to read, but I could tell that he was surprised. The Demys brothers looked rather amused, as did their mother, but when my eyes darted to Caedell's seat, I noticed it was empty.

"How good of you to join us." Dyani smiled as she approached, and Cat blinked up at her as if she was put under a daze.

"I thought Lady Catiline could come along today." I shrugged and then fell into the seat next to my friend, the one that Caedell had occupied the day before. "Though she plans on just observing, we thought perhaps it would be okay for her to sit in."

My brother's mouth opened to object, but Krayern stopped him. "Of course," he assured us. "After all, we sent a missive to her father, and should they answer our request, then her house will be involved in this war."

Cat's angular eyes widened, and I placed a gentle hand on her own before addressing the Heir of Demys. "When do we expect replies from the others?"

"The hawks will not return from the most southern of families for at least a fortnight, the others, a sennight." It was Aarik who answered this time, and I focused my eyes on the shining metal of his breastplate rather than his face. "But Caedell left last night with a small group to aid some of the northern families nearby. There have been reports that there are small groups of rebels moving through the villages."

My gaze lifted the moment his name rolled off of Aarik's tongue, and he held my stare. "Caedell?"

He nodded at my question, and I was sure I could hear a soft scoff come from Gwain's direction, though I ignored it. "Why him?"

"Why not?" Gwain snapped, finally pulling my attention to his discoloured skin, and I frowned at the bruises and split lip.

It would seem that Caedell had not pulled any of his punches, and judging by the damage he had done to the face I had once adored, I knew whatever Gwain had said about me must have been very cruel.

"I had planned to go myself," Krayern interrupted. "But Caedell insisted that he do it. He was particularly adamant since the number of disturbances has increased recently. He was concerned about my leaving Denimoore, should the reports be true, and certain he could travel across the northern province more inconspicuously than I."

Perhaps the reasoning was justified, but I couldn't help but think that I also had something to do with Caedell's fleeing from the northern capital.

"What if he runs into trouble?" Cat whispered from her place beside me, and my fingers curled around hers so tightly, she pulled her hand out from under mine. Not realizing what I had done before I had already caused damage, I whispered a quiet apology. But she ignored me and instead continued to look at the brothers.

"Caedell is well equipped to handle any issue that may arise, and he is not unaccompanied. He has some of his knights and your man, Donigan, as well."

"Donigan?" I asked with a frown, and they nodded. I had not seen my guard in days now and wondered why he had left without so much as a word to me. This was just not like him, and the change in his behaviour worried me.

"Your brother offered his service," Aarik explained. Well,

there was my answer. My knight would not fight my brother on a true and noble order, not that he could even if he wanted to.

"And when are they due to return?" I asked while disregarding the narrowed gazes of both my brother and Gwain.

"Why does that matter to you?" Skileer sneered, and I finally met his brown eyes from across the table.

"She worries for her men and for the heir of an Anointed," Dyani snapped, and I turned my head to look at her as she regarded my brother with obvious disdain. "That is a mark of a true and decent leader. Perhaps it would be wise to follow her example."

There was nothing worse she could have done than to suggest my brother seek guidance from me, and I watched as his entire body stiffened while his expression turned murderous.

Clearing her throat, Cat pulled all attention back to her, and I was so very grateful for my friend's interruption. "What do we do in the meantime?"

"We wait," Krayern said softly. "The rebellion has continued to expand, that we are certain of. But while our forces are split across the land, there is no way of ending this fight once and for all."

"So, we just wait for the other families to answer our request?" Her dark eyes roamed across the room as she looked at each man before her. "And what if they do not agree or if they are too late and the enemy has only continued to decimate Elrin?"

No one had an answer for my friend, and I swallowed at the sharp churning in my belly when I realized that the famed Anointed, the ones chosen by the Gods themselves, were truly just as powerless as any other ordinary men.

FORTY

It had been two days since the meeting, and there was a new air within the great walls of Denimoore, one that was heavy with tension and unease, and I felt crushed beneath the weight of it. However, it seemed that an escape from the castle was unlikely, and I instead settled for a quiet evening with my friend.

Glancing at her now, I watched as she lifted her needlework closer to her face. Studying it, she dipped her chin and then pinched the thread between her teeth before pulling at the string with a great grunt of displeasure.

"Embroidery is meant to be a lady's activity, and not one that usually involves the person's mouth," I drawled with a raised brow, and she released the strand of green from her grasp before offering me a sheepish smile.

"I fear I'm not very good at it," Cat admitted before tossing the wooden frame in my direction, and I glanced down at the mess she had created, trying to decipher exactly what it was I was looking at.

"Nor am I," I admitted as I turned the piece this way and that while I attempted to figure out what was the top and what was the bottom.

"Really?" Cat asked while moving to sit beside me, and I put her work on the table before us and shrugged.

"It is an activity meant to keep ladies' hands busy and our minds from drifting," I reminded her. "It is the hope that simple thread and a pretty design will keep us out of trouble. But I'm sure you know it would take far more than that for me. I have never been one to idle in place for long."

"Yes, you've had other, more exciting, pursuits," she giggled softly while her pale cheeks turned pink, and I rolled my eyes.

"I meant riding or walking," I muttered before grabbing at her embroidery once more and tossing it into her lap. "Perhaps you should spend more time practicing, if only to keep that salacious mind of yours from wandering."

Catiline's jaw hung while she stared at me with wide eyes and then she shook her head. "I have no such thing!"

"You just proved otherwise, sweet Catiline," I laughed.

The pink on her cheeks turned into a deeper shade of red, though she said nothing else on the matter. Choosing to cease my teasing, I went back to the book I had picked from the shelves and flipped through the pages while Cat plucked at the string once more.

It had been a quiet evening; we had taken supper in the library while the lords appeared to take their meals alone in their rooms. It was perhaps not usual for a host to do so, but given how strained everyone seemed to be, it was probably for the best. After all, we all seemed to be toeing an edge, and should one of us put a foot wrong, I was sure an argument would ensue.

Pressing in close to my side, Cat pulled me from my thoughts as she shivered, and I glanced at the fire roaring in the corner before turning to the faded words on the parchment once more. However, just as I was about to flip the page I had been on, I heard a great commotion coming from beyond the wall of glass that made up the south side of the library, and I pulled myself from our seat and hastily crossed the room.

My breath sent a thick fog across the cool surface of the window when I pressed in close, and I wiped the dampness away with my palm before gazing down below. The quaint little village was normally quiet at this time of night; usually its people had turned in for the day and the torches and lanterns that were scattered throughout the cobblestone roads would be snuffed out. However, now the town was set ablaze, and the glowing orange flames began to consume the endearing little shops and buildings as the fire grew.

"Holy Gods," I gasped before fleeing from the window. I rushed to Cat and grabbed at her arm.

"What is it?" she asked as she tried to pull from my hand while she looked towards the window I had just fled from.

Tightening my hold, I hauled her back to my side and her eyes widened with fear when she noticed my expression. But when my mouth parted to explain what I had witnessed, the screaming started, and she pressed against my side, seeking comfort while her fear rocked through her.

"We need to go," I ordered as I led us to the door. However, just as I reached the exit, I heard the shouting echoing from the halls, and I lowered my eyes to the brass lock before grabbing at it. Twisting the metal until I heard it click into place, I removed my grasp on Cat and hurried to the large chairs that sat in the middle of the room.

"Come help me with these," I instructed as I began pushing one towards the door, and she curled her arms around her torso while her wild, wide eyes bounced between me and the door.

"Shouldn't we go get help?" she whispered. "Shouldn't we find some guards or maybe Krayern or Aarik?"

"Whoever has come is already in the halls," I grunted as I pulled the heavy chair along behind me only to then freeze when a shrill scream came from just beyond the doors.

Jumping into action at the sound, Cat ran to me and grabbed the other arm of the chair, and then we pulled it across the room until it sat directly beneath the handles of the door.

"Now what?" she asked, and I glanced around trying to decipher a plan as fast as I could while the chaos beyond the library grew.

"Close the curtains!" I ordered before I ran to the fire. It was still burning strong, and there would be no putting it out anytime soon, which meant it would have to be left while we hid. Praying that the light and warmth would not be obvious from the crack of space beneath the door, I began to search for a weapon of some sort. Luckily beside the hearth sat an iron tool set, and I grabbed at the two stokers before racing back to Cat, who had just finished her task of covering the windows. Pressing one of the iron rods into her small hands, I then snatched her wrist and tugged her behind me as we ran across the library.

The walls were lined with shelves, but the rest of the room was a large open space, and our only real option of a hiding place was the enormous tapestry that hung from the ceiling in the back corner of the library. Thankfully, it reached the floor and was about two yards wide. However, the fabric lay flush against the stone wall, and if we were not perfectly pressed against the rock while remaining as still as possible, I was sure it would be obvious that we had sought shelter behind the heavy material. But knowing it was our only choice, I grabbed at the thick purple material before hauling it open and ushering Cat behind.

"Press back against the wall and try to be as still as you can," I demanded.

Following my instructions, Cat did just as I asked, and I stepped away and took note of how noticeable she was. Her body wasn't as obvious as I had thought it would be, and I thanked the Gods before joining her.

"What is happening?" she whimpered as she fought for breath, and I pressed a hand over her chest, letting my palm rest over her thundering heart.

"I don't know," I murmured. "But you need to calm down and slow your breathing."

Inhaling sharply through her nose, she held it for a pause before releasing the breath softly from her mouth and then repeated the motion twice more before nodding. Certain she was no longer fighting for air, I took a moment for myself and closed my eyes.

I had no idea how long we stood there; it could have been hours or moments, there was no way of telling. However, just as things would calm beyond the doors of the library and we would think it was over, another crash would echo, or we would hear another chilling scream and I would grab at Cat's hand while her body quivered. She was terrified, there was no doubt about that, and my touch did little to calm her, especially when my own fingers shook with fear.

I had faced many opponents over the years and was not one to cower from a fight. But during each of those instances I had been armoured, and the weapon clutched in my grasp had not been a measly stick of iron meant to push coals and wooden logs.

Tightening my hold on the metal, I tipped my head back against the stone wall and willed for time to pass as we waited for some sign that it was safe. However, it never came, and when my feet reached past the point of aching and my body strained to remain in the same position for any longer, I made the decision. We had heard nothing more since the last wail, which felt as if it had been hours ago, and I knew Cat was also struggling to hold her place.

"Catiline," I whispered while curling my sweaty fingers around her wrist, and I winced at the racing speed of her pulse. "I am going to go to the door and see what I hear."

"No——" She began to vehemently shake her head, but I pressed my nails into the skin of her arm, hoping the sting would pull her from her panic.

"It has been quiet for a good long while now," I muttered softly. "I think it is over and we can come out from hiding."

"I can come with you," she whimpered. "I remember my lessons, I can help."

A sob broke from her chest, and I flinched at the sound. "There is no need, I won't be but a moment. As soon as I see that it's clear, I will come back to get you."

Loosening my hold on her limb, I slipped out from the weight of the tapestry and carefully tiptoed my way across the stone floor and noticed the dying fire in the hearth. However, even with it nearly finished and the thick curtains closed, the room was alight, and I looked up at the glow that flickered from above the tops of the window coverings and noticed the way the orange reached across the ceiling. A light like that could only be created by an astonishing blaze and my heart ached for what I knew would be grave and permanent damage to the village of Denimoore.

And while I was lost in my worry for those who were suffering in the town below, I had not heard the quiet footsteps as they approached. It wasn't until a chorus of grunts sounded from behind the barrier of the door that I turned to face the exit. For just a heartbeat it was quiet again, but then a loud thud resonated through the room and the walls seemed to shake as something collided with the heavy wood.

With wide eyes, I watched the slabs of timber wobble and then noticed the small splinters that began to cover the floor as the men continued to slam into the door over and over again. Seeing that it would soon give way, I turned back to Cat, ready to sink beneath the tapestry once more if only to protect her from our unknown enemy.

However, just as I began to hurry to the far end of the

library, I heard the now-shattered door swing open and I froze. Glancing over my shoulder, I looked towards the party of men who rushed into the room and then my eyes met those of the leader of the group who wore a silver mask.

"Well, what do we have here?"

FORTY-ONE

I HAD SEEN THOSE WHO BELONGED TO THE REBELLION BEFORE. I had spilled their blood and taken their lives. I had heard their cries for mercy and witnessed their rage first-hand. I was more than what some might call familiar with our enemy. But these men looked nothing like those I had faced over the last year.

While they were young, they were also well-built and put together and did not appear to be part of the common folk, though I did not recognize their faces from the tourneys we had participated in either. I also didn't know the sigil that was stitched on their tunics and painted across their well-crafted shields. Eyeing the symbol, I took note of the long sharp beak of the raven's skull and the pointed tips of the crown that sat atop its head. It was a dark emblem, one that made my skin prickle, and the leader's covered face lowered so that he could look at the emblem sewed across his chest.

"Do you not recognize this symbol?" the man asked as his eyes lifted once more, and I clenched my jaw while my thumb stroked across the metal rod still grasped tightly in my hand. "It is of our commander's God."

Not caring to acknowledge his words, I gazed at the

stranger who stood at his shoulder instead. "Why are you here?"

The group of men shared a look and then some chuckled softly while others moved farther into the room. Doing my best to remain calm, I kept track of each of their movements, watching as they began to circle around me.

"We are here for the Anointed," the leader replied as he took a step forward, and I lifted my weapon in his direction and bristled when their laughter grew.

"As you can see, they're not here," I snarled. "It is just me in this room."

I prayed to the Gods Cat was listening closely and understood what I was trying to convey to her. I needed her to remain out of sight and away from these strangers who were now closing in on me.

"Yes, I do see that." The leader tipped his head slightly in an obvious but silent order, and when the man to my right stepped close, I held my breath and then swung. Though I had been armed, I knew they had not actually believed I would attack, and I was able to strike the man in the shoulder. Lodging the curved metal end into the muscle of his back, I tugged him roughly towards me, and once he had fallen to his knees by the force of the motion, I pressed my foot to his chest, dislodged the metal from his flesh, and then swung the rod into the side of his face.

By the amount of blood that spilled from the hit, I knew there would be no rising to his feet for him, and I turned to my next victim. This man was smaller, and though his blade was pointed at me, he was staring down at the body sprawled across the floor. Taking the opening, I lifted the rod high above my head and brought it down against his neck. The kill was quick—gruesome, but quick—and now I faced the rest of the group. Even with two defeated, I was still outnumbered by nearly half a dozen more. And while I did not love those odds, I would not surrender.

"Who's next?" I grinned, ignoring the gore that had splattered across my face while I waited for another to step forward.

Pulling himself from his shock, the leader shook his head softly and unsheathed his sword before pointing it at me. "It did not have to be this way; if you would have surrendered, we would have been gentle. We would have given you the mercy of an easy death."

My lips curled at the corners before I bared my teeth at him. "Then it's a pity for you that I will not offer the same." Steadily holding my weapon before me, I lifted a single brow. "I hope you are prepared to be united with the God your commander is so fond of."

The man pushed forward with his sword at the ready, and though it was craftily made, he was not accustomed to wielding such a blade. I could tell by the way he clumsily cut at the air in my direction, and I danced out of his reach now that my back was free from his comrades.

Following me in his pursuit, he hadn't noticed that I had lured him away from his men, and when I finally slowed my movements and let him close the space between us, I smiled. Stunned by such an expression, the man hesitated in his next attack and instead of bringing my weapon down from above, I swung towards his ribs.

The impact of the hit robbed him of air, and he choked out a pained gasp before staggering away from me. Pressing his hand against his torso, he wheezed, and I paused for a moment, watching as he pulled his bloodied fingers away from his side before gasping roughly.

"You shouldn't have laughed," I chided him with a shrug. "I bet it doesn't seem so funny now, does it?"

"I am going to kill you," he spat at me while lifting his sword in my direction once more. "But I will make you suffer first."

"I can appreciate your passion," I laughed softly. "And I will enjoy watching you try."

Reaching the end of his patience, the man swung the mighty blade of silver at me, and I dodged the attack carefully before closing in. Noticing the blood dripping from his side, I poked the end of my weapon against the wound and snickered when he wailed out in pain.

"By the Gods," one of his men gasped as he watched me toy with my prey. "What kind of creature is she?"

Angered and in pain, my foe shifted away from the steel I held and hacked at the air between us in a desperate attempt to hit me. However, due to his lack of attention to where he was going, his foot caught on the corner of the rug and he stumbled forward, nearly toppling headfirst into one of the chairs still left in the centre of the room.

Lifting both hands towards the seat, he dropped his blade in order to keep himself from colliding into the furniture. Diving towards the ground, I snatched the weapon off of the rug and held it before me.

"It's a pretty blade, one far more deserving of a better handler." Now facing me, the man choked on a rugged gasp, and then his eyes lowered to my blood-covered fist that was pressed against his wounded belly.

"Say hello to your Reaper," I whispered before pulling the blade from his gut, and the man fell forward, crashing to the floor in a heap as I stepped away.

Spinning on my heel, I looked to the remaining five men, all of whom were staring at their leader with surprise, and I grabbed at the skirts of my gown. Lifting the fabric, I carefully cleaned the metal free from blood and then waited for my next opponent.

"Don't tell me you no longer wish to fight?" I asked as I let my eyes roam across the group. "I was just getting started."

"You are from hell itself," one of the older men spat, and I rolled my eyes.

"Would you say that if I were a man?" I wondered out loud. "Or does my viciousness make me some sort of monster simply because it does not match the beauty of my face?"

The men pressed closely together as I approached, and I fed off their fear. I basked in the glory I was sure would come and ignored the bodies of those three who I had already slain.

That, however, had been my mistake.

Had I been wiser, I would have remembered another scenario in which I had been sure I would be victorious. But the man had somehow pulled himself free from the clutches of death. It had been impossible, but it happened, and yet I had somehow managed to forget.

So, when I neared the party, I wrongly assumed their widened eyes and pale faces were because of me. I had been certain that I was the foe they feared, and I relished in it. That is until I noticed their attention had shifted and I frowned just before a hand curled around my shoulder and grabbed at my throat.

Clawing at the wrist pressing into my breastbone while the strange fingers tightened beneath my jaw, I tried to kick out at my attacker. However, the movement knocked me off balance, and my enemy took the opportunity to pull me to the floor. Pressing me roughly into the stone, the man swung a leg over my thigh and straddled my hips while his free hand joined the other around my neck.

Crushed beneath his unyielding weight, I bent my legs at the knees and dug my heels into the ground in hopes of finding some sort of anchor to aid me in bucking my hips. But it was no use; the silk of my slippers slid across the cold rock floor, and I was forced to try another tactic. Growing desperate for air, I lifted my hands from the skin of his arms and reached for the silver covering his face while his cold, lifeless eyes watched as I choked beneath his palms.

My fingers were still coated in his blood and they left crimson-coloured marks on the silver as they slipped across the metal. Knowing it was no use, I let my arms drop and looked to the door in desperation. But there was no one there, only the broken wood remained, and I realized the other men had fled at the sight of their once-fallen friend rising to his feet.

Growing more frantic now that my mind had started to become hazy and my vision blurred, I moved my arms out at my sides, my fingers dragging across the rough surface of the stone floor while I searched for something, anything that I may use to help free me from my captor. But my nails scratched at the unforgiving rock to no avail, and I finally succumbed to the heaviness creeping into the corners of my consciousness and let my lashes flutter closed.

It was cold, the darkness I had been pulled into, and I felt as if I was floating, like I had been thrust into the strong currents of the Barren Sea rather than left on the floor of the library. Lost in the abyss, I did not sense another presence approaching until those hands which had been closing my airway disappeared, and were replaced by a warm and gentle touch.

Carefully tipping my head back, the fingertips stroked across the raw and bruised flesh of my throat, and then there was noise, some sort of murmuring next to my ear that tugged me from my trance.

"Rígan?!" The sound of my name sent me lurching forward, and I gasped as I buried my face into the shoulder of my saviour while they wrapped a strong arm across my waist before pulling me close.

"Easy," he whispered, his voice clear now that the haze had subsided. "You're alright, just breathe."

My body trembled and I clawed at the fabric of his tunic as I attempted to bury myself farther into his warmth. But even with my face pressed into the crook of his neck, the panic did not leave, and I panted desperately for air.

"It's alright," he cooed again before trying to pull himself away. But I snatched at the wool of his shirt and tightened my grasp until I was practically tearing open the material in my desperation to keep him with me.

Grabbing at my wrists, he gently untangled his tunic from my hold on his shoulders and brought my hands between us. Pressing my palm against his chest, he kept the other hand clasped in his own. Anchoring me to him with his touch and the rhythmic beating of his heart, he nudged my face with his, urging it back until our foreheads were pressed together and those amber eyes bore into mine.

"It's alright, just breathe," Caedell whispered, and when I quivered in his grasp, he strengthened his hold. "Just breathe for me, Rígan."

CHAPTER
FORTY-TWO

I WAS NOT CERTAIN HOW LONG WE REMAINED INTERTWINED ON the floor, but once I had managed to regulate my breathing, a wave of exhaustion slammed into me. Turning my head just slightly, I rested my temple on Caedell's strong shoulder, and his hand lifted to stroke the tangled mess of my hair.

"Is she alright?" Cat's nervous voice came from the far corner of the room, and I lifted my face to see my friend step out from behind the tapestry. Following my eyes, Caedell turned to her, and I pressed away from his warmth. However, Caedell's arms remained strong in their hold, and I pulled at his wrists until he slowly released me.

"Cat," I whispered with a hoarse voice while I struggled to my feet. Rising as well, Caedell placed a steadying hand on my hip, and we watched my friend race towards us.

Not caring for the blood or bodies that lay on the floor, she ran across the library and threw herself at me. Grunting at the impact, I stumbled back into Caedell's chest, and he wedged a hand between my friend and me to brace his palm on Cat's shoulder in an attempt to keep her from taking the air from my lungs once more.

"Careful," he warned sternly, and she blinked up at us, and it was then that I noticed the stream of tears.

"Oh, Cat," I sighed before wrapping an arm over her shoulders, and I pulled her close, not caring for Caedell's cautioning. "I'm fine."

"I was so frightened; I didn't know what to do!" She sobbed before burying her face into my shoulder, not at all concerned that the material was stained red.

"You did exactly the right thing," I assured her, though I ended up wincing at the tenderness of my throat. "I'm so glad you're safe."

"But you're hurt, I should have tried to help you! I know how to fight now, I should have helped you!" she wailed as she studied the raw skin of my throat and then looked to my left arm. The sleeve of my blue gown was ripped, and the jagged edges of the material were wet. Lifting my fingers to the shallow wound, I hissed through my teeth while I gauged how deep it was.

"I'll be fine," I told her, and she glared at me skeptically before looking at Caedell. His own eyes were assessing me closely, and I shifted under his penetrating stare before my attention moved on to the other bodies.

The first two men I had faced still remained where I had left them, but the leader was flipped over on his stomach and his head was a mere few feet from where we stood. Swallowing at the acid rising up the back of my throat, I moved away from the pieces of the corpse and pulled Cat along with me.

"We should find the others," I whispered while I forced myself to push through my shock, and Cat's face grew even more troubled.

"Shouldn't we stay here and let them come to us?" she asked quietly, and I squeezed her fingers gently.

"The others are fine and are the ones who sent me to find you after we realized your rooms were empty." Caedell placed a calm hand on the centre of my back and ushered us to the door.

"Skileer——" I began as Caedell led us out of the library, and the palm that pressed against me stiffened at the mention of my brother's name.

"In one piece," he murmured, and I noted the frustration in his voice as we crossed through the threshold.

The once-stunning halls of Denimoore were torn apart and covered with rubble. The paintings and sculptures that lined the walls were scattered across the floor, and the smell of smoke was heavy in the air. Frowning at the wreckage, I followed the Heir of House Reide as he guided us through the corridors, and Cat clutched at my hand desperately as she trailed along behind us.

"There you are!" Krayern called as we rounded the corner, and he sprinted towards us and then slapped a hand against Caedell's shoulder. Pulling his focus from his comrade, he gazed down at me and that smile of relief fell into a worried frown.

"By Gods, what happened?" he demanded as he examined my neck and then my gown, and I fought the urge to shrink away from his concern.

"Some of the rebels had a particular interest in books it seems," I muttered, though no one seemed amused by my comment. Turning to a group of people behind us, Krayern summoned one of the older men with a gruff command.

"See to Lady Rígan," he ordered. "Make certain she is cared for and comfortable. The rooms in the south wing are still in one piece, that is where they will stay."

"I will see to it myself," Caedell vowed, and Krayern's brows lifted.

"There is no need for that, I can assure you my healer is more than capable——"

"It wasn't a question," Caedell snapped. "I was simply informing you of what will be happening."

Confused by his misplaced ire, I peered at Caedell from the corner of my eye and noticed the set of his jaw and narrowed gaze as he watched the Lord of Denimoore, almost as if he was daring him to object.

"If that's what you prefer," Krayern relented.

"It is," Caedell answered, and Cat pressed in close to my side as we watched the tension build between the two men.

"As enjoyable as this has been," I drawled, "I would like to point out that I do not need an escort, nor do I want to be poked and prodded by your healer."

The men seemed ready to interject, but I glared at them both. "Just tell us how to find our new chambers so that I may rest."

A shadow of guilt clouded Caedell's face, and Krayern surrendered and murmured the directions. Tightening my hold on Cat's hand, we moved towards the south wing. And though each step created more distance between us and the corpse of the beheaded man who remained on the stone floor of the library, the fear curling in my gut only continued to grow.

My bones had been heavy with exhaustion, and yet, I had a horribly fitful sleep, and when the lady's maid had come the next morning to wake me in my chambers, I had nearly spat at the woman. Although it seemed I was not alone in my poor mood, and when I rolled onto my other side after dismissing the servant, the body next to me grumbled out a curse and lifted the sheets over her head.

"Cat?" I asked as I grabbed at the fabric before peeling it away and then frowned at my friend as she winced at the morning light. "What are you doing in here?"

Pulling herself up from the mattress, she ran her fingers through her long black hair and then wiped at her eyes. "I had awful dreams last night that kept waking me. When I reached my fourth attempt of falling back asleep, I gave up and decided to come here instead."

She had been in the room just next door, so it wasn't as if she had to venture far, but I still worried about her leaving her chambers alone and at night, especially just after an attack. However, as I studied her pale complexion and mussed hair, I decided to hold off on any lecture and then sank deeper into the warmth of the bed.

"Although, it's not as if I had a better rest here," she yawned while shimming back down onto the mattress. "You tossed and turned all night."

"I didn't have the best dreams either," I admitted, and she nodded.

"I figured that was the case when I stepped into the hall last evening." Not understanding, I furrowed my brows, and she lifted her head to peer over my shoulder in the direction of the door before shuffling closer.

"When I stepped into the hall last night, I had caught Caedell checking on you," she whispered, and my eyes widened. "He and Donigan were stationed outside our doors but apparently you had made some sound of distress that worried him."

"Was he in here?" I demanded, and she shook her head.

"No! It was not quite that scandalous," she swore, and I nearly snorted at her idea of scandalous. Especially when I considered just how many lines Caedell and I had already crossed. "He was just in the doorway, watching you with this very serious and, if I'm honest, rather sad look on his face."

"Oh," I muttered, and she curled her hands under her chin and nodded.

"You didn't make another noise while I was in here, just a lot of fussing about." Sighing, I offered her a half-hearted smile and watched as she settled once more before drifting back to sleep.

My own tiredness, however, was forgotten, and I wondered what could have possibly made the man who had just assured me of my insignificance to him come to my rescue…

Again.

THE HALLS WERE STILL LITTERED with debris, though it seemed that every working body besides Cat and me had been summoned to help repair the damage, and I watched as men passed by me, their hands full of stone and pieces of wood. But it wasn't just the structure itself that had suffered. Dozens had been attacked in the village, and though we had managed to be victorious against the rebels, it had come at a great cost.

However, since no one had bothered to actually inform me on the state of everything, nor was I aware if any of our enemies lived, I had spent the morning searching for my knight. Although Donigan had managed to evade my search, and I glowered as I prowled through the halls. Stepping over the remains of what must have been a statue of some sort, I peered down the hall and finally spotted the man in question. He, however, was not alone, and I curled my fingers around the smooth stone corner and then dipped behind the wall before carefully peeking at them.

They were quiet, their voices too low to hear, but whatever it was that they were discussing must have been serious because their conversation seemed heated, and I watched as Caedell and Donigan both glared at the Heir of House Demys.

"I didn't take you for the type to hide in the shadows and

spy," Dyani whispered from beside me, and I jumped at her voice and then spun around to face her.

"I wasn't hiding," I muttered, and she crossed her arms over her chest.

"Oh?"

"I was simply observing." The Lady of Denimoore rolled her eyes with a soft smile, and though she would appear to be in good spirits, I noticed that her silver irises seemed dull and weary and her normally meticulous appearance was lacking something. Her long lavender gown was stunning, of course, and her black hair was smooth and tied together in a pretty plait, leaving her shoulders free of its weight and that delicate golden chain with the shield pendant sat just above her breasts. But there was still something off, and I felt a pang of empathy for the woman.

"Well, why don't you come *observe* in the council room," she suggested before her attention lowered to my throat for a brief pause. Making certain that my own long hair was draped over my shoulders rather than tumbling down my back, I tried to use the dark strands as a cover of sorts. I hoped that it would work as a shield and that the worst of my injury would be somewhat concealed. However, judging by the sympathetic look Dyani sent my way, I was sure it was pointless, and I scowled as she turned from me.

"Is everyone else accounted for?" she asked as she led me towards the trio, and they hurriedly raised their heads in our direction.

Clearing his throat, Krayern then addressed us. "Aarik has decided to remain in the village. The repairs will take some time, and the people are heavy with loss. We think stationing him there for the rest of the day may ease their spirits or at least they will see that we support them."

His speech was heartfelt, or at least he tried to make it seem as much. But it sounded more like he was attempting to convince himself that his brother's presence would mean something to his people, and I scoffed.

"Do you have something to say, Lady Rígan?" he snapped, and both Donigan and Caedell straightened at his tone.

I took a deep breath, my eyes flickering to my knight, and wondered if Donigan would urge me to keep my mouth shut had we been in private. However, we were not, and I knew that after last night, the Lord of Denimoore needed honesty more than he needed pacifying.

"The villagers will notice your brother's presence, that is for certain," I agreed. "But do not mistake their attention for gratefulness."

"What do you mean?" Krayern asked, and I heard his mother sigh softly at my side.

"Although they made the effort to get into the castle, it wasn't until after they attacked the village. Their sights turned to us, but I don't think we were their only intended victims. After all, it was really the townsfolk who suffered the most, and I can't help but think their pain was not an unnecessary tragedy but rather an opportunity," I explained. "The rebels want to tarnish our names and abolish our houses. In order to do so, they must also destroy what support we may have, and that starts with the commoners of Elrin."

"Our people are smart and loyal," Krayern disagreed. "They will see this ploy."

"Perhaps," I muttered. "Or perhaps they will be overcome with their loss and poor fortune and will want to hold someone responsible."

Krayern's face grew troubled, and I noticed the other two men seemed solemn as well.

"There is no denying that Denimoore was the intended target of the raid," I continued. "They chose the home of the Protector's Anointed. Had it not been for us, your people would not be grieving."

"What would you have us do instead?" the Heir of House

Demys asked, and I was surprised that he would seek my advice.

Realizing I had no easy answer, I took a moment to think on it and then glanced down the hall and studied the destruction that still lay across the floors. "I would see that all efforts are sent to your people. As long as the castle is guarded and is not in any risk of crumbling down for the time being, send all able-bodied men to the village. Help your people before yourself."

"That is very wise," Dyani agreed.

"We should send food and supplies to them as well," Caedell added. "We should not be living frivolously while others go without."

"Loyalty can always be bought," I said softly. "And it is easier done if there is a promise of a full stomach."

Nodding, Krayern brushed past me and then strode down the hall. However, when he reached the very corner I had just been hiding behind, he paused and looked back at us.

"Cancel the meeting for today, we have bigger priorities," he ordered, and then his eyes lowered to my throat. "And see that Lady Rígan is seen by a healer this morning, I won't take no for an answer this time."

My mouth parted to argue, but he shook his head. "I think I will be needing your advice again in the near future, and you can hardly be of help to me if you are suffering and injured."

Caedell and Donigan assured the man that they would see to it, but I was still reeling by his admission and barely noticed the gentle hand on my shoulder that guided me towards another room at the end of the hall.

FORTY-THREE

"And does this hurt?" the man asked as he pressed his thumb into a particularly tender spot beneath my ear, and I clenched my teeth while Donigan and Caedell peered at me from the corner of the room.

"No, it feels delightful," I snapped, and the healer snatched his hand away as if the flesh of my throat had burned him.

"Perhaps a little less sarcasm, my lady," my knight suggested, and I glared at his handsome face.

"Considering I have rarely seen you since our arrival, I think you can keep your suggestions to yourself." I knew his lack of presence had not been his fault. He was at the mercy of my brother and thus the other lords since Skileer had seen it fit to pass the man around like a toy rather than a decorated knight.

"Apologies, my lady." His head dipped in a bow, and I inhaled through my nose while I tried to find some patience.

"None needed," I grumbled from my chair. "All of this fretting over a few bruises has made my mood sour."

"Few bruises?" It was Caedell's voice that now echoed in the room, and I noticed the harsh frown and dark look he gave me. "I would hardly classify this as such! You were nearly killed."

"And yet, here I sit, perfectly together and in one piece," I responded, and he glowered at me while my knight shifted on his feet. "I've never seen so many men make such a bother over something as minor as this. My brother does not feel that all this trouble is necessary, you heard him when we passed in the hall."

"You'll have to excuse me if I don't hold his opinion in high regard," Caedell growled. "After all, he needed half a dozen tonics a day for just a little scratch on his face."

Not bothering to point out the fact that it was more than a scratch and that he was responsible for said injury, I rolled my eyes before clearing my throat. "Well, perhaps I am just made of stronger stuff."

Frowning, he studied me closely and then lifted a brow. "Stronger than an Anointed heir who has been in the very centre of the rebellion?"

It was an odd choice of a rebuttal; it seemed as if he was daring me to say something about my brother's *role*. However, I just narrowed my eyes and stood from my chair. "Are you saying it's not possible, sir?"

"No," he answered. "Just unlikely."

He was looking at me again, the way he did when it felt as if he was trying to pry my secrets from me, and I nearly squirmed under the heat of his gaze.

"It's the bastard blood," I growled, annoyed that he still had this effect on me. "It is what keeps me strong."

Thrown by my words, the three men stiffened, and I plucked the salve the healer had been holding and offered the man a curtsey.

"Thank you for taking the time to see to my injuries," I said as I straightened once more. "But I can assure you there are others who need your attention far more than I do."

Turning back to my knight, I lifted a hand and gestured to

the healer. "See that he finds his way back to the village, Sir Taith. Lord Krayern asked that he return to the town as soon as he was finished here, and I do not think we should delay him any longer."

My knight bowed at my instructions and then helped gather the man's supplies before ushering him from the room. Now free from the healer's watchful and knowing gaze, I smoothed a hand down the bruised flesh of my throat and winced.

"Why were you not honest with him?" Caedell demanded, and I tore my hand away from my neck. "You should have told him how much pain you are actually in."

"It is nothing," I mumbled as I crossed the room. But Caedell chased after me and cupped my elbow before spinning me around to face him once more.

"It's not nothing, and you need to stop saying otherwise." Tugging my arm free from the grip of his long fingers, I narrowed my gaze at him.

"What does it matter? It's not as if you care," I snarled. "You made that clear, remember? You were sure to inform me of my insignificance."

Stepping back, Caedell turned away from me and ran a hand through his hair as he began to pace. Assuming that this was the end of the conversation, I shook my head and made for the door. But seeing my attempt to flee, Caedell lunged at me and grabbed one of my hands.

Turning towards him angrily, I was about to demand an answer for his odd behaviour. But when he tugged me forward and then cupped his hands over the wide curve of my hips, all thought was wiped from my mind.

The heat from his palms radiated through my gown. While I stood dumbfounded, Caedell took the opportunity to guide me back one step, and then another, until I was flush against the wall with him caging me in.

Unable to form a thought, I swallowed roughly, no longer

feeling any irritation in my throat. No, I felt nothing but the fire that he somehow lit within my veins with just a simple touch.

"You are right to be angry. I shouldn't have spoken to you in the way that I did."

His voice was soft, barely audible over the pounding my heart, and when I did not respond, his brows furrowed and he scrunched his eyes closed, almost as if he was in pain.

"You just don't understand," he whispered hoarsely.

"What don't I understand?"

"I know I mustn't," he answered softly. "And I have tried to stop myself."

Growing more confused, I exhaled, and when his eyes flickered open once more, I searched the burning golden irises. "What are you talking about?"

I did not think it was possible for Caedell to get much closer. But of course he had to prove me wrong, and he leaned forward until our chests grazed and his thighs brushed against my trembling legs.

"I do care, Rígan," he murmured as one of his hands slid up my side until it was resting against my ribs, and his thumb pressed just under the curve of my breast. "I have always cared."

Staring at him with wide eyes, I tried to gather my thoughts. He must be lying; those words couldn't be true. After all, he had said the exact opposite in the council room, and I had not detected a hint of deception then.

Noticing my inner turmoil, Caedell bent forward and held my gaze. "I know that I was cruel, I know it was beyond forgiveness. But you must understand, I didn't mean a word of it."

My lips parted, but Caedell took in a staggering breath and continued. "When we spoke after that meeting, I was prepared for you to hate me. I had accepted that outcome; I even wished for it. I knew the words I chose would cut you to the bone, and I said them anyway. But it is because that was an ending I could live with."

He was not making a lick of sense, and I glowered in irritation. "What are you saying?"

"I hurt you to push you away, and as much as I hated it, it worked," he whispered. "But then last night, when I saw you on the ground with that man's hands around your throat and you were just lying there..." My stomach turned at the retelling of events from the library and Caedell shuddered. "I knew then I could not go on without telling you the truth of it."

"Truth of what?" I demanded, and Caedell exhaled at the frustration in my tone.

"Since I was a child," he said tenderly while his eyes bore into mine, "I have thought of little else but you."

That was a declaration if I've ever heard one, but I still could not understand.

"Me?" I questioned as my head spun. "But you said—"

"I lied," he muttered softly. "You are not insignificant, Rígan, you are *everything*, and you have been for as long as I can remember."

The sound of the jar of salve shattering on the stone floor should have pulled us from whatever trance Caedell had put us under. But the racket did nothing of the sort, and now my hand was free to tangle into the hair at the nape of his neck while the other grabbed at the soft fabric of his tunic.

"You lied," I repeated. "But what you say now is the truth?"

"I don't blame you for not believing me," Caedell said gruffly, as if the words were difficult to get out. "However, I needed to say my piece, I needed you to know. I could not go on any longer acting as if you were nothing to me."

"And you have felt this way since you were a child?" I could hardly believe such a thing.

We, of course, had spent more time together as of late, and if I was being honest, he had only continued to surprise me. Not only had he come to my defence on more than once occasion, but he had also come to my aid and had protected me numerous times. Not to mention the fact that the great Heir of House Reide had even risked his life to save my own.

"Since the day I arrived in Noordeign when I was just a young boy. A boy whom you treated with kindness and respect," Caedell answered. "At that time, it was just a child's fancy. But over the years it grew, and then when I saw you that day, when you were five and ten—"

I nodded, remembering the time he spoke of. "I have never been so angry as I was when I watched your father strike you." One of his hands lifted to my jaw, and he cradled my face softly before running his thumb over the scar on my lips. "That was the day he gave you this."

"Yes," I whispered.

"Then at the tourney," he continued. "I watched the way your family treated you; the way Gwain treated you. It took everything in me to keep my distance, to watch your father push you aside or try and trade you like a piece of meat. Seeing their disregard for you and your well-being ate me alive."

"But that night," I murmured. "When I came across you at camp, you were so unpleasant."

"I seem to remember not being the only one," he chuckled.

"You teased me for my tears. You mocked my feelings." My eyes narrowed at him.

"It was not very well done of me, I will admit. But you can call it misplaced jealousy," he confessed, and then he moved his hand from my face and into my hair where his fingers tangled amongst the strands.

"And is *this* about jealousy?" I demanded, although my voice was far softer than I had meant for it to be.

"What?" His brows furrowed.

"Is this because you've received more word from her or

something?" The amber of his irises darkened at my suggestion, but I ignored it. "Are you doing this because of Ceara, because you want to hurt her or because you want to get even?"

"For once in my life, this has nothing to do with Ceara!" He spat the name, and his grasp on my hair tightened until I was tipping my head back. "I am doing this because I can think of nothing else. I dream about what it feels like to hold you in my arms. I imagine it is me who you think of when you seek your pleasure from your own touch. I pray that it is my face you long to see, or my voice that soothes you."

"Caedell," I murmured, and I heard the hitch in his breath.

"You so rarely call me by my name." His tone was deep and smooth, and my cheeks heated at the sound. "Say it again."

"*Caedell*—" My soft whisper was muffled by his lips, and my eyes closed as I moaned into his mouth. Pinning me to the wall, Caedell tightened his hold on my side, and then he used the hand on the back of my head to angle my face just slightly.

When he had kissed me in his bed, I had been sure his passion had been misplaced. But now, as he embraced me with more ferocity than I had thought possible, I knew it was for me. It was me beneath his hands, and it was me who he wanted.

Parting my lips with his tongue, he flicked the tip of it against my own and groaned when he heard my whimper. I was consumed by him, by the flames he had lit within me, and dear Gods did I want to burn. It was unlike anything I had felt before, and when he deepened the kiss, my knees buckled.

Refusing to be separated, he bent just slightly, and I felt the hand that had been stroking the underside of my breast lower to the skirts of my gown. Grabbing at the fabric, he lifted the hem until it had risen past my knee, and I shivered when the backs of his fingers slid across the delicate flesh of my thigh.

Smiling against my mouth at my reaction, Caedell moved his hand, twisting it slightly so that he was cupping the back of my leg, and then he lifted the limb until it was hitched around his hip. Struggling to balance on one foot—a foot that I could barely feel considering my entire body seemed to be tingling—I tightened my hold on his shirt and then tugged on his hair and he arched his back in response. Pinning his hips against mine, he pressed me against the stone wall, and my belly swooped at the feel of him pressed between my thighs.

We fit. We fit in a way I had not thought possible, in a way I had been searching for my entire life, and the feeling overwhelmed me.

Unable to fight back the sudden surge of anxiety, I pulled my face from his and turned my head to the side. Leaning away, Caedell looked at me with a dazed expression while he panted for breath.

"What is it?" he asked, and I peered at him from the corner of my eye, immediately noticing the deep flush across his cheeks.

"Nothing," I murmured as I pulled my hands away from his body.

"Did I do something wrong?" He pressed as his gaze searched my face worriedly. "Did I hurt you?"

Confused as to why he would ask such a thing, I tilted my head and frowned. "No, of course not."

Taking a step away, Caedell carefully lowered my leg back down, and when he was sure I was balanced, he took a clumsy step away.

"I shouldn't have gotten so carried away." The words were rushed, and he ran his hands down the front of his shirt nervously.

"Calm down," I muttered, and for a moment I was annoyed

by his overreaction. But then I watched the normally stoic man fidget like a spooked animal, and I felt the need to reassure him. "I'm fine, it's not as if I'm some blushing maiden."

The flush on his face darkened to a deep crimson. Assuming that my mentioning my experience had embarrassed him, I stiffened at his reaction. However, forcing myself to swallow my pride, I took another moment to truly observe him, and noticed just how out of sorts he was.

"Caedell," I called softly, but when those amber eyes of his would not meet my own, I figured my initial assumption was in fact backwards. "Have you not done this before?"

He turned from me then crossed his arms over his chest but did not deny my question, and I ran a hand through my hair. "That's not possible."

Stiffening, he glared at me from over his shoulder and I tried to explain. "You and Ceara..."

"Why do you keep asking about her!?" he seethed.

"I have heard—"

"Given how many lies are told about you, I would have assumed you would know better than to believe every whisper you hear!"

My assumption had hurt him, that much was obvious, but his anger only brought more questions. I had previously confronted him about the rumours I had heard, the rumours all of Elrin had heard, and yet he had not disputed them then. Though, I supposed he did not confirm them either.

But there was also the first-hand knowledge I did have. I had seen the pair together in the past; I had noticed the lustful gaze and lingering touches of Ceara Reide over the years, and deep down, despite his denial, I knew she was more than just his father's wife.

"You two have always been rather close." I shrugged, and Caedell's darkened gaze met mine.

"And do you fuck every man you are *close* with?" Flinching,

I sank my teeth into my ruined bottom lip and then lifted a brow.

"I suppose I deserved that," I admitted begrudgingly, and though I was taking accountability for my mistake, Caedell only put more distance between us.

"So, if she was not the reason..." His face shifted just slightly at the words and my brows furrowed. "If it wasn't because you regretted what happened that night in your bed, then why did you say those words in the council room?"

"I was doing it for you." Scoffing, I rolled my eyes, and Caedell scowled at my reaction. "You don't trust that?"

"I can't trust reasoning that has no logic to it," I rebutted. "How does loathing you benefit me?"

"Rígan—" Whatever he was about to say was interrupted by a loud pounding on the door, and we turned to see Krayern enter the room.

FORTY-FOUR

"Ah, there you are." His eyes bounced between Caedell's still-pinkened face and then to me. Thankfully I had enough practice to appear unbothered, however, he still lifted a black brow in my direction.

"Are you well, Lady Rígan?" There was no teasing in his tone, only concern, but I bristled nonetheless.

"Fine," I snapped, hoping my answer would signal my dismissal of his presence, but Krayern did not leave.

"What is it that you need, Krayern?" Caedell demanded when the man remained where he stood, and the Lord of Denimoore turned to his friend.

"We are gathering in the council room in a few hours." Frowning, I looked to Caedell in confusion, but when he seemed equally as puzzled, I focused back on Krayern.

"I thought the meeting had been cancelled for today." He nodded his head but lifted an arm, and it was then that I noticed a piece of parchment pinched between his fingers.

"It was, but we've received word." Caedell moved across the room and plucked the page from his friend.

"It is still early; we should not hear from the other families for some time yet." His eyes lowered to the letter, and I watched the way they roamed across the page and then his gaze widened.

"What?" I asked worriedly. "What does it say?"

"They must have sent this before receiving our own missive," Caedell murmured but that did not explain his expression.

"Well?" I growled impatiently before repeating myself. "What does it say?"

"It's from your father," Krayern answered, and I noticed just how grave his expression really was. "There was an attack on your lands."

My stomach sank while the air left my lungs, but Caedell began shaking his head.

"He is fine, Rígan," Caedell promised. "They were victorious against the rebels."

"Well, that's good news," I whispered and then my brows furrowed, and I sent him an accusing glare. "Why did you look so worried if it was good news?"

"He mentions that one of the men claimed to be the High Commander," Krayern answered, and when my mouth parted, the man's throat bobbed nervously before he continued. "Apparently your father joined the men for the battle, and when he faced their leader, the man claimed to be the High Commander. However, when your father struck him down, the man did not fall."

"What?" I whispered, certain I had misunderstood his words.

"Your father says the man cheated death a dozen times before he finally managed to take the stranger's head." A cold shiver of fear raced down my spine, and Krayern frowned when he noticed my body quiver.

"What are you saying?" I knew, of course. I had witnessed such a thing for myself, but I needed someone else to say the words.

"It appears our worries were correct. The rebels have

indeed obtained magic," Krayern whispered. "Dark magic, a power that could only belong to the God of Death himself."

"I DON'T SEE why we had to come back here," Catiline whispered as she wrapped her arms around her torso, and I stopped walking and peered down at her.

"I told you that I could manage on my own," I reminded her.

"I don't want you to have to go in there by yourself," she sighed and then looked to the doors ahead of us. "I just don't understand why we could not have a servant fetch them for you."

"Because, I do not need the castle to run rampant with whispers," I replied and then placed a hand on her shoulders. "Donigan assured me that the room has been cleared, but should you not want to risk it, you could just wait outside the doors."

"No," she argued. "If you are going in there, then so am I." I gave her a doubtful look but said nothing more on the subject and crossed the last remaining distance between us and the library.

Pressing my palms against the wood, I pushed open the doors with bated breath and braced myself for carnage. However, just as Donigan had promised, the bodies had been removed, though there was still a staleness to the air, and the pretty rug that had been on the middle of the floor was gone.

"Thank the Gods," Catiline whispered, and I hummed softly before stepping into the library.

"The book I was reading last night came from the second shelf on the far-left side," I explained. "If I were to guess, I would bet that the other texts about the Forefolk and the Gods would be there as well."

"Is there anything in particular we are looking for?" Cat asked as her gaze roamed across the room with uncertainty.

"I'm hoping we find something about the time before the Divine Triad shunned the dark God." Gasping, Cat turned her wide eyes to me, and I squared my shoulders. "It is important that we find as much information as we can about him and the powers he possessed."

"Does this have something to do with the men from last night?" she whispered, and I wondered just how much she had really witnessed from behind that tapestry.

"They mentioned that their High Commander follows… *him*." I was careful not to use the God's true name in hopes of not alarming her any more than necessary.

"But you don't really think that's true, do you?" Months ago, I would have thought the idea of any man worshipping something so evil would be impossible. The people of Elrin did not speak of the God, let alone wear his sigil. But the proof was there. The rebellion was not only gaining more power, but I had witnessed the unnatural occurrence twice, and now, so had my father. One man cheating death was an unexplainable marvel. Three men was a pattern, and we needed to find a way to stop it from happening again. If our enemies could not die the way mortal men should, then this rebellion was already won for our foes.

"I don't know what to think anymore, Cat," I admitted, and her face paled at the words.

"And what do the lords think?" Krayern had wanted the others to gather immediately after he had spoken to Caedell and me. But my brother had been well into his cups the night before and apparently, Gwain had joined him. Neither man was up to discussing such significant matters this morning, and I could tell that their carelessness and the delay in finding a solution angered the rest of the council.

"We haven't spoken at length about it yet," I sighed as I ran a hand over my face, and she frowned.

"Should that not be a top priority?" she asked with a raised brow, and I nodded.

"We will gather this afternoon," I assured her.

"We? You are joining them again?" Catiline asked in surprise, and I nodded.

"Krayern has extended an invitation to me for all future meetings, much to my brother's displeasure." Chewing on her lower lip, Cat glanced around the room and then peeked up at me from the corner of her eye.

"Do you think they would allow me to sit in again as well?" Krayern had not had a problem with it the last time, and though it was not custom, I could not see him or his mother allowing anyone to turn us away.

"I don't see why not," I muttered softly as I shrugged. "However, I will warn you that Skileer will most likely put up a fuss about it."

"I suppose that's to be expected." Cat sighed with a roll of her eyes.

"But—" Placing a gentle hand on her shoulder, I guided her towards the far end of the library. "Perhaps if we have something to bring them, something from the scriptures here, he would be less averse to our presence."

"Doubtful," she laughed, but then her eyes lifted to the rows and rows of books that surrounded us. "However, if the others take our side, he won't have a leg to stand on."

Happy with our plan, Catiline clapped her little hands together and then grinned up at me. "We best get to work; we have a lot to go through."

"WHAT IS it you are trying to say?" Gwain demanded from his seat, and I tipped my head so that it rested against the tall back of my chair and closed my eyes in frustration.

"I have explained it to you twice already, Dansby," Krayern growled, and Gwain finally had enough sense to look wary as the massive Lord of Denimoore glared down at him from where he stood.

"But it's not possible," Gwain argued, though his voice was quiet and weak. "A magic like that does not exist. I thought we all agreed on that."

Perhaps I would have been more understanding of his skepticism had I not been aware that Gwain knew better than to say such a thing. He himself had witnessed such magic at the tavern, and surely he now understood that it had not been a trick of our minds.

While the two men debated back and forth about the truth of it, I turned my head just slightly and glanced at Caedell. He had not chosen to sit in the only empty chair next to me, but stood against the far wall to my right, and I observed the space between us with a frown. Perhaps my focus should have been on the topic at hand, but every time I looked towards the other men, I was certain I could feel the heavy stare of those burning amber eyes.

"But what does it matter if the High Commander was defeated?" My gaze slid to Skileer in bewilderment, and the others turned to glower at him in turn.

"What does it matter?" Synrick repeated, and I watched the way his normally soft expression shifted into a fierce scowl.

"Their leader is dead," Skileer continued as he waved a hand in the air, as if the motion would somehow help us see his point.

"You think this rebellion stops with one man?" Aarik laughed coldly as he crossed the room, and my brother glared at him.

"Why would it not?" Gwain interjected. "They are fighting for him."

"They are fighting for an idea!" The words poured out of me before I could stop them, and all heads turned in my direction. Clearing my throat softly, I sat up straighter in my seat and then met my brother's furious expression. "They are not fighting for their commander, they are fighting for the things he is promising them, for the hope that he has instilled in their very beings."

"And what hope is that?" Skileer sneered, and I ran my hand through my hair while I gathered my thoughts.

Those boys we had taken prisoner before the tourney burned with the same hatred I had now seen time and time again. It wasn't just their fortune that enraged them, it was us, it was the Gods, it was the world. They had been taught to fight against everything they were meant to trust, everything good they were meant to adore, and not only had they turned on our Gods, but now they possessed a magic that could make their rebellion unstoppable.

"Hope that with this war, a change will come." *Change*— the word wasn't big enough to truly portray the chaos that would ensue should we lose. Chaos that those who turned on us couldn't seem to foresee. They couldn't see that the empty promises and delusions they had been promised would not be the reality of what would certainly occur. "They hope that we are nearing the end of the Anointed and the world as we know it."

"Which will be possible if they cannot be beat," Krayern added. "We cannot slay dead men."

"We can if we take their heads," Skileer murmured under his breath. "It worked for my father."

"That is not how a battle is won. It takes carefully planning and a solid strategy. Archers and cavalry play a vital role. Not to mention the fact that being in that close of contact with warriors who can withstand mortal wounds would risk us all!" Aarik snapped, and I fought the urge to rub at my temples and instead tried to think of a way to explain Skileer's ignorance of such things. Such things he should know, and judging by the faces of the others who surrounded me, they seemed just as exasperated by his lack of knowledge.

"He simply means that they are not truly unbeatable." It was Gwain who surprisingly jumped to my brother's defence, and I narrowed my eyes at him, wondering when they had grown close enough for him to do so.

"We do not know their limitations," Synrick pointed out. "We also cannot be sure just how many of the rebels have gained such powers."

"And while we have our assumptions, we cannot be certain as to where such an ability came from," Krayern added, and Cat, who sat across the table from me, shifted in her seat. Not understanding her reaction, I examined her closely and watched the way she avoided my eyes as she glanced down at her lap before wetting her lips.

"That we do know, actually," Catiline interjected, her voice high with nervousness, and both my brother and Gwain scoffed in unison.

"This is not a discussion for the likes of you," Skileer sneered. "You are here out of courtesy, not because we think you will have anything helpful to add."

Curling my fingers into fists, I waited for one of the Demys heirs to interrupt, or perhaps Dyani, but they remained silent, so I looked to Caedell. I hoped I would see some sign of support, some signal that he would step in. But the Heir of House Reide appeared to be lost in his own thoughts. His amber eyes were peering out the window before him, and I couldn't be certain he had heard anything that had been said over the last few minutes.

Knowing it would be up to me to defend Catiline, I straightened myself in my seat and my lips parted. But before

I could say a word, her dark angular eyes looked to me, and she shook her head softly and then rose from her chair.

"You are mistaken, Lord Skileer." Gone was the shrill crack of anxiety in her voice, and I watched with wide eyes as she lifted her small chin and peered down at the rest of us. "I have spent the morning scouring the library along with your sister, but I will have you know, I was already rather well versed in the history of Elrin."

Placing her hands on the table, she leaned over the wood just slightly and let her eyes move from one face to another as she addressed the room. "My family may not be of Anointed blood, and we may not be warriors, but we serve our Gods and their favourites in other ways. Our weapons are our minds, and they are sharp as steel."

Reaching down towards the floor, Catiline grabbed at something and then tossed it onto the middle of the table we surrounded. Shifting forward, I examined the leather-bound pages and then my gaze lifted to her in surprise.

We had left the library empty-handed; our search had been fruitless, or so I thought, and then we had parted ways before the meeting. When the time came to gather, she had beat me to the council room. In fact, she had been the first one seated, followed by myself, but had given no inclination she had brought anything along with her. Not once had she mentioned the book that sat before me, and I wondered why she would hide such a thing.

"I was able to find this," she explained sternly, and my brows furrowed at the fierceness of her expression. "I think you'll find it rather helpful."

Everyone moved towards the book, but I remained pressed against the back of my chair, peering at the stranger before me. Not caring for my bewildered expression, Cat smoothed a hand down the front of her gown and then cast a heated glare towards my brother.

"Perhaps the next time I am allowed to participate in a

meeting, it will be because of more than just courtesy," she snarled.

Snorting softly, Dyani caught my attention, and I watched as she turned to face me with a lifted brow. "It seems the shewolf has found herself a pack mate."

CHAPTER
FORTY-FIVE

Hurriedly moving to his feet, Skileer snatched the book from the table and brought it closer to his face before flipping through the text with a scowl. The others did not shift from their seats but watched my brother carefully as he nearly tore the pages in his haste to find exactly what answers Cat had thought she had discovered.

"What are we meant to do with this?" Skileer snarled before slamming the book back onto the table before him, and Aarik crossed the room and pulled on his wrist until his palm lifted from the leather. Pushing at his shoulder, he guided my brother back just a step and then slid the book back in Catiline's direction.

"Perhaps if you gave her the chance to speak, she would have told us what she has found." Skileer glowered at the eldest brother but said nothing as he sank back into his seat, and it was then that Caedell finally looked in our direction. However, his eyes did not seek out my own or anyone else's. No, they were solely focused on the deep brown leather, and I noticed the way he seemed to be almost entranced by the book before him.

Ignoring Caedell's bewildered gaze, Cat smoothed her

delicate hand over the cover before flipping open the pages. Carefully tracing the tip of her pointer finger along the words, her eyes followed her hand across the parchment, and then she paused and manoeuvred the text until it faced Krayern and his mother.

"Here," she said softly, and it felt as if everyone in the room stopped breathing for a moment, as if we were unable to do anything but stare at the page she pointed to.

Rising from her chair, Dyani pressed a hand against the wooden surface of the table while the other stretched for the book, and Catiline withdrew her touch and watched the Lady of Denimoore.

"Where did you find this?" Dyani asked softly, and though I did not move from my chair, I stretched as tall as I could in an attempt to see what it was they were looking at.

"What is it?" Krayern asked as he studied his mother closely.

"At first I thought it was just a simple passage, nothing of consequence really," Cat explained, and when we looked at her, she ducked her chin and tucked a piece of hair behind her ear shyly—the fierceness she had just displayed was now apparently forgotten.

"But?" Aarik asked as he rounded the table to stand in the space between his mother's chair and my own.

"But there is a word, it is not like the others." Confused, I frowned at my friend, and when she noticed, she cleared her throat. "The other scriptures—they talk about those who worshipped our Gods. They are called devoted or even followers. But this is different."

"Different in what way?" Synrick asked as he too crowded towards the book.

"*His* followers, though there were very few it seems, were all called servants, or worse." Her voice softened, and her face became solemn. "They were called slaves."

"Slaves?" Synrick repeated, and Dyani lifted the book and

handed it to the Healer's Anointed so that he may read it for himself.

"When I noticed this difference, I looked for other discrepancies between the scriptures of the first God and the Divine Triad."

"And what did you find?" Krayern asked, and Cat held out her hand. Hesitating for a moment, Synrick then returned the leather-bound pages to her, and we watched as she searched. Her eyes narrowed for a pause, and then she passed the book to the Healer's Anointed once more.

"Gifts are mentioned, there are many blessings from the Gods," she answered. "But when it comes to *him*, the word *payment* is used every single time, and it sounds less like a blessing and more like an exchange."

"Payment?" I asked as I finally rose from my seat. "Payment given by the God?"

"No." Catiline shook her head. "Payment taken from his followers."

"And you said exchange." It was Aarik who spoke now, and my eyes lifted to his brooding face as he peered at the pages clutched in Synirck's hands. "What were they exchanging?"

Slamming the book closed, the Healer's Anointed slid it across the table. Almost as if he was trying to put as much space between him and what he had just read, and I glanced at the dark leather curiously before lifting my eyes to his troubled face.

"Their lives," he whispered angrily. "He was trading immortality for their devotion."

"Why do you say that with such disdain?" Skileer asked as he reached for the book only to freeze as the rest of us glared at him.

"How could you ask such a thing?" Synrick growled, and my brother rolled his eyes at the man.

"Do our Gods not bestow their own gifts onto us in

exchange for our love and worship?" The room grew tense once more, and I glared at my brother in warning, but he paid me no mind. "Surely you can see how that may also be considered payment? We offer them our devotion and they bless us in return. It hardly seems any different."

"Perhaps that would be true if it came from one of our Divine Triad." Turning towards him, I watched the way Caedell prowled towards my brother and noticed the way his entire body was strung tightly, like a bow string ready to snap. "But nothing that comes from him is a blessing."

"I don't know," Skileer chuckled softly. "I think living forever seems like a rather—"

Grabbing on to the back of my brother's chair, Caedell pulled it until it faced him. Slamming his palm against the panel next to Skileer's head, Caedell then bent down until his face was a mere two inches away from my brother's.

"Nothing"—the word was quiet, but the roughness of his tone made me shiver—"that comes from *his* hand is a blessing. He is darkness. *He is death.*"

Skileer shrank away from the burning amber eyes, and I remained frozen, unsure if I should do something to separate them. However, before I had to make a decision, Krayern moved to his friend and placed a gentle hand on Caedell's strong shoulder. The touch was enough to pull him out of his sudden rage, and he moved back to the window he had been so lost in just a few moments before while the Heir of House Demys addressed the room.

"We will meet with the Grand Elder and will have the rest of the scriptures searched. We will not stop until we know what has truly transpired. As of right now, we know that some of these rebels have found magic, but that is not to say for certain that it has come from the God himself. He was banished centuries ago, so we must assume there is another possibility." Krayern was right, of course, there had to be another explanation. However, looking at the others who surrounded me, it was easy to see their uncertainty as well.

"The missives from the other families will be here soon," Aarik added. "We will need to have plans in place for when they come. Perhaps that should be our focus while the Grand Elder and his men investigate. After all, the more we delay our battle plans, the more time we give to the rebels to strengthen their forces."

"Agreed," Krayern said with a nod, and then the pair exited the room followed by Dyani. Gwain and my brother were next, though he threw a nasty look towards Caedell just as he stepped through the threshold.

Left with Catiline and Caedell, I looked between the pair. But before I could pick who to address first, Caedell turned from the window, offered us a quick bow, and then strode out the room without a second glance in my direction.

"He seems rather off today," Cat murmured while she reached for the forgotten book, and I stood from my seat and crossed my arms over my chest before narrowing my eyes at her.

Noticing my ire, she clutched the leather to her chest. "What?"

"You know what, Catiline." My voice was cold and sharp, and she winced at the sound.

"You're mistaken, I don't have the slightest idea." Not interested in playing this game with her, I crossed the room in four long strides and shut the doors before spinning to face my friend once more.

"Why did you not tell me?" I demanded.

"Tell you?" Her head tilted to the side, and I nearly snarled at the perplexed expression on her face.

"Were you not the one who said your mind was as sharp as steel?" I snapped. "Do not pretend to be so obtuse, it is exasperating."

"I don't see why you are so upset about it, I'm the one who

found it," Cat grumbled while her eyes lowered to the floor, and I scoffed.

"I'm not upset about you finding the book," I explained. "I'm upset about you hiding it from me. Why would you do such a thing?"

"Does that really matter?" My arms lowered to my sides, and I searched my friend's face for some clue as to what she was thinking.

"It matters that you did not think you could be honest with me," I answered, and she exhaled roughly before her shoulders sagged.

"I wanted a chance is all." Not understanding, I furrowed my brows, and she chewed on her bottom lip before taking a step closer. "I wanted a chance to prove my worth."

"To whom, the others?"

Shrugging, Cat finally peeked up at my face. "To all of you."

"Cat—" I started but she shook her head.

"Don't." One of her small hands lifted towards me and my mouth snapped shut. "Don't act as if you are not part of it, do not pretend as if you do not have the same opinion as them."

"Catiline, you are my friend," I reminded her. "You do not have to prove anything to me."

"Yes I do," she argued. "We are friends and I know that. I know that you care, Rígan, that has never been a question. But you do not see me as one of you. You said as much yourself. You have overlooked my value, and I wanted a chance to show you all that I can do more than sit silently and be a proper lady."

Guilt weighed heavily on my shoulders, and I watched as my friend shifted from foot to foot nervously before she sighed.

"You have been given more here," she said. "The others, they don't treat you the way your father does, the way the nobles do when we are in the south. They see beyond your pretty face and your bloodlines; they see your worthiness."

Swallowing, I glanced at the now-empty chairs in the room, and Cat closed the last bit of space between us before grabbing at one of my hands. "I just wanted to be seen too."

Squeezing her fingers, I waited until her dark eyes met my own and then I nodded. Interlocking our hands, Cat offered me a blinding smile and then tossed the book back onto the table and pulled me towards the door.

THE HALLS WERE QUIET, and I turned my head to peer at the thin crack of space under the heavy wood of the doors. The torches were lit in the hallway, which was easily seen by the soft orange light flickering across the stone floor of the room, but it was silent. And perhaps I should have found solace in that, in the fact that even after the attack on Denimoore and the information we had learned today, the others were not roaming around the castle, worried and panicked. But the stillness within the mighty stone walls only sent my mind wandering, and I sighed before resting my head against the cold glass and peering up at the great northern mountains. Their snowcaps seemed almost blue under the glow of the moon, and I studied their peaks before tilting my head back so that I may get a better look at the stars while my hands curved over the corners of the leather cover of the book that sat in my lap.

Krayern's men had made quick work of the library; they had found every text that even so much as mentioned the God of Death, but it had not been much help. There was no clear explanation as to why the rebels had been entrusted with immortality, and as far as we knew, there was another reason for how they came to possess such power. After all, we were still fairly certain the God they now turned to had not truly returned, and though that brought some relief, we were still left with more questions rather than answers.

Lost in my worry, I continued to search the stars, hoping to see some sign, some signal from the Gods above before I whispered, "Huntress, please guide us."

My breath fogged the glass before me, and I watched as the mist expanded across the window before slowly fading into nothingness, just like my prayer.

"Do you think she'll hear your plea?" Standing from the ledge I had been perched on, I spun towards the door. Not caring that the book went tumbling to the floor, I placed one palm on my beating heart while the other braced against the frigid glass to help me keep my balance.

"What are you doing here?" I demanded once I finally caught my breath, and Caedell stepped farther into the room and then pressed the doors closed behind him with a resounding click.

"Should you not have a guard with you or at the very least Donigan?" He took a step towards me, then another, and I watched his movements with narrowed eyes as he rounded the table.

"You didn't answer my—" The words caught in my throat as Caedell herded me backwards, and when my hips pressed against the cool stone, my knees buckled, and I fell back onto the sill I had been sitting on.

Following my movements, Caedell bent at the waist until either hand was pressed into the rock beside my hips and his face was a mere inch from my own. Blinking up at the burning amber, I swallowed roughly and watched as his gaze lowered to my mouth.

"I couldn't sleep," he whispered, and my eyes fluttered shut as his warm breath fanned across the lower half of my face while one of his thumbs stroked across the skirt of my gown, though the touch was so soft I wondered if it was perhaps a figment of my imagination.

"So what, you decided to find yourself a distraction?" I asked weakly, and when Caedell lifted a brow at the sound, I swallowed before glaring at him. I had been taken by surprise and that had left me defenceless against my body's reactions to his proximity.

"Are you offering?" His head tilted to the side just slightly while he flashed me that smile that made the dimples hollow out in his cheeks, and I blinked up at him as if in a daze.

"What?" I spluttered, and his grin grew at my lack of decorum.

"Are you offering to be a distraction?" he asked again as he closed the space between us, and one of my hands lifted to brace against his chest, ready to push him away. However, when the warmth of his body seeped into the chilled skin of my palm, my fingers fisted the wool of his tunic.

"What if I am?" I murmured quietly, and Caedell trembled beneath my touch.

"And is that *all* you would offer me?" My brows furrowed while I watched that smile fall from his face, and then he lowered his chin and studied the hand that was curled in his shirt.

"What else would you have of me?" I breathed, and the pounding of his heart quickened.

"Everything," he replied. "I would have everything you would be willing to give me."

The air left my lungs, and I blinked up at his face while I tried to gather myself. To a maiden his words would be sweet, poetic even, but I saw his answer for what it was.

He was right, he would take everything from me. He would collect bits and pieces until there was nothing left but an empty husk. And despite his pretty declaration of caring for me, I did not know what I would receive in return. Would he give *me* everything in exchange? Or would I be gifted some lovely words and a few nights of his warmth before I was pushed aside for another?

Knowing I could not risk it, I spread my thighs and pulled on the material clasped in my fist until he was standing between my legs.

"A distraction is what I offer," I muttered softly. "But do you think you can handle me?" I questioned, and though there was a look of disappointment, a flush covered those strong cheekbones.

Lowering his head, he pressed his brow to mine, and I tilted my chin towards him. However, he did not meet me halfway, and when I noticed his hesitation, I searched his face.

"Are you sure, shewolf?" he questioned, and while I was certain he had meant to sound far more confident, I could hear the tremor in his voice. Raising my other hand, I tangled my fingers into his hair and tugged on the strands.

"Stop talking," I snarled and then I crushed my lips against his.

CHAPTER
FORTY-SIX

A distraction, I reminded myself. That was what was decided and was all it would be. However, that did not mean I was not going to make certain I seized the opportunity.

Lifting a leg, I pressed my knee against his waist while I canted my hips towards him, and then I ran my teeth across his lower lip. Surprised at the sensation, Caedell panted into my mouth, and I flicked my tongue against his while my hands tightened their hold on him.

The warmth that had been burning between us the last time was now an inferno, and I was determined to devour the flame until it burned me from the inside out.

"Rígan," Caedell groaned as he pulled his mouth from mine, and finally his hands were moving. One cupped the back of my head as he angled my face away so that he could run his lips across the sharp bone of my cheek and down to my jaw. The other grabbed at the skirts of my gown. However, the heavy material of my dress restricted my movement, and I released my grip on his tunic so that I could gather the fabric and pull it higher.

Following the hem with shaking fingers, Caedell smoothed his palm over my knee and up my thigh and then sank his

401

fingertips into the plushness there. Tipping my chin, I cast my eyes to where he seared me with his touch and watched the way flesh gave way to the firmness of his hold.

"Is this alright?" he breathed against my ear, and I smiled to myself before grabbing at his wrist.

"A little higher would be ideal," I murmured back before tugging on the chestnut strands that were still tangled in my other hand, and his eyes flickered closed for a second as his jaw clenched.

"I can't think when you do that," he admitted with a growl, and my grin grew as I noticed the fluttering pulse in his throat.

"You aren't meant to be thinking." The words came out huskier than I had meant for them to, and for a moment I worried I had exposed what little control I desperately clung to. However, the tone only seemed to encourage Caedell, and he squeezed the thick muscle of my thigh before hitching it over his hip in the same way the other had been and my skirts pooled around my waist.

Now free from the barrier, Caedell pressed closer to me, and I linked my ankles behind his back and urged him forward. Not prepared for the sudden movement, his hand slipped from my leg, and he braced himself against the glass next to my head while he pressed exactly where I wanted him to. I was unable to contain the groan that broke from my lips, and I heard Caedell's sharp inhale.

"My Gods," he whispered as he buried his face into my neck. "Make that sound again."

Turning my chin just slightly, I caught his earlobe between my teeth and gave it a sharp nip.

"That is a privilege that is earned," I told him while my hips rocked into his own as I sought out more friction. "If that's something you want, you will have to work for it."

Pressing his teeth to the side of my neck in retaliation,

Caedell ran the sharp edges across the tender flesh and then laved the skin with his tongue. "Tell me how."

I knew of his inexperience now, but I would be lying if I said it did not still surprise me. Clenching my eyes closed, I struggled for composure, and then I loosened my legs from around his waist. Straightening to his full height, Caedell peered down at me with burning amber eyes, and I took in the deep flush that was painted across his face and the way his muscular chest rose and fell with every breath.

He looked positively wrecked and devastatingly beautiful, and I wondered how he had gone so long without being touched.

"You want to know how to please me?" I asked as I lifted a hand to stroke the backs of my fingers down my throat and across the neckline of my gown, and his eyes followed the movement.

"Need," he growled, and I tilted my head.

"Need?" I repeated the word slowly as I tried to understand.

"I don't want to know; I need to know. I demand to know, and I demand to be shown." The hand that had been pressed against the window curled under my chin, and he tilted my face up as he stepped closer once more.

"You demand?" I scoffed, and his fingers tightened around my jaw before he bent towards me again.

His mouth was hot, his kiss filthy, and for a moment, all arguments—all thoughts—left my head, and I was left mindless and trembling.

"You said I had to work for it," he whispered against my lips. "Well, consider me your ever devoted servant. Teach me how to make you feel good."

Had I been a person of more humility, I may have told him he was well on his way to becoming a master at the art of my pleasure. But I was not, and I refused to admit as much to Caedell the Undying, the great Heir of House Reide. No, I would have him on his knees before I would confess such a thing.

"You truly know nothing?" I asked, skeptical that he had been fully truthful about several things during our last conversation, one of which being his virtue, the other, his feelings for me. But that was a subject for another time. For now, I would focus on the burning heat simmering low in my belly.

"Not nothing," he said softly while his thumb stroked across my bottom lip. "But any of my previous knowledge does not matter now."

"Meaning what?" I demanded as I pulled my face from his hand. "You said you had not done this before."

"And that's the truth of it," Caedell snapped. "But that is not to say I have not been privy to information from others."

"Men and their conquests, always boasting and bragging," I scoffed with a roll of my eyes, and Caedell frowned at me.

"Is that how you see it?" He no longer stood between my legs, and I shivered at the sudden loss of warmth.

"That is the way of things," I muttered while I smoothed a hand down my long hair, hoping I appeared unbothered rather than regretful for the way things had begun to turn.

Caedell searched my face for a long moment, and then his eyes lowered to the stone floor beneath his boots. "And is that how you would see me?"

"See you?"

"Would I be a conquest?" I nearly flinched at the hurt in his deep voice, and I knew I needed to act quickly before this *thing* between us was ruined beyond repair.

"No," I answered honestly as I stood, and then I reached for one of his hands that hung at his side. "Despite what is said about me, that is not how I view things."

"And how do you view things?" he asked. "How do you view Gwain?"

"Gwain?" I nearly spat the name, and whatever hurt that

had been reflected in those golden irises was now concealed behind a wall of sorts.

"Do you still care for him?" His question threw me, and I released his fingers from my hold as I backed up a step.

"Why are you asking me such a thing?" Whatever flame that had been burning between us was now snuffed out by ice, and I shivered as I crossed my arms over my chest.

"Because I deserve to know," he replied. "You know of my feelings; I have been forthcoming with them."

"Forthcoming?" I chuckled dryly. "You have been nothing more than unclear about your feelings."

"That is not true!" he argued. "I told you how I felt, and yet I am in the dark about your own desires."

"I think my desires were rather obvious," I growled as I waved a hand toward the sill I had been pressed against.

"Perhaps *desire* was the wrong word," Caedell said as he ran a hand through his tousled hair.

"Caedell," I sighed. "You said this would be a distraction, that is what was agreed upon."

For just a heartbeat, his shoulders sagged under the weight of my words, and then it was as if he pushed his frustration away and he was standing tall once more with a mask of indifference covering his face while he stared at me.

Swallowing nervously at his hardened gaze, I struggled to organize my thoughts in a way that would make sense. "I don't understand what you want. You go back and forth between loathing me and proclaiming you care. You save me, you tend to me, and then you shut me out. You cut me with your words, then you say you only did so for my own well-being. Your indecisiveness makes me dizzy, and I just don't understand."

He didn't deny any of my accusations, but just continued to glare at me. "So what would you have of me?"

What I would have and what I wanted were two very

different things, I realized. But only one could hurt me, and now, I was not willing to risk it.

"Give me what you initially offered," I whispered. "Give me a distraction."

Caedell was moving as soon as the words left my lips, and I clung to his shoulders as he lifted me into the air. Pulling me flush against him, he walked us to the round table that sat in the middle of the room and lowered me onto the cool wood. Blinking up at his unreadable face, I waited as he pulled my hands from his body, and then his palms were smoothing down the length of my arms until they reached my neck. Pressing one hand against my racing heart, Caedell urged me back until I was lying across the hard surface and I looked down at him.

Holding my gaze, he kept his palm against my chest, pinning me in place while the other grabbed at the hem of my dress once more. Lifting the fabric, he eased the skirts up, and when the pale flesh of both legs was exposed, he released the material from his fingers and moved them to my left knee. Carefully, that big hand cupped the joint, and he guided it up and then out, making space between my limbs again.

"Tell me," he whispered as the tips of his fingers stroked across the skin of my thigh, and I wet my lips before parting my legs even farther.

"Touch me," I answered, though I could not hear my voice over the pounding of my pulse, and his face remained impassive as he waited. Raising a shaky arm, I moved to the laces of my bodice, and then I plucked at the ribbon until the knot released.

Though I wore a corset and stays beneath the dark blue dress, the neckline hid a great deal of cleavage, and now that the tie was undone, the soft skin spilled out. Inhaling sharply, Caedell gazed down at my chest and the hand that rested against me slid lower until one of my breasts was filling his palm.

"You are stunning," he sighed into the silent room, and when he traced the edge of the corset, my back arched into his touch.

"More," I demanded, and the leg that was free from his hold wrapped around his hip. Urging him forward, I pressed my heel into the back of his thigh. "Touch me."

"Where?" he questioned, though judging by the way his eyes danced between where his hands rested on my body, I was certain he knew exactly where I meant. Growing impatient with this game, I reached for his fingers, the ones curled under my knee, and when I clutched at his wrist, I pulled.

But he did not give and instead, shook his head and then tightened his hold. Growling in annoyance, I tried once more, and he lifted a brow, but his hand remained where it was.

"Tell me or show me." His voice was deep with longing, and my throat dried at the sound of it. "Those are your options."

Eyeing him for a moment, I tried to decipher if this was a battle I would win. But when I was left unsure, I pulled away and slowly traced my own fingers up my leg. Noticing the movement, his eyes darted to follow their path, and I slowly slid my touch higher and higher until I was pushing my gown up to the apex of my thighs.

"Here," I said softly as I ran my index finger over the warm wetness between my legs, and Caedell's hold on my knee tightened to the point of bruising. However, the stinging pain only added to the pleasure building, and I felt a wave of arousal at the knowledge that I was slowly making him lose control.

"Touch me here, Caedell." The words were firmer than they had any right to be considering the fact that my entire being felt as if it was on the cusp of shattering, and Caedell's eyes snapped to my own.

"Are you certain?" I had not anticipated that he would ask for my consent again. Most men would not bother after receiving it once from a woman who obviously was so ready and wanton, and his thoughtfulness made me soften just ever so slightly.

"I am," I promised with a small smile. "Are you?"

He searched my face for a moment, as if he was not expecting me to ask the same. Hoping my expression showed my honesty, I waited, and he offered me a soft but earnest smile before leaning over my body. Slowly, as if he was nervous about spooking me, he lowered his face, and when his lips pressed against my own in the gentlest of brushes, I sighed.

He kissed me for a moment, but soon it wasn't enough, and when I responded in kind, he deepened it. While we battled for dominance, the hand that had been resting on my knee finally moved. Warmth followed the path of his touch, and my veins burned with lust as he finally reached the place I had been so desperate for him.

Pulling from my mouth, Caedell rested his forehead against my own, and I held his heated stare as he fought for breath. "You'll tell me if I do something you don't enjoy?"

"You won't hurt me," I assured him while my arms lifted to wrap around his shoulders, but he did not move. In fact, my words seemed to have struck a nerve, and I soothed the stiff muscles of his back with one hand while the other cupped his jaw.

"Caedell," I whispered, and when he relaxed into my embrace, I kissed him again. "I will tell you what I want, that was the agreement, remember?"

Pulling himself from whatever daze he had been in, he nodded, and I settled against the table once more while I waited for him to finally begin.

CHAPTER
FORTY-SEVEN

The first touch of his fingers was hesitant and far too delicate for my usual preference, but there was something about the man himself that elicited responses that were out of my control, and my mouth parted with a whimper.

"Like this?" Caedell asked as he studied my face closely, and I tipped my head back as my hips rose towards his hand.

"More," I demanded, and his eyes darkened at the neediness in my voice, but he did not give in to my order.

"Should I not ease you into it?" he questioned while he ran the tip of his nose along my own, and I glared up at him in annoyance.

"You are taking pleasure in this," I snapped, though the fierceness disappeared when Caedell circled the tips of his fingers again.

"I am," he admitted. "You must forgive me for wanting to indulge my desire by taking my time. I have thought of this for years, I don't plan to spoil it with impatience."

He called it impatience, but it was really desperation, and my fingers curled into claws and I tore at the fabric covering his back as I dragged him closer to me. Crushing his chest against my own, Caedell chuckled softly, but his pace did not change, and my entire body tensed as he teased me carefully.

"You demanded to be taught," I panted. "But now you defy me?"

"You sound displeased," Caedell said quietly before pressing a kiss to the scar on the right side of my mouth. "But I think your body says otherwise. You are quivering, and I've hardly touched you."

As much as I hated to admit it, he was right. My skin was on fire, my muscles trembled, and desire ran through my veins. And while delayed gratification was often more satisfying, I was not certain how much longer I could tolerate this pace.

"Teasing me does not generally bode well for others," I warned with a weak voice as I fought to focus.

"I am well aware of that," Caedell chuckled, and those fingers that had been circling the bundle of nerves slid lower and dipped into me hesitantly before returning to their previous place once more. "But I think this time I will take my chances."

Left to his mercy, I pressed into the wood beneath my body and took a deep breath as his lips trailed from my mouth, to my cheek, down my neck, and to my pulse point. Staying there for a moment, he sucked at the skin and flicked his tongue across the fluttering beat that pounded against the flesh.

"You're going to leave a mark," I groaned while my head tilted away in order to give him more access.

"I'm aware of that too," he muttered against my throat before focusing back on his task, and my fingers curled into his hair.

"I thought this was not about conquests." My eyes flickered shut as he hummed against the spot he had been fixated on while his fingers slowed their circling between my legs.

"I've had my share of victories and triumphs." His teeth

slid across my jugular and I whimpered. "But this is not the same."

Finally, the hand that had nearly stilled picked up a quicker tempo, and I cried out as he sought out my entrance with his middle finger while his thumb took its place above. Carefully he entered me again, and though he may not have had the skill of a more practiced lover, my body had been so desperate to be filled that I nearly wept at the sensation.

"I am not marking you for others to see. It is not to show them that I have had the privilege of having you like this," he continued. "I am doing it for you."

Confusion and desire fogged my mind, and I lifted my hips off the table as I encouraged him to press deeper into me. Following my silent request, Caedell slid a second finger in and held them there for a pause before tentatively moving his hand in a gentle thrust. It was what I had been needing, and now that I was full of the long, thick length of his fingers, I opened my legs farther and groaned when he put more force behind his movements.

"I want *you* to see my marks," he breathed while his free hand curled around the top of my corset before he tugged it as far down as the boning would allow, and then his fingers squeezed the supple flesh of my breasts. "I want you to see them and know you are the only woman worthy of them. The only woman I have ever wanted to carry them."

His declaration was heady. But despite the haze I was under, I was still aware that desire made even the proudest of men say things they did not mean. I had been given promises and pretty words before, and though I was desperate for him, I knew better than to believe anything he said while his fingers were buried in my cunt.

Knowing I needed to pull his attention elsewhere, I called out for him.

"Caedell." It came out in a gasp as his thumb swiped

across me roughly, and I tugged on his hair until his face lifted and his eyes met mine. *"Please."*

The word came out of me broken and pathetic, but his eyes darkened and he moved so that he could see the hand nestled between my thighs.

"Does it feel good?" he whispered as he pressed deeper into me, and my back arched sharply as his fingers clumsily stroked across that spot along my inner walls.

"Yes." I nodded, and my thighs splayed further open as my hips began to rock into his touch.

"And this?" The question was immediately forgotten when he pressed his fingertips upwards at the same time his thumb circled, and my mouth fell open but no sound came from me. "Tell me, Rígan."

"Yes!" I sobbed, and his thrusting slowed to a halt.

Not understanding why he remained still, even after my confirmation, I lifted my head to glare down at him.

Burning amber eyes peered up at me, their colour sharp in contrast to the dark lashes that framed them. However, it was the heat at which he looked at me that left me stunned. It was the stare of a hunter, a being that was set on its prey, and the intensity of his eyes made me quiver.

"Tell me you feel it too," he whispered into the dark room, and I ran my tongue across my bottom lip.

"Feel what?" I inhaled sharply as he bent his head towards my legs and pressed his mouth to my inner thigh before picking up his rhythm once more.

"The pull between us," he murmured against my skin while his thumb touched me just perfectly.

I did feel it, that tie that somehow had wrapped itself around both him and me. The same thread I had been trying to ignore since the tourney. However, confessing as much would not benefit me, not after I had witnessed his uncertainty and just how easily he could switch from supposedly caring for me to disregarding me all together.

Instead of answering, I reached for him once more, and this time did not allow him to resist my touch as I pulled him over me. Curling one arm around his shoulder, I brought my other hand to his cheek and guided his mouth to mine.

Consumed by the heat of our kiss, Caedell continued to move his fingers, and I was lost to the pleasure of it all. His mouth, his taste, the feel of his body over mine, the touch of his hands as he dragged me towards the edge of my desire. It was otherworldly, and when he softened our embrace and his lips ghosted over my scar, I finally reached my peak.

Burning heat swam through my veins, the flame licking at my skin while I fell over the edge, and then I was floating. Whatever tension had been in my body melted into nothingness, and I buried my face into Caedell's shoulder as I fought to catch my breath.

"Shh," he soothed as he slowed his movements, though he did not withdraw from me. "I have you."

Comfort after a climax was not something I had enjoyed often as it was so rarely given. Usually, my partner would pull away from me and worry about dressing themselves or doze off while I gathered myself. Caedell, however, tucked my face into the crook of his neck and pressed a kiss to my sweaty forehead while he carefully removed his fingers and then pulled the skirts of my dress back into their place. Smoothing the fabric over my thighs, he eased my shoulders from the table but kept me pressed against his chest while the trembling of my body slowed.

"Are you well?" he asked as my breathing returned to normal, and I leaned away from his body before peering up at him with a raised brow.

"Stop fishing for compliments," I muttered while I ran a hand through my hair, and he frowned and then stepped away.

"I was asking in earnest." His face was pinkened, and his eyes had lowered to his boots. Realizing he felt embarrassed by my testiness, I sighed and then slid from the table. Making certain my legs would not give out from under me, I reached a hand out towards him and cupped his face. For a moment, he nuzzled into my palm, and then he met my gaze with uncertainty.

"It was enjoyable," I said, though the term did not do the experience justice. "Now, what about you?"

Caedell pulled his face from my touch, and I frowned. "What?"

"Did you expect some sort of exchange?" he asked as he studied me closely, and I wrapped my arms around myself and shrugged.

"Not an exchange necessarily, but I figured we would continue on."

"Continue on to what?"

Nearly everything this man said or did came as a surprise, and I exhaled roughly before answering. "To the main event."

"As far as I'm concerned, that was the main event." He ran a hand through his dark hair, and then those eyes of his lowered to the bodice of my dress. Following his gaze, I realized my bust was nearly pouring out of its constraints, and I hurriedly retied the lace.

"I just mean, are you not wanting to…?" I had not felt this unsure since the night I lost my maidenhead, and I wondered how Caedell had the power to turn me into a babbling lass rather than the experienced woman I had been for nearly a decade.

Caedell finally looked away from me and let his attention roam around the room before he glanced at the window. Looking over my shoulder, I noticed the sky behind the great mountains had begun to lighten, and my brows rose when I realized just how close we were to dawn.

"As much as I would love to *continue*"—the word poured out of him in a purr—"we do not have the time I would like to take to truly enjoy such a thing, and remaining in this room for much longer puts us at risk for being caught."

"It would be your first time," I muttered with a roll of my eyes. "I think you are overestimating how long it would really take. Most men are rather *quick* at getting the job done."

Scoffing, Caedell crossed his arms over his chest and lifted a brow. "I think *you* are underestimating my stamina," he growled. "And what have I told you about comparing me to others?"

Perhaps it was the lust-filled haze I was still recovering from, but I couldn't remember speaking of such a thing. Scowling, I watched as he closed the space between us, and then he cupped my chin in his hand before pulling me towards his face.

"There is no *duty* I cannot perform and no contest I won't measure up in," he reminded me. "Do not assume I will be like the others."

Then his mouth was on mine, and I sagged into him as he kissed me deeply. However, before we could go any further, he pulled away, and I panted as I glared at him.

"It was not two minutes ago that you were asking if I was well while your cheeks turned crimson," I pointed out. "How do you go from that to this?"

I waved a hand at him, and he tipped his head to the side. "To what?"

"To this arrogant creature?" Caedell laughed softly and then grinned.

"I don't like being compared to men who are beneath me," he said. "It brings out my competitive streak, and winning is something I am confident in."

"You are not at all what I thought you were," I admitted softly, and his smile suddenly faded.

"We should get you to your room." Grabbing at my hand, he interlocked our fingers and then pulled me towards the doors.

Pressing the wood open, he peeked his head out through the crack and then led me through the space. Carefully he guided me through the hallways, never once letting go of my hand, and then we turned the corner that led to our rooms. Walking me to my chambers, he finally loosened his hold, and I paused at the door.

"You should try and get some sleep," he murmured while he ran a hand down the length of my hair. "We have no plans to meet until this afternoon, you have time to rest."

Feeling oddly nervous, I chewed on my lower lip and nodded, but remained silent, and Caedell leaned forward to press his mouth to my cheek.

"I will see you later then." Again, I nodded in reply, but just as I turned towards the door, his hand caught my shoulder, and he spun me to face him.

"I want you to know—" He paused and took a deep breath. "That was not just a distraction to me."

My brows furrowed as I searched for the right words, and Caedell examined my face.

"I don't understand," I confessed, and his eyes lowered to the floor. "Nothing you've said or done has made much sense."

"I know," he whispered.

"I'm beginning to feel like a plaything." My voice was sharper now, and Caedell swallowed.

"You aren't."

"Can you not give me a better explanation than that?" I could see that wall forming in the way his body had begun to stiffen, but he still would not meet my gaze. "Can you not give me anything?"

"Rígan," he sighed, and I clenched my jaw before running a hand over my face. Perhaps it was my blood that kept him from being completely honest with me. Maybe he truly felt something for me, felt what I felt, but kept distance between us because he knew I would only sully his reputation.

That had always been my fear with Gwain, a man who was not half as important as the one who stood before me, and it had been true. So why would Caedell be willing to risk something that Gwain had not?

"I understand," I snapped, and Caedell's lips parted while his eyes widened. "There's no need to protect my feelings, I see now."

"You don't," he argued while he took a step forward.

"You may not think so, but you *are* just like the rest of them," I snarled.

"I'm not!" His nostrils flared and the amber of his eyes turned heated. "I am nothing like them, nothing like *him*."

"Oh really? Tell me how you are different."

"I told you I care about you," he growled. "That was not a lie, and you know it. You feel that. I know you feel that *here*." One of his hands pressed against the beating of my heart, and that simple touch sparked the warmth I was growing familiar with. "For now that has to be enough. Please just tell me that is enough."

It shouldn't have been. I should have needed more; I should have demanded a better answer. But as I looked at his face, I realized perhaps I didn't care about the risks. There was something beneath my ribs, a dull flickering that told me to damn my worries, to cast aside my apprehension, and let that heat that he carried in his touch, thaw the ice within me.

Rising on my toes, I pressed my lips to his. Gone was the ferocity of our lust, and instead we were left with something slow and sweet. Cupping my face, he held me to him, even after our mouths parted and I gazed up into the deep golden hues of his irises.

"It won't be for long," I warned quietly. "But for now, it is enough."

CHAPTER
FORTY-EIGHT

"YOU SEEM RATHER RAVENOUS THIS MORNING," CAT remarked from across the table, and I paused my chewing to look up at her.

"I'm used to breaking my fast earlier than this," I murmured around the mouthful of bread, and she wrinkled her nose at my poor manners.

"And you had a very late night." Crumbs tickled down the back of my throat, and I slammed my hand against my chest as I began to cough. Startled by my choking, Cat rose from her seat and rushed to my side before hitting the space between my shoulder blades with her palm.

"Thank you," I croaked once I swallowed the lump of food, and she carefully backed away and then moved to her chair once more.

"Maybe that was your sign to slow down," she said with a pointed look towards my now-empty plate, and I narrowed my eyes at her.

"It wasn't my pace that made me choke," I grumbled. "It was your comment."

"My comment?" She had the gall to pretend to look surprised, and I glowered at her. "I didn't know such a little thing could cause that kind of a reaction. I was just pointing out how late you were coming to bed."

"And I was unaware that you were so observant of my comings and goings." Cat pressed into the back of her seat and looked at me with a thoughtful expression.

"It wasn't as if you were trying very hard to be inconspicuous," she said after a long moment. "The two of you were rather obvious, you should be glad that I had dismissed the guards just a few minutes before you arrived. If I hadn't, whispers would be spreading like wildfire by now."

I knew when I was caught, and though my cheeks burned, I kept my face as impassive as possible. "Well, I appreciate your consideration."

Rolling her eyes, Catiline dismissed my comment and then she placed her arms on the table in the most unladylike fashion and leaned forward eagerly. "Alright, enough of the pretences, tell me what happened."

"What do you mean?"

A delicate black brow rose. "You told me not to comment on him or the two of you during the meeting. Yet the next thing I know, you are kissing outside your room while you both look rather dishevelled, might I add."

"It is nothing, Cat." The disbelief was evident on her face, and I shifted in my seat. "It is not worth worrying over."

"That was a little more convincing," she laughed. "But try again."

Sighing roughly, I lifted a hand to rub at my temple. "I don't know yet what it means or what it will result in."

"Not quite what I was looking for." She smiled brightly as she clapped her hands together. "But now that you are beginning to be honest, tell me, how was it?"

"How was what?" I asked, and she giggled softly and then rose from her chair once more before racing to the one next to me.

"Was he how I pictured him to be?" she asked. "What did

he say? Was he gentle? I feel like he would be a very good lover."

"Catiline!" I gasped in dismay, and her pale face pinked but her smile did not falter. "You are not to speak of such things! How are you even so knowledgeable about what goes on between a man and a woman?"

My chiding was half-hearted, and she swatted at my shoulder before pressing in close. "Tell me already."

"The road has changed you," I scolded as I shook my head. "What would people say if they heard you now?"

"They would probably call me a harlot." She shrugged as if the insult would be nothing to her and then gazed up at me expectantly.

Glancing around the empty room, I made certain the door was closed and that the guards could not overhear us before I shifted towards her. "We did not lie together."

Her brows furrowed. "But you two came back to your room so late, and the way you embraced seemed as if there was some familiarity between you."

"I said we did not lie together, not that we did not find some enjoyment in each other's company." Catiline looked even more perplexed, and I realized she really did not have much knowledge about such affairs.

"There is more than one act that can happen between a man and woman," I explained. "Things that are just as pleasant, maybe even more so."

"And you did these things?" she questioned and I chuckled softly.

"We did one, yes."

"And he cares for you?" Whatever humour I had slowly slipped away, and she frowned when she noticed the change.

"He says he does."

"And you care for him?" I had not admitted as much to Caedell, and though I dreaded to reveal such a thing to anyone, I could not bring myself to deny it. Cat took my silence for an answer and her smile grew once more.

"Well, that makes me very happy indeed."

"Does it?" I asked in surprise, and she nodded.

"And I can't wait to see the look on Gwain's face." A twisting sensation erupted in my chest, and I grabbed at her hands.

"Catiline." The seriousness of my tone made her tense immediately, and she looked at me with wide eyes. "Please do not speak of this to anyone. Do not speak of it at all once we are out of this room."

"Why?" I could understand why she was confused, especially after such a blatant display in front of my door this morning. But we had not noticed any witnesses, and I was sure if we had, we would have parted differently.

"I do not want anyone to know," I explained, and her expression shifted into a scowl.

"You deserve more than that, Rígan." Her tone was hard but sincere. "You should not be kept in the dark like some sort of dirty secret."

"Please, Catiline," I whispered. "This is my choice; promise me you will keep this to yourself."

She did not look happy at my request, but she nodded anyway. And though I should have felt some relief at her acceptance, I couldn't help but notice that the flicker of a flame Caedell had ignited just this morning had already cooled to a glowing ember.

KRAYERN PACED AROUND THE ROOM, and I couldn't help but let my eyes drift from the edge of the table to the window.

Now that the sun poured into the room, I noticed a very large handprint on the glass and my cheeks heated.

"We should have received some word by now!" Krayern growled as he slammed his palm against the back of his chair, and the sound of the impact made me jump.

"Winter has arrived, poor weather always delays news," Dyani reminded her son, though judging by the tension in her expression, she too was worried.

"What about the other issue?" Synrick asked softly from his place directly across from me.

"We have found no other evidence that explains how those men had come to learn such magic," Aarik responded, and the blood that had rushed to my face suddenly fell away as I was reminded of the reason for meeting in this room again.

"And have our men or Donigan said anything about the villagers?" Krayern asked, and my brows furrowed at the mention of my knight. "Oftentimes the most useful information is passed through the common folk."

"They are worried, of course. They fear another attack will come and we will be just as unprepared." Aarik ran a hand over his jaw, and I realized just how exhausted he looked. His normally tan face seemed ashen, and his dark eyes were tired. "But nothing of substance has been heard."

"So, we will just continue to sit idly and wait for the worst to happen, I assume," Skileer scoffed with a roll of his eyes, and all heads turned in his direction.

"It is not as if we are pleased about this delay, but winning a war takes time and careful planning," Krayern snarled.

"You keep calling this a war," my brother laughed dryly. "But I don't see it as such. Despite all your worry and talk of magic and the Reaper, they are in fact just common folk. They are nothing more than farmers with their pitchforks and scythes and are easily beat. I can, however, understand why you wouldn't be aware of that fact considering you have spent your time hiding up here in the north."

Synrick looked to the Heirs of Denimoore with uncertainty, and I noticed the unconcealed loathing in their eyes as they regarded Skileer.

"We have had our own battles to fight, Lord Baxteel," Aarik reminded my brother, and I prayed to the Gods he would heed the warning in his tone.

"And yet you were surprised when your home, the castle of the *Protector's Anointed*, was ambushed by a group of rebels!" He rose from his seat with enough force that it sent his chair crashing to the ground. "They scaled your walls and ransacked your halls. They killed your people, and you were somehow not only blindsided, but ill-equipped as well!"

"We should have been better prepared for such things; you are correct." It was Dyani who spoke, and I shivered at the coolness of her tone. "But what do you call an attack on the Gods' chosen, if not war?"

"Poor leadership," my brother snarled. "We are all facing this rebellion but only my family is facing it head-on. Had you handled your own *difficulties* the way we do, it would be over by now."

"And how is that?" Krayern demanded as he strode towards my brother.

"By seeking the rebels out!" he growled. "Not by sitting in this castle and having little discussions. Not by summoning us here to do nothing!"

"We summoned you here so we could be a united front as we confront our enemies," Aarik answered as he flocked to his brother's side.

"And what confrontation has happened?!" My brother was an impatient, foolish man, but I did not think him stupid enough to try to take on the rest of the Anointed. "We are wasting time!"

"You did not seem so eager just a week ago when your men and I went west to rid the neighbouring villages of the criminals." My eyes slid to Caedell as he finally rose from his own chair, and Cat grabbed at my hand nervously. "You were not so keen when those deviants kicked down the door of the tavern, or when that creature snatched your sister. Where was your bravery then?"

Skileer's dark eyes slid to my face in accusation, as if Caedell listing *his* wrongs was somehow my doing. Holding his gaze, I forced myself to remain still and unaffected. But my brother must have seen something as he glared at me and then he shook his head in disbelief.

"Have you spread your legs for another already, sister?" I heard Gwain's sharp inhale from two seats over. I dared not move my eyes from my sibling, but I squeezed Cat's hand tightly in question and then saw her shake her head in my periphery.

"How dare you speak to her like that!" Dyani shouted, but my attention was back on the face that so resembled my father's.

"I knew he was growing desperate to bed his precious *shewolf*," he hissed the name at me with venom, but I still did not look away. "But I did not think you would be so stupid as to let him slip between those thighs of yours. Especially not after what happened with the last one. But you do have a habit of falling for pretty words and empty promises."

His head tipped to the side as he studied me. "Though I suppose he is a step up, and I would be lying if I said I wasn't a little impressed. I mean imagine, *you*—a bastard—managed to lure a true Anointed to your bed. Father was right, despite your blood, you do have some use."

I did not notice Caedell move until his fist collided with my brother's jaw, and though the first hit sent Skileer crumpling to the ground, Caedell followed him to the floor. For a moment, no one else moved; they stood rooted in place while they watched my brother get struck over and over again. However, when I heard Skileer's cries of pain, I broke and rushed to the pair who remained on the floor.

"Enough!" I shouted as I grabbed at the back of Caedell's tunic. But I had seen the way he fought. Once he set his sights on his opponent, he would not let up until he deemed himself the victor. This time was no different, and I was certain the only victory in his eyes would be my brother's death.

"Help me!" I demanded as I frantically looked to the others, and the door to the council room burst open at the sound of my cry for aid.

With one hand on the pommel of his weapon, Donigan searched the room, and when our eyes met, he ran to my side. Wrapping his arms around Caedell's middle, he hauled on the man, but it was no use, even with the two of us, Caedell would not let up. However, seeing how serious the situation had turned, Aarik and Krayern finally jumped into action and helped my knight separate the two, though Caedell continued to thrash in their hold.

"Skileer?" I whispered as I kneeled at his side. His scarred face was bloodied, and his hands were lifted in an attempt to block the blows he anticipated. However, when none came, he cracked a rapidly swollen eye open and peered up at me.

Hurriedly, I cupped a hand under one of his elbows and tried to ease him up, but he shook off my touch and slowly pulled himself to his feet. Turning to the group of men, my brother wiped the back of his hand across his nose and then spat in Caedell's direction. Enraged by such insolence, Caedell fought against his captors, but before he could break free, Skileer turned on his heel and strode out the room.

For one long moment, only Caedell's panting could be heard, and I lifted my eyes to his. His face was twisted with fury, and I narrowed my gaze.

"You had no right," I snarled, and the arms that had curled around him like a cage loosened until they fell away from his body.

"I had every right, every Godsdamned right." Despite the

quietness of the words, I could still feel the sharp edge of rage, and the others flinched at the sound.

"He did not insult you, sir," I spat, and when he moved towards me, Donigan made to follow him. However, Krayern intervened and placed a strong hand on my knight's shoulder, halting him a few feet away.

"Back to *sir*, are we?" Caedell sneered.

"That is how I address those who pose a threat to my family." Lifting an arm, Caedell ran a hand through his hair and tugged on the dark strands.

"Even now you defend him?" He said the words as if he couldn't quite believe it to be true, and I curled my arms around my torso. "Why?"

"My duty is to him. He is my kin," I replied. "He is my blood."

"And what am I?" he demanded, and my heart pounded in my chest.

"You are asking for too much, sir," I warned him softly, and the amber of his eyes blazed.

"Damn it, Rígan!" Caedell snarled as he came towards me. "What am I to you?!"

The rest of the room and its occupants faded away while he raised his hand towards my face, and for a moment I almost leaned towards his touch. However, when I saw my brother's blood coating his knuckles, I flinched away, and Caedell's arm lowered to his side. And with one last longing look, he turned his back to me and stormed out of the room.

CHAPTER

FORTY-NINE

"What is happening between you and Caedell Reide?" Gwain growled as he followed at my heels, and I quickened my pace while I ventured farther down the hall. After the chaos my brother and Caedell left in their wake, Krayern had called the meeting to an end, and I had fled from the room and the suffocating stares of the others.

"Rígan!" Gwain shouted, and then his hand was curling over my shoulder, and he pulled on the joint roughly until I faced him. "Answer me!"

Livid that he would not only have the audacity to demand anything of me but to also touch me in such a way, I slammed my palms against his chest and pushed him away. "Leave me be!"

His face grew thunderous, and his green eyes studied me from head to toe. "Was what your brother said true?"

"Go away, Gwain." Turning from him once more, I continued down the hall, but he was not satisfied with my dismissal.

"It was, wasn't it?" Gwain ran after me, lengthening his strides until they matched my own, but I did not turn my head

427

to look at him and instead searched for my brother. Skileer was embarrassed and enraged, a poor combination, and I knew if I did not get things under control quickly, the ramifications would be dire. "You're fucking him."

The hurt in his voice would have been laughable had I not been so annoyed by his pestering, and I swiftly halted and then shifted to face him. "So what if I am?"

His jaw fell open at my question, and I narrowed my eyes. "What do you care if he warms my bed, if he strokes my skin and kisses my body?"

I was baiting him cruelly, but I no longer cared about the feelings of Gwain Dansby. "Why does it matter if I call out his name in the throes of passion? Surely that should mean very little to you."

"You are mine!" Lunging forward, he reached for me. But I was faster, and I snatched his wrist from the air and twisted it to the side. Having no choice but to curl his body in the same direction to keep the limb from breaking, he crumpled to the side.

"I am not yours!" I snarled as I watched his face contort in pain. "Do not dare to ever claim otherwise again."

Releasing my hold, I watched as he fell towards the floor, and then I continued on with my search. Room after room passed with no sign of my brother, and I grew more worried as time went on.

"Lady Rígan!" Donigan called from the far end of the corridor as he rushed towards me, and when I saw the panic on his face, I ran in his direction.

"What is it?!" My eyes bounced around the space, looking for a sign as to why the man before me seemed so concerned, and his large hands cupped my shoulders with a familiarity he would not usually dare display when the risk of witnesses lurked around every corner. However, given what had been said about me not just over the years, but in the council room before the other Anointed themselves, it was safe to say my tarnished reputation was beyond saving.

"Are you alright?" Pulling from his touch, I rolled my eyes and then brushed past him.

"Fine," I seethed and Donigan followed after me. "But I need to find Skileer."

"He's in the yards." Grabbing at my elbow, Donigan directed me towards the doors that would open to the grounds and did not release his hold until we were through the threshold.

Donigan had been right, my brother was there, screaming at our men as they hastily began organizing our things, and I frowned. Pressing a hand against my guard's shoulder, I gave him the silent order to stay where he was, and then I took a deep breath.

"Skileer?" I called as I approached carefully. His back stiffened, but he did not turn to face me. "What is going on?"

"Go to your chambers and collect your things, sister." His voice was eerily calm considering what had transpired, and when I reached his side, I noticed the skin below the drying blood had begun to bruise.

"What are you doing?" I asked, ignoring his order, and he looked at me from the corner of his swollen eye.

"What does it look like? We are leaving." Focusing back on our men, Skileer barked out more orders, and I glanced around the manicured yards of Denimoore while I tried to come up with a way to soothe his anger.

"I don't think we should be so hasty," I said softly while I reached for him. But Skileer dodged my touch and laughed.

"I don't care what you think," he spat. "I am the Heir of House Baxteel and I have given the orders."

"Skileer, you have not thought this decision through," I tried once more, and my brother whirled towards me so swiftly, I took a step back in surprise.

"Get your things and say your goodbyes." His dark eyes

were murderous, and for the first time I was truly afraid of my brother.

"We need the others to fight this war," I argued before lowering my voice to a whisper. "I cannot win—" His jaw clenched at the words, and I swallowed. "*We* cannot win this on our own."

"You underestimate the power of our house, sister," he growled. "And they are not winning anything from their place in that room. Let them stew and plan, we will return home and defend our lands. We will defeat those who oppose us and the rest of the Anointed can be damned."

"But the rebellion has grown in size and power," I reminded him, praying to the Gods that he would hear me. "We need to be united."

"We will protect that which belongs to us, they can deal with the rest."

"That is not wise," I warned him, but he scoffed.

"Our father has done a fine job so far; he has held our position, and now it is time we return to Noordeign and join him. Let these fools argue amongst each other while their home is torn apart by their enemies, I no longer care."

"*Our* enemies," I corrected. "And if their attacks are victorious, what do you think they will do next?"

Skileer didn't bother to answer, and I ran a hand through my hair. "They will join those in the south and set their eyes on us. Their target is *all* of the Anointed, not just the Protector's."

"Then we will make certain to rally the lesser noble families when we arrive," Skileer replied. "We will offer them better trade agreements and land. We have the biggest province; we could do so. And if the houses of Demys and Reide fail while they remain here in the north, well then, we can use their Anointed title when negotiating with our other allies."

"We can do no such thing. The Gods themselves chose the

Anointed," I whispered, shocked that he would say something so blasphemous.

"Then they chose badly," he snapped. "We will honour our Huntress by returning home and protecting what is ours, and she will smile upon us as she has done each time before."

"You think she would be pleased by this," I muttered, and Skileer lifted a brow.

"We have been victorious in every battle; we have survived every attack. If she was not satisfied by our efforts, why would she continue to guide our swords? Why would she bless us with the strength we have been given?" My eyes moved to the guards who were rushing around the yards as they prepared for our departure. "We insult her by staying here."

"You are turning your back on the Gods' other favourites."

"No, sister, *we* are," Skileer replied. "And I have a feeling they will not be favourites for long."

CAT CHEWED her bottom lip while she watched me toss my things into the trunk and then looked to Donigan in desperation.

"Surely he would listen to you!" she cried. "Tell him he is making a mistake; it is not safe to leave on your own. Not now when we know our enemies are out there!"

"Our enemies have been there the whole time," I reminded her as I closed the heavy lid and she sniffed.

"But you will have a quarter of the men you arrived with and there was just an attack!" I turned to her in frustration and watched as she flinched away from my glare and then sought out my knight once more.

"I do not have a say in this, Catiline, he has made his decision," Donigan replied softly, and then to my surprise he moved to her side and wrapped a strong arm around her shoulders. For a moment, she did not move, but when his thumb stroked across the sleeve of her gown, she fell into his chest as she wept.

Raising my eyes to his face, I lifted a brow, and he blushed but did not push her away. The two had grown closer during our journey, and I knew he had continued his lessons, though they were infrequent and short given how many eyes were on us while we remained in Denimoore, but I did not think they were this acquainted.

"You could stay," I offered, and Donigan frowned at me. "Cat needs better protection here. She needs someone who can lift a sword without being winded, and someone who is loyal to her and not Krayern or anyone else."

"Fynn will remain," Donigan argued, and I shook my head.

"He is Caedell's man, and while he has shown us his kindness, he would not prioritize her should another attack happen."

Moving her head from his chest, she wiped her hands over her cheeks and then pulled from my knight's embrace. "I can come with you!"

"It would not be safe for you," I argued. "And Skileer does not want anyone else but our men with us this time. He wouldn't hear of it."

"Then stay," Cat whimpered. "Let him go home if he must, but stay."

"I cannot leave my brother, Cat." I knew she couldn't understand why, she did not know the true extent of it, and even now, I could not tell her. "But I may be able to convince him to leave Donigan."

"That would put you both at greater risk; he would not be willing to lose a man, and not such an important one at that," Donigan disputed.

"He would if he thought your allegiance was in question." He flinched as if I had slapped him, and I swallowed my guilt. "You have been spending a lot of time with Aarik and his men in the village and you are close with Fynn. It would be easy to convince Skileer."

"I have been nothing but devoted to you and your family!" He straightened his shoulders before taking a step towards me and I nodded.

"I know that," I assured him. "You have been the most faithful and trustworthy friend."

"And yet you would cast me aside?" I gave him a sad but sympathetic smile.

"Skileer is being rash in his decision and he will not see sense. We both know how this is likely to end." Cat whimpered as she listened to our conversation, and I glanced at her for a second before seeking out my knight's dark eyes once more. "A lost cause is not a worthy one, and I would not have you perish for my brother's pride."

"Rígan, if you think I am going to agree to this—" I shook my head and then cleared my throat in hopes it would ease the tightness there.

"There is nothing for you to agree with, Donigan," I murmured. "This is not a discussion, it's an order, and we both know you can't refuse to follow a command once it has been given. It's not in your nature."

Donigan looked like he was going to be sick but did not interject further, and my attention lowered to the ground. "Catiline needs someone here, and I would trust no one else with her," I said softly. "But you both must make me a promise."

My eyes stung as I lifted them to study my friends.

"Should my house fall—" The words burned my tongue as I said them, and Cat gasped, but I carried on. "Should my house fall, I want you to promise me you will not let them sing songs of my brother's honour or allow a Grand Elder to tell the tales of his supposed courage."

My grin grew despite the stinging behind my eyes, and I lifted my chin. "Make certain everyone knew what a bastard *he* was, even if his blood was pure."

CHAPTER

FIFTY

CAEDELL AND KRAYERN WERE NOWHERE TO BE SEEN AS THE others stood outside the castle's entrance, and I lifted my eyes to the windows above for just a moment before I noticed Dyani moving towards me.

"You could stay," she whispered while her gaze flittered to Skileer quickly, as if she was making certain he could not hear her suggestion.

"I belong with my brother," I replied, and she searched my face for a long pause and then nodded.

"Well, then I insist you take this," Her hands moved under her long black hair and to the back of her neck. The delicate chain that hung there loosened, and she reached for my hand. Flipping my palm over, she lowered the piece of jewellery into my grasp, and I looked down at the dainty shield and the tiny blue stone that sat in the middle of the pendant.

"The Protector's shield," she said softly.

"I can't accept this," I gasped, and she curled my fingers over the metal and held them there.

"The set has been a part of this family for centuries." She shifted her hand to show me a ring that sat on her middle finger. Like the necklace, it was made of gold and there was a

435

soft blue rectangular stone set in the metal that lay across the width of the digit.

"They have been passed down through generations and mean a great deal to me. So know that I would not separate the pieces if I wasn't sure." Dyani's tone was firm, making it clear she would hear no argument. "It will keep you safe, and if you insist on this decision of yours, well then, I fear you will need its protection far more than I do."

"Thank you," I whispered, and she gestured for me to turn around then plucked the necklace from my fingers. With nimble fingers, she pushed my hair over my shoulder and redid the clasp and the chain pressed against the back of my neck while the pendant dangled just above my heart.

"You are an impressive thing indeed, Rígan Baxteel," she murmured as I faced her again. "But do not let your courage cloud your judgement. Even the most fearsome of creatures run when they know they are beat."

"That may be so, but I've never been one to flee, no matter how bad the odds may be," I replied, and her dark eyes held mine for a long moment before she nodded.

"I do not envy your enemies." With that she fell into a graceful curtsey and then moved back to the entrance of the castle and placed a hand on Aarik's arm. The man turned his head just slightly in my direction, but his face remained stern, and I lowered my chin in a subtle nod before finally looking at Cat and Donigan.

My assumption had been right; Skileer had been eager to leave Cat behind, and though I was certain he was furious that one of our men may have found new fidelity, I managed to convince him that Donigan was not worth bloodying his sword. Especially when we were surrounded by those who would not take kindly to such an action. Much to my surprise, and despite his arrogance, Skileer had decided that this particular battle was not one he should bother with.

Instead, he now sat upon his mount and glared down at

the man who had grown up with us, and I noticed Donigan held his stare, not showing an ounce of weakness. Worried this impasse may provoke another spat for my brother, I moved to my friends and embraced Cat quickly.

"Be safe and look after him for me," I whispered against her ear, and she sniffed into my shoulder but nodded. Pulling from her, I glanced at my knight from the corner of my eye.

"Legends will be written about you, Donigan Taith," I said faintly, just loud enough for the pair to hear. Finally, that stoic expression cracked just slightly, and when I noticed the tremble of his lower lip, I offered him a soft smile. "Make sure they mention that despite your fate and the doubts of those around you, you always managed to be a man others envied."

Worried the last thread of strength I clung to would begin to unravel, I turned from them and took a deep breath. Passing my brother, I ignored the nasty look he sent my way and then grabbed the reins of my horse from one of our men and hoisted myself up into the saddle.

"You do not need to leave, Skileer Baxteel," Dyani called gently, obviously left to be the voice of reason, and I admired her determination, though I knew it was pointless. "You can stay, and when the time comes, we can fight this together."

"I wish you and your people luck," my brother laughed as he glanced up at the looming walls of Denimoore castle. "I will be sure to tell others of your grand home, rest assured you will not be forgotten."

Aarik's fingers curled over the pommel of his weapon, but his mother placed a steadying hand on his shoulder before straightening to her full height. She looked every bit a grand lady as she said farewell, and my brother turned his horse as he led our party away. I, however, hesitated for just one more moment and I searched the panels of glass for a flash of chestnut hair or piercing amber eyes. But only the reflections of the mighty mountains were visible, and I looked to my friends once more. And with one last longing gaze and a small wave, I turned from my family and followed my duty.

BESIDES THE GUSTS OF WIND, the camp was quiet, and I gazed at the fabric of my tent while I hauled the heavy furs to my chin. It had been just over a fortnight since our departure, and the men were struggling as we travelled through the northern province now that the weather had turned. However, it wasn't just the snow that slowed our pace. We were also hungry. Game had been scarce even this far north, and though we had hoped to find something in order to make our supplies last longer, our hunts had proved to be fruitless. Now we were forced to ration what was left of our food, although I was certain I had seen Skileer sneak a pack into his tent on more than one occasion and I hoped the others hadn't noticed.

Pulled from my musings by the growl of my stomach and the whistle of the northern wind, I tucked my legs to my chest. "Gods be good, it's freezing,"

The temperature had dropped significantly tonight, and although my skin felt like ice and my belly was empty, I tried to will myself to sleep. Softening the tension in my muscles, I sank into my bedroll, but just as slumber crept closer, I noticed a quiet shuffling. I had been barely able to hear it between the gusts of wind, but it was in fact getting louder, which meant the person was close.

Slowly, I slipped from my bed and crawled across the floor. Once I was next to the entrance of my tent, I rose so I stood next to the entry and then I waited. Now that they were within a few feet, I was certain I had not been wrong in my assumption, and I searched the dark for something that would work as a weapon should it come to that.

"Fucking snow, fucking cold," my brother slurred. "Fucking north!" One of his hands crashed into the canvas near my head and then he was hauling on the flaps as he tried to pry them open.

"What in the Huntress's name are you doing?" I demanded while I loosened the tie and then pulled him through. Not prepared for my touch, my brother stumbled forward and fell onto my bed, and I glared down at his sprawled form for a moment before I peeked my head out into the winter night. The rest of the camp remained silent, and before I was blasted by the frigid wind, I stepped back into the shelter and secured the entrance once more. It was then that I noticed the sharp smell of wine, and I exhaled roughly before stepping over Skileer. Carefully, I lit the lantern and held it in his direction.

"You're drunk!" I snapped in accusation, and Skileer groaned before lifting himself onto his hands and knees unsteadily. "Where did you find wine?!"

I had made certain there was none packed along with the rest of our belongings, and he had appeared to be on his best behaviour over the last few weeks, minus the stealing of food. However, when it came to my brother, I would take thievery over drunkenness. A full belly would ease his temper, wine would not.

"I would have you know, sister, I am very resourceful when I want to be." He slowly shifted until he was sitting on the furs and then glared up at me. "Stop looking at me like that."

I was surprised he even noticed my glare given the way he swayed back and forth, and I took a step closer and then bent at the waist. "What are you thinking?"

"What do you mean?" He rolled his eyes and my nose wrinkled at the state of his breath, but I did not move away.

"Skileer, being a drunkard is one thing when we have the safety of numbers, but to be so careless when we are out here—"

"Wine is the only thing that makes this Godsforsaken land tolerable." His head lolled and then the corner of his mouth lifted in that way that warned me he was about to say something cruel. "I fall into my cups, and you fall into beds, such is the way of the world."

There was no point in trying to defend myself when he was in this state, so instead I lowered myself onto my knees next to him and held out my hand. "Give it to me."

He leaned away from my body, but I grabbed him by his cloak and pulled him closer. "Give it to me, Skileer."

Huffing, he curled one of his hands around his side and then he was pulling the wineskin out from its hiding place. However, he did not place it in my waiting palm and instead lifted it to his mouth, tugged the cork free with his teeth, and then rushed to finish what was left in one large swallow.

"Here." Slapping the now-empty leather pouch into my hand, he hiccupped, and I tossed the wineskin into the corner of the tent.

"I can't believe you would be so foolish," I scoffed under my breath, and his dark eyes narrowed at me.

"I will not have the likes of *you* judge me!" he snarled, and then began to scramble to get up. Watching him struggle to get his limbs to cooperate, I remained where I knelt. However, just as he managed to lift himself onto his knees once more, I noticed a flickering of light amongst the shadows outside my tent, and I rushed to grab a hold of my brother and then tugged him down.

"Unhand me!" he shouted as he thrashed in my hold, and I slammed my body into his and then covered his mouth with my hand.

"Shut up," I hissed while I managed to pin him down. But my order only seemed to anger him further and his efforts to escape my clutches grew tenfold. Lifting my chin, I searched the area I was certain I had seen the light. However, it was no longer there but had moved to the right and now I knew for certain we were not alone. Glancing at the lantern on the ground, I knew there was no point in blowing it out. In fact, doing so may only alert our visitors that I had noticed them. Instead, I rolled my brother onto his back and prayed that he would listen to me, just this once.

"Skileer," I whispered while my fingers tightened over his jaw and finally those dazed eyes met mine. "You must be quiet, and you must be still."

Perhaps it was the urgency in my voice, or maybe he could see it in my expression. Or maybe the Gods finally heard my prayers and decided to answer them. Falling still, my brother took a deep breath through his nose and then blinked up at me in confusion.

"I will release you, but you must do as I say." I lifted my attention once more, and I watched that tiny spot of flickering light for a moment before I slid my hand from his face.

"What is it?" he asked as he turned his head towards the side of the tent.

Straightening my spine, I rocked back onto my heels and took a steadying breath. "Someone is out there."

FIFTY-ONE

My brother froze under my weight, and then his wide eyes turned to me. Now that I was sure he would heed my advice, I moved away from him and glanced at the heavy wool of his cloak.

"Hand me your sword," I demanded, and his brows furrowed. "Your dagger then."

Skileer's frown deepened, and he shook his head, and I narrowed my gaze. "Tell me you did not walk across camp unarmed."

"Use your own," he growled quietly as he sat up, and I ran a hand over my face.

"I do not have them, Skileer," I reminded him. "I may be a bastard, but I am still a woman and having a weapon strapped to my hip would not be considered proper."

"You've done it before," he scoffed, and I wondered how he could still be so thick-headed.

"In secret and when I have the security of our father!" I snapped. "I cannot rush to your rescue and take your place when there are so many eyes on us without his protection, without any plan in place to keep our secret hidden."

"So what do we do?" Skileer demanded as he eyed the

tent once more, and I checked to see that the light had not moved.

"You will have to carefully wake the men and devise a plan and then defend us," I whispered and my brother paled. "Was that not what you wanted when we left Denimoore? You wanted to take action, now is your chance to do so."

"I did not think—"

"No, you did not," I interrupted. "You never do."

Glowering at me, my brother rose to his feet and then reached for the lantern, but I slapped his hands away. "You cannot take that with you!"

"It's dark," he argued, and I was certain tonight would be the end for us.

"They will be able to track your movements, they will know you are alerting the rest of our men and will attack before you can make it across camp." His eyes widened as he realized how foolish that decision would have been and then he searched my face.

"Tell me how to do this," he demanded, and I wondered for what had to have been the thousandth time, why our fates had not been switched.

"The men on watch, they may already be aware," I said softly. "We chose our guards well and they are more experienced than most. Go to them first, tell them what we have noticed. Then carefully rouse the rest, do so quietly and quickly. Have them armed and ready."

"What will you do?" Skileer asked as he began to move to the exit of my tent.

"I will stay here until we know for certain what is happening." I grabbed at my cloak and pulled it over my shoulders. "Should a battle come, I will do what I can to help you, but I will need a weapon of sorts to do so. Bring one to me and leave it outside the tent when you are done waking the men."

"I thought you said you should not be armed," Skileer argued, and my head throbbed.

"Not when there is no reason to be, but I hardly think the men will notice me if they are fighting for their lives." Skileer shivered at my words but nodded and then he turned to leave. However, something twisted in my gut, and I called out for him.

"Skileer." Turning, he looked at me, and I searched his scarred face for a moment before exhaling roughly. "Be careful."

He ducked through the flaps of canvas, and I moved to the trunk in the corner of my tent. Lifting the lid, I pulled out the breeches I had buried in the bottom and quickly changed out of my thick wool gown. Certain I was dressed for a fight, I moved my attention to my hair and hurriedly braided the long dark strands until they fell in a single plait down my back.

I was as ready as I could be given the fact I had no weapons or armour, and I moved to the front of my tent and listened closely. There were no hushed whispers or rustling of fabric, and for a moment, I worried Skileer had failed his duty. Or perhaps he fled into the night, leaving me and our men to fight our visitors.

But then the screaming began, and my stomach fell.

Every man sounded the same when he died. Their voice was always sharp and shrill as fear consumed them, and I wondered if the others knew, that despite their courage and strength, they too would cry out just the same.

So, considering that, there was no way to decipher who was being attacked, and I looked at the lantern sitting on the ground and then grabbed it. It would make no difference if they saw the glow disappear now, and I blew out the flame and tossed it to the floor before rushing through the exit.

Chaos erupted in the dark of night, and I watched as our men rushed through camp, their swords ready as they charged south. But there were no hoof beats, no whinnies or signs of battle, and that glowering ember in the distance remained where it had been.

Despite that, the man's screaming continued, and I followed the group to the edge of our site. Together they gathered close, and I pressed towards them and lifted onto my toes so that I may see what it was that had caught their focus.

A body lay across the snow, the white surface now a deep maroon as the blood spread around the corpse, and one of the older knights approached the fallen man carefully.

"Who is it?" a squire asked, and carefully the knight nudged the face with his boot until the dead eyes of the man fell onto us.

It was a bannerman, one I recognized from our journey to the tournament, and now that I knew his identity, I looked at the rest of him. His torso was ripped open, but not in a way I would have expected. Swords cut flesh cleanly, the wounds were often long and narrow and this injury was the opposite. It appeared as if he had been shredded apart, and given how quiet the camp had been prior to his death cry, I wondered how that was possible.

"What could have done such a thing?" my brother gasped from his place behind a line of men, and there were quiet rumblings in response, but no one had a true answer for him.

"We must light the torches," one of the men demanded. "We cannot see what lurks in the dark."

He was right. We had an enemy watching us and now it was too late to try and remain concealed. Quickly our men moved into action, and soon the group was exposed by the burning orange flames, and I looked to the forest once more. Still that glowing orb was visible and remained unmoving but that was no longer my concern.

"Turn our backs together," another man ordered, and quickly the party gathered in a circle while they faced the dark of night, and I was soon pressed shoulder to shoulder with our knights. They, however, paid me no mind now that they were consumed with fear.

For a long moment nothing happened, and all I could

hear was the pounding of my pulse while I searched the black for some sign of our enemy. And then it was there.

First it was just a hint of movement, and had I not had a hunter's eye, I would have assumed it was just a tree blowing in the wind. But these branches did not shift like the others, and although it seemed to be made of bark and leaves, it moved the way a human would.

"By Gods, what is that?" a knight choked out, and I watched as a massive wooden hand curved around a thick trunk and then the hefty tree was bending to the side, and the sound of its roots cracking echoed in the air. Tossing the tree away, the beast slid into the now-empty space and then turned its glowing grey eyes onto us.

The creature was almost as tall as the rest of the forest that surrounded us, and I tipped my head back to study it as it loomed over our camp. Its massive body was dark in colour, and I realized that its long limbs and thick torso were made up of twisted vines and thick branches that were braided together until it created a manlike form. However, it was its face that really terrified me.

The bark was haggard, its cheeks were hollow, which made the sharpness of its features even more pronounced, and those sunken grey eyes were haunting. The beast was something from a nightmare, and I shivered as it watched us carefully while the long taloned hand that hung at its side dripped with blood.

It was unlike anything I had seen before, and my knees knocked together while I trembled with fear.

"What do we do?!" someone gasped in panic, and the creature's eyes slid to the man and then his mouth clicked open.

"Come meet your fate, children of the Huntress." The voice slithered out of the beast, and the sound made my skin prickle painfully.

Frozen in fear, we did nothing but watch as the monster

took one step closer, and then another, and I had to tip my head back to look up at its face. Sneering, it peered down at our group, and then one of its mighty hands swung, and the man next to me was plucked from his place as if he was nothing but a frail weed growing from the earth. Holding him near its face, the creature curled its fist, and the guard barely had a chance to gasp out in pain before he was crushed in the monster's clutches.

Then panic finally set in and all hell broke loose.

Our circle scattered in every direction, and the monster laughed and then began its hunt. Bending at the waist, it chased after its prey on all fours, and I watched in horror as it crushed another knight beneath a foot while its great mouth lowered to the ground and then it scooped up a young squire and snapped him in two between its sharpened wooden teeth.

Frantically searching the men for my brother, I spotted him running for the woods, and I chased after him. Though his fear was strong, his stride was slow given his inebriated state and I easily caught his shoulder. Startled by my touch, he swung his arm back in alarm and his fist caught the edge of my jaw.

Ignoring the sharp pain, I wrapped my arm around him and tackled him to the snow. Gasping for breath, Skileer twisted beneath me, and I fisted a hand in his hair and tugged his head back.

"Quiet," I snarled into his ear, and he stopped moving and glanced at me from the corner of his eye.

"Rígan?" he whimpered, and I moved off of him and then grabbed at the arm he had struck me with. Guiding him back to his feet, I pressed a finger to my lips and looked towards camp where the screaming continued.

"We must hide," I whispered and then searched the shadows for someplace that would conceal us both.

"It will find us," Skileer protested weakly, and I tugged him forward and ushered him towards a thicket. The bush was dense and large, and though I could not fit alongside him, it would be enough to hide my brother.

"Stay here," I ordered, but just as I backed away, his fingers snatched at my wrist.

"What about you?!" he asked with wide eyes, and I shook my head. "I cannot face it alone!"

"You either stay here and have a chance of survival or we both die," I growled and his throat bobbed.

"But…" For a moment I wondered if he truly cared about my demise. "How will we beat the rebels if you die?"

My lips curled and I laughed coldly. "Should I die, I suppose you will have to win the war yourself, brother."

With that, I pulled my arm from his touch and turned to meet my fate.

CHAPTER
FIFTY-TWO

THE AIR STUNK OF SALT, AND I FOLLOWED THE PATH OF carnage. The monster was at the end of the bloody trail and was dragging a finger across the chest of a man, and I watched the way it revelled in the screams of its victim. Distracted with its task, the monster did not seem to notice my approach, and I searched the remnants of our camp for something that would aid in its defeat.

The men and their weapons had all but disappeared, and I bent down towards a lifeless body and pried his sword from his hand before I noticed a torch that still burned despite being forgotten in the snow, and I hurried to pick it up before it could go out. Lifting it in the air, I examined the shredded tents until I found my answer.

Keeping my eye on the beast, I backed away from it and tossed the sword to the ground in exchange for the oil lamp that lay next to a shredded piece of canvas. It was still heavy with oil and the wick was unused. Thanking the Gods for my good fortune, I pried the lid off the lamp and peered down into its opening. The liquid was thicker but somehow not yet frozen, and I clutched the container to my chest and then looked at the beast once more. His victim no longer made a sound, but he remained in his place, and I moved towards the large trees in hopes of remaining undetected despite the flickering light I held in my hand.

"Do not bother to hide from me, Triad's daughter," the beast sneered from where it still knelt. *"I can smell your fear."*

Pressing my forehead against the rough bark of the tree I hid behind, I closed my eyes while I gathered my courage and then tucked the lamp behind my back and stepped out into the clearing once more. The monster had not moved from its position, but glanced over its shoulder at me with glowing eyes, and I pressed my knuckles into my spine while I lifted the torch high above my head.

"Tell me why you face me alone," the monster demanded as he studied me closely. *"Why do your men let you do such a reckless thing?"*

"I do not wait for permission before I act," I snarled. "And I will not run from an enemy like some coward."

"The Divine blood runs strong in your veins." Moving to its feet, the beast turned to me but did not approach, and I felt my stomach churn at the gore that covered the twisted roots of its body. *"I hope you taste as pure as you smell."*

My lips curved up at the edges despite my terror, and I lifted my chin as I peered up at its terrifying face. "You are about to be sorely disappointed," I laughed softly. "Purity is no virtue of mine."

Its eyes narrowed but it said nothing else and then straightened to its full height. Quivering, I lifted my gaze higher towards the sky, but I did not move and waited for my foe to act first.

Striding forward, the creature approached, and my fingers slipped around the lamp as my skin turned clammy. However, I was able to keep a decent enough grip on the metal as the last of the distance between us closed.

Much to my surprise, the beast did not snatch me from my place, nor did it lift a foot to crush me. Instead, it tilted its head to the side and then its wooden face cracked into a smile, and I felt my breath catch when I saw the sharp row of teeth that were crimson in colour.

"Why do you stand before me like some sacrifice?" it asked. *"Is that what this is? Have your shepherds led you to slaughter, little lamb?"*

"I told you I do not ask for permission; I am here on my own accord." My voice was far stronger than I thought it would be, and I felt a flicker of pride at the sound.

"But that is not the whole truth of it," the monster argued. *"Perhaps men do not lead you to your death, but duty will. It guides you into the dark and you go willingly."*

"There is honour in that," I whispered. The monster's head fell back, and a great laugh rumbled through the forest.

"You humans and your honour." My jaw clenched and it looked at me once more. *"How easy you are to manipulate when your right-eousness is at risk. No wonder the Divine Triad has ruled for so long. Who could stop them when they have such devoted servants?"*

"What do you know of our Gods?" I snarled as the beast glared down at me.

"I know they have fed on your fidelity for centuries, but not for much longer." More questions sat on the tip of my tongue, but before I could ask them, a mighty hand was moving, and the fingers of the beast curled around my hips.

Lifting me into the air, the monster held me before its face, and I shrank away from the piercing stare while the hand behind my back tightened its hold on the lamp. My timing would need to be precise if I was to be successful with my plan, and I forced myself to slow my breathing while I tried to remain calm.

"I will be sure to send them your regards after I've torn your heart from your chest," the beast promised. *"They will be saddened to lose such a dutiful child."*

"Perhaps I shall send them your regards instead!" Bringing my hand forward, I smashed the oil lamp against the knuckles that curled around me and then brought the torch to the thick substance that covered the twisted roots. The moment the flame kissed its hand, the fire caught, and for a moment I feared I too would be consumed by the blaze. However, the beast released me just as the heat licked at my skin, and I fell from its clutches and landed into the snow in a heap.

Gasping, I rolled onto my knees and pressed my forehead into the snow as I fought to take in enough air to fill my lungs. My body was still running on adrenaline, so despite my struggle to breathe, I did not feel the extent of any injuries I may have suffered from the fall. And while that was ideal in a situation like this, the haze also distracted me from the beast whose limb was now engulfed in flames. In fact, it wasn't until a large piece of burning root crashed into the ground next to my head that I lifted my face from the icy earth.

Narrowing my eyes at the bright burning flames, I watched the monster grab at the shoulder that remained free from the blaze, though the decision was precarious considering that the fire was spreading higher and higher at a rapid rate. Coming to the same realization, it curled its hand around the joint and then it tugged and suddenly the limb was torn from its body and tossed into the woods.

"I would have been merciful," it growled while those glowing eyes met mine. *"I would have made it quick, but now I will bask in your suffering."*

Scrambling to my feet, I began to back away, too fearful to take my gaze off it, and it prowled towards me, its steps slow but confident, and given the size of its stride, there really was no reason to rush.

"Perhaps I will start slow," the creature seethed. *"Break your bones one by one and then bleed you carefully, making certain you feel each drop as it leaves your body."*

My gut churned as one of its feet landed just inches from my body, and the ground shook beneath me as the earth struggled against its crushing weight. Knowing I could no longer risk a slower pace in order to keep an eye on the beast, I turned on my heels and then pushed my legs as fast as I could. But just as I gained momentum, the clasp of my cloak dug into the tender flesh of my throat, and I was lifted into the air.

Flailing, my hands sought out anything that I may be able to grab on to so I could pull myself free from its grasp, but my fingers remained empty and then I was being tossed back onto the ground as if I was nothing more than a plaything. Although I supposed now that I had failed at my attempt to vanquish the beast, that would be my fate.

Bracing myself on my hands and knees, I dragged myself through the drifts, not caring that I sunk down to my belly in the snow or that the cold bit at my skin. None of that mattered, considering if I stopped, I would surely meet my death far sooner, and I knew I could not give up; I would not surrender. Not if it was to be my final action in this life.

"That's right, crawl away like the vermin you are," the creature laughed, and then I was being flipped onto my back. I blinked up at the night sky, taking in the treetops and dusting of stars before its monstrous face loomed over me.

Lifting its hand, the beast moved a finger towards me slowly, as if it was savouring my terror, and just as the giant wooden claw snagged on the fabric of my tunic, a whistle rang out through the night. Raising its chin, the monster searched the area that surrounded us, and then I saw what appeared to be a flash and a burst of orange came from its left eye. For a moment I didn't understand, but when the creature clutched at its head just in time for another arrow to lodge itself into its jaw, I realized what had happened.

Standing, the monster staggered back a step, and then three more arrows notched into the roots that made up its body and the beast screamed in pain as the fire began to consume it. Ashes fell from above, and I rolled away from my place and rose unsteadily to my feet once more and then began to run.

I didn't know which direction I headed towards or where I

planned on going. All I knew was that I needed to leave this place and find safety. Ducking my chin, I tried to avoid the bitter wind that blew against my face, and warm tears leaked from my eyes as I continued to flee into the dark woods.

Weaving between the trees and heavy brush, I pushed myself harder and just when I thought I was free from danger, I heard it. It was not the shrieking or heavy footfalls of the beast. No, I could decipher the noise now, the deep snorts and sound of galloping through the snow was familiar, and I turned to glance over my shoulder.

They were close, far closer than I had anticipated, and I watched as the hooded figure kicked at the barrel of his steed, urging the animal faster towards me. In the shadows, I could not tell if they were friend and foe, I could not see if there was a mask beneath that hood or what sigil they wore.

And it did not matter. In the end it would be my body that betrayed me, and suddenly my knees buckled, and I crumpled into the snow. Curling on my side, I finally surrendered and braced my hands over my head while I prayed that the Divine Triad would forgive my cowardice.

CHAPTER
FIFTY-THREE

"Rígan!" the gruff voice was muffled by my arms that covered my ears, and I pressed deeper into the snow while I waited for my death. "Rígan, stand, damn you!"

Cracking an eye open, I blinked at the white surface before me and then twisted my face to peer up at the figure who sat upon his horse. The hood was lowered, and the greying curls appeared darker in the night. However, the furious scowl and heavy brows were immediately recognizable, and I slowly sat up and gaped at the man before me.

"Father?" The word was soft and disappeared into the next gust of wind, but still he dismounted from his horse and stalked towards me.

"Get on your feet," he demanded. "Now, we do not have time!"

He reached for me then, grabbing at my arm, and then hauled me to my feet, and I swayed under his touch, which only made that glower of his deepen. Uncurling his hand, he pressed the palm roughly against the space between my shoulder blades and shoved me towards the dark bay who pawed at the snow in agitation. The animal was obviously eager to leave this place that reeked of death, and I felt the

455

same. Staggering to its side, I shakily lifted a foot to the stirrup and hoisted myself into the saddle.

"Slide back," my father ordered, and I did as he asked and then waited for him to move in front of me. The horse snorted at the added weight, but my father pulled the reins to the left and then dug his heels into its side as he urged the mount into a gallop once more.

Lowering my head, I did my best to shield myself from the frigid air and held on as my father guided our steed back towards camp. The smell of smoke was heavy in the air, but it was far more welcome than the scent of blood, and when the horse slowed to a walk, I took in our surroundings.

Our site no longer resembled what a camp should look like, and the ground was a deep pink colour. However, the bodies had been moved into a pile and I searched the men who remained. Taking count of those who had been in our original party, I realized only eight of the twenty lived. Swallowing down the acid creeping up the back of my throat, I scoured the crowd for my brother.

The injured groaned in pain and orders were being shouted at others, but I could not hear, nor see my sibling, and I felt dread twist in my chest. Clutching to my father's back, I turned towards the thicket where I had left him and prayed that I would find him there. But the bush remained still, and though I was certain he had cowered behind the shield during my confrontation with the monster, surely, he would come out of hiding now that we had been saved.

"Father," I croaked out, and he halted his horse and glanced at me from over his shoulder. "Skileer…"

I trailed off not knowing what else to say, and my father's brows furrowed as he glared at me and then he urged me to dismount before doing the same. Now standing, he tossed the reins to one of his men and then spun towards me once more. Lunging forward, he grabbed at my face with one of his enormous hands and held me still while he snarled at me.

"Is fine," he growled. "Despite your actions."

My mouth parted as I searched his face, and he scoffed before releasing his hold and then crossed his arms over his chest. My eyes stung as I studied the disapproval painted across his face and felt the weight of shame press onto my shoulders.

"I was trying to protect him," I whispered, praying that he would hear the sincerity in my words.

"By leaving him on his own?" my father asked and shook his head. "I have taught you better than that, Rígan."

"We are just lucky you came when you did, Father," Skileer's voice called from behind me, and I sniffed and ran a hand over my face before I faced him.

Skileer sauntered towards us, not at all appearing to be the snivelling mess I had left behind, and I looked him over, noticing he appeared to be no worse for wear before I turned my back on him once more.

I had taken it upon myself to protect him with what I thought would be my last breath, and as always there was not a hint of gratitude. If anything, his face matched our father's, and I bristled as he came to stand next to me.

"Because without him you would still be trembling behind that bush," I snapped as I glared at him from the corner of my eye.

"I am the Heir of House Baxteel," he sneered. "If I die, so does our lineage. We cannot risk my life."

"You say that as if all the other Anointed heirs do not fight their own battles. They do not hide in the shadows in fear." It had been my idea, of course; I knew that Skileer would not be of any use against the creature or any other enemy for that matter, but still, I wished he would see some value in me or at the very least, admit what he really was.

"Enough of your squabbling," my father demanded, and we froze at the anger in his tone. "We do not have time for petty arguments." His dark eyes turned to me. "You know what is expected of you, and you failed."

I heard my brother's soft laugh, but I said nothing, and my father came towards me slowly. "But be that as it may, I do not have the time or patience to reprimand you. We must be leaving."

"For home?" Skileer asked hopefully.

"Yes." My father nodded, but the tension in his body told me there was more to it.

"But what of the others?" I asked quietly, and they both turned to face me with similar expressions.

"What others?" my father questioned, and I swallowed.

"The other Anointed, what of them?" I had hoped that once my father learned about our desertion, he would reprimand my brother for being so foolish as to leave our comrades behind. But judging by the look of disdain on his face, I realized he had the same opinion as Skileer.

"They do not matter," my father said, and my brows furrowed. "What is important is our family and our lands. That is where your loyalties should lie. Let the others take care of the war, we will worry about our *own* battles."

"But the Gods—"

"Will protect us from our foes as they have continued to do," my father interjected. "You will see, we will come out of this victorious and will have more power than we could ever dream."

"Was this your idea all along?" I snapped as I pressed forward towards him until our toes were nearly touching. "Why send us north if you had no plans to uphold any alliance?!"

"I could not very well turn away an invitation from House Demys, not when they have shunned us for years," my father growled. "But they continue to curry favour with House Reide and peer down their noses at us. I had hoped perhaps they would see the error in that decision, especially considering Carlel Reide has been killed."

"Caedell's father has been killed?" My father rolled his eyes at my question.

"It should surprise no one. It is a time of great risk for us, and if I am being honest, I am surprised it had not happened sooner, though no one seems to know exactly what happened." My father ran a hand over his face and then fixed me with a pointed stare. "I had thought maybe House Demys would see it as an opportunity to ally with another great house who still has their true lord and not a boy of four and twenty. However, given what your brother told me, that was a misjudgement on my part."

My eyes slid to my brother in accusation, and he held my stare. "When did you write to him?!"

"When I noticed just how close you grew with Caedell Reide." He shrugged. "The moment I heard him call you that little name, I knew you could not be trusted to see things clearly."

"And so you decided to come retrieve us?" I asked when I looked back at my father.

"You should be thankful I did, Rígan!" my father snarled. "A warrior you may be, but a man you are not. You are too easily swayed, and despite my lessons and guidance, your heart remains weak."

"Think of this as a favour, sister." Skileer grinned. "We are saving you from yourself and aiding you in putting this family first."

I had always put my family first, that had never come into question. But I had thought we shared the same vision. I had thought peace was our objective, but now I saw the truth.

It was not peace that my father longed for; it was power.

THE MOOD of the men was sullen and tense, and I felt my heart ache in sympathy when I thought of their fallen brothers. Many had gone up through the ranks with each other, and though a dozen men were not considered an immense loss during a time of war, I still felt the effects heavily. Fighting others on a battlefield was something one could prepare for, but to face a creature that was unlike anything we had ever seen before, to be so unprepared for the carnage, meant pushing the memories into the back of our minds was all that more difficult.

Moving through the narrow lane we had left between tents, I lifted my hood over my head and clutched at the skirts of my gown. Nothing more had happened on the road, and though it had been days since the last event, I could not seem to settle and was forced to pace across camp when the sunlight began to fade.

"Are you well, my lady?" one of my father's captains asked as I passed, and I stopped and turned to him.

"Fine, sir." My voice was softer than normal, and the sound made the man frown.

"You should be resting," he suggested. "After everything you've been through, being out in the cold will do you no good."

Something about his concern made my shoulders sag, and I pressed a hand against my chest. Without Donigan, I was alone, and though the men had never been truly cruel to me, they usually did not pay me any mind either. That is unless they hoped to gain more than my *favour*.

Even when I led them into battles, I had Donigan take charge. He was the one who barked orders and made certain that my identity was protected. And while leaving my knight behind may have been a poor choice for my own benefit, I took comfort in knowing he would not be tied to me and whatever fate the Gods saw fit.

"Yes." I nodded. "I think I will do that."

Curtseying, I turned back around and followed the same trail I had just made. However, before I could reach my tent, I heard my father call for me. Spinning towards his voice, I watched as he beckoned me closer with a flick of his fingers and sighed as I prepared for whatever he was planning.

Since our rescue, he had not spoken to me beyond giving me orders to stay away from my brother and to not cause any more problems for him. However, watching as he ducked into his tent, I knew that was about to change.

The enclosed space was warm and bright, despite the other structures not having more than a single lantern, and I frowned at the lavish set-up of his chambers before I moved to the chair he gestured to. Carefully I perched in my seat and waited until he rounded the table and fell into his own.

"Our scouts say there is a settlement of rebels just three days' ride south from here." Snatching his glass of wine, he raised it to his mouth and took a long sip.

"And what would you have us do?" The question came out sharper than I had meant for it to, and I shrank back at his cold stare.

"If we had the choice, I would ignore it. They are far from our lands and would be someone else's problem," he muttered. "But the winter has limited our routes, and there is no getting around them without being noticed. I will not have them telling others that we fled at the sight of them."

"Is that not exactly what we have done though?" I whispered under my breath, and my father slammed his palm against the table.

"We did not flee, we returned to our people." I did not bother to lift my eyes to his face; I already knew what I would see if I did, and so I nodded. "The other Anointed have a better chance of victory than we do. I had thought this would be nothing more than keeping a few common folk in line, but you've seen how it has grown, you've heard about what has changed."

I swallowed and then lowered my chin. "The others, they have more men, more coin, and more experience. Remaining in the north would not benefit us, not now when the stakes have changed. It left our lands open for an attack and put your brother at risk. He would be expected to fight alongside the other heirs, and though they may be willing to risk such a thing, I am not."

"So why send us in the first place?" I asked, still not at all understanding his decision to do so.

"I could not very well decline an invitation in front of the others at the tourney, and even before Carlel's death, I had thought perhaps it would offer us an opportunity." Chewing on my lower lip, I thought over his words and then finally raised my eyes.

"An opportunity?" Sinking back against his chair, my father nodded.

"For you," My confusion only grew, and he exhaled roughly. "You met Aarik, the bastard son?"

I nodded.

"I had hoped they would see a potential there, that perhaps we could unite our houses. Which is why I had sent word that I planned on giving you a title. I had thought maybe with that, a union would be more likely and then they would have no choice but to forget about Elrin as a whole, and instead focus on what was important. Their home and our own."

"A union?" I muttered and he nodded.

"A marriage," he replied. "Had that happened I would have insisted they let the other nobles and Anointed worry about the rebellion. They could make the plans and fight the war, and we would have waited it out while they did so. That had been my expectation, it would have been ideal. Then Skileer would be spared, and you would fulfil the role meant for you."

"They would have never agreed to such conditions." I had meant allowing us to remain neutral, but my father took it another way.

"Not after you had wasted yourself on Caedell Reide!" His temper was back, and I readied myself for his wrath. "The Dansby boy was unfortunate but could be overlooked. However, an Anointed? Well, that took every option from us. No one will have you now."

Rolling my eyes, I chuckled softly, and I heard my father's sharp inhale.

"You will continue to do what you have been; you will put your family first, and then when this is all over, you will accept whatever punishment I see fit." Rising from my chair, I reached for his wine and lifted it to my mouth while I held his stare. I was not safe if he had no use for me any longer, and thankfully that time had not come yet. So, I swallowed the rest of his drink, not caring about the consequences my future held, and he leaned forward and snarled. "I hope whatever time you spent with him was worth it, Rígan."

Running the back of my hand across my ruined mouth, I dried my lips and then smiled. "I can assure you, it was."

FIFTY-FOUR

Though we were mere half siblings, I wondered if I actually had something in common with Skileer, despite my unwillingness to admit it. However, the very thought, no matter how hazy or fleeting, made me frown, and I tightened my grip on the neck of the bottle and then lifted it towards my face. Eyeing the contents, I shook the glass, watching as the red liquid sloshed against the smooth sides, and then brought the top to my lips. I had nearly finished the entirety of the wine in the last hour, and though I loathed what a drunkard my brother was, I could certainly see its appeal.

My mind was light, and my skin prickled pleasantly, but despite my intoxication, there was that unfamiliar yearning beneath the surface that I had not managed to smother even with the amount of wine I had consumed. Frustrated by that, I pressed the glass to my mouth once more and finished the last swig before tracing the opening with my tongue, seeking out every drop before I finally declared it empty. No longer any use to me, I cast the bottle aside and stood on unsteady feet before beginning my hunt for another.

The room spun as I crossed the small space, and I held my arms out in an attempt to steady me while I moved about.

However, my coordination was worse than I thought, and as I turned to search the other side of the tent, I rammed my knee into the small table that had been placed at the end of my cot.

"Godsdamn it!" I groaned as I lifted my leg and curled my hand around the throbbing joint to try to ease the pain. That, however, would end up being another mistake. Only having one foot on the ground did not help my balance, and when I began to lean too far to the left, I tried to correct myself but overcompensated and ended up stumbling before I crashed into the side of the tent.

"My lady?" a voice called from the door, but I was too busy trying to right myself again to notice a man had entered my room. In fact, I didn't notice him at all until I saw the toe of his boots step into the space beside where I sat on the ground, and I studied the leather toes with a frown.

The laces were frayed, and the boots themselves looked worn and not nearly warm enough for the weather, and I wondered if his feet were cold. Tracing the material with my eyes, I scanned up his legs, to his hips, and then tipped my head back to examine his strong torso, wide shoulders and then his face. He was not the usual young guard my father had stationed to follow me around since our rescue. No, this was one of his favourites, and while he was still considered rather youthful compared to many of the others, my father obviously saw something in him that made him rise in ranks despite his age.

Or perhaps that was just what my father did. He sought out young impressionable lads who would be at his beck and call and offer him their lives for just a fraction of affection and praise. After all, isn't that exactly what I had done all these years? I had given him everything, and though I believed it was my duty to our Gods to do so, there had always been another reason tucked deeper within my chest. I longed for his love and approval, but even after twenty-six years, I still did not have it.

Frowning at the depressing direction my mind had wandered off to, I looked up at the worried face before me once more. His hair was a light brown, and his eyes were a plain muddy colour. But his jaw was chiselled in the way I fancied, and though his nose had most definitely been broken a time or two, he was handsome enough.

Holding up a hand, I waited for him to take my fingers. But when our palms touched, I realized there was no warmth between us, and my frown deepened as he helped me to my feet. However, I was not ready to give up. Standing before him, I slowly raised my arm until it rested over his shoulder. Settling the limb there, I pushed forward until the curve of my breasts grazed his chest in the gentlest of brushes and then sighed softly.

"I think you should get to bed, my lady." His voice cracked, and I noticed the way his eyes moved to the space just past my head. His face looked impassive, but I could feel the change in his breathing, and I curled my arm around his neck.

"Is that so?" I whispered before rising onto my toes, and I brought my face just a few inches away from his own. "And will you be so gallant as to help me?"

The words were low and sultry, and I knew they had their intended effect when I felt his arm wrap around my middle. However, despite his actions, he did not make another move to close the distance between our lips and instead began to lean away from me.

"I am not certain that is a wise idea." He was right, of course, it was not, but I still longed to feel a hint of that spark. I grew desperate for the blaze that had evaded me since that night in Denimoore, and when the winter winds blew against my tent, my yearning for that flame only grew.

"Tell me," I said softly. "How long has it been since you've enjoyed a woman?"

His eyes widened at the brazenness of my question, but I

offered him my most seductive smile, and his throat bobbed before he cleared it. "Half a year."

Clicking my tongue against the roof of my mouth, I shook my head slowly and ran my fingers through his hair. "Much too long."

His eyelids had lowered, and he seemed dazed by my touch. Thrilled by how easy this would be, I lifted my other hand to press against his chest. However, my fingers remained cool, and my heart, though beating, did not race.

And yet, I continued.

"Are you not desperate to feel? Are you not eager to touch?" His head nodded and I smiled. "Tomorrow, you go to battle, and we can never be certain of the outcome."

His eyes searched my own, and I held his stare while I tilted my chin. Carefully, I swept my mouth across his, watching the way his gaze darkened at the touch. Exhaling shakily, he tightened the arm around my middle and then his mouth was on mine.

There was no delicacy to the kiss, it was a rough and brutal thing. It was the type of kiss I had often sought out in the past, the kind that I would *need* in order to feel something. But now there was nothing but ice. There was no thundering pulse or burning in my veins. Just a void of cold nothingness, and when his tongue ran across my scar, I pulled from his embrace.

"I will see myself to bed, sir," I grunted as I ran my sleeve across the moisture on my lips, and the knight's brows furrowed.

"But—" Crossing my arms over my chest, I glared at the man before me, and his eyes widened.

"Did you hear me, or must I repeat myself?" I snapped with more venom than was needed, but I did not care, and the man hurriedly offered me a bow before fleeing from my tent.

Perhaps if I was not drunk or so frustrated, I would have felt some guilt. After all, it wasn't his fault. In fact, he most likely would have made for a decent distraction had this taken place a few months ago. At that time, I was sure I would have even enjoyed it.

But now I knew what was possible. And despite my intoxicated state and his willingness, he could not give me what I so desperately desired. He could not chase away the frost that filled my very soul, and I worried no one could.

No one, but Caedell Reide.

THE ARMOUR FELT foreign on my body after not wearing it for so long, and I rotated my shoulders under the heavy metal. My father, who was just an arm's length away, stood still while my brother finished strapping up his own suit and watched me closely. Setting my jaw, I took a deep breath and then met his gaze.

"I will lead the command," he reminded me for the fifth time since dawn broke. "It has been a while and I am sure you are out of practice disguising your voice."

Part of me wanted to divulge the truth, that Caedell's father had been correct at the tourney, and the rumours were not wrong. I had never barked orders at the men but rather allowed Donigan to do so on my behalf. I wanted to tell my father that my friend knew of our ploy the entire time and that he had been wrong to assume we could not trust anyone with our secret. I wanted to tell him that if you inspired affection and nourished a friendship, a person would not betray you, no matter what was offered.

Doing so, however, would only enrage him further, and I did not have the energy to deal with that as well as fight this battle. Instead, I bowed my head slightly in understanding.

Let him lead the fight, let him have the glory. It was not as if he would allow me to relish in it anyhow.

"How many more small groups of these men are there, do you think?" Skileer asked while handing my father his sword.

"It is hard to say. Most have marched north to take on the Anointed, and if I did my job well, they will still think you remain there."

The mention of the others drew my attention, and my gaze moved to my brother. "It was rather devious of you to pretend it was action you longed for." Skileer stiffened at my words, and I searched his face. "I even believed you. I was convinced you were being rash and impatient. Of course, little did I know that you had another plan altogether, and it wasn't a fight you ran to but rather what you ran from."

"I'm pleased you were so easily tricked," he snapped, and I snorted.

"Yes, I was very much a fool. I forgot that cowardice is your nature, though I don't understand how. After all, you always were craven." My father lunged towards me, and his fingers curled over the edge of my breastplate.

"You do not need a tongue to fight, Rígan," he snarled as he tugged me forward. "I do not know what has gotten into you, but I suggest you remind yourself of exactly who and *what* you are before I lose my patience."

"Why do I need to remind myself when you so often do it for me?" The slap across my cheek was expected, but it did not take the sting away, and I closed my eyes before taking in a deep breath.

"Where is your respect? Where is your sense of duty?" he demanded, and one of my brows lifted.

"You speak to me about *duty*?" His eyes narrowed at my tone, but I remained firm in my position.

"Your obligation is to this family!" my father roared, and I shook my head.

"It was, when you were upholding your position as an

Anointed," I replied. "But you have turned your back on your responsibility, and I will not betray the Divine Triad nor our promise to them."

"But you will betray your own blood?" he asked, and I grabbed at the hand still holding on to the metal and pulled it from me.

"My blood is sullied, remember?" My grasp tightened around his wrist. "So what is it that binds me to you?"

My father's mouth hung open, and Skileer looked equally as shocked. Pleased to have finally silenced them both, I pushed my father's arm from me roughly and snatched my own sword from the table at my side.

"I will fight this battle; I will aid you in this." My voice was steady and cold, and I hardened my expression as my gaze bounced between them. "But when it is done, I am returning to aid my true family, and you will not stop me."

CHAPTER
FIFTY-FIVE

THE GELDING BENEATH ME SWUNG ITS HINDQUARTERS BACK AND forth while it tossed its head, and I tightened my hold on the reins as I watched my father address the circle of men that surrounded him. They huddled close, listening with rapt attention as my father went over the battle plans once more, and I swallowed before glancing at the tent that concealed my brother.

For just a moment, I thought about calling out. I thought about screaming to the others that they should not listen to their lord. That they had been fooled by him for years, and that the Anointed heir was hiding away like some snivelling coward while I took his place. It would be amusing—no, *gratifying*—to see the horror on my father's face when they realized who they followed. It may even ease that resentment brewing in my chest.

But would it be worth it? My duty to my family may no longer hold any importance, but my obligation to Elrin and its people did. That and our promise to the Huntress and her fellow Gods was now my priority and I would not turn from it, not like they did. Especially not when the men we were about to face endangered the peace the Anointed had kept for hundreds of years.

Frowning, I glanced at my father again and wondered what his ancestors would say if they could see the way he betrayed them and their oath. Perhaps he would answer for it should we not be victorious. There was that chance, of course, the scouts had reported the group of rebels as being rather insignificant, but we had undermined them before and I had learned there was no telling just how prepared they would be.

Moving my attention to the rolling hills that surrounded us, I searched for any sign of our foe in the light of dawn. The air remained frigid, and the snow was heavy, making the white drifts look more like a blanket coating the ground. However, now that the first rays of sunlight peeked over the horizon, the earth almost shimmered. The icy surface glistened under the soft glow, and I took in the beauty with a smile, deciding that should we not come out of this as triumphant, today was a decent day for it to end.

"We are nearly set to march," my father advised as guided his horse next to my own, but I did not face him. Instead, I was lost in my musings, now wondering if blood would melt the snow in these temperatures or if it would freeze and ruin the stunning landscape.

Perhaps the Gods would see fit to send another blizzard in order to hide the carnage we would most certainly leave behind. Maybe they would make it look as if we were never there to begin with, and whatever happened here on this day would go unnoticed by the rest of Elrin.

"Are you ready?" my father asked, and I finally turned to him. The visor of my helm concealed my face, so I did not need to worry about my expression. Taking advantage of that freedom, I scowled at the man before me and wondered when he had changed. When did his own interests become more important than his vows and honour? Or had he always been this way and just kept it from me until that was no longer an option?

In the end, did it matter? This is who he was now, and I would never trust his reasoning or decisions again.

"Are you listening to me?!" His patience had grown thin, and my silence must have snapped the last thread.

Straightening my spine, I gave him a nod, and he cursed under his breath before kicking his steed forward while bellowing more orders. The men scattered from their cluster, hurrying to their tents to grab their weapons and shields. The higher-ranking knights mounted their horses while the others fell into line next to the bannermen, and I glanced at the blowing sigil of my family before taking in the group as a whole.

They looked every bit the part of an Anointed's army. They appeared proud and stoic, and yet, they did not know who it was they fought for, and I felt a twinge of guilt. They were offering up their lives for a man who saw them as a means to gain power. In the end, they were nothing—*we* were nothing—more than pawns, and that stung despite my fury.

"These rebels will answer for their betrayal!" my father's voice called out across the group. "We will see that they are brought to justice and then we will return to our homes!"

The men lifted their swords into the air, thrusting the metal high above their heads while they shouted alongside my father. I, on the other hand, remained silent and still, keeping to myself as I observed the small army.

I knew they were skilled and would fight with all their strength. I had seen as much for myself over the last year. Each time we faced our enemy, they proved to me that they were ready and willing to do what it took to uphold our promise, despite not being the ones to make it in the first place. They were loyal, easily fooled by the family who had been charged to lead them, but loyal.

Like dogs.

And should I not escape after this battle was won, I would be looked at as being even less than that. Feeling the rage twist in my chest, I inhaled and then forced myself to push my wrath aside and thought of my plans instead.

I would wait until the threat was dealt with and then I would flee. A pack of supplies was hidden amongst the snow just south of camp. Once the guard had run from my tent last night, I had taken the opportunity his absence gave me and journeyed my way there before hiding the bag. As soon as I had made certain that I would have what I needed to make the journey north, I returned to my bed. However, even with that task completed I could not ease my nerves, and I had spent the rest of the night trying to think of what I would say once I returned to Denimoore. Thankfully the trek would take me some time and I would have days to perfect my speech.

If I made it that far.

I pushed that voice from my mind, not willing to dwell on the what-ifs and the likelihood of my survival. I knew the odds; I had seen just how perilous the road north could be and that had been with a group. This time I would be on my own, and yet, despite the risks, I knew I would go regardless.

There was nothing left for me here. There was no longer a reason to remain once this was finished. The others, however, needed me. They needed my help to face the war that was coming and when that was done, I would let the rest of the Anointed decide my family's fate.

"To victory!" Glancing at my father, I watched as he spun his horse and then looked at me from over his shoulder. Pressing my heels into my mount's belly, I urged the animal to his side.

The rest of the men fell behind, and as we approached our enemy, I lifted a hand to press against the steel of my breastplate. Under the metal, buried beneath the chainmail and gambeson, sat the necklace Dyani had given me. And though it was separated from my palm by a number of layers, I swore I could feel its power echoing against my heart.

"What are you doing?" my father whispered as he narrowed his eyes at my chest. "Stop that at once."

My fingers curled at the tips, almost as if they were claws, and for a long moment, I left them there. Letting the ends push against the solid steel while I held my father's gaze and his face grew furious, but there was not much he could do without risking exposure. However, when I looked back at our party, I noticed some of the curious stares slowly melted into worried frowns and my hand fell back to my side. I no longer cared if I upset my father, but our men found strength in our confidence, and it looked as though even the most subtle of gestures could change their perception of our certainty.

Facing ahead once more, I focused my attention to the lightening sky, noticing that the sun had risen as we marched forward. Tilting my face towards the warmth, I closed my eyes for a moment, and I prayed that despite my family's betrayal, the Gods would see my devotion and guide me as I led our men towards our enemy.

CHAPTER

FIFTY-SIX

Frowning at the valley before me, I examined the muddy tracks and the mess of hay and manure they had left behind and heard my father curse under his breath. It was obvious that our enemy had fled from this place, and considering they had not passed us, it was most certain that they had continued south.

"Perhaps this is a blessing," my father murmured softly, and I peered at him through my visor. "There are many roads south of here, the Gods' Passage forks towards both coasts. They may not turn towards Noordeign. Not after what happened to the last group who decided to try to pillage our lands."

I could hear the doubt in his voice but said nothing, and he glanced at our men before sighing. It had not been what we prepared for, and while not having to fight would usually be the best scenario, something felt off about this particular situation. Clicking his tongue, he urged his mount down the steep hill, taking his time not to rush through the blanket of snow, and I moved my eyes towards the horizon before following behind him.

Slowly we reached the valley that had been deserted, and I

took note of the fire pits that were scattered across the space. Given the number of them, this camp had been far larger than we had originally anticipated, and I swung my leg over my horse and dismounted before moving closer to the abandoned site.

The snow had been disturbed and flattened where the tents had been placed and that spanned for nearly two dozen yards. Also, the amount of manure and hay told me these were not just your average foot soldiers, many of them had been mounted. Moving through the camp, I examined the rest of the space closely. They had not left anything of value behind, just signs that they had been there, and as I wandered towards the south end, I smelt it.

The other embers were cool, obviously having been put out hours ago, but there was a hint of burning in the air, and I looked at the pile of broken twigs and coals that still wafted a heavy stream of smoke. This one had either been forgotten about, or had been left for last, and if that was the case, I had been wrong—they had not fled long ago.

"Come now, Skileer," my father called, and I turned to him, answering to my brother's name. "Let's not waste any more time and return to camp."

He turned his horse on its haunches and kicked the animal into a steady trot, putting more space between us while the men hurriedly followed. I, however, remained where I stood and watched him guide the others towards the hill.

The men were far more eager to leave than they had been to arrive, and I noticed that their formation grew sloppy as they ascended the hill. However, just as they began their climb, I felt it, that unnerving shiver that travelled under one's skin when they were being watched, and I moved my gaze from our army and looked to the hilltops that surrounded me.

All was quiet, not even the wind whistled through the air, but I knew without a doubt there was someone there. Striding to my horse, I mounted the beast, but it scurried forward the moment my weight settled into the seat of the saddle and then shied to the side. It was a temperamental gelding, but I had ridden it for months, and the only time it was so hot-headed was when we were facing a foe at a tourney or on the battle-field. In fact, he had been spooked the entire morning, almost as if he could sense some force I could not, but I knew better than to doubt its instincts.

Shortening my reins, I sat up straight and narrowed my eyes as I searched my surroundings once more and then looked to the peak my father was scaling. They were nearly halfway up the side but had not noticed the figures that waited to greet them, and I felt my heart stop at the sight.

"Fuck!" I snarled and then I kicked at my horse's barrel and leaned forward, giving him his head as we galloped across the valley and to the base of the hill.

However, by the time I reached the bottom, my father had finally noticed our enemy and turned his mount around before racing back towards me. The bannermen and those on foot had already started screaming; they had no chance of outrunning our attackers, and now they would succumb to their fate while the rest of their brethren hurried back down to the dale.

Frightened by the wave of horses who charged towards us followed by the cloud of snow that clung to their hindquarters, the gelding below me snorted and then rushed backwards. Hauling on the reins with as much strength as I could muster, I tried to keep the animal from leaving, at least until my father came to my side. But it was no use, he champed at the bit and then threw himself to the side and bolted.

"Godsdamn it!" I swore as the cold air blew through the small slits of my visor, momentarily blinding me with tears as my eyes stung from the gusts. When my vision had cleared, we had managed to put a great deal of distance between us and the men who just reached flat ground, and I felt my stomach churn as they turned to fight their foes.

And then the sound of battle erupted.

When one was in the midst of it, it was almost as if the Gods had plucked you from your body. It was as if you were no longer in control, like the heavy breathing and thudding of your pulse were the only things that tied you to this life. Even time itself seemed to slow. Nothing was as it should be when you were in combat; you did not notice the heaviness of your sword or the sweat that coated your skin. Nothing else mattered, nothing else existed—besides striking your enemy down.

But looking at it from the outside, that was another thing altogether. My heart raced, and given the ache in my chest, I was certain I was not taking in enough air. But that was not at the forefront of my mind. Not when I could hear the ringing of steel; not when I could see the viciousness of it all.

In the end, I realized I had been wrong. There was no beauty in battle, only brutality.

Watching for another moment, I noticed the way our enemy fought. They were quick and skilled, and while their ambush had taken us by surprise, I was not so certain they had needed it to gain the upper hand.

On and on they fought, decimating our men like we were the ones who were nothing more than commoners and they, the Gods' chosen. Watching them now, it was hard to imagine that they did not have the favour of a higher being. They cut our men down, one by one, ending their lives by a simple swing of a blade and yet, I remained here, at the other end of the valley. I had never, not once in all my time fighting for my father, turned away from a battle. I had never cowered from a challenge or avoided the end of a sword. But now, as I watched our army slowly face defeat, I could not help but think that this was my chance.

I could flee from this very spot and go north like I planned. I would not have to worry about my family's fate, it would already have been decided. I would not have to answer for my desertion; my father would not survive this and Skileer was no threat now.

I would be free.

My eyes filled at the thought, and a single tear ran down my cheek, its warmth finally startling me from the daze I had been under. Blinking back the rest of the moisture, I noticed a brown banner billowing in the wind and watched as it came towards me. The fabric curled in on itself, dancing gracefully with the breeze until the gust slowed to a stop and then the material drifted slowly to the ground before my horse.

Our sigil, the bow made of antlers and the line of trees below with the words—honour, duty, family—stared up at me, and I reread the banner again as the air rushed from my lungs. Our family's words, the words of House Baxteel, pounded through my body like they followed the very beat of my heart, and that pendant that hung from around my neck sat heavily against my chest.

I could not run, not from this, not after I had given my word that I would see this through. Doing so would be no different than my family breaking their own promise to the very Gods who had chosen us to uphold the peace of our lands. And although my brother and father may have been disloyal to the Divine Triad, I was not.

Looking back at the battle, I unsheathed my sword and then moved my horse forward. Bending to the side, I lowered my armed hand and carefully buried the tip of steel into the material before lifting my weapon once more. Plucking the banner from the metal, I grabbed the corners and flicked the fabric over my shoulder before tying it just under my chin.

My father may have betrayed our oath and my blood may not have been pure, but I would be the hero. I would honour our Gods the way an Anointed should, and then I would meet my fate. And in the end, even if my face was forgotten and my name disregarded or replaced, I would be the one they wrote ballads about for years to come.

I could not think of a better end.

Holding my sword high above my head, I urged my horse into a gallop and charged at our foe. The snow beneath the hooves of my mount lifted into the air, surrounding me in a dusting of white as we crossed the valley, and the sunlight that bounced off the steel of my blade flickered like a beacon from the Gods themselves.

Clenching my jaw, I tightened my hold on the hilt of my sword and searched for the best opening. The number of our men had dwindled significantly in the time I had wasted, and the ones that remained struggled against the constant onslaught of attacks from our enemy. Searching the crowd quickly for my father, I noticed that he remained on his horse, and although there was an arrow protruding from his left shoulder, he still managed to keep his opponent at bay with his sword. However, I could tell he could not continue for much longer.

I thought that I was prepared to see my father fall, that I had accepted that outcome and would be all the gladder for it. But now, as I watched his face twist in pain while his assailant notched the end of his sword into the muscle of my father's thigh, I felt an icy wave of dread fill my stomach. I could not let him perish, not without trying to aid him.

Steering my mount around the group, I readied myself to race into action. I would worry about his attacker first, then move on to the others. Satisfied with my plan, I lifted my chin and then angled my sword in preparation. However, just as I began to approach the pair of men, I noticed a massive black horse race towards them from the opposite direction, and my eyes widened as I watched the rider hoist his axe over his head and then he swung.

The blade sank into the space between my father's neck and shoulder, the metal wedged so deep that the man could not dislodge it from the flesh, and the weight of the weapon made my father crumple forward. Seizing the opportunity, the other man twisted his blade and shoved the length of it into my father's chest and I felt my heart stop as those dark eyes widened and then lifted to me. For a moment, he held my stare, and then the deep brown dulled, and he toppled from his horse and fell into the chaos.

That haze that came from battle fell over me once more, and I could hear nothing but my wheezing breath. I could see nothing but my father's horse, who was now riderless, racing from the madness of the fight. Watching as it fled, I felt my gut twist and then my dazed vision slid to the disarmed man. His eyes were searching, looking for some sort of weapon to use now that his axe was stuck in my father's corpse, and I snarled before I guided my horse towards him.

The gelding no longer fought my direction and finally submitted to my every request. He turned when the man turned, he opened his stride when the man noticed our approach, and he slowed when I hauled on the reins after I had lobbed the enemy's head from his body.

Covered in blood, I seethed with anger as I set my sights on my next victim, and it was as if time finally slowed. Looking at me, the rebels watched as I lifted my sword high once more and they paled as I pushed through the crowd. Back and forth I swung my blade, cutting and slashing at those who were brave enough to face me, and I revelled in their pain as they crumbled to the earth.

Dashing through the crowd, I made it out to the other side and then twisted, urging my horse to turn once more so that I may repeat the process. Aiming for the middle of the madness, I forced my mount as fast as the animal could go, and just as we neared the battle, I saw him.

He was across the battlefield, his face covered in a silver mask like the man from the library or the one from the tavern, and his black cloak blew in the winter wind. He sat tall and proud atop his horse, and I knew he had to be my next target.

Keeping my eyes locked on silver covering, I panted for breath and his head tilted and then his arms rose.

Pulling back the string, he nocked an arrow and then aimed it towards my body. Knowing I had to move, I pulled on the leather reins, guiding my gelding to the left as I prepared myself to dodge his shot. However, this man was skilled in the art of battle and had anticipated my plan. Instead of releasing the arrow at me, he angled the bow down, and I heard the point make contact with the flesh of my horse and then the front half of my mount disappeared, and I was thrown through the air.

The world turned on its head, my vision blurred, my lips parted with a grunt as my body finally crashed into the earth, and then, everything turned black.

CHAPTER

FIFTY-SEVEN

MY LEFT LEG WAS BEING JOSTLED AROUND AND THEN LIFTED, and I felt the clumsy fingers slide across the buckles behind my calf before a voice grumbled out a curse. Another set of hands came to my thigh, hoisting the leg higher in the air at an awkward angle, and I winced at the ache in my muscles.

"It's a fine suit of armour, to be sure," a man grunted as he raised the limb back towards my chest. "But these damn clasps are a pain."

"What if we just cut them?" the other asked, and a shadow passed over my covered face.

"We don't have a smithy who has enough skill to replace them with anything so sturdy." The touch grew rougher as their patience waned and then they were shoving me over, urging me onto my stomach so that they would have easier access. "Armour without fastenings is useless."

"We should try drying them, they would be less slippery then." It sounded as if one of them stood, and then I heard footsteps near my head and I finally cracked open my eyes. Despite my helm and half of my face being pressed into the snow, the sunlight was bright, and the sudden glow made the pounding in my head worsen.

Standing above me, the stranger surveyed my form. "Think he's really the Heir of Baxteel?"

"Who else would wear their banner as a cloak?" the other scoffed, and finally the metal clasp opened, and he pulled the greave away from my shin.

"I hear his face is deformed." There was amusement in his tone, and I held my breath as he bent towards me. "They call him Skileer the Marked now."

"I heard it happened at the tourney, and the wound was so deep, it took his entire nose and an eye," his friend laughed and then moved to the metal that covered my thigh.

"How fortunate we are to have come across them, I thought they remained in the north with the others." Fingers tapped against the side of my helm now, and the echo made my stomach roll. "I bet Petyr will be pleased. Perhaps we will even be given the chance to meet the High Commander himself."

"We should present his head on a spear," the man at my feet chuckled. "His father's body is no longer in good enough shape; he was trampled into the snow during the battle. But this one looks like he is all in one piece."

"Who thought a fall from a horse would be the end to such a great warrior." Those fingers near my ear were moving, searching for the buckle beneath my chin, and I held my breath when I felt them stroke under my jaw.

"Better warriors have died from less," his friend responded, but the man touching my skin did not answer and instead hummed quietly. "What is it? Do you feel his scar?"

"His skin is soft," the stranger replied, and his companion laughed again.

"Taking a moment to enjoy him, are you?" The fingers prodded at the flesh of my throat and then drew away.

"There is no trace of hair." Moving from my legs, his friend came to join him at my shoulder.

"He was said to be a pretty boy before the scar, perhaps he

did not like the look of a beard covering his face?" Rolling me onto my back once more, one hand tilted my head roughly and another went to my jaw and then the leather loosened, and the metal was being lifted from my face.

"By Gods!" one of them gasped and my eyes fluttered open, and I struggled to adjust to the light and the ringing in my ears.

They were young, no older than myself, and I narrowed my gaze at their shocked faces and then went to move. However, my body was cold and stiff, and though I could not feel any significant injuries, the fall from my horse had left me dazed. Sensing my plan, the one who held my helm in his grasp reached for my waist, unsheathed my sword, and then placed the blade against my cheek.

"Don't!" His friend grabbed at his wrist, and the sudden change in weight made the edge gently kiss the delicate skin of my face. It was the barest of scratches, but I felt a droplet of blood form beneath the metal and then it raced down towards my jaw and pooled in the curve of my ear.

"She is one of them!" the armed man argued, and I glared up at him.

"She may be worth more alive," his friend whispered and then turned his chin and lifted an arm high above his head as he waved someone over.

I remained still, watching them as they waited with anxious expressions, and then I heard the soft hoof beats. The animal snorted as it approached and then cast a shadow across my face, and its rider peered down at me. Now closer in distance, I could see the intricate markings of his mask and I peered up into pale blue eyes.

"What do we have here?" His voice was muffled by the steel covering, but I noticed the way his gaze seemed to darken and then he was leaning over the neck of his horse.

"It is the rider you shot down, sir," the man with the sword explained, and his leader lifted a hand to remove the hood of his cloak and then kicked his horse closer. Remaining steady, I forced myself not to recoil when the dark hooves stepped just half an inch away from my head and the leader chuckled.

"Not just a rider, boys," he replied, and those cool irises travelled down the length of my body before returning to my face. "This Lady Rígan, the bastard born to House Baxteel."

The metal blade lifted off of my face but remained close enough that my breath fogged the steel, and both men peered down at me with surprise. Keeping still, I waited for the leader's decision, glaring up at him as I did so, and he tilted his head and then peeled the mask from his face.

I did not recognize his light hair or pale complexion but then again, I did not pay any mind to many of those who noticed *me*. They often just blurred in the background, becoming nothing more than part of my surroundings. However, judging by the coldness in his eyes, I would wager he did not see me as such.

"Take the rest of her armour and find her something warmer to replace it," he ordered. "Make certain you keep a weapon at the ready at all times and be sure to bind her hands."

"With rope?" the unarmed man asked.

"No, you will need something stronger than that to contain this beast." My lips quirked at the insult, and the leader spat at the ground next to my temple. "Do not let your defences down, not for a single moment. She is not to be trusted."

The men stiffened at the advice, and I lifted a brow. "You sound afraid, sir."

The blond man snarled at me. "Any intelligent man would be."

"And why is that?" I asked with a grin.

"Because I've heard the whispers and I know what they call you," he snapped as he moved his horse back a step and then another. "The *shewolf*."

THE METAL CUFFS chafed at my wrists, making the skin beneath the heavy weight burn despite the frigid cold. Looking up at the man who held on to the chain, I glared at his back and wondered if I could manage to rip the link free from his grasp and then attempt to flee. The problem, of course, was the dozen others who trailed behind us, and despite having more stamina than most men, I could not outrun a herd of horses.

Sighing roughly, I followed along behind his steed, keeping my chin held high despite the snickers I heard when I staggered and slipped my way through the deep snow. They enjoyed taunting and mocking me, or they had tried to. But despite their best efforts, I pretended to be unbothered though I secretly made plans in my mind. Brutal and nasty plans for each and every one of them, and the worse they insulted me, the slower their death would be.

"We shall make camp here," my captor called out to his men. "See that the cage is constructed for the beast."

He had meant it as a slight, but I took it as a badge of honour. It was a title of power and would only fuel my wrath when the time came.

Dismounting from his horse, he tugged me along with him and pulled me towards a tree. Watching me from the corner of his eye, he tied the chain securely around the trunk and then turned to me with a sneer.

"Stay here and behave," he ordered, and then a hand lifted to cup my jaw. "And do try to face us. You may be rabid, but at least you are lovely to look at."

Pulling from his grasp, I lunged forward and sank my teeth into his fingers, clenching down on the digits until his warm blood bloomed in my mouth. Crying out, he yanked his hand free from me and brought the other fist down, striking me in the jaw.

"You filthy creature!" he screamed, and I watched as he cradled his bloodied fingers to his chest.

"You should be more careful around a rabid shewolf," I laughed, flashing my crimson-covered teeth at him.

"And you should mind yourself," he growled as he glared at me. "You are only alive because I have decided you are worth more that way. Do not prove me wrong."

"I'm not afraid of the likes of you," I snickered and then lifted my chin. "You hit like a woman."

His cheeks flushed and his mouth parted but he said nothing more on the matter and instead turned from me and strode towards the men who had observed the exchange with interest. Noticing their attention had been on us, the leader began barking orders and the men scattered, fleeing from his temper while I watched in amusement.

Quickly the party put together the camp with practiced ease, and then they settled around the fires they had constructed while their leader hid away in his tent. A few of them pulled their dinner from their saddlebags and began cleaning the rabbits before putting them on a spit. The smell of meat cooking made my mouth water, and I watched with envy as they shared their game amongst each other.

"Hungry?" I had not noticed one of them approaching, and I turned to look at his face, immediately noticing he was the one who had tasked himself with stripping me of my armour at my capture. At the time his touch and longing looks irritated me, but now, as he scanned me from head to toe, I felt queasy.

"No," I growled, and he lifted a roasted rabbit towards me.

"Are you sure?" His voice was soft and smooth, but it did little to ease my dislike of him.

"Certain," I snapped before moving a foot away.

"You know having an ally here would not be a poor choice

for you." Scoffing, I pressed my bound arms against my chest and then glared at him.

"An ally?" He nodded while extending the meat to me once more. "And what do I have to do to earn such a thing?"

"Nothing you haven't done before," he whispered, and I swallowed down the bile rising up the back of my throat.

"I think I will pass on that arrangement and take my chances," I snarled at him, and his hand lowered to his side.

"I was certain you would be wiser than that." The cooked rabbit fell to the snow beside his feet, and I blinked down at it. "It was a fair offer."

Growing annoyed at his persistence, I tugged at the chains and strode as close to him as I could. "You saw what I did to your leader, imagine if my teeth had more access." He swallowed roughly and I eyed the flesh of his neck for a long moment. "The first chance I had, I would rip out your throat."

The man staggered back a step. "You may look like a lady, but you really are nothing more than a mangy bitch!"

I grinned. "Be sure to tell the others what I think of your offer."

Forgetting the meat on the ground, the man turned from me and then raced back to camp, and I bent down. Grabbing at the cool carcass, I lifted it from the snow and then looked at the men who gathered by the fire. Watching them, I brought the rabbit to my mouth and sank my teeth into it before tearing away. The meat may have been cold, but it tasted heavenly, and I tore another chunk of it from the spit with a growl.

The group studied me with wide eyes and slack jaws, and I paused in my chewing and then narrowed my gaze before smiling around the mouthful. *"Woof."*

FIFTY-EIGHT

THE COLD SEEMED TO SINK INTO MY BONES DESPITE THE PELT beneath me and the heavy wool cloak that covered me from my chin to my toes. Curling onto my side, I brought my chained hands to rest beneath my icy cheek while my teeth chattered. Wrapping my arms around my knees that were pressed to my chest, I eyed the bars that surrounded me with a frown. The cage was made of heavy iron, and I wondered why they had bothered to travel with such a thing. It would have been a pain to transport, but then again, considering their excitement when they shoved me into the cell, it wasn't too difficult to see how much they had longed to find a captive, and such a lucrative one at that. Though I doubted I had been the one they had really hoped for.

Skileer would most certainly have been the target had they had a choice, and I thought of my brother, wondering what had become of him. Only three men had stayed behind at camp, and as far as I was aware, they had no idea he hid away in one of the tents. Surely by now they knew, and they must have realized what had happened to us. Or perhaps our enemy managed to slip past our forces and attacked the camp first, and that is why the valley had been empty.

I had thought to ask one of the men where they had hidden when we had marched towards their site, and I even sought out who I thought may be the weakest and most tempted to get in my good graces by answering my questions. However, I bit my tongue in the end; my curiosity would only draw attention, and should my brother have somehow made it out alive, I did not want to risk alerting them to that small possibility.

Rolling onto my back, I blinked up at the dark sky and sighed. The fires of camp had dimmed to glowing embers and the men had turned in for the night, leaving me alone in the quiet and cold with no escape from them, or from the thoughts that waited amongst the shadows, ready to take their place in the forefront of my mind at the first chance. Thoughts that would soon twist into regrets, and despite the heavy wave of exhaustion that accompanied the ache in my bones, I could feel it already begin.

The image of my father's lifeless eyes crept in first, which of course brought an onslaught of guilt that I had not sooner alerted the others of my findings in that valley. That shifted to wishing I had not wasted so much time contemplating running away like some craven. Perhaps then I could have stopped that axe from splitting my father's flesh.

Or maybe, had I remained in Denimoore, nothing from today would have transpired at all. My family would be whole, and I would be with my friends. I would have had another opportunity to bask in the warmth I had found in the north. I may have been able to hold on to that touch for just a moment longer, and maybe even respond honestly when he asked me that question in the council room—the question I had fled from the last time I saw him.

Though even now, I wasn't certain I had a true answer.

A shrill scraping noise came from the end of the cage, startling me from my pondering, and I swiftly rose from my bedroll and searched the dark for my visitor. The edge of a dagger was being dragged across the bars, and I narrowed my eyes at the pale fingers that curved around its handle and waited.

"It is a shame to see such a stunning creature caged like this." It was a man I had not interacted with though I had noticed his stares throughout the day, and I rolled my eyes at his stupidity.

"I would think by now you would see the reason behind such a decision," I scoffed before lowering myself back down onto the pelt.

"I disagree." He stepped closer to the bars, and I glared at his broad nose and dark eyes and then dragged the cloak over my legs as I tried to appear unbothered by his presence. "A cage isn't necessary if you know how to invoke loyalty."

"Loyalty?" I laughed. "What makes you think you could inspire such a thing from me?"

He grinned, flashing his crooked teeth at me, and the sight of such joy on his ugly face only put me more on edge. "Because I know what it takes to handle a wild animal," he explained.

"I get the feeling you boast about things you don't have experience in," I argued. "If you had a lick of sense, you would turn around and leave me be."

"I'm not frightened of the supposed *shewolf*," he hissed, and I scoffed.

"Because you have never handled one." That smile fell from his face, and he scowled at me.

"Does not matter, wild beasts are all the same," he sneered. "And if you strike enough fear into them, they will not turn on you."

My lips curled at the corners, and I shook my head, but then I noticed the others who stood behind my guest, one being the man who had brought me the rabbit. Holding his stare for a moment, I let him see my hatred, and he lowered his chin and then shifted behind his friend. Dragging my eyes away from the group, I looked to the camp, searching for the blond hair and silver mask, and it was the armed man's turn to chuckle.

"If you are looking for Petyr, you won't find him," he whispered before pressing his face against the bars. "We do not take kindly to threats from noble blood, even if he did abandon his title to side with us."

I swallowed at his words and then examined him closely while I tried to decipher if he was speaking the truth. The man had worn all black as almost all of the rebels did, and there was nothing to distinguish him from the others beside the way he looked at me with such familiarity.

"We had thought perhaps he was different, maybe he could see the vision we had for a new beginning. But it turns out, he was just like the rest. You can take the noble boy from his house, but you can't change his upbringing it would seem." Rising to my feet once more, I straightened my shoulders and watched as one of his friends stepped forward and began to unlock the chains that had secured the door shut.

"He ordered us away from you, like you were above us and not our captive." The metal links slackened and then fell from around the bars, and I curled my fingers into fists while I readied myself.

The door was opening now, and the man stood at the threshold and grinned. Taking a step back, I eyed him warily, and he lifted his hand and pointed the end of the dagger at me.

"He had plans for you, he hoped to present you to the High Commander in exchange for more authority, as if he was the one to find you." The man scowled. "And while we did not appreciate losing our turn to finally meet our leader, we had hoped he would at least see fit to reward us now. But when we asked about what to do with you in the meantime… well, you could see on his face that he saw you as more than just a pawn to bargain with. I would even go as far to say that maybe he was once sweet on you. Why else would he threaten the entire camp?"

I swallowed and the man narrowed his eyes at me. "He promised to take our heads if we went near you. He said it with such conviction, one would almost believe he had the power to see it through."

"I did not know that man, I had never seen him before in my life," I snapped, and the stranger shrugged.

"That doesn't mean he hadn't seen you." Stepping into the space now, he lifted his hand closer to his face and admired the metal blade of his weapon. "And that in lies the problem, doesn't it? You lot never seem to acknowledge those around you."

"Who do you speak of, sir?" I demanded, hoping to distract him long enough to come up with a plan.

"You, them, the Anointed and the nobles."

"I am not one of them," I growled. "I am a bastard, not a highborn."

"That is true." He nodded and then looked at his friends. "You have sullied blood and yet are still somehow too good for us. How poorly you must see the people of Elrin. You must really believe we are no better than the dirt beneath your feet. Why else would you turn a blind eye to our suffering?"

"You're wrong!" I snapped as the rest of them stepped through the doorway, and I moved back again and pressed against the cold bars. "I have wanted nothing but to protect the people! I want to keep harmony amongst us all and end this rebellion."

"Ending the rebellion will not help us," he chuckled. "The only solution is to accept the Reaper and abandon your Gods."

"The Reaper?" I spat out and he nodded. "You think he will save you? He is death itself!"

"And yet," the man sighed and then lifted his free hand towards me. Flinching away, I turned my head but watched from the corner of my eye as he pressed the tip of the dagger into the flesh of his palm. The cut was deep enough to bleed, but just as he pulled the weapon away, I noticed the edges began to close and he wiped the flesh across his pant leg and then showed me the uninjured skin of his hand. "He has given us never-ending life."

The man took another step forward, cornering me against the side of the cage, and I felt the tip of metal press into my lower belly.

"Now, you can be agreeable, or—" Suddenly a great burst of glowing light came from the right and we both turned towards the flames when voices began calling out.

"Fire! Fire!" men screamed as they ran from their tents, and the blaze grew and spread across the rows of canvas faster than I thought possible.

Looking to his friends, the leader gestured for them to leave and moved the dagger up my body until it pressed against the skin at the bottom of my neck. "I will be back and then we can finish this conversation. Perhaps this time will allow you to think over your options."

The group filed out of the cage in a rush, and slammed the door behind them, and I watched them leave and run towards the fire that now engulfed the camp. Certain they were well and truly gone, I took in a deep shuddering breath and then darted to the door of the cage. In their panic, they had not remembered to wrap the chains back round the bars, and I curled my fingers around the freezing metal before pushing it open.

For a moment, I did nothing but stand there and stare, almost as if my body could not decide between remaining still or fleeing from this prison. It was an odd thing, to be struck still by your mind while your heart begged you to run. Especially when I knew what awaited me here should those men come back. However, I was more than aware of what could lie in wait in the darkness of the forest too. Looking at the tall trees I silently weighed my options and then slipped through the open space.

Crouching low to the ground, I watched as the men attempted to save what they could of their camp before I turned to look for the makeshift pen they had built for the horses. Of course, I could try to escape on foot, but I would not get far without supplies or a weapon, and though my body was growing more and more desperate to flee, I reminded myself of the last time I had ventured off and knew that I would not survive for long if I was not wise about this.

Slipping back into the cage, I grabbed at the pelt and cloak and then turned for freedom again. Still my captors had not returned, far too preoccupied with the disaster at hand, and I wrapped the wool and fur around my shoulders and crawled across the snow.

The horses were whining, frantic to get away from the bright orange flames that lit up the night sky, and I shuffled across the icy earth as quickly as I could. However, some of the group had apparently decided that there was no more to be done and had come for their mounts, and I froze when I saw half a dozen figures approach.

"Hurry, boys!" one of them shouted, and I slunk back towards the treeline as they reached the wooden beams that had managed to keep the horses corralled despite the panic amongst the herd.

Thinking they were distracted enough by their task, I decided to wait nearby in hopes of managing to grab one of the horses that were now being released. However, the light of the blaze was bright compared to the darkness of the forest, and once the first man mounted his steed, he spun the animal towards me and our eyes locked. Gasping, I kept my gaze on the very stranger who had just held a dagger to my throat while my heart pounded beneath my ribs. Knowing I had to do something, I dove behind a tree.

But it was too late, I had been caught, and I doubted my

poor attempt at hiding would dissuade him from pursuing me. He didn't seem like the type to forfeit such a challenge, and when I heard his voice call out, I knew my assumption about him had been right.

"She's escaped!" the man shouted to his comrades, and so, the hunt began.

FIFTY-NINE

THE DRIFTS WERE HIGH, AND I STRUGGLED THROUGH THEM AS I fled from my hunters. I could hear the horses closing in now; their hoofbeats were quieted by the amount of snow, but their heavy breathing and the shouts of their riders were loud, and I searched for someplace that would conceal me from their eyes.

But the problem with snow was that it left tracks, and it would not matter which way I went when they could simply follow my path without issue. Especially since the blanket of white that covered the narrow space between trunks was undisturbed. My jaw clenched in frustration and my eyes stung, but despite that and the fact that the length of my legs from the knees down were now numb, I did not slow.

"Where are you going, shewolf?" a voice called out from behind me, and I peered over my shoulder at the group who were now just a yard or two away and who had brought their mounts to a walk. There was no point in wasting their horses' energy when their prey was so easily caught, and I panted for breath before facing forward once more.

A scattered pattern of thick trunks and snow, that was what surrounded me, and despite the calmness of the forest now, I knew what dangers lurked amongst the darkness. I had decided that I would rather place my fate with those monsters rather than the ones who chased me currently. But that choice no longer existed, and it was obvious what my end would be. Taking in a deep breath, I gathered my wits and then spun on my heel.

"Well," I sighed. "Let's just get on with it, shall we?"

The leader looked to the man at his side, it was the one who had offered me the rabbit just a few hours ago, and nodded his head. Following the silent instruction, he dismounted and then unsheathed his sword as he approached.

"I bet my offer looks good now, doesn't it?" he asked with a grin, and I rolled my eyes.

"You have a rather high opinion of yourself," I snapped, and the man's steps faltered and then rage clouded his expression and I watched him carefully.

"I'm sure you'll change your mind when I'm through with you," he growled as he twirled the blade swiftly, and I scoffed at the action.

"Is that meant to impress or frighten me?" I asked. "Because I can assure you, it does neither. I mastered little useless tricks like that at the age of five."

There was no point in keeping my secret now, not after they had found me wearing my brother's armour and especially not when this was most likely my last night in this life.

Lifting my gaze from the man before me, my attention moved to the others. There were seven of them, and had I been armed, I would have wagered on myself being victorious, despite that making me rather arrogant. However, my hands were still bound, and I did not have so much as a dagger with me.

Snarling, the man rushed forward, following the trail I had made, and without the high drift, he moved with more speed than I had anticipated. He swung his sword at my middle, and I leaned back, missing the edge by just a hair. However, given the weight of the weapon and the force he used to cut at me, the man stumbled clumsily, and I narrowed my eyes at his sloppy footwork.

The others in the party may have been battle savvy, but this man was not, and I wondered why his leader would send him rather than handle me himself. Lifting my eyes to the stranger, I watched as he scowled at us, and then laughed softly.

Hearing my chuckle, the swordsman righted himself once more and lifted his weapon high above his head and then brought the steel down. But I had time to anticipate this move, and I raised my own arms, turning them in such a way that the metal of my cuffs kissed his sword and though the vibrations from the contact rattled my bones, the blade bounced off of the iron and slipped from the man's hand.

The man was surprised by the sudden turn of events, and when his jaw went slack, I lifted a knee into his groin. Gasping, he doubled over, and I thrust my arms down, striking him in the ribs with the sharp points of my elbows, and then lunged for the sword that remained forgotten in the snow.

Catching his breath, the man turned to me with wide eyes, and I dove forward, burying the blade into his chest. Wet gurgling came from the back of his throat, and I eyed the skin there and then smiled.

"This is a far cleaner death than the one I had imagined for you," I whispered. "A shame perhaps, but at least it will be slower with your throat intact. Enjoy choking on your blood."

Hauling the metal from his torso, I wiped the blade across his shoulder and then pressed a foot to his crimson-covered chest and kicked him back. Falling to the ground, he took in one last heaving breath, and I looked to the others.

"Who is next?"

Two came at me this time, one slightly older and more skilled, the other, just barely a man and obviously nervous. Knowing I would be better off to kill the challenge first, I lured him away from his anxious comrade and we began a dance of steel.

Back and forth we went, and while he may have had two free hands, I had stamina and speed on my side. Panting for breath, the man jabbed the tip of his blade at me in a last effort to fight me back, and I slid away from the point and then swung my blade at his neck, taking his head clean off.

No longer attached, his face rolled across the snow towards the young man, and he quivered at the sight. At another time I would have perhaps found it in myself to show him mercy, but there were still four of his friends left, and I knew displaying any amount of weakness would not bode well for me. Besides, he may have been young, but he had joined the rebellion that wished to extinguish my family and the other Anointed. And though I may have made excuses for them in the past, I could not now. This man had attacked my father, he had allowed the others to take me hostage, and I was sure he would not step in and keep his leader from acting on whatever vile thoughts sat behind those dark eyes. No, I was better off ending him now, and so, I granted him a quick mercy and watched as his head fell next to his friend's.

"You are impressive," the leader called from where he sat atop his horse. "Had I not been here to witness it, I would have thought it impossible for a woman to be such a fearsome warrior."

"Perhaps you do not give women enough credit," I muttered as I examined the remaining men carefully.

Ignoring my suggestion, he sat back in his saddle and studied me. "Tell me, why are you so skilled in combat? How did you become such an expert in something you have no business participating in?"

"You really want to discuss such boring matters at a time like this?" The man shrugged his shoulders.

"I would like to know why your father allowed you to

master the sword and take your brother's place. Surely, he knew it was you beneath that fancy armour."

Swallowing around the tightness in my throat, I tipped my chin high and sniffed. "He did."

"And he allowed you to do so?" The man's eyes widened and then he shook his head slowly. "No, he didn't just allow you, did he? He ordered you to."

My jaw clenched at his words, and a great laugh burst from him and echoed through the woods.

"For centuries you Anointed have acted as if you were so holy, like you were a part of the Divine Triad themselves." He wiped a finger under his eye and sighed. "But in actuality, you are just as corrupt as the rest. Your own father would rather sacrifice his bastard daughter than make something of his son."

"Does allowing a daughter to fight make someone corrupt?" I growled while my hands tightened around the hilt of my weapon.

"Allowing? No," the man responded. "Forcing her to take her brother's place and then lying about it? Yes."

"I did so willingly, sir," I muttered, and one of his dark brows lifted.

"Is that what you would like me to tell the others when this is done?" he asked softly as if he was wanting a truthful answer. "Despite your name, shewolf, you have no pelt to take as a memento for this fight. If I cannot have furs to prove my victory, I might as well have the true story to share."

"I take pride in what I have accomplished for my family," I said, raising my voice so that perhaps the Gods themselves would hear my words. "I have honour and have done my duty. I have fought for our Gods, and I will do so until I take my last breath."

"That will be soon, I promise, Rígan Baxteel." Slowly the man slid from his horse and the others followed.

My heart began to race, pounding against my chest as

they approached. Their movements were slow and careful, that of predators who had finally cornered their prey, and despite the cold, my palms became damp with sweat.

"Where are those fangs now, shewolf?" the one on the far left asked with a snicker, and I glared at him, watching as he slithered towards me like a serpent of death. Their leader remained in the centre of the group, slowing his stride while he let the others carry on.

"Why don't you come and see for yourself?" I spat and he laughed again.

"Tempting offer, but my life means more than my pride, and I have seen what you can do in one-on-one combat." He unsheathed his sword and then the others did as well. "But let's see how you do with three of us."

At once they charged and I lifted my sword to meet them. I had experience in fighting off multiple men at once, but never with my hands shackled or without armour. And while I managed to dodge their lethal blows, I was clumsy and far slower than I would usually be.

Ducking from a swing aimed at my neck, I rolled across the snow. But the chain that dangled from my cuffs dragged behind me, and one of the men grabbed at the metal and hauled. Twisting around, I fell onto my belly and lifted my chin to see them come forward once more. Scrambling onto my knees, I went to rise to my feet. However, the toes of my boots could not find purchase on the icy ground, and I fell forward again.

Seeing my struggle, two of the men lunged for me, pinning my shoulders down to the snow while the third stepped towards my head.

"What shall we do with her now?" the man above me asked, and I heard the leader move across the snow.

"Whatever plans I had are not worth it," he answered. "She is more rabid than I had anticipated and it is obvious she fears nothing. Keeping her alive is too large of a risk. We will have to find another way to finally gain an audience with the High Commander."

I looked up at the man who stood by my head from the corner of my eye. He held his weapon steady, aimed directly for the back of my neck and, though part of me wished to close my eyes, I knew I had to see this through. I had spent my life facing my foes head-on and this could be no different.

Bringing both hands to the pommel of his sword, he lifted it higher in the air and then paused and smiled down at me.

"Any last wor—"

For a moment my mind could not process what it was I was looking at. He still stood above me, his face tilted down, even that grin remained though it was slowly falling. But instead of two eyes peering at me, one was now a bloody mess, and I watched as the feathers at the end of the shaft blew in the winter breeze.

The sword that had been held high slipped from his fingers, landing into the snow behind him, and then he crumpled, following his weapon to the earth. Suddenly, the hands on my shoulders loosened, and I heard a sharp intake of breath and then the man on my right toppled face first into the ground beside me.

The man on my left staggered back a step, and now that I was free from their hold, I pushed myself to my knees. Both remaining men spun around in circles, their eyes wide as they searched the dark for our attacker. But no sound came, no person stepped forward, and instead another arrow flew, missing the leader by just an inch.

Clambering to my feet, I did not bother to join their search for the assailant and instead saw the blessing from the Gods for what it was and bolted. No longer caring about their plan, the men also scattered. One ran for the horses while the leader ducked behind a tree when another arrow flew in his direction, and I was free from their pursuit as I made my escape.

Now that I had somewhat of a trail to follow, I was able to quicken my speed. However, my tied hands still made keeping my balance difficult, especially since I had to keep them at my sides so that the chain was less likely to curl around my feet, and I glared down at the heavy iron. I had thought I may be able to survive with my wrists cuffed, and while I had managed well against those men, I knew I had no choice but to return to what was left of the camp in hopes of finding something that would aid me in getting rid of these shackles.

Looking at the bright orange flames that still rose high into the sky, I raced towards them, and when I reached the edge of the treeline, I took in a staggering breath. Most of the tents were nothing but kindling now, the once-white ground looked more like soot and the heavy flakes of snow that began to trickle down from the sky danced with the embers that blew in the winter wind. It was beautiful and devastating, and although the blaze should have been terrifying, I couldn't help but appreciate the warmth the massive fire offered.

Gathering the chain into my hands, I lifted my arms towards my head and nestled my face into the sleeve of my tunic and then squinted against the smoke. I would have to be careful, though the south end of the camp had become nothing but a pile of ash, the fire still ate at the other half.

Moving slowly through the site, I scoured the ground of some sort of instrument I could use to pick at the locks of my cuffs. However, what the others had left behind had been burned beyond recognition, and I winced as a strong gust of smoke blew against me. Blinking the sting from my eyes, I gasped for clean air, but the thick grey clouds were too heavy, and I lowered myself to my knees and went to turn back for the forest once more.

However, just as I had crawled a step, I noticed the dark iron bars a few feet away. The cage remained standing, tall and proud despite the devastation that surrounded it, and I looked at its base. The chains were there, the ones that had secured the door, and twisted in their lock was a key.

Grunting, I pulled myself across the snow, doing my best to take in small breaths of air rather than a lungful. I had hoped that it would ease the ache in my chest, especially now that most of the smoke was above me, but it seemed that my body had nearly reached its limit. By the time I was within reach of the lock, I was dizzy with exhaustion. Closing my eyes against the smog, I ran my hands across the dirty ground, searching for the metal I knew was before me.

Stinging heat, that was the first thing I noticed, and I hissed in pain as my fingers smoothed over the burning metal until they found the loop of the key. Despite the discomfort, I pushed a finger through the loop and then twisted the key, and when I heard the click, I pulled it from its place.

Slowly, I moved again, slithering my way across the earth and away from the blaze and the ruin it left in its wake. Not stopping until the air finally felt as if it was no longer trying to choke me, I then shifted onto my knees and carefully brought the end of the key to my face. Grasping the metal between my teeth, I adjusted my hands so that they were in front of me and then aimed the end into the tiny hole.

For a moment, nothing happened, no click, no release, and I thought perhaps this key would not work. But then I tilted my face at a slightly different angle and one of the cuffs dropped open. Taking the key between my fingers of my free hand, I bowed my head.

"Thank you, Gods." I sniffed as a tear leaked from my eye and then I unlocked the other.

The skin was red and raw, and though the joints should have ached, I felt nothing but joy. Looking down at my arms, I sniffed again while my lips curved at the corners. But my smile would grow no bigger, and instead an arm shot forward and a massive palm covered my jaw before I even had a chance to scream.

CHAPTER

SIXTY

FLAILING AGAINST THE HOLD OF MY ATTACKER, I SWUNG MY arms behind me, pounding my fists against his solid back while their strong limb wrapped around my hips. Opening my mouth, I attempted to scream. But with the warm hand covering my face, it came out as nothing more than a muffled sound. Not bothering to try again, especially since there was no one to come to my rescue, I instead pulled my lips back and then sank my teeth into the flesh of his palm.

Yelping in pain, the man released my jaw and pressed his hand against my chest instead, and I looked down at the long fingers that twisted in my tunic. Desperate to get away, I curled my own hands into claws and began tearing at his arms.

"No!" I screamed, my voice high and shrill. "Get off! Don't touch me!"

Had I been in a better state of mind, I would have noticed that his hold had loosened. But I could feel nothing but cold, icy fear running through my veins, and I shivered as warm rivers began to pour down the sides of my face.

"Get off me!" I bellowed into the night. "Don't touch me!"

His hands had disappeared, so had the body that I had

508

been pressed against, and now that I was free, I threw myself forward. I didn't get up, I didn't run. I just laid my forehead against the freezing ground and kept repeating the words over and over.

No. Don't touch me. No. Don't touch me.

It was like a chant I could not stop, a hymn I could not swallow. It was a spell or a ballad. Something broken that I clung to, as if it was the only thing keeping *me* in one battered piece.

"Easy, shewolf," a voice whispered, and I flinched at the name, curling into a ball while my arms covered the back of my head.

The sound of shuffling came from my side, and I whimpered as he moved until he was in front of me, and then those hands that I had clawed at pressed into the snow beside my head, almost as if he put them there so that I could see them from my position. Taking in a shuddering breath, I eyed the long fingers and then frowned.

"It's okay now," he whispered. "You're okay, Rígan."

I felt anything but okay. I couldn't move, I couldn't breathe. I couldn't do anything but curl into a ball and whimper. Yet still, he waited, and when the pounding of my heart slowed and the tears stopped, I lifted my chin.

"Caedell?" I gasped as I peered up at him. His face was pale, his hair a mess, and those amber eyes seemed dull as he searched my own.

"I'm right here," he swore, and I swallowed at the soothing sound of his voice before my face crumpled once more. I couldn't decipher his expression through the welling in my eyes, but I did notice the way he lifted his hands, holding them up with their palms towards me, as if he was trying to assure me that he would not touch me. A broken sob tore from my throat at the gesture, and then I was reaching for him. All but crawling into his lap, I clung on to his shoulders and buried my face into his neck.

Still, his arms remained in the air, and I pressed my damp face against the warm skin beneath his jaw and sighed.

"Please," I cried, and I felt him swallow but still he did not return my embrace.

Growing desperate, I pulled at his cloak, twisting the wool in my fists, and he swallowed again and then tilted his head so that it rested on mine. "It's okay, I won't touch you, just take what you need from me."

Frowning, I realized how meek I sounded when I had said the word. My begging could have been misunderstood, and I shifted against him and then closed my eyes.

"Hold me, please." Those strong arms curled around my body the instant the request had left my lips, and I slumped against him.

For a long moment, we stayed there. Me against his chest, moving with it as it rose and fell with every deep breath, as if we were breathing as one, and him, completely wrapped around me. It was a comfort unlike any other I had ever felt before, and though my trembling had nearly stopped, more tears sprang to my eyes at the overwhelming release I felt.

"Are you hurt?" His voice was low, and I could hear the simmering rage beneath the concern.

Pulling my face away from the warmth of his skin, I blinked up at him and shook my head. His eyes scanned me, and then narrowed at the cut on my cheek. Pulling an arm from around my waist, he cradled my jaw in his hand and then swiped his thumb over the wound.

"Yes, you are," he argued, and I felt my lower lip tremble.

"It's nothing," I swore, and that was the truth of it. Compared to the guilt and fear still twisting in my gut, the small scratch was nothing.

Caedell scowled at me, but before he could press the issue, I shifted onto my knees and brought a hand to the back of his head. Curling my fingers into his thick hair, I guided his mouth to mine.

It was soft and slow, and I could feel his uncertainty in the way he held himself still. However, despite the stiffness in his shoulders, those long fingers of his had moved down to rest against the base of my spine. Sighing at the heat that seeped into my chilled skin, I brushed my lips against his again, and then he was pressing his palms against my back as he dragged me forward.

Whatever indecision he had felt was now gone, and he deepened the kiss, stealing my breath from my lungs and sending my mind to dizzying heights. He consumed me, wholly and completely, and I moaned against him as he ran his teeth against my bottom lip.

"Dear Gods, Rígan!" he groaned in answer, and then suddenly he was gone, and my eyes flickered open in confusion.

His face had regained colour, those amber eyes were bright and burning, and I watched in satisfaction as he panted for breath. Narrowing his gaze, he held my stare and then released his hold on me so that he could run a hand through his hair.

"I can't think when you make noises like that." Shrugging, I tucked a dark strand behind my ear, and he brought his fingers down to his jaw and then traced them over his lips.

"You were trying to distract me," he accused, and I could do nothing but shrug again. "Why?"

Crossing my arms over my chest, I felt my face drop into a scowl, and the lust in his gaze melted into concern once more. Hating the look of pity, I lifted my attention to the smoke that billowed behind him and tried to find a way to redirect the conversation.

However, it would seem I didn't need to. Just as my mouth opened, Caedell lunged for me, and for a moment, I thought he had changed his mind. But when he pressed me back into the snow and covered my body with his own, I realized it wasn't because he wanted to continue our kiss, he was shielding me from something.

There was a dull thud, the sound of something making contact, but Caedell's eyes remained locked on the treeline, and he gave no indication he had been hit or injured in any way. Lying still beneath his weight, I watched as he snarled at something before him and then he was pulling himself to his feet and bolting towards the forest. Rolling onto my belly, I moved to follow him and saw the man from before, the leader of the group who had chased me into the woods. He stood there, his hands clutching a bow as he aimed another arrow at Caedell, and my breath caught as he released his shot.

But he was Caedell the Undying, an Anointed of the Gods, and just like every other time he faced an enemy, he remained protected. Dodging the arrow, Caedell unsheathed his sword while he ran towards our enemy with more speed than I would have thought possible, and I watched the way the man's eyes widened.

Struggling to nock another arrow, the man began to shake as Caedell neared. And then the Heir of House Reide was there, standing before our enemy with his mighty blade piercing through the man's middle until it protruded from his back. Pulling the blade free from the body, Caedell stepped away and watched as his victim crumpled and then he cleaned his blade on the wool of his enemy's cloak and turned to face me. However, he had just taken three steps in my direction when I heard a groan echo and fear twisted in my chest when I remembered a very important detail about the man Caedell had struck down.

"He is immortal!" Looking back at the stranger who was now dragging himself across the snow, Caedell cursed under his breath and we both watched as the man brought his hands to the stain on his belly. Holding them there for a moment, he lowered his chin and then pulled his crimson-covered fingers away so that he could study them.

"Blessed Reaper, his gift is true." The man grinned and then his eyes lifted.

"Not for long." Swinging his sword, Caedell cut into the side of the man's face, and then pulled the metal free only to attack again. Looking at the carnage, I was certain there was no coming back from it. However, Caedell still took the time to behead him and then turned from the mess he had made, and I studied his expression.

Just as concern had stolen the lust from his gaze, anger had now taken pity's place, and he marched towards me, his jaw clenched and body stiff. Stumbling to my feet, I watched the way he prowled across the snow with dawn breaking at his back, and the beauty of him under the soft glow of the sunrise stole my breath away.

"Are you well?" It was my turn to ask him, and his brows furrowed.

"Fine." His tone was clipped, and he appeared uninjured despite a rip in the sleeve of his tunic. In fact, now that I saw it, I noticed that the dark blue frayed edges looked almost black, and I frowned.

"Did he hit you?" His amber eyes lowered to the arm I gestured to, and then he shook his head.

"It's old." Rolling his shoulders, he took a deep breath, but I remained unconvinced.

"Show me," I demanded.

"Rígan, we need to leave this place, we do not have time for this." He sheathed his sword and then brought his hand to the rip in his shirt, and I narrowed my eyes at him.

"I'm not going anywhere until you show me." Sighing, he lifted those fingers from his arm and curled them into a fist but then let it fall back to his side before angling towards me. Pinching the cool damp fabric, I moved it away and noticed a wound that had scabbed over.

"I told you it was old," he snapped, and I scowled at him.

"Why are you upset at me for being worried?" I demanded, and the air left his lungs in a great rush.

"I'm not upset, not at you," he promised, and then he was cupping the back of my neck and dragging me forward until my forehead rested against his own. Closing his eyes, he took a steadying breath, then another one, and I waited until he gathered himself.

"Are you sure you're well?" I whispered. Those long dark lashes fluttered open, and I searched the deep golden colour while he nodded against me.

"I am now that I know you're alright." Tilting his chin, he pressed a long, lingering kiss to my temple, but before I could react to such an unexpected gesture, he grabbed my hand and pulled me along behind him.

CHAPTER
SIXTY-ONE

Caedell's attitude was slow to change despite the distance we put between us and the ruins of the camp. In fact, he seemed more uneasy the farther we ventured into the woods, and I frowned at the tension he carried in his shoulders.

"Are you certain you are not injured?" I pressed again and then watched the way his entire body seemed to stiffen.

"I don't know how many times I can convince you I am fine," he muttered, and I crossed my arms around myself at the sudden chill in his tone.

"Perhaps that is because you are doing a rather piss-poor job at it," I growled, and his head hung for a moment before he spun on his heel to face me.

"I am just tired," Caedell assured me, and I took in the pale colour of his face and the ragged expression he wore. He was still handsome, there was no denying that, but he looked worn down, and I suddenly felt ashamed that I had not taken it upon myself to remember the journey he must have faced to reach me. Though now that the threat of the rebels had passed and the adrenaline had worn off, I found myself left with even more questions.

"Why are you not in Denimoore?" Caedell frowned for a moment and then ran a hand through his hair.

"I thought that was rather obvious," he answered softly, and my eyes narrowed at him and he continued. "I came for you."

My chest tightened but I ignored the feeling. "But why? There are far more important things that you should have been worried about. Why would you bother coming after my brother and me when we turned our backs on the rest of the Anointed?"

"Because I will always come for *you*." My heart stuttered in my chest, and I felt the air leave my lungs in one fell swoop.

"But the others—"

"It doesn't matter right now," Caedell interrupted sharply. "We need to focus on finding shelter before nightfall. We both know what lingers in the forests of Elrin, and I don't think either of us are eager for another run-in with the beasts that hide amongst the shadows. Whether they be man or monster."

"I have come to the realization that they are often one and the same." Caedell sighed roughly but nodded.

"I don't think I can argue that point," he agreed and then held his hand out for me to take.

Glancing down at the long fingers before me, I lifted my own. However, just as our palms were about to touch, I brought my arm to my chest and pressed my fist against the pounding that echoed just beneath my knuckles.

"Just one more question," I murmured before I tilted my chin and glanced up at the burning amber eyes that studied me closely. "How did you find me?"

His lips lifted at the corners and his gaze turned gentle. "I have been tracking you since you left Denimoore. I was only half a day's ride behind."

"What?" I gasped while my brows rose in surprise. "But

how? You weren't there to see us off and I never noticed someone following. None of our men did."

"Did you really think I could stand to say goodbye to you that day?" Caedell asked. "Did you think I could watch you leave without begging you to stay?"

"Caedell—"

"We were only parted for a mere few hours and yet the ghost of you haunted me at every turn. I knew that letting you leave was a mistake and it was not one I was willing to regret for the rest of my days."

"I had no idea, none of us did." My brows furrowed, and Caedell took a step closer and then curled his fingers around the wrist that was pressed to my breastbone. Easing my arm away from my torso, he carefully interlocked our fingers and then used his other hand to cup my chin.

"I can't say I'm overly surprised. Your brother and your men are rather hopeless without having you and Donigan to lead the group." I tightened my grasp on him, and he stroked his thumb over the sharp angle of my cheekbone.

"Now, if that answer satisfies your curiosity, can we continue on our way?"

"I suppose so," I answered, and he pressed a quick kiss to my mouth.

"Should any other questions arise, perhaps you would be better off saving them until we have found somewhere safe. I do not want us to be followed."

Nodding, I offered him a smile, and he turned from me once more and led me farther into the forest.

WE SPENT the rest of the day trekking silently through the woods. Hour after hour passed, though time seemed to drag at an even slower rate when my legs began to protest and my teeth started chattering from the bitter cold. Thankfully, however, we had the light of the sun to accompany us, and the golden rays at least offered slivers of warmth, though those were few and far between as the forest grew more dense and their branches captured the light for themselves. By the time we reached Caedell's destination it was dark once more, and I wondered if I ever spent so much time in the shadows as I had since meeting him.

Curling my fingers around his own, I looked through the thick cover of pine needles and frowned at the structure before us. It was tall and mighty, its stone walls impressive and imposing, and I searched the small glowing windows for some sign as to who this manor belonged to. There were no men stationed out front, no banners hung, and if it hadn't been for the flickering orange behind the panel of glass, I would have thought the building was abandoned.

"Where are we?" I whispered, and Caedell glanced over his shoulder at me.

"Halfway between Noorde Point and Rushander," he replied as he faced the building once more.

"So, the middle of nowhere," I muttered, and he squeezed my hand. "Why would such a place be here?"

"It was built by the very first of the Forefolk," he explained, and my eyes widened in surprise. "It was once a trading post and a great village. However, over time it became apparent that the winters were too harsh for travellers to visit on foot, and since it is landlocked, it was soon abandoned. The rest of the town has been overtaken by the trees, but the manor remained."

"And who is in there now?" I frowned as I examined the back of him.

"You do not need to be afraid, Rígan," Caedell promised as he raised our joined hands to his mouth and then pressed a kiss to my fingers. "It is just my men, you are safe."

Swallowing roughly, I took a moment to study the stone walls once more and then exhaled. Looking back at me, Caedell waited until I offered him a soft smile and then he tugged me forward.

Rather than taking me towards the grand front entrance, he guided us around the back of the building, towards a door that would have gone unnoticed had he not led me directly to it. Standing in front of the worn wooden plank, he turned to me once more and my brows furrowed.

"Why are we trying to enter without being detected?" I asked and Caedell's mouth curled half-heartedly before he tucked a long strand of hair behind my ear.

"I figured you would prefer to go unnoticed and have some space to yourself rather than be ambushed and fussed over." His words took me by surprise, my mouth fell open.

He was right, of course; I would much rather not be swarmed by strangers after everything that had happened over the last few days. I did not want to have to answer any questions or retell the events that had led up to our arrival. But what startled me was the fact that he knew all of that without me having to say a word. He somehow anticipated what I needed and made certain to see it happen.

The warm feeling of gratitude curled in my chest, and I tilted my face so that I could press a kiss to the corner of his mouth. Returning the favour, he brushed his lips over mine for just a moment and I lifted a brow.

"Will you still be there to fuss over me?" I asked, watching smugly as his tongue darted out to wet his lips.

"Only if you will have me," he whispered back, but the words were not full of heat and longing. They were soft with nervousness, and I curled my free hand around our joined fingers and then lifted them until the back of his hand was pressed against my mouth.

"You're the only one I want," I promised as my lips ghosted over his skin, and his lashes fluttered closed while a forlorn expression crossed his face. Hoping to ease the burden that had suddenly taken hold of him, I pressed another kiss to his fingers and then cleared my throat.

"Lead the way."

SIXTY-TWO

CAEDELL SWIFTLY GUIDED ME THROUGH THE QUIET HALLS, only checking on me when he rounded a corner too roughly or when I failed to keep up with his pace because I was distracted by the ancient art that hung along the walls. The corridors were narrow and winding, and I knew should the need arise, there would be no way for me to trace our steps back to the entrance on my own. I was left with no choice but to surrender to the man who held my hand, and though I would have once thought it impossible, I realized now, I would happily follow him anywhere.

Swallowing down the heady wave of emotion, I sniffed and the tension on my arm loosened as he slowed his stride.

"Are you well?" His amber eyes searched mine, and I blinked up at him before nodding silently. Exhaling, he glanced at the door before us and then used his free hand to press on the handle. "This will be your room."

The chambers were dark, but I could make out a large bed and a vanity. There was a great fur rug that nearly covered the entire floor and a mighty fireplace in the corner, though all of it had certainty seen better days.

"It is not Denimoore, but it will do," I whispered as I

stepped into the room, and Caedell stiffened as I passed him. Waving at him to follow me, I waited until he was out of the way and then closed the door carefully, making certain not to make too much noise.

"What did I say to upset you just then?" I asked, and his dark brows furrowed. "Is it because you are worried for them in the north?"

His eyes lowered to the ground. "The rebellion has gotten out of hand."

I knew that, I had seen as much even before the attack on my family, but I worried sharing the news of my loss would only add the weight on his shoulders and so I decided to save it for the morning. Reaching for him instead, I placed a steady hand on his chest and waited for his gaze to lift once more.

"I am sorry you left them behind, perhaps you should have stayed." His frown only deepened at that, and he shook his head.

"I do not regret coming for you, Rígan," he whispered. "As I said, I will always come for you."

"Yes, you've proven as much." My hand slid up to his shoulder and then traced across the muscle there until I reached his neck. Cupping the back of it, I swallowed and then pulled him towards me. "Thank you."

I had tilted my face towards him in a silent invitation, and though I heard his breath hitch, he did not meet me. Confused, I slowly withdrew, and my face flushed.

"I'm sorry," I murmured under my breath while my fingers began to fall from their place. But he grabbed at the wrist that rested over his collarbone and held it against him, letting his thumb slowly stroke across my pulse point.

"Don't be sorry," he sighed. "But don't thank me either."

My eyes widened at the hard edge of his voice, and his shoulders sagged while he hung his head. "Do not do this because you think you owe me something."

Snorting, I rolled my eyes and then tucked my free hand

under his chin. Pressing my knuckles against the sharp edge of his jaw, I lifted his face and narrowed my gaze. "I'm insulted that you even thought I would do such a thing." Moving my thumb, I ran it across the tender flesh of his lower lip.

"I don't trade my affection. I give it to those I choose, and everything I do is because I want to." The relief was evident, but I still waited, taking a long moment to study him closely. "Is this something you want, Caedell?"

"Would you judge me harshly if I said that, though I know I have no right to, I have wanted nothing more? It has been a constant thought in my mind since that night in Ferri when you entered the great hall in that *fucking* sinful gown." My eyes widened at his admission. I had been so preoccupied that night, I had not seen him in the great hall. In fact, the only time I remember noticing him that evening was when I had stumbled upon him after learning of Gwain's betrothal.

My heart raced but I kept my expression calm. "I would say your priorities may need some work."

Caedell tipped back his head with a laugh and the sound of it warmed me from the inside out. Still smiling, he reached for me and pulled me close before nuzzling his nose against mine. "Before we get ahead of ourselves, how do you feel about a bath?"

My eyes widened at the word, and he chuckled again when I nodded dumbly. Fresh water and clean skin sounded divine, and he grabbed my shoulders and then spun me around before ushering me towards a door that sat flush against the wall. Opening it, I stepped into a smaller room that had a large tub sitting in the middle of it, and he released his hold on me and began to light the candles.

"It's not hot, but it will do the trick, and I will get the fire started in your room to keep the chill away for when you are finished."

He pressed a quick kiss to my cheek and then ducked out

of the room, and I placed a hand over my chest, savouring the warmth that spread there.

THE WHITE SHIFT that had been left behind did little to conceal my body, especially since my skin was damp and the droplets of water that had clung to my flesh seeped through the cotton, leaving the material nearly translucent. Looking down at the fabric, I decided to part my wet hair and pulled half over each shoulder, in hopes that the dark strands would cover my breasts. I was not usually shy about my body, and in truth, Caedell had already seen it. But this felt different somehow, and for the first time that I could remember, I was nervous about what may happen once I walked through the doorway. Ignoring the trembling of my hands, I pressed the door open and then stepped into the room.

The fire had been set, and the warmth wafted across the room while the orange from the flames illuminated details I had not noticed before. The curtains were a pretty green colour and the bed was far more lush than I had thought it would be. However, what truly caught my eye was Caedell.

He was sitting on the furs before the fireplace and his hair looked damp and his clothes had been changed for a simple loose-fitting tunic and breeches. But that's not what drew my eye. It was the blaze behind him. It was the way it flickered as the flames danced in the hearth and the glow only illuminated his sharp jaw, perfect nose, and amber eyes. He looked ethereal, utterly and devastatingly beautiful, and my breath caught at the sight of him.

"Feel better?" His voice broke me from my trance, and I crossed the room.

"Much," I whispered as I knelt beside him.

The room went silent besides the odd crackle from the fire, and I studied the stone of the mantel while I gathered my courage. Seemingly to be one step ahead once again, Caedell reached for the hand closest to him, and then plucked it from the floor before urging me to turn. Following his guidance, I shifted until my knees brushed against his and chewed on my lower lip.

Bringing my hand to drape over his shoulder, he repeated the process with the other arm and then leaned forward. His kiss was soft and sweet, first a brush of lips, then a little more, and then he deepened it until it grew into an inferno. No longer able to sit idle, I guided him back until he was splayed across the furs, and then I lifted on to my knees and straddled his waist. Groaning into my mouth, he cupped my wide hips, digging his fingers into the supple flesh there, and I captured his lower lip between my teeth and gave it a gentle tug.

"By Gods, Rígan," he panted once I had released him, and I grinned as I lowered my focus to his neck.

His skin was warm under my tongue and teeth, and I paid careful attention to his reactions as I teased him with my mouth. A flick of my tongue against his pulse point would make his hips lift, while a scrape of my teeth under his jaw made him gasp out my name and those hands on my body would tremble. If I ran my fingers through his hair while sucking at the skin just above his collarbone, he would whimper, and I would be lying if I said the sound did not make my toes curl.

I took my time, chasing every noise, every response, and when I finally moved back to his lips, his forehead was damp, and his eyes were dazed as they gazed up at me. Rocking my hips into his, I watched the way he looked up at me, as if I was something precious that was meant to be adored, and I reached for one of his wrists and then pinned it next to his head.

"Do you want to continue?" He had taken charge that

night in Denimoore, and while I had loved every moment of it, this time I wanted to be the one in power.

"Only if you are sure," he whispered huskily, and I nodded.

Releasing his arm, I brought my fingers to the hem of his tunic and then slowly dragged it up the length of his body and over his head. I had admired him before, both in armour and in clothes, and had even seen him shirtless a time or two. But still, I had not been prepared for what lay beneath now that I was close enough to truly enjoy the view. The long length of his torso was not bulging with mass, but the muscles were larger than one would have assumed they'd be. His chest was wide and strong, covered in a light dusting of hair, and his waist and hips were narrow. The rest of his torso was solid, but not flat. It was very defined, and I wanted to trace the grooves of his abdomen with my tongue.

"You seem pleased," he laughed softly, making the muscles of his stomach shift beneath me, and my mouth dried at the sight.

"You're very…" I trailed off, not knowing how to finish the sentence, and one of his eyebrows lifted.

"So, you are?" My eyes rose to his handsome face, and though he may have appeared confident, I could see a hint of nervousness. "Pleased, that is."

Tossing his tunic towards the bed, I placed a hand on his chest, taking a moment to enjoy the racing rhythm beneath my palm, and then I bent forward and kissed him gently. "Very."

He exhaled roughly at my confirmation, and I kissed him again, making certain to take his mind away from his nerves and back to the task at hand. Now that there was nothing in my way, I ran my fingers across his skin, tickling and stroking the warm flesh while our tongues fought for dominance until I reached the lace of his breeches.

Pulling from my mouth, Caedell fought to catch his breath

while he tipped his chin so that he could look down to where my hand had stopped. My fingers remained on top of the fabric, not going any further until I had his agreement, and his brows furrowed.

"Should we not do something else?" he asked, and I frowned in confusion.

"I'm not sure I understand what you mean," I replied, and then carefully shifted so that my weight was no longer pressed into his hips but rather just an inch or two above him.

"I don't want this to be bad for you," he explained. "I want to make sure you enjoy it."

My eyes widened in understanding, and I took one of his hands in my own and then slowly brought it to the cotton that covered the top half of my thigh. Dragging our fingers underneath the material, I let him take a moment to stroke the muscle there and then I urged him higher. Slowly his touch crept up my leg, making my skin rise as he tickled my flesh, and then his fingers slid across the warm wetness at the apex, and I whimpered at the sensation.

"I am enjoying it," I murmured softly once I was able to make my tongue cooperate, and I noticed the way his eyes darkened. "Can I continue?"

Swallowing, he nodded his head, and I pulled his hand out from under my shift and then plucked at his laces. Once they slackened, I grabbed at the waist of his breeches and began to lower them. Planting his heels on the fur beneath him, he lifted his hips, and I eased them down the length of his legs, not allowing my eyes to move away from the dark material until I had passed his feet and he was free from them. Kneeling at the end of his body, I took in a deep breath and then slowly moved my gaze. Large feet, strong calves, thighs heavy with muscle and—

Shaking my head, I pinched the bridge of my nose in frustration and amusement. Of course Caedell fucking Reide would be blessed in every aspect, but more specifically that particular area, and I chuckled at the unfairness of it all.

"Is there something funny?" Caedell's voice was quiet, and I lifted my hand from my face and noticed the stiffness in his body as he lay before me.

"I just can't seem to understand how you have managed to not bed every woman in Elrin." I shrugged, unable to be anything but honest, and then I crawled up the length of his legs and straddled his waist, careful to sit above his navel.

"I haven't wanted anyone else." It was his turn to be truthful now, I supposed, and the corner of my lips lifted at his admission.

"Does it bother you that I have?" I asked earnestly, and Caedell frowned for a moment, and his expression made me hold my breath.

"It does not bother me that you have bedded others." He paused as he gathered his thoughts. "I suppose it bothers me that they have been undeserving of your attention. Though I suppose, so am I."

Sliding a little lower, I felt his hard length brush against the curve of my ass, and then I curled a hand into his hair and tipped forward until my mouth was an inch away from his own.

"I told you, I give my affection to who I want." I slanted my mouth over his, bringing his lower lip between my own and then flicked my tongue across it. Allowing me entry, Caedell surrendered to me fully, and when I was satisfied that my kiss had sent him into a daze, I pulled back. "And you are who I want."

Straightening once more, I leaned back and reached for the end of my shift. However, before I could begin to lift it, Caedell sat up and pushed my hands away. Letting them fall to my sides, I watched as he pinched the hem between his fingers and then slowly, just as I had, he pulled the cotton from my body.

There was a flash of white as it passed my face, and then my hair was falling down around me while the necklace rested against my chest, and I was left bared for Caedell's heated gaze. Bringing his trembling fingers to my waist, he held me still and took in a deep, shuddering breath.

"My Gods, you are glorious." I preened at the compliment.

"I will always accept flattery." I smiled. "But I would appreciate it more if you would touch me."

Wetting his lips, Caedell nodded and then smoothed his palms up my sides until they reached the curve of my breasts. Cupping the heavy weight of them, he stroked his thumbs over the peaks, and I let my head fall back with a moan. His palms were large, and his fingers were long, but the fullness of my chest still spilled out of his grip, and he tightened his hold before moving his mouth to my shoulder. Tracing my skin with his lips, he showered my body with kisses. Starting at the curve of my arm before moving to my collarbone, then my neck, up to my jaw and then my cheek. Once he reached my temple, he lowered his chin, brushed his mouth against my own, and then repeated the entire process on the other side.

The intimacy of it all was unlike anything I had experienced, and by the time he finished, I was a quivering mess. Pulling his hands away from my breasts, I urged him onto his back once more and then carefully moved until I hovered above his length.

"Are you sure?" I asked, needing to make certain that he wanted this. I needed to know that this was not some rash decision, that this night would not end up being a secret he hid, or worse, a regret. Nodding, he lay flat against the floor, and I reached between my thighs before guiding the head of his cock to my entrance.

I thought I did not need any more preparation, after all I had been desperate for him since the first touch. But despite my wetness, it took some time to work the thick length of him into me, and I steadied my breathing as I rolled my hips. Caedell, however, panted below me, and those hands had been at his sides, grabbing at my thighs roughly, as if he was trying to use my flesh to anchor himself while I worked my way down.

My skin prickled as he finally filled me, and while the stretch had been uncomfortable at the beginning, it was magnificent now. Holding myself still, I braced my palms on his muscular chest and then swallowed while I allowed myself a moment to adjust.

It truly was overwhelming, the way he seemed to reach inside me, almost as if we were pieces of a puzzle meant to come together, and when I could bear it no longer, I began to move.

It started off as a gentle rocking, just a slow twist of my hips really. But when the tingling heat licked at my skin and the blood in my veins began to burn, I hurried my pace, and Caedell tipped his chin towards the ceiling and groaned.

The sound of his desperation sent another wave of arousal crashing into me, and I closed my eyes as I chased my own blaze of ecstasy that was now just out of reach. Curling my fingers, I let my nails scrape across his skin while my brows furrowed in concentration.

I was close now, achingly close, but each time I neared the edge, it would move further away from me. Growling in annoyance, I clenched my eyes shut. However, before I could change my rhythm again, a hand cupped my jaw and my lashes fluttered open.

"Look at me," Caedell whispered hoarsely. "Let me see you."

Pulling my lower lip between my teeth, I held his stare, letting that burning amber sear into my mind, and then his other hand moved to press over my fingers, flattening my palm against his heart.

"Do you feel that?" he asked, his voice cracking as I

rocked into him again, and I looked down to where our hands lay across his chest. "That is yours."

I gasped at the words and that cliff came barrelling towards me now. Noticing how near my release was, Caedell shifted my chin so our eyes could lock once more.

"No matter what happens, that is yours." His jaw clenched and his lower lip quivered before he spoke again. "I am yours."

His declaration was my undoing, and I dove headfirst over the edge with his name on my lips.

SIXTY-THREE

My cheek was warm as I lay across his chest, and he ran his fingers over my spine, stroking the flesh as we both gazed at the fire. We had not moved from the floor yet; we were far too comfortable to even bother, and I let my eyes close as his hand drifted to the damp strands of my hair.

"It's still wet," Caedell whispered as he twirled a piece before tickling my shoulder with its ends.

"It takes ages to dry, especially with how long and thick it is," I murmured, letting my lips graze the muscle of his chest while I nuzzled closer. "It's just another reason why my father always insists on me cutting it."

My body reacted before my mind even had a chance, and the suppleness that had taken over my frame from my earlier release shifted into ice. Noticing the change, Caedell curled his arm over my back and cupped my shoulder gently before guiding me to the side so that he could see me more easily.

"What is it?" My brows furrowed as I studied the slope of his collarbone, and he moved his hand so that it was tucked beneath my chin and then he lifted my face.

"I said insists," I answered, my voice hoarse from having been pushed past the sudden tightness of my throat. Clearly not understanding, Caedell frowned, and I wet my lips. "I should have said insisted."

His expression darkened but he remained quiet, and I took in a shuddering breath before closing my eyes. "You probably think me monstrous for not saying something sooner, or for falling into your bed so easily given what has happened."

"I think nothing of the sort," he swore, and I laughed coldly.

"I don't see how that could be possible," I murmured. "My father is dead, my brother left abandoned, and instead of picking up the broken pieces of my family, I came here with you."

"Do you regret that?" Caedell asked, and I noticed how stiff he had become beside me.

"Would you be able to look at me the same way you did tonight if I said no?" That was the truth after all, but I still kept my eyes closed as I braced for his disgust.

"Rígan," he sighed and then I was being moved onto my back. Sinking into the soft furs, I slowly opened my eyes and gazed up at him as he braced himself above me.

"Despite your masks, your fangs and claws, I see what lies under here." One of his fingers caressed the skin of my chest, and I glanced down at his hand. "I know everything you do is for the right reasons. You have only ever wanted to be honourable and good. You wanted to do your duty, and whatever you are feeling or not feeling right now does not make that any less true."

"How can you be so sure?" I whispered doubtfully.

"Because I see you," he answered before brushing a kiss to my forehead. "I see what lies deep beneath the surface, and I recognize the same thing I know I carry myself."

"Caedell the Undying truly cares about being honourable? I thought that was just a rumour," I laughed softly, but he did not join me, and I lifted my attention and searched his face.

"Perhaps I have not always been the most honourable, but

my duty to the people of Elrin has been the most important thing in my life," he muttered.

"Has?" My brows furrowed and his palm cupped my face. Stroking his thumb across my jaw, he tilted it just so and then slanted his mouth over mine.

"Now it comes second." My pulse raced as my breath caught in my throat, and he grinned before sitting back so that he straddled my hips.

"But before I make any more declarations or let this get any further…" His smile grew until those dimples became evident, and I felt a warm flutter in my belly at the sight. "Do you want to tell me what happened?"

"No," I replied. "Maybe tomorrow, but not now."

Placing his hands on his bare thighs, he watched me for a long moment, and I realized while I did not have to go into detail, seeing he was an Anointed, I owed him more than that.

"I had already decided that my loyalties no longer belonged to them, even before the battle began and we had been defeated," I whispered. "And while I will grieve the man he could be, my father was not someone who I would have chosen to keep in my life. He was not who I thought he was, and I do not want to give him any more of me."

"And your brother?" Skileer's fortune was not so obvious. I had no idea where he was or if he even survived. But I found myself no longer carrying the burden of worrying for him and the consequences of his actions.

"I do not know of his fate, but I hope he lives." The muscle in Caedell's jaw twitched at that, and I realized he probably could not understand such a thing considering how poorly my brother had treated me during our journey. "But I do not want to be tied to him any longer."

"What do you want?"

"Now, or?" Caedell rolled his eyes at that, and I sat up and reached for his shoulders. Pulling him over me, I shifted my legs so that my thighs sat on either side of his hips, and then I raised my head to kiss him once more.

"Right now, I would like to teach you a few other things." I slid my nails across the strong muscles of his back and his eyes fluttered closed while a groan poured from his mouth. "And then, I'd like to lose myself in your warmth."

"I'm not so sure I need to be taught." He smirked and then he ran his tongue up the length of my neck and caught my earlobe between his teeth. It was my turn to moan, and I clutched at him while my hips lifted.

"One deflowering and you think you are proficient enough to take charge?" Caedell laughed against my cheek while his fingers tickled across the skin of my inner thigh.

"I'm a quick student," he murmured, and that hand of his moved higher. "Besides, I don't remember any complaints when I had you sprawled across that table."

A witty retort had been on the tip of my tongue when he finally sought out the wetness between my thighs. And though his touch was soft and teasing, he did not hesitate before seeking out that place that sent sparks shooting through my veins. Circling it carefully, he then lowered his face to my shoulder. Grazing his lips across my chest, he moved down, not stopping until he reached the peak of my breast. Closing his mouth around my nipple, he pinched the flesh gently between his teeth while sinking two fingers into me.

His rhythm was smooth and slow as he took his time to build my pleasure, making note of every whimper and gasp and then repeated the actions responsible for such responses. Thrusting sharply after a particularly breathy sigh, he curled his fingers and my hips snapped towards his touch just before I reached my climax.

I could feel the dampness on his hand as I came back to myself, and he cupped his palm under my knee. Melting into the floor, I watched while he widened the space between my legs, and I lifted both limbs and pressed my thighs against his waist before bringing a hand to the curve of his ass.

"Are you sure?" he whispered, though he did not fight my encouragement.

"Are we going to do this every time?" I chuckled with a raised brow, and those amber eyes held my own while he nodded.

"Yes," he answered simply. "I never want to assume, so I will make sure that you are clear with what it is you want."

"What I *need* is to feel you fill me," I breathed while urging him forward, and I felt his body quiver at my words.

Taking his length in his hand, he brought it to the wet heat of my cunt and then eased in. He was careful, pressing one glorious inch in at a time, and I grew impatient with his restraint. I was burning for him, nearing delirious desperation, and though his body trembled, and his breathing sounded laboured, he did not seem anywhere near as far gone as I was.

Refusing to wait any longer, I locked my legs around his hips and dug my heels into his back. Seeming to reach the end of his own patience, he braced his weight on his hands next to my head, and snapped forward, thrusting the remainder of his cock into me.

"Caed!" I cried out as my back arched, and he lifted his head at the sound.

The amber of his eyes was liquid gold and the heat in his stare set me ablaze. Needing more, I wrapped myself around him. One hand slid into his hair, tugging on the strands as my hips lifted to meet his own. The other remained on his backside, my nails clawing at him as I urged him faster, and he pressed his forehead to mine as he panted.

"Caed?" he gasped. "Is that what you would like to call me, my heart?"

Rolling his hips, he brought a hand to where we were joined and circled his thumb against me. Flushing at his own term of endearment, I nodded, and Caedell's smile was blinding as he watched me race towards my third release of the night.

"Does that mean I can keep you, Rígan?" he whispered, his voice full of longing. "I am already yours, but will you be mine?"

Tightening my fist in his hair, I steered his mouth to my own for a brutal kiss and then, as I hurtled towards the edge, I nodded one final time and his warmth enveloped me.

A SOFT GLOW trickled into the room from the gap between the green curtains and I rolled towards the window and studied the light with bleary eyes before glancing around the rest of the chambers. The fire, which once burned bright, was nothing but embers now, and I shivered before looking at the furs laid out before the hearth and frowned.

The pelts somehow seemed duller from my place on the bed. Their surface did not appear nearly as soft and plush as they had in the flickering light of the flames. I also noticed the clothes that had been strewed across the floor were missing, as were their owner.

Sitting up in the bed, I ran a hand through my long hair and searched for some sign as to where he could have wandered off to. The door to the adjacent room was open slightly and no sound came from there and his boots, which had been left near the chair in the corner, had also vanished.

For a moment I sat there, clutching the covers to my chest, my thumb stroking across the pendant while I just listened. The hall outside was silent, eerily so considering the time of day, and the longer I waited the more uneasy I felt.

Throwing the fabric off of my legs, I stood from the bed only to hiss when the soles of my feet kissed the cold stone of the floor. Wrapping my arms around my naked body, I fought the frigid sting of the air and searched for something to wear. My clothes from the day before had vanished along with Caedell it seemed, and I bent down to snatch at the shift I had worn after my bath. It was dry now, though still thin, but besides the furs or the covers of the bed, it was the only other option. Pulling it over my head, I let the length of it settle along my form and then crossed the room to the door.

Bracing my hand against the frame, I curled the other around the cool steel handle. But before I could haul it open and begin my search for Caedell, I heard someone speaking as they approached the door.

It was not the deep timbre I had grown fond of, but a woman's voice, soft and sweet, and I frowned. It grew louder as it neared only to stop altogether, and then the handle beneath my palm was moving. Stepping back, I moved out of the way just as it swung open, and then she stepped forward.

Her hair was tied back in a neat plait and her dress was a deep navy, but it was the silver that covered her face that startled me. A metal mask, identical to those the two burly men at her sides wore, and I took a step back, then another as they entered farther into the room.

"She is going to try and flee," the woman said quietly. "Grab her, but be careful, we've had too many issues as of late. He will not forgive another mistake on our part."

Lunging forward, the guards reached for me, and while I was able to dodge the first set of hands, the other grabbed my arm. Twisting it painfully behind my back, he shoved me forward and then his friend came to my side and snatched my other wrist.

Their hands were strong, unbreakable like the cuffs had been, and though I kicked and flailed in their hold, they still managed to drag me from the room.

Glancing over her shoulder, the woman curled two fingers,

beckoning us along, and then men followed as she led us down the narrow hallway.

Having turned back around, the woman kept her face forward, not bothering to offer me a second glance, and I eyed her long blond hair. Should I break free, the braid would be easy to grab a hold of, and if I was able to slip a dagger from the waist of one of her men, she would have no defence against me. I imagined the entire scenario, going over exactly how I could do it, though I still had not come up with an idea that would result in my hands being free for long enough to set it into motion.

"In here." The woman gestured to a room just ahead on our right and then moved to the side so that we could pass.

"Yes, Commander." My heart plummeted at the title, and while they dragged me through the threshold, I glanced back at her, watching as she plucked the metal from her face while she followed behind.

"Ceara?" I gasped, and her pretty light blue eyes lifted to mine while her lips curled into a smirk.

Stepping through the doorway, she moved across the room and pointed to a chair. It was then that I noticed I had been brought to the manor's great hall, and the men followed her silent order and moved me towards the seat.

"It's been a long time, Rígan," she replied as she tossed the mask onto the table in front of me and then her guards roughly pushed me into the chair and held me there by my shoulders. Caught by surprise, I no longer braced myself against my captors' strength and my skull knocked against the solid back of the seat, the sound making Ceara giggle.

"You are not how I imagined you would be." She grinned as she sat directly across from me, and I watched while she smoothed her hands down the front of her dark gown.

Satisfied that it was pristine, she studied my face and then her eyes lowered to my chest and she frowned at the pendant for a moment before speaking again.

"I had expected a rabid beast, not something so compliant. Maybe the fight has finally been knocked out of you, or perhaps it's just the afterglow from a night of fucking. Though surely with all of your experience, you've had better than Caedell Reide."

She spat his name out like venom and my stomach twisted at the sound. But despite my rage and worry, I clenched my jaw, hoping it would be enough to stop me from playing her game. Noticing my reaction, she tipped her head to the side.

"Tell me, how was it?" Resting an elbow on the wooden surface of the table, she perched her delicate chin in her hand. "I've never had a virgin."

Remaining silent, I continued to glare at her, watching as the amusement slowly melted from her face. Lowering her arm, she pulled it from the table and sighed.

"This is going to be very boring if you refuse to speak to me," she muttered with a pout. "Perhaps I will have to *pull* it out of him, I have the means necessary to do so, you know."

She was baiting me with the threat; I could see it in the way she peered at my face when she said his name. And though I said nothing, I knew her men could feel the stiffness in my shoulders at the thought of her harming Caedell in any way.

"She didn't like that," one of them rumbled from above me, and Ceara clapped her hands in glee.

"Where is he?" I seethed. There was no point in remaining silent now that my feelings were out in the open. "What did you do to him?!"

"Who would have thought Rígan Baxteel, the bitch, would have a soft spot," she chuckled while shaking her head in disbelief. "Though if the rumours are true, you have more than one."

My brows furrowed, and she stood from her chair before placing both hands on the table and then she leaned towards me.

"Most would assume your brother or father, though the latter was probably more likely. Even I had expected as much. After all, they are your kin, your very blood, and we all know the words of House Baxteel."

Grabbing the discarded mask, she lifted it from the table and held it before her face, peeking at me through the holes for her eyes. "But it's not them, is it? It's the highborn girl and that handsome guard of yours."

Knowing she may have Caedell locked away somewhere was hard enough to cope with, but the mention of Donigan and Cat had me throwing myself forward, and despite the heavy hands trying to haul me back, I nearly made it across the table before they could stop me.

Eyes wide with fear, Ceara took a step away from the wooden edge, clutching her mask to her chest as her guards fought to bring me back to my chair. But despite the roughness of their touch, I clawed and spat, nearly mindless at the thought of her hurting anyone else I cared for.

"Enough!" one of the men bellowed, and I felt the cold edge of steel under my chin. Freezing, I leaned away from the dagger, and Ceara smoothed her gown once more before clearing her throat.

"Now then, let's get back to the conversation at hand," she suggested casually, but I heard the nervous trembling in her voice.

"I will say nothing until I know they are all alive and well." One of her delicate brows lifted and she crossed her arms over her chest. "If you promise not to harm them, I will tell you whatever you want to know."

"I may know of their importance to you, but why would I get to decide their fates?" Grabbing a hold of the arm rests, I let my nails dig into the wood while I gathered the courage to say the words I now knew to be true.

"Because you are the High Commander," I spat. "You would have the power to make certain that they are spared."

"High Commander?" she repeated and then her eyes widened, and she tossed her head back with a laugh. "I may have a crucial role in all of this, but the High Commander I am not."

Swallowing, I tipped my chin and glared at her pretty face. "Then who is?"

Despite the hatred I directed towards her, Ceara's grin grew and then her gaze lifted to the door behind me. For a moment, I thought it was her avoiding my penetrating stare, but the way her eyes brightened and the prickling on the back of my neck told me someone was there. Shifting to the side, I took in a staggering breath and then brought my chin to my shoulder and lifted my eyes to the man who had just stepped into the room.

His entire form was covered in black. Black boots, black breeches and tunic, and a black cloak that flowed out behind him while its hood covered his hair. The only thing not covered in the morbid colour was his face. No, his face was concealed by a shining silver mask, and I felt my body quake as he lifted his gloved fingers to the metal while his eyes remained on the floor.

And then the steel was gone and his gaze lifted and suddenly the only colour I could see was a bright burning amber.

ACKNOWLEDGMENTS

Ballad of Broken Banners has taken 1095 days, at least three litres of tears, and every ounce of brain power I have. That being said, none of it—and I mean none of it—would have been possible without *you*. Usually in this part I go on and on. I thank my friends, and family, and those who helped me during my writing journey. And while I will be getting to that, I wanted you to have this first.

So, dear reader, thank you.

Thank you from the very pit of my heart. Thank you for reading, thank you for posting, thank you for reviewing, and thank you for supporting me. I may be a stranger to you, but I see you as part of this little family we have created. You have given me the grace to share tiny parts of myself, tiny minuscule parts that I tuck away in fear of being rejected or teased. I would have never had the courage to continue this dream if it wasn't for you. I would have kept these characters, who reflect some of the very things I hate about myself, away from the eyes of others, and instead put this book in the trash like I did with many that came before it. I will forever be grateful to each and every one of you. Thank you. Thank you. Thank you.

Now, moving on to my husband, family, and friends. Thank you for loving and caring for me. Thank you for pushing me when I need it and pulling back when it all becomes too much. Thank you for your understanding and patience. I am lucky to have so many of you to love.

To Jaqueline, this cover is insane. You are so talented and kind. I am lucky to call you a friend. I cannot wait to see where your journey takes you and hope you know how much I appreciate all your hard work.

To my beta team, you fit in the friends and family category, but I think you deserve your own paragraph. You each earned a medal for dealing with me. Thank you for your hard work and for your cheerleading, it means so very much.

To Beth, my trusty and lovely editor. Thank you for always taking these books on. Without you, they would be a mess. I am forever grateful to you.

That's it. The mushy part is done.

About the Author

K. Godin is the Canadian author of *The Chosen Series* and *The Anointed Duet*. She lives in beautiful Ontario, Canada, with her husband and her four dogs.

Her passion for writing started very early. Even as a child, she had a keen interest in creating new worlds and fantastical stories and that has only continued in adulthood.

When she isn't in her office typing away, she spends her time running her small business or is taking time for photography or spending her afternoons out at the barn where she keeps her horse.

PRONUNCIATION GUIDE

People:
Rígan Baxteel: RYE-gan BACK-steel
Skileer Baxteel: sky-LEER BACK-steel
Caedell Reide: CADE-el REED
Catiline Norse: CAT-i-line NOR-ees
Dyani Demys: DYE-an-ee DEM-ease
Aarik Demys: AIR-ick DEM-ease
Krayern Demys: CRAY-urn DEM-ease
Synrick Mooreel: sin-RICK MORE-eel
Places:
Noordeign: NOOR-dean
Denimoore: DEN-i-more
Wahstand: wa-STAND
Rushander: RUSH-and-er
Other:
Valkhag: VALK-hag
Gloomhor: GLOOM-or